Ritual Abuse - Summer

Spiritual Warfare

Lynda L. Irons

Irons Quill

Lynda L. Irons

Cover by H. Gene Irons

This is the fourth of a four-book series and is a work of fiction that is loosely based on some actual events from the author's life. Names, characters, places, and incidents that resemble that of any actual persons, living or dead, business establishments, locales, churches, and so on, is purely coincidental and are the product of the author's imagination.

This story is not for everyone. It contains some very disturbing information. Unfortunately, while this book is purely fictional, it depicts the tormented lives of far too many ritual abuse survivors who live in our communities. The representative characters in this book give voice to these amazing survivors in a way that only hints at the horrors that they have experienced day in and day out. This narrative is not meant to be sensational, rather to raise awareness that these people exist and desperately need the help of the Church.

WARNING: If you are a Satanic or Witchcraft Ritual Abuse survivor, please be aware that some of the contents in this book could trigger unresolved programming.

Lynda L. Irons

TABLE OF CONTENTS

Key Characters from Ritual Abuse – Autumn, Ritual Abuse – Winter, and Ritual Abuse - Spring

Abigail Steele, a widow and pastoral counselor, started her life over after the deaths of her husband and three sons by purchasing a small farm in a remote area of the county.

Earl and Jan Milner are elderly neighbors who live north of Abigail. Earl was a World War II sharpshooter who taught Abigail how to shoot.

David and Martha York, also elderly, live on the other side of Abigail to the south.

Carrie Sue Wagner was born to Satanist parents, Ron and Susan. Her oldest brother, Danny, died at age 25 in a traffic accident. Her other brother, Billy, was recently killed by the cult.

Fuchsya Amy Bolton, another SRA survivor, is working with Abigail. Her very closed and secretive internal system resembles a prison complex.

Prinz, the regional master, resided in the capital of the state and had risen to power over the decades. He was reputed to be well over a century old before his recent death.

Daggett and Darod, area masters, are now vying for Prinz' position along with Luxor and Amalek.

Zorroz and Herrak are local masters who reign under Daggett and Darod respectively.

Charlie Fletcher and Levi Blevins are lower level Satanists along with many others who are respected pillars in their communities as family men and businessmen, professionals and even church-goers.

5

Reigning above all of them is Xerxes, an influential congressman who is currently being groomed for the American presidency.

Gary and Cindy McCord are good friends of Abigail Steele and the parents of little Traci and Bryan. Cindy and Abigail are prayer partners and attend the Baptist church in Springfield where Daniel Spalding is their pastor.

Gary's cousin, Lee Norris, recently made the decision to move back east from Montana to be near his extended family. He sold his ranch and purchased a farm across the road from the Milners and Abigail Steele. He is courting Abigail Steele.

1

Thursday, June 21, Summer Solstice

The clock ticked from 11:59 p.m. to midnight, from Wednesday to Thursday, but no one was ready to settle down. The deputies had left so the area was dark and quiet again. Abigail was wearing out the floor with her pacing. Amy sat wide-eyed and silent in her chair with her hands instinctively soothing her unborn baby while Lee either dozed off or watched Abigail.

"I can't stand not knowing what's going on next door!" Abigail burst out for the umpteenth time.

"Well, they called an ambulance for the Yorks. If Earl and Jan were hurt, surely, they would have called an ambulance for them, too."

"Um, why would someone shoot the Yorks?" Amy asked. "I mean, you said you hardly see them and never talked to them, so why would Charlie Fletcher or some other cult guy shoot at them, too?"

"Good question," Abigail answered.

"That *is* a good question," Lee echoed as he lifted a heavy eyelid.

Abigail refocused on Earl and Jan. "It's just too weird that the sheriffs went up there and left. If they're not hurt, why don't they answer the phone? Why wouldn't they call us?"

"Well, here's a paranoid thought," Amy chimed in. "What if they *are* hurt and *couldn't* answer the door and the sheriffs just left thinking no one was home?"

"That might make sense," Lee concurred. "And that deputy did ask about the shooting from a couple of months ago. This might be payback to Earl and they could cover it up by saying that no one appeared to be home when they investigated."

"That's right," Abigail added resentfully, "they sure didn't acknowledge our statements about the shooting starting up there and our concern about them not answering. They'll just lose these reports like they lost all the others."

Suddenly, they were all energized and, without verbalizing it, they were going to see about the Milners. Right now. One final look out of the living room window that was not hit by the hail of bullets confirmed that the lights were still out on the next hill.

"Amy, you stay here. We don't know what we'll find up there and there's no sense in jeopardizing you or your baby."

"Okay, but let me know something right away."

"No problem."

Grabbing flashlights, Lee and Abigail were soon in his truck and heading up to the Milners. It was dark except for the lone yard light. Lacy shadows covered the front lawn. Lee gave two soft toots because he knew that they knew that he tooted whenever he approached Abigail's house and they would know it was him. Headlights illuminated Earl's car as they pulled up to the house.

"Oh, my! Look at the car! They've got to be home." Abigail was the first one out of the truck.

"Yeah! Just what happened up here?" Lee was both puzzled and alarmed as he shone his flashlight around the property. "Their windows are shot out, too."

"Earl! Jan! It's me, Abigail."

Lee tried the front door. "It's locked."

8

"Wait! I know where they keep their spare key." Directing her flashlight to the windmill in the flower garden next to the porch, she reached into the compartment behind the blades and pulled it out.

"Earl! Jan! Lee and I are coming in."

"Let me go in first," Lee said protectively as he firmly pulled Abigail back. His flashlight was shining into the living room.

Abigail was right behind him and flipped on the lights. She knew where the switch was.

Earl moaned.

"Earl!" Abigail rushed to his side. "Where are you hurt?"

His bloody fist was clenched over his heart. He was pasty and gray.

"Let me check him," Lee said as he shifted into his paramedic mode. Placing his fingers on Earl's carotid artery, he checked his pulse. "Kind of weak. Earl! Do you have nitro?"

Earl was able to make a feeble nod.

"Where would he keep his nitro?" Lee asked as he glanced around the room.

"It might be on his night stand. I'll go check."

"I'm calling 911." Lee pulled out his cell phone and made the call. "What's the address here?"

"1964 York Creek Road," Abigail yelled over her shoulder from the hallway. She charged into their bedroom to look for the nitroglycerin and to find out about Jan.

"Jan! Oh, dear Jesus!" Abigail found Jan slumped on the floor in her blood-drenched nightgown. She knelt down beside her and checked for a pulse.

9

Lee sprinted toward them not knowing what to expect when he got there.

"She's alive but I don't know where all this blood is coming from!"

"You work on her and I'll get back to Earl," Lee said as he moved over to Earl's nightstand. He was relieved to find the small vial. "Praise the Lord! Nitro!"

Abigail could hear Lee telling the dispatcher about Jan and the need for two transports as she moved Jan into a more comfortable position. Putting pressure on her wound with a shirt that she pulled out of a nearby drawer, she waited for help to arrive.

Like the rest of the shaken community, Pastor Spalding had heard the news about the shootings of the previous night. He called to check up on Lee and Abigail that morning. Abigail had called Cindy and assured her that they were a little rattled but otherwise unscathed. They all suspected that this was yet another attack by the cult. Probably Charlie Fletcher. The attacks were definitely escalating.

By mid-morning the media from the larger cities had gotten wind of what they were calling the York Creek Shooting Spree. They were beginning to circle like vultures looking for tasty scraps of news. It did not escape their notice that this was the same community that they had descended upon not all that long ago for The Taco Tower Tragedy. What was going on in that area? Was it just a coincidence?

Sheriff Bynum was unsettled as he peered out the front window at the gathering crowd. The phone never stopped ringing as the office was bombarded with calls.

Rubbing his temples, he thought about the official statement he would have to make sooner or later. He had a suspicion about the shooting spree which he did not share with his deputies.

They knew that Bynum hated those trouble-makers on York Creek Road and they were all too willing to respond slowly or badly. Or not at all. They were just as corrupt as he. Not all of them were Satanists but all five of them feared Sheriff Bynum. Warily watching Bynum, the deputies quietly went about their duties, or at least looked as if they were.

"I'll be back; I'm going to make a follow-up run," Bynum informed the deputy who was manning the desk. "And keep those lousy reporters out of here. I'll make a statement when I'm good and ready!" Letting a string of curse words fly, he donned his cap on his way out the back door.

Cruising down back roads that led from Springfield and through Kingston, Bynum turned left onto York Creek Road. He slowed around the final curve before Charlie Fletcher's long driveway and made the turn. With his windows rolled down, Sheriff Bynum noted the eerie quiet that was punctuated by the distinct raucous caws of a flock of crows and the quiet crunch of gravel as he cautiously rolled up to the house.

Charlie's maroon pickup truck was parked at an odd angle, partially on the front sidewalk with its driver's side door slightly ajar. A closer look revealed that the keys were still in the ignition. Bynum made a slow rotation and looked for anything amiss. The big horse nickered at him from his usual place in the corral next to the barn.

Seeing nothing obvious out of place, Sheriff Bynum approached the house with his right hand poised over his weapon. "Charlie Fletcher! Yo! Charlie!" Rapping loudly on the weathered wooden door, Sheriff Bynum heard no response and tried the door knob. It was unlocked so he slowly opened the door and cautiously creaked over the floorboards as he entered. "Charlie! It's me, Sheriff Bynum. Just checking on you, buddy. You all right?"

The only answer was the piercing sound of the crows coming from somewhere up the lane.

Bynum warily moved through the old farmhouse and searched for Charlie Fletcher. Not finding him, he went to the barn; the very barn where Carrie Sue had surprised him at that ritual. Charlie was nowhere to be seen. *Blast him!* Looking agitatedly from side to side as if he were about to be ambushed, Bynum's jitters were getting the best of him as he cautiously walked up the path toward the pentagon-shaped rock that sat in the shade of the ancient oak tree at their ritual site. Subconsciously reaching for his throat and rubbing the scar, his rage toward Carrie Sue and Abigail Steele was ignited once again.

Clamorous caws of the crows startled him out of his thoughts. The flock was gathered in a wing-flapping flurry under the large oak tree. "What the ..." Bynum gasped. He picked up his pace and focused on the site.

Entering the clearing, he disturbed the insolent crows. Some were strutting with strips of raw pink flesh swinging from triumphant beaks while others were still in a feeding frenzy. Walking away, looking over their shoulders, black tails swinging from side to side with each step, they reluctantly retreated. Almost

12

as one, they rose and then the sound of flapping wings ceased as they found perches in the nearby trees and watched like vultures for an opportunity to resume their feast.

Sheriff Bynum gazed at sightless empty sockets that stared back from Charlie's disfigured face. The large caliber weapon lay silently glinting in the sunlight after having done its loud and lethal job.

"Aww!" Bynum cursed as he removed his cap and slapped it hard against his thigh. *This is getting stickier and stickier.* He thought about how, as Sheriff Bynum, he needed to handle this situation with the community and the reporters. He thought about how, as Zorroz, he would have to handle this situation with Daggett and Xerxes.

The normally decisive man was rattled. There did not seem to be a risk-free solution. He couldn't leave Charlie's body to the crows. He couldn't just bury him.

He squatted down resting his right elbow on his right knee. His chin rested on his fist as he considered his options. *Think! Think!*

After calling for back up from a deputy who had celebrated many rituals with him under this very tree, he suddenly realized that the rock, the five-sided altar, was no longer there.

Speed dialing another number, he waited through six interminably long rings.

"Judge Roberts," an officious voice answered. "This better be important."

Sheriff Bynum apprised Daggett of the complicated situation and received his instructions.

"Mom! Calm down, Mom. Daddy's going to be all right." Rob held her hand lightly and tried to soothe his mother as she thrashed her way out of oblivion and back to consciousness. Jan mumbled something about having to check on Earl right now.

"Robbie?" the disoriented woman queried. "What are you doing here?"

"We're all here, Mom. Someone shot up the house and managed to get a couple of bullets into you in the process."

"Who..." Jan drifted off again.

"Let her rest," the nurse instructed gently. "She'll come around pretty soon. What's the word on your father?" Almost everyone in the small-town hospital had already heard about the shootings.

"He's up in the ICU. They patched up his hand – I don't know if it was a bullet or glass or both that tore up his hand – and they're monitoring his heart. They think he may have had another heart attack."

"I'm so sorry. What a shame."

"We're just grateful that they survived."

"Well, I'll be praying for your family. Call me if you need anything. I'll be back to check on your mother as soon as I finish passing meds."

"Thanks. We could use all the prayers we can get right now." Rob returned to his watch at his mother's bedside and continued his bed-side vigil until the next interruption.

"Cripes! What the heck is going on around here?" Michelle burst into the room in her usual bottom-line, no-holds-barred manner.

"Don't know for sure," Rob answered slowly.

"Did they catch the guy? And who would want to shoot up the neighborhood anyway?"

"Don't know."

"Well, I'm going to get some answers. I'm going to the sheriff's office."

"Slow down, sis, they got enough going on without you getting in their faces."

"Hello! This is Mom and Dad we're talking about."

"I know. They're investigating now. They'll get it all sorted out."

"Did you see the house? Yellow tape all over the place! We can't even get in to board up the windows." Jan moaned.

"Calm down. Mom doesn't need to hear you all worked up."

"Fine. By the way, Lori and Kevin are up by the ICU with Dad. They'll be down soon."

"Thanks. I'm glad Lori is an OR technician. She'll understand all that medical jargon."

Richard was weary from his long drive, but he did not stop until he arrived at the hospital in Springfield. His father was in critical condition from a bullet wound to the chest. It missed his heart, but his lung was nicked and it had collapsed. Loss of blood exacerbated the elderly man's condition.

Martha looked up at the sound of footsteps hoping that it would be a familiar face. "Oh, Richard." The physically weak and emotionally fragile woman could let down now; Richard was here. Tears seeped and then rolled steadily down her weathered cheeks.

15

He settled his tall frame down next to her on the worn waiting room sofa and put his muscular arm around her, pulling her fragile form to himself as they reversed roles. "Ma, Pa's going to be all right. He's strong. He'll make it."

"I don't know, son," Martha York quavered, "he lost so much blood and it took them so long before they let the ambulance come."

"What do you mean? That doesn't make any sense, Ma. What are you talking about?"

Martha tried to recount the events of the previous night, but her exhaustion compounded her diminishing mental capacity and she drifted into her vacant place. Richard insisted on taking her home after they visited David York for their allotted ten minutes.

"Well, I'm glad they're finally doing something up there," Abigail said as she peeked out of her kitchen window.

"Yeah," Amy's cynical side kicked in, "like hiding evidence and trying to figure out how they can pin it on you or Lee."

"You think too much." *Ooh, that is a possibility.*

"All right, I'll stop thinking and let you think about that for a while," Amy quipped with a twinkle in her eye and a half smile.

"Hey, seriously now, let's change the subject. How are you doing? You've been through a lot, plus this is another ritual night. How are things inside?"

"Well, it's been a bit quieter since Original Fuchsya made her ultimatum to level six. I'm not sure if they're thinking about agreeing to what she said or conspiring to overthrow her."

"What do you say we do a session later today?"

"Sounds good."

They chatted over a late breakfast and then Abigail had to make some phone calls. She contacted her insurance agent to inquire about coverage and repairs. After satisfying herself that the siding and the old hardwood underneath the siding had not been penetrated by any of the rounds, Abigail took more pictures and did a more thorough cleaning just in case they missed any tiny shards of glass.

"The insurance guy said that the window guys will be here tomorrow morning first thing, so I'm going over to see how Misty is. Call me if you need anything or if you see anything suspicious."

"Gotcha."

Lee heard the sound of Abigail's four-wheeler coming up the path and smiled. Walking out of the barn where he had been tending to Misty, he squinted in the bright sunlight. "Good morning!"

"This is the day," Abigail began.

"That the Lord has made," Lee continued.

"We will rejoice and be glad in it." They finished the verse in unison as was becoming their custom.

"How's Misty?"

"Limping a little and a bit spooked. I'm going to take her to the vet today. You want to come along?"

"Sure. How serious is it?" she asked as they walked into the barn.

"Not serious at all other than the fact that she was shot. I mostly want it documented."

"Good idea."

They took their time loading Misty into the trailer. There was plenty of time before his appointment with the vet who was a short drive away. Parking behind the veterinarian's clinic where the vet tended the large animals, Lee went inside to register.

They did not have to wait very long before the energetic boot-wearing, denim-clad doctor emerged from the back door with a clipboard in his hand.

"Hello there! I'm Dr. Wallings," he said as he extended his hand to Lee. "Call me Doc, everyone else in this county does."

"Lee."

"You said your horse got shot?"

"Yep. A casualty of the big shoot-out last night."

"O-oh," Doc replied with new understanding. "Let's see what we've got here." He slowly moved over to Misty who was now tied to the back of the trailer nervously stamping her hoofs. "Hey, little lady, let's see what's going on here."

He completed his examination and confirmed Lee's assessment that it was a flesh wound that just needed to be watched. "She'll be a little stiff for a couple of days. I wouldn't worry about her. She's healthy. Just keep an eye out for infection."

"Sounds like a plan. I just wanted to be sure," Lee said. "I've never had a horse get shot before."

Lee and Abigail were soon headed back to the farm. He told Abigail that the new house did not suffer any damage from the shooting and that he could not detect any damage to the barn or other out-buildings either. They made plans to have supper together and then Abigail headed back home for her session with Amy while Lee brought Misty back down to the pasture.

"You ready?" Abigail asked Amy as they finished clearing their lunch dishes.

"Ready as I'll ever be."

They got settled in the living room and after opening with prayer, Abigail looked expectantly at Amy. She saw the subtle shift in her posture and countenance and knew that a different personality had switched into executive control.

"Hello. I haven't talked with you for some time." Abigail greeted Head Warden. His distinct military bearing was familiar to her.

"I've mostly been watching while Tiara and Original Fuchsya have been taking care of things."

"So give me some feedback. What's going on with your group?"

"Nothing new, really. Everyone's gotten healed and integrated including those teenaged hold-outs from Mayor's area."

"What are you sensing? Why are you up today?" Abigail had a hunch that he wanted to collapse the ground level prison and integrate everyone much like Mayor did with his town.

"I, we, that is, me and my leaders think it's time that we shut down our part of the system and integrate."

"I'm not surprised," Abigail said with a big smile. "Your strength and experience will really help Original Fuchsya for sure."

"Well, she's going to need it for the level six mess."

"Oh?"

"I got wind of a rumor that Apollyon and Joktan and about a third of the ones on that level are not going to comply with Original Fuchsya's announcement. They think that they can still escape and take over and finish their assignments."

"Even with the demons and programs removed?" Abigail silently reflected on the similarity between the demon-loyal third of Amy's system and the Satan-loyal third of demons that had rebelled against God. It was reassuring to know that no matter how many legions of angels were created, there were two good angels for every fallen angel.

"I'm not sure they're all gone. Somehow a bunch of them held onto their demons."

"Thanks for the heads-up. How about if we pray a minute and ask the Lord if there's anything that needs to be addressed in your area before we ask Him to close it down?"

"Good idea."

They prayed briefly and after listening for a few minutes, they agreed that there was nothing else that needed to be taken care of prior to integration and the removal of the ground level prison.

"Let's pray!" Once again, Abigail marveled at the internal communication that went on between the various personalities in her dissociated counselees. Amy's system had been extensive and complicated which only confirmed the horrendous ritualized abuse that she had endured all of her life. She asked the Lord to complete and correct anything prayed inadequately and then she asked Him to do whatever needed to be done to clean up the ground level prison area.

"Hello," a softer voice said after a few moments.

"Tiara?"

"That's me."

"Head Warden said that you and Original Fuchsya are doing a great job."

"I'd thank him but he's nowhere to be found."

"I'm guessing that they went into the original."

"Probably. I didn't feel anything."

"What happened to the prison?" Abigail was quite curious about the changes in the system. What started out as a six-story prison with crowded cells on each floor had later been reduced to one story, and now it was gone.

"Well, it was like watching a huge invisible bulldozer push the building way off to the side," she waved her right hand to the side twice. "It kind of just crumbled down to pebbles and became like a paved road and the place where it was standing is now just a plain yard with a small building in the middle of it."

"A building?"

"Yeah, kind of like an ornate gazebo."

"Interesting."

"I think it might be right over the central hub of the subterranean levels."

"Very interesting. I wonder if that's how everyone will come up and out."

"Could be."

"How's Original Fuchsya?"

"Why don't you talk to her yourself?" With that, Tiara abruptly disappeared.

"Hi," Original Fuchsya said with a little more strength than Abigail remembered.

"How are you? Did Head Warden and all his people integrate into you?"

"I think so. I feel fuller... more solid. I don't know how to describe it."

"That's okay. You sound stronger. You have some really strong characters in there."

"Thanks. What's next?"

"Let's ask the Lord. Tonight is the big summer solstice ritual. I would imagine that the level six guys are a bit agitated."

"I can feel it. I know some of them want to defect out of Satan's kingdom, but with Apollyon breathing his threats, they don't want to tip their hand."

Abigail was curious about how she knew what was going on in level six. It was supposed to have been sealed up, but then, Original Fuchsya did make that announcement last time. Internal communication. What a mystery! "Let's ask the Lord for a strategy for dealing with level six."

Original Fuchsya surprised Abigail by launching into a prayer. "Lord, I need Your help with Apollyon and Joktan and all the others who are still Satan-loyal. Please let us know how to deal with them, Amen."

"What are you sensing?" Abigail asked. She had an impression about Joktan but she did not want to make any leading statements.

"I'm getting the words 'false front' or something like that. What does that mean?"

"Let's keep praying. Lord, would You illuminate that thought and bring clarity?"

"It has something to do with Joktan."

"Okay. That makes sense. I was getting something about Joktan, too, but I wanted you to confirm it first. When you said that about the false front, it made me wonder if Joktan might be a demon masquerading as an alter - a pseudo-alter. Or maybe there's a part named Joktan who has a demon with the same name."

"That sits right with me. What do we do about it? Never mind. Pray. Would you? I'm not sure exactly what to ask for."

"Lord, on behalf of Fuchsya Amy Bolton, we ask that You would show us what is going on and how to proceed. We believe You have revealed that Joktan is a demon and as such, he is trespassing. We plead the blood of Jesus the Christ of Nazareth over Joktan and ask that You would separate any human part of Joktan from any demonic being, amen."

"Amen."

"Anything happening?"

"Whoa! Yes! The guy I thought was a part of me *is* a demon. There is no human part. Ew! Gross. Does that mean I've had a demon in charge of all the subterranean levels all this time?"

"It happens."

"Now what?"

"I think it's time for him to go wherever Jesus wants to send him."

"I'll do the honors," Original Fuchsya announced. "God, I renounce whatever so-called legal right Joktan had to rule inside of me and I ask that You would demolish strongholds from covenants or agreements that were made on my behalf against my will. I renounce Joktan and ask that You would send him and his entire hierarchy to a place where he will never hurt anyone ever again. Fill me with Your Holy Spirit and all the good stuff from Your kingdom. Thank you, Lord Jesus. Amen."

"Amen. Wow! You've been taking notes!" Abigail was astonished at how quickly Original Fuchsya was taking back her life.

"Maybe it's because Head Warden knew this stuff and now I have it."

"Of course! That should really encourage you about being able to handle life once everyone is back inside."

"Yeah," she said with a smile. "Now what?"

"Let's see what's going on with Apollyon and the other hold-outs."

Original Fuchsya conferred internally and then reported, "He doesn't seem as resistant, but he and a whole bunch of parts are still holding out. And then there are hold-outs from the other levels, too."

"I wonder if we can ask the Lord to separate the two camps," Abigail mused.

"Good idea! We should ask God to collapse the six levels and make it all one level with a divider between the cult-loyal ones and the ones who want to defect and integrate."

Abigail could not stifle her delighted chuckle. "You don't mess around. Go for it."

Original Fuchsya prayed again and then reported that the cult-loyal parts – about a third of all remaining personalities – were isolated in their own area and that the God-loyal ones were together in another area.

"Whew! I'm exhausted," Amy said.

"I guess so. That was a lot of work. And I would guess that the fact that you're back in charge is a clue that we're done for the day."

2

Friday, June 22

Abigail was delayed by the glut of traffic on the two-lane roads to Springfield and was a few minutes late for her ten o'clock appointment. Pastor Spalding and Max were waiting for her when she finally arrived.

"Good to see you," Pastor Spalding greeted her. "I was beginning to worry about you after all that excitement last night."

"Traffic! What's going on?"

"Sheriff Bynum is having a press conference. I'm curious about what he's going to say. I sure hope they caught the guy."

Max looked back and forth between the two of them, but did not voice his question. He was pretty sure that whatever happened had something to do with the cult. He was still feeling guilty for his part in harassing Abigail when he was a cult member.

Getting right into it, Abigail turned to Max and said, "Well, it's been a couple of weeks since we met. Before we get to the dissociation stuff, how's your physical therapy going? How's your job and your relationship with your folks doing?"

"Pretty good. I'm slowly getting this leg back," he said as he patted his left knee. "The therapist thinks that the brace might not be a life sentence if it keeps getting stronger."

"Excellent!" Pastor Spalding joyfully chimed in. He had a hard time containing his enthusiasm.

"I'm working almost full time again. Dad's trying to show me some of the business stuff, but I'm not really into that."

"What do you want to be when you grow up?" Abigail asked with smile and a twinkle in her eyes.

"I'm not sure. I'm pretty sure I don't want to take over the dealership. That'd hurt Dad's feelings, but it's just not for me. I was thinking of working with high school kids, but I'm not exactly sure how. I see them hanging out in the park looking for trouble like I used to. I want to be able to direct them away from cults."

"If you don't mind my saying something," Pastor Spalding injected, "I just had a thought. Most of those kids don't have jobs and they find trouble or trouble finds them. What if you and your dad could set up some kind of an apprenticeship at the dealership? I mean, at the very least they could learn how to change oil and fix flats."

Max brightened at the idea. "Thanks. I'll definitely give it some thought. Maybe Dad would have some ideas about that too."

"We'll certainly pray with you and I'm sure God will give you direction. Meanwhile, we need to take care of this dissociation." Abigail shifted back to the matter at hand. Looking at her notes from the previous session, she said, "Let's see... last time you asked God to put General Maximillian and the Caesar and others to sleep so they couldn't agitate, and you said that it got real quiet inside."

"Yeah, but last night it was like everyone was awake again." He frowned at the thought.

"Ritual night."

"I could tell."

"Let's open with prayer and see where the Lord takes us." Abigail prayed and then looked expectantly at Max.

Max looked up uncertainly and said, "I got a word – senate. What's that supposed to mean?"

"Interesting. It seems like your internal system is patterned after the ancient Roman political system." Abigail looked at Pastor Spalding and asked, "Didn't they have a senate?"

"Sounds right to me, and don't forget proconsuls and governors. I wonder if there's a Herod in there?" he mused as he mentally scrolled through the various Roman leaders that were mentioned in the Bible.

Max suddenly shifted in his chair and another personality emerged. "We are quite weary of being summoned in such a common manner."

"Herod?" Abigail asked.

"Do you not know that I could have you executed for such impudence?"

"Do you not know that you can't do a thing unless Jesus Christ permits it?" Abigail retorted more as a reflex than as a challenge.

"Jesus Christ! We put Him to death!"

"Perhaps the Romans had a hand in it 2000 years ago, but Jesus the Christ of Nazareth was raised up by the power of the Holy Spirit."

"Satan reigns!" he growled.

"Let's not argue that now," Abigail replied evenly. "I suppose you are one of the twelve or thirteen Senate leaders. Maybe with Titus and Philip, Quirinius and Pilot, and the others?" Abigail was getting words of knowledge and she let them flow. It seemed that every ritual abuse survivor had an internal system that was

27

configured around twelve or thirteen leaders who had three above them and one top leader. She supposed it was a mockery of Jesus and the twelve disciples. She always marveled at the mysterious mix of personal experience and God's revelations that allowed her to work effectively.

Herod was visibly jolted with each name she mentioned. He was clearly shocked and disappeared as suddenly as he appeared. Max shook his head as he tried to make sense of what had happened.

"Well, it looks like we're beginning to figure out what your system looks like and who some of the key players are."

"Yeah," Max replied. He was clearly bewildered. "What are we supposed to do with this?"

"Let me give you kind of a general overview. You, the original Max, were dissociated as a little guy because of the trauma of the leukemia. As a teen, you got hooked into the cult and that's where you get cloudy with your memories because the cult was able to drug you, hypnotize you, and traumatize you effectively enough to intentionally create the cast of characters that are now coming to the surface."

"Okay."

"Our job is to have all that damage reversed."

"How?"

"Remember how we dealt with Little Max and his horrible hospital memories?"

"Yeah."

"We need to do the same thing with these guys. It's a little trickier with them because they have been programed and demonized. Jesus needs to heal them.

They need to be set free from the deceptions and lies they've believed. They need to be integrated."

"Sounds like a big job."

"It might get intense, but the good news is that you seem to be the original Max and you have the authority to pray on their behalf for them."

"Can I just do it right now? For all of them?"

"I wish it were that easy. We can definitely go for it, but in my experience, we probably have to do some work in the trenches to get at the specific assignments and covenants. Sometimes they install some unusual programming."

Max frowned. "Then what *can* we do?"

"I think that we can start with that comprehensive three-page prayer of renunciations and affirmations. We can see what happens and go from there."

"Sure."

Abigail pulled three copies out of her file and gave one to Max and one to Pastor Spalding. She obtained Max's permission to pray on his behalf in case he was unable to continue for any reason, and then Max began the prayer. It took about twenty minutes and when he was finished he sagged in the chair.

"How do you feel?"

"Besides tired? Kind of mixed. I feel a little lighter, but I also feel like stuff got stirred up inside."

"That's to be expected. I think that was significant and we'll see what kind of fallout happens."

They made their appointment for the following Friday and then Max left. Abigail and Pastor Spalding debriefed and then went their separate ways. Abigail grabbed a snack and waited for Kristin Kelly.

Kristin showed up at noon and poked her head into the room uncertainly. "Am I in the right place?"

"Are you Kristin?"

"Yes."

"Then you're in the right place," Abigail smiled at the blue-eyed, raven-haired young lady. "Come in and have a seat. I'll let you fill this out and then we can get started."

Kristin accepted the clipboard and an ink pen. Quickly filling in the information, she was soon seated in Abigail's office.

"Tell me a little bit about yourself and why you're here," Abigail prompted her.

"Well, I work with Jason at The Taco Tower and he and Mr. Bell explained salvation and prayed with me. I've been coming to church here since then."

"Yes. I've seen you a couple of times. I saw you go up front with Jason one time."

"That was me. I want to get baptized now that I'm saved. Anyway, we work together and he told me how you helped him. I'm still having nightmares about the murder. I, I can't look at that utility closet without seeing Gabrielle and all that blood."

"It's been about a month now. I remember seeing you there. You were one of the quiet ones."

Kristin blushed and looked away. "Yeah, I'm a little shy, but what you said there really helped a lot."

Abigail went on to explain to Kristin that they could ask the Lord to minister to her in that past event and release her from the painful emotions and body memories – especially the sight of Gabrielle's lifeless body in a pool of blood. "So, you might see Him with your spiritual eyes, hear Him with your spiritual ears, or just sense His presence. Your job is to release the pain to Him and receive whatever it is He wants to give you in exchange."

"Okay." Kristin was not sure that she wanted to intentionally focus on the brutal murder of her co-worker, but nothing she had done so far had erased the memory. She was tired of the recurrent nightmares.

"You focus on the memory and I'll pray for a little bit and then wait while you kind of look around in the memory." Abigail prayed aloud and continued silently asking the Lord to show up in the memory and bring this precious teenager some freedom from her pain.

After several minutes of silence, Kristin looked up with a quizzical expression on her face. "How does He do that?"

"Do what?" Abigail never knew what creative thing the Lord might do to demonstrate truth.

"I saw Him there and He was kneeling by Gabrielle. He kind of moved His hands over her and all the blood just disappeared and she started um, like, glowing and then He scooped her up and walked out the back door with her and the floor was clean."

Abigail remained quiet and let Kristin absorb what she had visualized in the memory.

"Did I make that up?"

"No, I don't think so. God uses our senses and our imagination, our thoughts and minds to bring us truth that sets us free. It's kind of like a personal parable. Look back at the memory now – think about walking into The Taco Tower and going to the utility closet. How does that feel now?"

A puzzled frown creased Kristin's forehead briefly. "It's okay. I mean, I don't have that big knot in my stomach and I really can't even make myself see Gabrielle or the blood."

"Good. Before you believed that you would always see that gruesome scene and always have that awful effect whenever you were at work. What's the truth?"

"She's okay. She's not there anymore. Actually, I can picture her standing by the counter smiling at a customer. She was always so nice to everyone."

"Try to pull up that bloody scene."

Kristin closed her eyes and then gasped, "I can't! I tried, but I just see a smiling Gabrielle. How does He do that?"

"I'm not sure how, I just know that He does. For some people He just speaks or conveys some words. Some people just know; they have a realization. I just know that I don't suggest anything and you couldn't have made that up."

"I sure couldn't! I feel so much better! I can hardly believe it. Thank you so much!"

"What's the name of the shooter?" one brash reporter shouted as soon as Sheriff Bynum emerged from the building. He was flanked by two of his deputies who stood slightly behind him with frowns on their faces, feet spread wide, and gorilla arms like parentheses at their sides.

"Is he in custody?" another one followed up.

"Is this community safe?"

"Is this related to The Taco Tower shooting?"

"How many people did he shoot?"

Sheriff Bynum held up both of his hands to silence the crowd of citizens and reporters. They pressed in and quieted.

"Now folks, I know you have a lot of questions. I can answer some of them right now and the rest will have to wait until we look at all the facts. Some things will have to remain confidential until the investigation is complete." He had their attention.

"We don't know what set the man off, but he is dead of a gunshot wound. We are still investigating his death. We won't know until the coroner finishes the autopsy whether it was a self-inflicted wound or if someone shot back at him. His name will be withheld pending notification of his family. That's all I have to say for now." He turned and started to walk back into the building.

"Sheriff Bynum! How long before the autopsy is finished?"

"Sheriff Bynum! How many murders have there been in this county this year?"

"Sheriff Bynum!"

Bynum turned sharply and glared at the reporters. "I told you that I was finished. We have work to do here. If you don't want to be arrested for interfering with an investigation I would suggest that you disperse immediately." He turned and walked through the door that was being held open by a deputy.

Richard York was standing near the back of the crowd. He picked up something with his intuition that was based on decades of investigations. He could read people, and what he was sensing was worth probing. Dad was right; something was going on in this county.

By the time the last rays of sunlight disappeared, evil spirits had roused their hosts into action. It was yet another ritual night because of the first quarter moon. Rituals, rituals, interminable rituals. Moon phases and celestial phenomenon, Judeo and Christian holy days, Sabbats and demon revels, numbers and birthdays drew the Satanists and wizards, witches and warlocks to their festivities.

Christians by day and Satanists by night, the faithful ones began to assemble at their designated ritual sites by ten o'clock that night. They were on a mission to rise as high as they could in Satan's kingdom and as high as they could in God's kingdom. They were blinded by the god of this world and could not see that by embracing that very quest they nullified their desperate mission.

The entire cult fell for the deception. Judge Jeff Roberts by day, Daggett by night. Sheriff Bynum by day, Zorroz by night. Prosecutor Ed Jeffers by day, Herrak by night. County Commissioner Mark Miller by day, Darod by night. Congressman John Davidson by day, Xerxes by night. Levi by day, Leviathan by night. The list of ordinary and professional citizens would have astounded the unsuspecting communities that were home to these who held dual citizenships.

Xerxes heard about the situation in Zorroz' area and decided to join the local festivities. His sleek black car snaked down the highway with little regard to posted speed limits. He drove with impunity because of his status as a congressman as well as his status in the dark world of Satanism. He briefly recalled his last visit to the area which resulted in damage to his car from a freak hail storm that seemed to target him and Prinz as they drove past Abigail Steele's property. They were prevented from inflicting any harm and that thought fueled his rage and renewed his vows to destroy that woman and everyone near and dear to her.

He made his way through the thick grove of pine trees and walked surreptitiously up to a cluster of hooded men. They communicated briefly and then a signal was flashed. Chanting and drumming increased in tempo and volume. A pregnant teenager was brought forward and lashed to the altar. After viciously violating her, they induced labor and did unspeakable things to the tiny sacrifice.

The dazed girl had been drugged and hypnotized. The trauma of the inky night caused her to dissociate into many more alternate personalities. It was routine for the Satanists. They had long ago figured out how to leverage physical pain, mental anguish, and emotional agony into splitting out a programed, controlled, and predictable pawn.

If she survived to adulthood, the dissociation would eventually break down neuro-physiologically, the flashbacks would begin, and the body memories would continue to mysteriously emerge. She would think she was crazy or making up stories, and just having nightmares or a wild imagination. But the body does not lie. It tells the truth. Someday she would believe it and if she were blessed, she would find someone like Abigail Steele who would know how to deprogram her and bring the deep healing she would need.

3

Sunday, June 24

The rising sun shot pink and coral arrows into the dawn sky. Abigail stirred in her bed and stretched lazily before her feet hit the floor. Donning the shorts and shirt that were hanging on hooks on the inside of the old, varnish-crazed closet door, slipping into her shoddy tennis shoes, she walked through the dew-drenched grass past the lush garden and orchard. She heard the chickens cackling impatiently in their coop. They were nine weeks old and needed about another nine weeks before they started laying eggs.

"You pretty little freeloaders can be early bloomers if you want to," Abigail said, anticipating fresh eggs.

All she got were a few cackles as they rushed past her into the claw-worn dirt. Abigail scooped out some cracked corn and tossed it in an arc that alarmed and temporarily scattered the chickens. Soon they were scratching and pecking contentedly.

"It must be nice to be a chicken. You have only one mission in life. Lay eggs. Eat, sleep, and lay eggs." Abigail was jealous for a few seconds. Right now, her life seemed to be very complex. Amy's trailer had been burned – probably by cult members, Carrie Sue would soon join Amy and live in her house, Abigail was getting married in less than two weeks, plus there was the prayer ministry, and Ministerial Alliance activities. Earl and Jan were living with their son, Robbie, while their house was being repaired and their bodies were recuperating, her own house would be repaired tomorrow, and on top of it all, the cult was continually harassing her. And now they were coming after her neighbors, too, it seemed.

"No weapon, Lord; You said that no weapon formed against us would prosper. But they sure do some damage. Abba, please don't let them hurt Lee or Carrie Sue or Amy or the Milners or the Yorks or our critters. Hasten the healing for all our neighbors, too."

By the time she finished her prayers, she was back in the house. Amy was in the shower and getting ready for church. This was new for Amy. It helped that Carrie Sue was further down the healing curve, attended church, and would soon be living here, too. There were so many triggers in church. The cult designed portions of their rituals to have mockeries of Christian ceremonies and sacraments, symbols and services. It was amazing that any of the survivors ever showed up for a church service.

Amy was wearing one of her maternity outfits and looked at Abigail for a reaction. She was still shy about her appearance. Being an unmarried woman who was starting to show did not help. She had been reading material and looking at charts about the development of a baby. "How come I look this big when this baby is barely six inches long and not even half a pound?" she asked as she smoothed her top and looked down at her growing belly.

"I'm not sure. I just know I gained about twenty-five or thirty pounds with each of my pregnancies. It took me nine months to put it on and nine months to take it off. You look great and you're barely showing."

"Thanks, but the view from up here looks different," she said as she eyed her belly. "I used to be so skinny."

"Emaciated might be a better word. Hey, sorry to change the subject, but are you taking your own car or do you want to ride with Lee and I?"

"I'll go in my own car, but I do want to sit with you guys. I want to stop at the store and pick up a couple of things. Carrie Sue and I will probably grab lunch somewhere."

"Hey, why don't you invite her over here for lunch? I haven't seen her in a while and we need to figure out a time-table for her moving in here while I'm moving over there." She tossed her head in the direction of Lee's property.

"I'll ask her."

The parking lot was nearly full by the time Lee and Abigail got there. It seemed like new people were coming to church every week. It was hard to keep up with all of them. Abigail saw Kristin and Jason and gave them a wave and a smile. It was obvious that they were becoming an item.

Lee ushered Abigail into "their" pew which was already occupied by their friends. Gary gave a semi-salute to Lee from the far end and Cindy smiled as she leaned forward and mouthed her greeting to Abigail over Carrie Sue and Amy who were whispering animatedly about the shooting spree.

After a time of praise and worship, Pastor Spalding bounded up to the podium with his patented big smile. "Welcome, everyone! Isn't it good to be in the house of the Lord today? We're especially glad to see the York Creek Road folks here in one piece. Please remember to pray for their neighbors who are recovering from their injuries."

That drew the attention of the congregation and many of them looked toward Lee, Abigail, Carrie Sue, and Amy. Amy wanted to crawl under the pew. The lady directly behind Abigail patted her on the shoulder. After he had their attention again, Pastor Spalding made a few brief announcements and then launched into his sermon.

"If you're like me, you don't want to be reminded of your sins and failures, but that's part of life. Despite rumors to the contrary, none of us has arrived yet. Today I want to talk to you about King David, a man after God's own heart, and how he failed. I mean, really failed. We're talking about the big ones: adultery and murder! We can learn some lessons that will help us when we sin. Notice that I said, *when,* not *if,* we sin."

Pastor Spalding had them turn to the passage in Second Samuel eleven that described how David saw Bathsheba, lusted after her, got her pregnant, and then had her husband, Uriah, murdered as part of an attempt to cover up his sin. He then had them turn to Psalm fifty-one.

"Folks, this was David's prayer after he was busted by the prophet. Let's look at some of the verses here and see how we can apply them to our own lives. First of all, repent of your sin to God. Just admit it and confess it to God. Look how David recognized it as sin against God and assumed full responsibility for it. Be totally open and honest before God. By the way, repent means change of thought. I thought it was a good idea to kill Uriah, now I'm confessing, that is, agreeing with God, that it was a bad idea." He continued to make several more points about receiving God's forgiveness and making restitution wherever possible.

"Let's look at verse eight and see if I can explain it. It says, *'let the bones which You have broken rejoice.'* What does that mean? I broke my arm when I was a kid and I can assure you that my bones were not happy." He paused and looked at a number of puzzled faces before he went on to answer his own question.

"Remember that David was a shepherd. When a willful little lamb decided to wander away too many times, he would take his shepherd's crook and break the front leg of that lamb." He paused as he heard startled gasps from some of the women. "I know, I know. It sounds cruel, but David didn't just leave the lamb in the middle of the trail; he splinted the bone and then he put the little lamb in a sling and carried the lamb on his chest until it healed. After weeks of close contact with the shepherd, that little lamb would never wander away again. The lamb was disciplined out of love, not hatred."

Pastor Spalding saw expressions of understanding and then wrapped up his message. "Folks, if you feel like you're about to get a broken leg because you've failed, or sinned, or fallen short, and you think God might be about to discipline you, come on down for prayer and make it right with God. Take heart! He loves you as much as He loves David. *'Create in me a clean heart, O God, and renew a steadfast spirit within me.'* May this be the cry of all of our hearts because that's when God can use us more effectively."

He made some more points and then invited them to come down for prayer. Several people made their way up to the front while many more edged their way toward Lee and Abigail to talk to them about their harrowing experience. Amy and Carrie Sue found a way to slip through the crowd.

By the time Carrie Sue and Amy and Lee and Abigail had reassembled at the farm, they were hungry.

"Lee, would you fire up the grill?"

"What can I do?" Carrie Sue asked.

"Oh, how about setting the table? I've got some burger patties ready to go. You can set out the tossed salad and the potato salad. Oh, and grab that quart of applesauce. It's in the door with all the condiments."

It was not long before the burgers were done and they sat down to their very summery meal.

"Are you packed? Is everything okay with the landlord?" Abigail asked Carrie Sue.

"Almost. I have one little problem." Carrie Sue did not want to impose on Abigail but she could not avoid the direct question.

"Oh?"

"Well, the end of the month is Saturday and the landlord changed his mind about letting me stay until July eighth. He was going to prorate my rent but he just told me that he wanted me out by Saturday or he'd charge me for another full month. I think he has a friend who wants to move in right away."

"Is that legal?" Amy asked with a tinge of outrage.

"I don't know, but I don't have the resources or the energy to fight him."

"Well, you'll just have to move here by Saturday, then." Abigail said it in a tone that conveyed that the matter was settled.

"Are you sure? I mean that's only a week away from your wedding."

"What's a little more chaos?" Abigail laughed. "You can take the bedroom upstairs until I move out and then you can either stay up there or move into the front bedroom. What other options do you have?"

"Well, I was thinking of staying with my mom for a week and putting my stuff in storage."

"That is *not* an option!" Abigail scolded her with an exaggerated frown. "Your mother could switch back into Dorkas and kidnap you again and hand you back over to the cult. She could mince you up and bury you in her rose garden with all your father's skeletons. She could..."

"All right! All right!" Carrie Sue laughed and put her hands up in surrender. "I'll be here by Saturday. Is it okay if I start bringing stuff over in my car?"

"Sure. Anytime. I'll get an extra key made for you."

"How much furniture do you have?" Lee asked.

"Oh, just my bedroom stuff and a couch and a stuffed chair from the living room. Then there's the kitchen table and two chairs. I'm going to donate the couch to the resale shop where I work. You said you're leaving your couch here, right?"

"Yes. And Lee's got a nice kitchen table so my bigger one can go in the dining room and your little one can go in the kitchen. We're taking my dining room stuff over to Lee's, er, our place."

They continued to discuss the logistics of the move and where all the furniture would end up. Lee offered to use his truck and trailer to move her. Amy felt badly because she had nothing to contribute. Her mobile home had been burned to the ground with every stick of furniture in it. They presumed it was yet another cult attack. They presumed it would remain yet another unsolved case.

Plans were set. Dishes were cleared. Carrie Sue and Amy relaxed in chairs on the back porch, carefully positioning the angle so that the sun would tan them evenly. Lee and Abigail positioned their chairs on the front porch so that they could hold hands. They enjoyed the balmy breezes and contentedly filled their afternoon respite with talk of their upcoming wedding and honeymoon, their animals and crops, the shooting and the sheriff.

Richard York was pleasantly surprised to see his father sitting up in his bed and snapped a crisp salute as he entered the private room.

"Semper fi!" David York rasped and returned the salute. He was proud of his son who had nearly followed in his footsteps. They each joined the FBI after their Marine careers were completed. Richard put in ten years and then went to college on the G.I. bill and became an attorney before his father lured him into joining the FBI. Richard moved on to the Department of Justice after that.

"You look better, Dad. How are you feeling?"

"Like I've been shot. Not the first time but I sure hope it's the last!" He was feisty and angry and talked in clipped sentences because of the shortness of breath that came with his wound. "I'm worried about your mother. How's she doing? She's been slowing down mentally, and I don't want to leave her alone. That's why I quit that maintenance job a couple months ago."

"She's settling down. She misses you, of course, and she keeps asking the same questions over and over. She keeps telling me about that big horse and keeps peeking out the windows looking for it. What has been going on? Why would anyone want to shoot you and the neighbors? And what does that horse have to do with anything?"

"I've got a hunch and it'll sound like a fairy tale, but there are a lot of things that don't add up along with all the suspicious characters around here." He looked at the open door, frowned, and then motioned for Richard to close it. Pressing the bandage on his chest with his large hand, he coughed and winced.

Abigail happened to be in the house when the phone rang Monday morning. She screened the phone call and listened to the message warily. It was from Sherry Samuels – the SRA survivor who was sent in last fall to distract or harm Abigail. Abigail received that word of knowledge from the Holy Spirit at the time and confronted the cult-loyal parts of Sherry. She added another knife to her collection when the part named Abaddon pulled it on her. Another Abaddon. They all seemed to have an Abaddon or an Apollyon.

Abigail finished listening to her message and then decided that she would have to pray about whether or not she would call her back. Through her contacts with the Ministerial Alliance, she found out that Sherry, the six-foot-tall woman with ink-black hair, sometimes attended Rev. Don Wilmore's Hillsdale Baptist Church.

Abigail played the message again after Sherry was finished: "Hello? This is Sherry Samuels. You saw me a couple of times last fall and I'd like to come back and work on my issues." She left her phone number.

Lord, is this another set-up? Another attempt to destroy me? Should I see her again? Abigail prayed silently as she drifted out to her garden. She called it her prayer garden because that was what she did as she battled the weeds or tied up the undisciplined tomato plants. Rolling slowly down the bean rows on the little garden cart, she plucked weeds and squished bugs. Thoughts tumbled in her mind. She thought of the probability that Prinz was dead and how that might have weakened the grip of the demon-driven parts of Sherry. Perhaps Sherry's call was a confirmation that the tide was turning. Abigail was loath to give up on anyone.

By the time she got to the end of the long row of beans, she decided to call Cindy. She made it a practice to consult God before she consulted with anyone else when she had weighty matters to decide.

"Hello there." Cindy picked up on the second ring.

"Have you got a couple of minutes?"

"Sure. What's up?"

"Do you remember me telling you about that six-foot-tall SRA survivor who pulled a knife on me last fall?"

"Yes. Scary."

"Well, she just called and wants to see me again to work on her issues."

"Wasn't she sent in to destroy you?"

"Yes, but they all have a few personalities who are supposed to do that. The Lord just happened to bring that out right away."

"Oh." Cindy connected the dots. "Do Carrie Sue and Amy have parts that are supposed to hurt you?"

"Yes. It's all part of the programming. Sometimes it's against particular people and sometimes it's general programming against all Christians or all nice people or anyone who is helpful."

"I had no idea."

"I've observed a lot of similarities in them over the years. I've worked with survivors from all over the country, plus a bunch of local ones. It seems that no matter what particular cult they come from, the masters seem to work from the same book. There are variations on the themes of course, but I just expect it when it comes up. Anyway, I just wanted to pray with you a little bit and see if God confirms anything to you."

Richard York accompanied his mother to the hospital for his father's discharge. Wanting to maintain a low profile, he drove their car. He was like so many people who worked in D.C. and lived in Virginia or Maryland. He liked the Eldersburg, Maryland area. With his high-pressure job, he liked to come home to his isolated five acres. He remodeled the original old farmhouse and found a vintage Allis Chalmers tractor to go with it. Having been raised on the old York farm, he found comfort in being close to the land whenever he could.

After settling back into his own home, David was confronted with the reality of his situation. The much-relieved Martha was bustling around the house trying to fluff and straighten and offer him food as she chattered on and on about the same things she had prattled about for days.

"Martha, honey," the beleaguered man said, "I'm fine. Let me just sit here and talk with Richard for a little bit. I'll call you if I need anything."

She looked back and forth between her husband and her son and then sighed. The fickle cloud that had momentarily lifted settled back down and fogged her brain once again. She sat in her easy chair and stared vacuously out the window.

Richard was beginning to realize just how quickly his mother was deteriorating. "Dad, I think I'm going to take some vacation time and hang around here if that's okay with you and Mom."

"That would be good, son. I could use a hand with your mother while I'm recuperating. I'm also in the middle of a hornet's nest here. I'm not sure how I got in it and how I'm going to get us out of it. I could use your expertise."

"Tell me what's been going on here. Mom keeps rambling about the big horse and trouble next door. Who lives up there now? Why would someone target you and her and the Milners and whoever bought up that place across the road?"

"Slow down, son." David almost laughed, but the seriousness of the situation and the soreness of his chest caused him to control his breathing. "Can you go to my desk? There's a false bottom in the center drawer under all the pens and pencils and such. Pull it all the way out and you can lift it from the back. There's a notebook in there."

"Still don't trust computers, eh?" Richard smiled at his father as he crossed the room in front of him.

"Actually, there's a thumb drive in there, too."

47

The movement roused Martha and pulled her out of her empty place. "Do you need something, dear?" she warbled her query.

"Not now, honey; just relax." He smiled warmly at the love of his life.

She settled back down and soon drifted back into her ever lengthening vacant mental state.

Placing the slim notebook into his father's hand, Richard returned to his chair and waited for him to begin the debriefing.

Looking directly at Richard, the elderly man began to debrief him much like he would have done years ago as an FBI agent. "The lady next door is a widow. Steele. She bought the place from Willy and Lisa after they split up. You remember his crazy old man?"

"Sure do. Is he still around?"

"No. I heard he drank himself into the ground. Willy's brothers seem to be following in his footsteps. They're kind of wild, but none of them are as mean as the old man was."

"Yeah. I remember when he bit the tails off those Doberman pups. He said he'd save himself the vet bill and then laughed like a hyena." They reminisced about some of the antics of that wild family for a couple of minutes and then got back on track.

"Anyway, about three months ago," David paged through his notebook and then continued, "a man on the big horse went by and waited at the end of her property. He shot at her. I don't think he hit her or it would have been all over the news. There was a second shot which I'm real sure came from Earl Milner. Now why he would be shooting at a man who was shooting at the widow is beyond me. I can only guess that he was already aware of trouble between the shooter and the widow and was watching out for her. The leaves were down and I could see that she was coming up her back steps onto the deck."

"Okay."

"Then there's the fire that someone started in her woods. Martha and I saw them cut through the corner of our property."

"Who were they?"

"We didn't recognize them. They seemed young by the way they walked and carried themselves, but they had hoods on. They crossed the creek and headed down the road to the south."

"We saw someone on that big horse hiding in the rough behind us too many times to count. I guess they didn't think we would notice. Whoever it was seemed to be watching the widow's property."

"Why would she be under anyone's surveillance? What does she do?" Richard puzzled out loud.

"There's nothing that stands out that I can see. I used some of my old contacts and nothing stands out to them either. I've seen her in the sheriff's office several times filing complaints or asking about her cases."

"Cases?"

"It seems that there was a break-in last year and the man who did it disappeared. I saw him in the jail cell when they brought him in that day. They had to stop at the hospital first. Rumor has it that the widow took out his leg."

"So, who was he?"

"Just some local kid as far as I could tell."

"How'd you find all this out?"

David grinned at his son. "No one is as invisible as an old maintenance guy. Everyone at the sheriff's office thought I was blind, deaf, and stupid. The folks at the courthouse complex seemed to have had the same opinion."

4

Friday, June 29

Abigail had mixed feelings about making the phone call. On one hand, she wanted to minister to every SRA survivor that she could. On the other, she remembered her last encounter with Sherry Samuels very clearly. She was not anxious to add another knife to her collection, but she and Cindy had prayed about it and had peace about the decision to try again.

"Sherry?" Abigail asked.

"Yes."

"This is Abigail Steele. I'm so sorry it's taken me this long to get back to you. Are you still interested in coming for counseling?"

"Yes. My grandmother just died and I think I need some help."

"I'm so sorry for your loss. I know this seems like a long way off, but do you think you will be okay until Friday, July twentieth? I'm going to be unavailable for a couple of weeks and that's the first opening I have."

"I guess I'll have to be. What time?

"Will noon work for you?"

"Yes."

"Good. I'll see you then."

Abigail hung up and got ready to go to town. She had several appointments as well as her usual Friday errands. Amy and Carrie Sue had been busy all week with transporting whatever belongings fit into Carrie Sue's car. Bit by bit she was getting settled in the upstairs bedroom while Amy became unsettled about *not* being able to help much. She was so accustomed to being strong and vigorous, but she did not want to risk any more complications with her pregnancy.

"Hey, you two, don't work too hard. Lee can load the rest of the stuff on his trailer. We'll do that after I get home this afternoon."

"Okay. Sounds like a plan."

Abigail was soon cruising down the road. Traffic was light and she was able to enjoy the lush greenery as she passed through the familiar terrain. Max and Pastor Spalding arrived shortly after she did and they quickly launched into the session. Max was somewhat on edge, but then, Saturday was another ritual day. Full moon.

"How is it inside?" Abigail asked.

"Mostly quiet, but I feel like something or someone is lurking around."

"Let's ask the Lord to show us who or what it is." Abigail prayed to that effect and waited a moment for Max's response.

"It's that Maximillian guy. He's upset about being put out of commission."

"Well, let's see if he'll come up and talk with us."

Max cleared his throat and shifted his posture making it very evident that another personality had assumed executive control. He immediately challenged Abigail. "What do you mean by putting us to sleep and making all those declarations for us? Who do you think you are? I ought to call the Praetorian Guard and order your immediate execution."

Praetorian Guard. Abigail tucked another scrap of information away before addressing the general. "Max has to be able to function."

"Max! Max! Who the blazes is this Max character?"

"Max Berryman happens to be the original person from whom you split out. You are a part of him and he has the obligation to do whatever is best for everyone concerned. And that includes you."

"You are not making any sense."

"Are you interested in understanding what I'm talking about?"

"I am interested in resuming my command and fulfilling my assignments."

"I don't think that would be in Max's best interest and, by extension, yours."

"Woman! I've tolerated enough of your dialogue. Hold your tongue."

"How about if I talk to Caesar then?"

"I should cut off your head right now!"

"Sorry, but that's not going to happen. Let me talk to Max again."

General Maximillian sputtered as he disappeared back into his internal place. Max returned shaking his head. "That guy has quite an ego. And he has no clue about reality."

"That's what programming does to the parts. He probably visualizes himself wearing Roman sandals and has a sword in his belt. That *is* his reality."

"Actually, when I visualize him, that's pretty much what he looks like. He's got one of those helmets with the bristles, or whatever they are, sticking up like a Mohawk and he's wearing some kind of a metal vest thing." Max was getting much more comfortable with describing his internal world.

"It seems that we are at an impasse with him and all the others in there. Are you up for asking the Lord to break the lie of multiplicity for these guys and let them understand the truth of the dissociation?"

"Yeah. Um, could you help me with that? I'm not exactly sure what to say."

"Sure. I'll pray and then you pray in agreement. Lord, we ask that You would go through Max's system and let the Caesar, the generals, the Praetorian Guard, the Senate, and anyone else in there be released from the lie of multiplicity so that they no longer believe that they are independent from Max, and would You allow them to understand the truth about the dissociation?"

"Yeah, God, I agree. Please let them get it, amen." Max kept his eyes closed for another minute and then he reported, "They're all just milling around looking real confused."

"Let's see if General Maximillian will come back and talk to me again."

"Sure." Max closed his eyes in a long blink and soon it was evident that he had been displaced once again by the general.

"Hello. Are you okay?"

"I don't know what in Hades you did, woman! What kind of treachery have you worked on us with your sorcery?"

"It's not sorcery. It's truth. I serve Jesus Christ of Nazareth and He is the one who unveiled your eyes."

"We crucified Jesus of Nazareth and now you're telling me that He's alive. How do I know that this is the truth? How do I know you're not tricking me?"

"You don't; although you may have a gut feeling about it. You seem to be a bit less hostile toward me right now."

"Something seems to have changed."

"Yes. Would you be willing to have me ask this Jesus Christ to bring you more truth?"

"About what? What do you have in mind?"

"Can you tell me about your first memory?"

General Maximillian suddenly looked at the floor. It was apparent that what he was remembering was not pretty. Clearing his throat, he said, "I was flogged until I passed out. When the men revived me, they said that I had two choices: I could be a whipping boy or I could rise in the ranks and be a whipper."

"You chose to be a whipper."

"Yes."

"It was not much of a choice, but it certainly came with a price."

"Yes. Every advancement in rank came with tests. If I passed them, I'd advance. They compelled me to do things that I will not convey to a woman."

"I can pretty well imagine. And I have a feeling that under all that hard-core military armor there's a soft heart."

General Maximillian hung his head at the words. He had barricaded his heart behind thick armor. "I couldn't get out of it. They had me flog Jesus the Nazarene. I saw Him crucified. And then they told me that Satan had won. If I wanted to survive, I had better not throw in with a dead man."

"You were hopeless and didn't see another choice."

Maximillian nodded. His mouth kept opening and closing, but he could not utter a word.

"Maximillian," Abigail gently addressed the stricken personality, "they lied to you. They used you to do their dirty work. The true Jesus Christ *was* crucified about two thousand years ago, but that is not the end of the story. Jesus Christ was raised from the dead and ascended to Heaven. He has defeated Satan."

Maximillian raised his eyes slowly and looked at Abigail as he processed the implications. If what she said was true, then he had been royally duped. Used. Manipulated. And that got his attention.

"Would you like for me to ask this risen Savior, Jesus the Christ, to introduce Himself to you and bring you truth about your choices?"

"Yes, please," a much humbler general answered.

"Lord Jesus Christ, would You come to this part of Max that has been programed to be and do what the cult chose for him. Let him see You with his spiritual eyes or hear You with his spiritual ears or just sense Your presence and Your truth as You answer his questions about his identity and his purpose and his past, amen." Abigail briefly glanced at Pastor Spalding who was intently focused on Max and then she turned her attention back to Max.

General Maximillian looked up at Abigail. He was distraught as he hoarsely whispered, "Whom then did we crucify?"

"What do you mean?" Abigail was fairly sure that he would be referring to a ritual sacrifice that involved a crucifixion, but she waited for the general to give the details. It would be a variation on a story that she had heard far too many times from various ritual abuse survivors over the years.

"I just know that I helped flog a man. They had him stripped down naked and... and I don't know how he survived it. We kicked him and spit on him. Someone stuck a crown of thorns on his head and... and he was bleeding... there was so much blood." Maximillian shook his head and put his face into his hands and wept loudly. "I did it. I did it. I killed him. I should have died."

"How did you kill him?" Abigail asked. She sensed that there was more to this story.

"I'm the one that shoved the killing dagger into his heart. I did it." He was disconsolate as he sorted out the details of the memory without the programing to confound his thoughts or numb his emotions.

"Would you be willing to go back to that memory and ask the true Lord Jesus bring you the truth?"

"I have naught to lose," he said hopelessly.

"Lord Jesus, You are the same yesterday, today, and forever. You were there that day. Would You cover that event with Your cleansing blood and flush out all darkness and deceptions of the enemy so that he can see You with his spiritual eyes, hear You with his spiritual ears, or sense You in such a way that he would realize the truth. Lord, did General Maximillian kill that man? Is he responsible? What is the truth that will set him free?"

After several prolonged, silent minutes Maximillian slowly raised his head. "That wasn't the real Jesus. I don't know why I can remember this now and I couldn't remember this before, but I remember seeing them, uh, the hooded ones, drag a man out of the van. He kept yelling something about suing the sheriff and screaming that he wouldn't get away with this. He was pointing at Zorroz."

"Interesting. How would he know that Zorroz was the sheriff?"

"Zorroz was not wearing his hood."

"Huh." Abigail filed that bit of information away. "So, what's the truth? Did you kill the man?"

"Well, it was my hand on the dagger, but now I know that I had a killing dagger in my back. It was do or die. Kill or be killed." He put his head down and clasped his hands behind his neck. "Why didn't I just let them kill me?"

"Let's take that to the Lord, too."

"Sure."

"Lord would You address this kind of agony and bring him truth?" Abigail and Pastor Spalding waited quietly, prayerfully, for the response.

"He said that they were going to kill the man that night. If I hadn't done it, someone else would have been put into that position. Jesus said that it's not my fault."

"You were set up."

"This angers me!" he said as he straightened his posture. "I want to kill them!"

"And that would make you exactly like them," Abigail gently chided. "They'd love it. And so would Satan. His agenda is to kill, steal, deceive and destroy."

"It's a no-win situation."

"Ah, that's where you're wrong." Abigail smiled compassionately at him. "How about if I lay out a plan that will be win-win for you. No more duplicity. No more double-binds."

"I'm ready," the general surrendered. "What do you have in mind?"

Abigail laid out the big picture of how Max Berryman was dissociated as a child because of the trauma of the leukemia and his subsequent issues that made him an easy mark for Levi. She talked about the specifics of how Maximillian was created for, and programed to do the bidding of the cult and Satan. The information further inflamed Maximillian.

"What do I have to do?"

"Is there anything left that's still uncomfortable for you in that memory?"

"Not really. I'm just angry at them."

"What do you want to do with your anger? Do you want to keep it or let it go?"

"If I let it go, it's as if they get away with it."

"Let me talk to you about anger and forgiveness."

"Forgiveness! How can I ever forgive them for what they've done?"

"Give me five minutes." Getting the nod, Abigail taught Maximillian the principles of forgiveness and its associated issues of reconciliation and trust, and of letting God execute timely, creative vengeance.

"Okay, that makes sense. I'm ready to choose that."

"What about those under your jurisdiction? The Praetorian Guards and the other soldiers?"

"Well, there are a couple of hold-outs, but the rest are on board." He thought for a moment and then said, "Humph! My last order as a general is to all the hold-outs. There will be no insurrection in the ranks. We are no longer serving Satan or the Satanists."

Barely suppressing a grin, Abigail asked, "Why don't you do some business with the Most High God and then if there's nothing left, we'll see who needs to be integrated."

Maximillian forgave the cult members and reported a peaceful sense of relief. Abigail then prayed her comprehensive prayer for all those under Maximillian. When they prayed about integration, Maximillian sensed that there needed to be consolidation of some key players into himself. The rest should be integrated while he remained dissociated with a new assignment.

He warned Abigail that the Caesar was very demon-loyal and cult-loyal as were the other two generals. He named Brutuz as one of them who was very traitorous. "Look out for him!"

Max was a little more encouraged by the end of the session. He left for work while Abigail and Pastor Spalding debriefed.

"Who do you think they flogged and crucified? Could it have been an actual person? How recent do you think it was?" Pastor Spalding asked with concern.

"There's no telling. I mean, sometimes the cult can use one event and incorporate elements of it into the person's mind through hypnosis and programming. It might have been an actual person who was really flogged and crucified or it might have been programed in. Programing is tricky. In some ways it doesn't matter if they actually did or saw something because it will have the same effect. In this case, though, I'm leaning toward an actual event based on his visceral response to the memory."

"So, if the guy in his memory was pointing at Sheriff Bynum and threatening to sue him..." Pastor Spalding lapsed into a thoughtful silence as he thought about the ramifications.

"It makes you wonder how recent that ritual was. If it was recent, then someone was abducted somewhere around here."

"Maximillian said that the man said that the sheriff wouldn't get away with it."

"I hope that's prophetic," Abigail asserted. "I just wonder how the man was lucid enough to recognize Bynum. But then, it might be God working to take Bynum down."

"Okay, is that it?" Lee called out as he stood poised to close the trailer door. He lifted his cap and wiped the sweat from his brow before replacing it.

"Let me do a dummy check," Carrie Sue replied.

"A what?"

"A dummy check. That's where you go back and look in all the closets and drawers to make sure that you didn't miss something obvious and have to smack yourself on the forehead and say, 'Dummy!'"

"Right." Lee nodded his head slowly as he said it.

Carrie Sue quickly completed her check and came out with her thumb up and a big smile. "We're good to go." She was excited and ready to finish the move. Of course, the move would complicate things with her mother; but then, everything with her mother was complicated. She did not want her mother to know where she would be living. She did not want to jeopardize Abigail's property or Amy or the neighbors by having her mother – particularly the cult-loyal Dorkas part of her mother – come onto the property.

Carrie Sue slid into her car and followed the trailer that Lee and Abigail were pulling. It had gotten a lot of use hauling livestock and household goods since he moved from Montana. Once Abigail was moved into their new house he hoped that he would be finished with the moving business for quite a while. He was ready to marry Abigail and settle into married life. Eight more days.

It was not long before they were creaking and bumping up the gravel driveway to Abigail's old farmhouse. The SUV that had followed them at a discrete distance slowly rolled by shortly after Carrie Sue turned up the driveway. The driver continued to snake down the road past the York's home, past Charlie Fletcher's property, and on to the windowless building to make a report.

Lee expertly maneuvered the trailer so that the end of it was at the foot of the ramp. Using the dolly, he handled the heavier pieces of furniture and then stacked boxes on it for the transfer to the base of the stairs. Carrie Sue and Abigail brought whatever he unloaded to the upstairs bedroom and got other things settled in the appropriate rooms.

"This is so nice and airy!" Carrie Sue exclaimed happily as she surveyed her new digs. She had chosen to occupy the bedroom on the north end of the upper floor. Her window looked out on a broad valley that swept up to the Milner's house on the next hill. It would be cooler in the summer and she would not feel self-conscious about creaking the floorboards right over Abigail. There was a small landing at the top of the stairs with doors which opened to each bedroom. By leaving both doors and the windows wide open, it was light and breezy. The large tree that was centered over the southern end of house gave ample afternoon shade.

Once Lee was finished unloading the trailer, he closed it up and said his good-byes. "I'll just leave you ladies to do the finishing touches, but before I go, is there anything heavy that you need help with?"

"No, we're good," Carrie Sue called down the stairs. "Thanks so much for all your help. I don't know what I would have done!"

"You're welcome. See ya later." He gave Abigail a quick hug and a kiss, and then headed out the door.

"You'll be back for supper, right?"

"Wouldn't miss it."

5

Saturday, June 30

Breakfast was livelier with the addition of Carrie Sue. Amy was excited about having someone who could fully relate to her. Carrie Sue was relieved to be in a relatively safe place. Abigail was happy, content. She was finally seeing the beginnings of one of her dreams: providing a place of sanctuary for her beleaguered ritual abuse survivors. *Lord, I will not despise the day of small beginnings and trust that if I am faithful with little You will entrust me with more.*

"One more week! Are you nervous?" Carrie Sue asked and shook Abigail out of her thoughts.

"More like excited. It's like we're throwing a big party and all our favorite people are coming." Abigail beamed. "And that includes the two of you!"

"I'm not sure what to wear," Amy said. "I mean, you got me some nice things, but they're not exactly fancy-smancy wedding clothes."

"Hey, this is informal. As far as I'm concerned if you show up in something purple, I'll be happy."

"Wait a minute," Carrie Sue said, "I thought *you* were wearing purple. Aren't the guests supposed to *not* wear the same color as the bride?"

"Not at my wedding. I'm not going to be a Bride-zilla about it, but my favorite color is purple, and if everyone wears something purple, I'll be happy."

"You're a hoot."

"Thanks," Abigail replied and gave her a cheesy grin. "Changing subjects. What do you have planned for today?"

"I'm going to finish unpacking. There's not much left to do. But first I need to go back to the apartment and make sure it's clean and turn in my keys."

"I'm going to calmly keep making this baby. I'll probably go supervise the cleaning. Do you need us to help you with anything?"

"Actually, I could use some help with some of the wedding decorations."

They were interested and excited about helping their friend and benefactor. Abigail explained how she wanted the silver and purple foil-wrapped chocolate candies made into little favors that would be at the guest tables. "We'll need at least one hundred of them. Whatever is left over will go into candy dishes."

"We can do this," Amy said as she eyed the scissors, the silver and purple ribbon, and the netting that were needed for the project.

"Thanks. I made a few already. They're not hard, just time consuming."

They finished breakfast and lingered a little while at the table talking about the wedding plans and the division of labor around the house once Abigail moved in with Lee.

"Lee and I are going to get some last-minute things taken care of and then we'll meet you back here tonight for supper."

"Hey, why don't you let us make supper?" Amy asked as she looked at Carrie Sue for confirmation.

"That would be great. Check the freezer. There's ground beef and chicken in there. Oh, and check the garden, too." Abigail was pleased at the offer. It was one less thing for her to do and it was a gauge of how well the ladies were learning basic home-making skills.

The soft toot of Lee's horn ended the conversation as Abigail grabbed her wallet and headed out the front door. She was down the steps and opening the truck door before he had a chance to open it for her. "Hey, hey," he laughed, "what's the big rush?"

"I don't know. Maybe I'm just thinking that we're one week away from being married. That's seven days. That's like seventy hours that we have to do stuff."

"What's left to do?"

"Well, mostly wait, I guess. Today we meet with Pastor Spalding to finalize everything. He told me that he's picked out two or three ceremonies for us to choose from."

"I vote for the shortest one!" Lee laughed again. He was in a very good mood. "I can't wait to start our married life together."

"Me too, but I want to savor the whole process even while I hurry up and wait. I hear of so many people who are so focused on the wedding that they haven't prepared for the marriage."

"Well, we've both been married before and I sure know how to do things wrong, but I also know how to do a few things right."

"I guess we could all say that. So, we'll just have to decide if an issue is so important that it's the hill we want to die on. That would save a lot of headaches."

Lee agreed, and then said with mock seriousness, "You do squeeze the toothpaste from the bottom, right? After all, I actually read on one of the boxes that for best results one must squeeze from the bottom and roll it up."

"So, I get more cavities because I squeeze it in the middle?" Abigail replied with mock horror.

"Oh, baby, we're in trouble."

"I have the perfect solution."

"What's that?"

"Two tubes. His and hers." Her triumphant grin evolved into a giggle.

By the time they got finished with purchasing the silver and purple candles and some of the other items that she and Cindy and Ginny were going to use to decorate the church and fellowship hall it was time to meet with Pastor Spalding.

"Come in! Come in!" He shook Lee's hand and gave Abigail a light shoulder hug. "Have a seat," he said as he waved to the two chairs that faced his desk. He hustled around to his chair and sat down as well.

It did not take them long to agree upon a ceremony that was meaningful to both of them. They went over the order of service and other details. Pastor Spalding reminded them to eat a good meal before the wedding so no one would pass out. He had a check-list that he had used over the years.

"No ring bearer? No flower girl?"

Lee and Abigail looked at each other and laughed before Abigail explained, "We've both seen too many cute little kids upstage the bride and groom. I know it sounds selfish, but it's our day and we don't want to take any chances. Besides, this is a second wedding for both of us. We're trying to keep it simple."

They talked about the wedding logistics for a few more minutes and then he made it a point to go through his list. "I don't want to insult you, but just because you're a counselor, it doesn't mean that we can assume that you know it all," he said as he smiled in Abigail's direction and winked in Lee's.

"No problem. You've been married for a long time so I really respect that and expect to learn from you."

"Thank you. Well, my list is considerably shorter than it would be if you were going to raise a family or blend a family. Let me start with the number one marriage breaker: finances." He stopped and raised an expectant eyebrow.

After Lee apprised him of their convictions about finances, Pastor Spalding went on to the other items on his list – intimacy, biblical roles of the husband and wife in the home, communication, handling conflict, different styles of expressing anger and forgiveness, and more. Finally, he prayed for them. He blessed them and their future together. "I'm really looking forward to next week. I'm just tickled that the Lord has brought the two of you together."

One of the breeders was in the seventh month of her pregnancy. She had been impregnated at a previous ritual. She knew the drill; this was not the first baby that she had borne for the express purpose of providing a sacrifice for a ritual. Of course, her other personalities experienced the pregnancy like any other woman whose hormones kicked in and whose maternal instincts flared. Having been dissociated as a child, there were many personalities within this young woman who were oblivious to the reality that the pregnant ones knew and dreaded. They were programmed. It was their job.

Xerxes decided that the full moon ritual should take place at Charlie Fletcher's farm despite Charlie's death. Or, perhaps, because of Charlie Fletcher's death. Something was going on in that sector of his territory and he wanted to get it under control. He knew that it had something to do with that woman. What made her untouchable? She had to have a weakness. He would find it and exploit it.

As the local master, Zorroz was on edge. With all the irregularities that had occurred in the last couple of months, he was doubly anxious for this ritual to be a success. He had to impress both Daggett and Darod. They were vying for the place that had been vacated by the death of Prinz. Xerxes also needed to be impressed.

As Sheriff Bynum, he was able to commission one of his like-minded deputies, Andy Lockman, to use Charlie's tractor to drag the ceremonial rock back up to its place under the oak tree. Charlie Fletcher had been estranged from his family for a long time. He never called them. They seldom visited. No one had filed a missing person report, and even if they did, his body would never be found.

The faithful ones felt stirrings from their demonic hosts. Restless with anticipation, they prepared for their roles in the ritual that evening. Russ Ranson's normally docile wife switched into a vixen, a demon-driven shrew, and accompanied him to the ritual site. Carrie Sue's mother switched into Dorkas and drove the short distance down the back roads.

Others mounted horses or drove their four-wheelers through the well-worn trails through the woods along the river bottoms and along the edges of the fields that checkered the countryside. To the ordinary citizens in the area, it looked like a great time for a night ride with the light of the full moon. They would converge discretely around ten that night and by three o'clock in the morning curses would be dispatched using the diabolical winged couriers.

The day flew by for Carrie Sue and Amy. By noon the apartment was immaculate and they went to the office and faced a grumpy supervisor. Sitting behind the disordered desk, he barely acknowledged Carrie Sue's request. At last he mumbled something about checking the apartment next week and then if it had no damage, he'd mail her the deposit.

"Uh, excuse me, Mr. Young," Carrie Sue said as nicely as she could, "but I need for you to inspect it before I give you this key."

"I don't have time to do that now."

"I gave you full notice and besides, that's part of the rental agreement that I have here." Carrie Sue held out the papers.

"I told you I don't have time."

"I'm sorry, sir, but I've heard too many horror stories of people not getting their deposit back because the management claimed damage that did not exist."

"Are you calling me a liar?" He puffed furiously on his cigar and blew smoke in her direction.

"No sir, I just want to make sure that I'll get my full deposit back." She tapped the paper and said, "These are *your* rules."

"Fine, let's go now." Snapping his cap off of his desk, slapping it on his head, he stomped to the door and briskly walked the fifty feet to Carrie Sue's apartment door. "Gimme the key!" he demanded as he turned and held out his hand.

"I'll get it," Carrie Sue responded assertively. She moved past him and opened the door.

He walked in and made a show of inspecting the apartment. For a man who did not have time for an inspection, he took his sweet time looking behind every cabinet door and into every drawer in both the kitchen and bathroom. He opened the closets and looked high and low. He kicked at the living room carpet where he noticed a stain. When he finished, he begrudgingly conceded that the apartment was clean and only had normal and expected wear and tear.

"Thank you. Will you sign my rental paper now?"

"Huh?"

She pointed at the bottom of the last sheet. "Here. This says you're supposed to sign it to certify that you inspected it and found no damage and that my deposit will be sent within two weeks."

"Geez, lady, you some kind of lawyer or something?" he asked through teeth still clamped to his cigar. "Gimme the paper," he huffed as he grudgingly reached for the pen in his pocket.

"No. Just got burned too many times." She forced a smile and handed him the paper. Once he signed it, she handed him the key and then she and Amy made a bee-line for her car.

Once inside, Amy dissolved in a fit of laughter. "Geez, lady, you some kind of lawyer or something?"

she mimicked the manager. "Carrie Sue! Where did you get the nerve to get in that guy's face like that?"

Carrie Sue was grinning from ear to ear. "I guess I've been going through Assertiveness Training 101 dealing with Mom's many and varied personalities – especially Dorkas!"

"Woo! That was a thing of beauty! Just wait until Abigail hears about this."

They rehashed and celebrated the victory all the way back to Abigail's house. After making a quick lunch, they set some chicken out to thaw and then Amy started on the wedding decorations while Carrie Sue finished unpacking upstairs. They wandered down to the chicken coop to see how the peepsters were doing and then meandered through the garden to pick some of the ripe tomatoes.

"Abigail showed me how to make Grecian Chicken. It's really easy and really tastes good," Amy informed Carrie Sue.

"What's in it?" the leery woman asked. She was like so many survivors who were triggered by any number of food colors, flavors, or textures. Even though she was presumably fully integrated and healed, her mind and brain still worked by association. Some things would naturally resolve; other things would require intentional adjustments to overcome negative triggers.

"Basically, just chicken and lemon juice and oregano. Simple." Amy looked at her wary friend and reassured her, "Look; if I like it, you'll like it. Trust me. Besides if you could eat Abigail's kale quiche, you'll love this."

"I'll try it. I guess I just have to get past handling raw meat."

"Let me do that part. Once it's cooking, I'll show you what else we need to do. Why don't you start on the salad? Do you think we should do mashed potatoes and maybe some green beans?"

"Green beans? There aren't enough ripe ones yet."

Amy laughed, "Sorry, I keep forgetting that you just got here. Let me show you all the canning jars in the basement after I get this started." Amy efficiently got the chicken started while Carrie Sue made the salad. After moving the completed wedding decorations to a box in the living room and setting the table, they were ready for the next step. Beckoning to Carrie Sue and opening the door to the basement, Amy flipped on the light and made her way down the stairs.

"I was wondering what was behind that door. Wow! I had no idea."

"Check it out. She has a bunch of tools and stuff over there," Amy said as she gestured toward the workbenches. "Here's the good stuff – applesauce, jam, beans, tomatoes, spaghetti sauce – she has pumpkin in some of them, too."

Carrie Sue was impressed. "I guess we won't starve. It looks like a lot of empty jars waiting to be filled."

"Abigail mentioned that she wanted to teach me how to can."

"Maybe she'll teach me, too."

"I'm sure she will."

They heard the toot of Lee's horn and the crunch of gravel as he parked his truck. Grabbing a quart of green beans, they returned to the kitchen.

"Yum! What are you two cooking? It smells great in here," Abigail said as she greeted them.

"I'll second that," Lee added. "I'm so hungry my stomach thinks my throat's been cut."

The women responded with groans and rolled eyes.

The dinner conversation was spirited with Amy's animated reenactment of the encounter with the grumpy apartment manager, drawing laughter at her exaggerated impersonation. Amy felt like she had a family; like she was finally home. Carrie Sue did not feel so alone, so isolated, so vulnerable. Lee and Abigail felt the smile of the Lord on their decision to make this place into a haven for these deeply wounded survivors. Who knew how many more would pass through these doors?

Darkness was falling on the region and the leaders of darkness were gathered in the dimly lit windowless building waiting for the right time to move out. Xerxes was looking for answers. Daggett was on the hot seat since he was now the highest-ranking master of this territory. Darod was not off the hook since he lived at the farthest edge of the county and was the county commissioner. His territory covered several counties further east.

"We know that they're both living up there with that woman. The word is that she and the man that lives across the street are getting married. That'll leave them alone up there eventually."

"What about Milner? You remember what he did to Viper." He was referring to Earl's shot that practically destroyed Charlie Fletcher's hand just as Charlie shot at Abigail.

"We'll just have to find a weak spot."

"Yeah, they have to go to town sometime."

"What about that York fellow?"

"He's out of commission thanks to Viper."

"Zorroz, what's your take on York?" Daggett asked.

"You've probably seen him around the courthouse complex, at least until he retired a few months back," Zorroz answered. "I heard his wife wasn't doing so well and he had to take care of her."

"He was in the courthouse?"

"He was one of the maintenance crew both there and in the sheriff's office. Quiet. Spooky quiet. You didn't know he was there until you looked up or turned around. I kind of had the idea that he was sharper than he let on."

"What's his relation to that lady?"

"None that I know of – other than being neighbors."

"Why would Viper shoot him?"

"Not sure. Maybe Charlie got paranoid and thought the guy saw him and could finger him. Maybe he was just on a roll and decided to shoot up the whole neighborhood."

"We'll get some of our young men to pick up where Max and Charlie left off."

"Speaking of Max – why isn't he here?"

"That woman has got him deprogrammed somehow. He meets with her and that pastor. I'm afraid that if we don't do something pretty soon we're going to lose another one. He's not responding to any of the pumper commands."

"Another one?" Xerxes asked.

"Max's recruit, Nathan, was killed; and then his other recruit got with that pastor and that woman. Max didn't handle his recruits well."

75

"He'll pay for that."

"That woman filed some complaints against Max but the files disappeared, if you know what I mean. They could reappear."

Malevolence and malice were palpable in that inky room. The demons intensified the wickedness and spite in that bitter atmosphere. It was as if the human beings were inhaling and exhaling the foul spirits with every breath.

———————————

Earl and Jan Milner had been home for a couple of days. The repairs had been made to their house but the repairs to their bodies and souls were still works in progress.

"How's your hand, honey?"

"It's a little stiff," he said as he balled his fist and then extended the fingers and thumb on his right hand three times, "but it'll be back to normal in no time." He kept three fingers curled as he made a trigger-pulling gesture and added, "That snake better not show his face around here again. Next time I won't be so nice."

"Now, Earl," Jan chided, "we don't even know for sure that it was him."

"I know who I saw. Who else would it have been in a maroon pickup? Look at who got shot up: Lee, Abigail, and us." He paused and then added, "and the Yorks." He chewed on that unexpected twist until she interrupted his thoughts.

"Why did he shoot at the Yorks? I mean, they just stay to themselves. I'm pretty sure that Abigail doesn't interact with them. She's probably never even been on their property."

"It doesn't make sense." They lapsed into silence as they each pondered the events of the last week.

At last Jan got up and moved to the phone. "I'm going to call Abigail and just ask her," she announced decisively and then dialed the phone number that she had memorized long ago.

"Jan! How are you? And how's Earl? We've been thinking about you two. I'm so sorry I haven't checked on you sooner."

"Fine, fine. We're almost back to normal," she lied only slightly and added, "of course, normal at our age isn't exactly like being spring chickens. We'll have a new normal that we'll have to get used to." Her gentle laugh reassured Abigail.

"Listen, if you need anything, please call any one of us. Carrie Sue is moved in already."

"Oh? Well you have been busy and you have your wedding coming up in one week."

"It's been crazy but we're all ready. Carrie Sue's landlord was being a jerk-face. The end of the month is today and her landlord wouldn't give her an extra week. She would have had to pay for another whole month. But that's a long story I'll let her tell."

"Well, how are you all doing up there? Did you have much damage?"

"All the windows up front were shot out and we got a few holes in the siding. One of Lee's horses got grazed, but she's okay now."

"I'm glad you and Amy weren't hurt. Listen now, Earl and I were wondering about something. We were trying to figure out why the Yorks got included in the shootings. We're assuming that it was Charlie Fletcher. Do you ever talk to them?"

"No. I don't think I'd know them if I saw them. I mean, they just stay to themselves and I'm afraid that I haven't been a very good neighbor. I guess with the woods between us it's kind of like out of sight, out of mind. It's funny you asked because we were talking about that at supper tonight and we were wondering the same thing. I don't know anything about them."

"All we know is that the York family has been on that property for generations. David and Martha raised their son there, but he was in the military so they moved around a bit. Someone took care of the property while they were gone. He worked for the FBI and lived somewhere around D.C. I think."

"FBI? Huh! Well, what do you know?" Abigail was surprised by that information. "It makes me wonder if maybe Charlie and the rest of the cult might have thought that they saw something they weren't supposed to see."

"I guess that's a possibility. After all, they probably cut through their property or behind it. It wouldn't take a genius to make a connection between that big horse you keep talking about and all the troubles around your place."

"Yeah, and Max used to park across the street from them while he was watching my place. They probably would have noticed that, too."

Abigail slept soundly through the night. Amy did not. Amy felt her baby stirring in her womb. Normally it did not awaken her, but tonight it did. She glanced through sleepy eyes at the clock on her night stand. Three o'clock. She was alert enough to recognize the connection between the darkest hour of the night – the hour that curses were sent out – and the impact on her baby. *Lord, You said that a curse without a cause shall not alight. If there's any cause, I ask You to show me. If not, I ask that You would just tell the demons and whoever sent them to shut up and leave me and my baby alone.* Soon the vigorous kicking stopped and Amy drifted peacefully back to sleep.

Carrie Sue did not sleep soundly through the night either. Tossing and turning, willing her uncooperative mind to stop thinking about everything, she startled at every new sound. Her window was open and she was subjected to the endless cacophony of every cricket on the property. She identified croaking frogs. Maybe. The haunting hoots of a distant owl added to the night sounds that assailed her ears. *I thought it was supposed to be quiet in the country!* She fumed at the strange sounds. All she heard in her apartment was the white noise of her air conditioner and the occasional muffled tones of someone in the next unit speaking.

Just as she fell back asleep shortly after three o'clock, she was awakened once again by the sound of traffic. Someone had a loud muffler. Someone else thought it would be a good idea to lay a patch of rubber while accelerating past the house. Four-wheelers gunned their motors not too far away. There was a full moon tonight. Were they the typical night riders that Abigail talked about or were they ritual participants heading home? She shivered in the night.

6

Sunday, July 1, Demon Revel

It was difficult for Lee and Abigail to get through the foyer to their seat that morning because of all the people greeting them and making comments about their upcoming wedding. It was the talk of the church. Many confirmed their intentions to be there while some expressed their regrets that they had other plans. Eventually they made it to their pew and settled down for the service.

After the music died down, Pastor Spalding sprang up and quickly mounted the steps. Opening his Bible on the podium, pressing a folded paper flat, he peered at the expectant crowd. "What a beautiful summer day! Isn't it good to be in the house of the Lord?" He waited for the amens and other responses to die down before he made some announcements. "I saved the best for last. This coming Saturday at four o'clock Abigail Steele and Lee Norris will be married right here. I just want to remind you that you are all invited to come and there will be light refreshments afterward in the fellowship hall." He was beaming his delight and the congregation broke into light clapping as they looked toward Lee and Abigail.

"Speaking of weddings and marriage, I want to talk to you this morning about an aspect of marriage that all of us men, as spiritual leaders in our homes, and women, as spiritual partners, need to consider." He saw the slight uncomfortable shift as some of the men and women squirmed, hoping that they would not be a target. He was always gentle with his admonishments and graciously pointed his finger at himself first. Even so, there were some guilty consciences represented in this crowd.

"I'm calling this my spouses-who-suffered-because-their-spouses-made-poor-decisions sermon. I guess it goes both ways and we actually should add all kinds of other relationships that suffer because of one person's decision. Anyone here besides me ever made a mistake that caused your wife or other loved one to suffer?" He held his hand up and looked hopefully around the auditorium. "Now don't leave me up here all alone. Please! Tell me that I'm not the only one!" He let out a chuckle and thanked the transparent men and women who were willing to support him with raised hands.

"Let me start with the guys. God admonishes us men to live with our wives in an understanding way. He says that they are weaker vessels. Now ladies, don't get in a huff on me. You women are very strong in so many ways. I mean, if we men had to go through labor and delivery, this planet would be empty!" He let their gentle laughter subside before he continued. "Science and medicine back up the fact that men are physically stronger. Did you know that we even have more red blood cells? That's why some of you ladies tire a little sooner. God wired the male and female brains differently. God made men taller with broader shoulders." He continued with several other points before moving on.

"Let's look at the garden of Eden where Adam and Eve ate the forbidden fruit. Adam, who was mandated by God to be the leader, was there with Eve. What happened? Was she just too quick and he couldn't stop her? Did he have a lapse in his judgment? And once she partook, he knew that she would die. God just gave her to him and he knew that there was no one else suitable for him. Did he just decide to die with her? We can only guess since we were not there. But I wonder if I would have done any better if it were me instead of Adam. Their decisions have affected all of mankind." Pastor Spalding briefly let the questions linger before moving on.

"God picked Abram out of the world and told him to leave his family and go where God would lead him. What did he do? He took his nephew, Lot, with him. I won't go into it, but Lot caused him a lot, ahem, sorry, a lot of trouble along the way. Now maybe Sarah didn't suffer too much about that decision, but there was the time Abram told Sarai - God hadn't changed their names yet - to lie, not once, but twice, and say that she was his sister rather than his wife so he wouldn't get killed."

He leaned over the podium, raised his eyebrows and asked with a mischievous grin, "Now wasn't that an opportunity for Sarai? Maybe she would have thrown him under the bus if those incidents had happened after Abraham had agreed to use Hagar to conceive Ishmael. And she was the one who suggested it! There is nothing mentioned about either one of them consulting God about the suggestion or acting upon it. Wasn't *that* a nightmare for Sarah, Abraham, and both of their sons? Incidentally, Isaac and Ishmael - Israel and the rest of the middle-east nations - are still at war and the whole world is affected by their decisions." He paused again to let that sink in.

"We could talk about both Isaac and Rebekah and their favoritism of Esau and Jacob, respectively, and their descendants' animosity that continues to this very day." Pastor Spalding expanded on those dynamics and then after pointing out some of the decisions that various kings of Judah and Israel made that affected not only their wives, but the whole nation in some cases, he began his concluding remarks.

"Okay, let's see what the Bible has to say about how to respond if a spouse, child, parent, sibling, or employer makes an adverse decision. Turn to 1 Peter 3 and start in the first verse. It tells wives – who *hope in God,* according to verse five – to be submissive to their own husbands. Now don't get rankled on me, ladies. The word submissive means to stand under. In this case it's a protective husband. It means he's the point man and takes the shots so you don't have to. It's not! Hear me! It's *not* being smooshed under his thumb," he said as he stuck out his elbow and twisted his thumb on his pulpit as if he were squishing a bug.

"Now these verses specifically mention wives, but the principles apply to all of us. Go back up to chapter two and look at the last couple of verses where Peter gives us the example of slaves or employees being mistreated while doing right, and of Jesus who *'kept entrusting Himself to Him who judges righteously'* and then urges each of us to keep returning *'to the Shepherd and Guardian of your souls.'* That's the bottom line when someone suffers because of another person's choices."

Seeing some "aha" looks and nods he finished his sermon encouraging both the men and women to make prayerful decisions, admonishing both the husbands and wives to trust God for protection when and if their spouse made an adverse decision. Walking down to the floor level, he invited people up for prayer and then dismissed them.

Lee and Abigail, Amy and Carrie Sue headed home for lunch. It was a simple meal and when they were finished, both Amy and Carrie Sue retreated to their rooms for a nap. Lee and Abigail ended up on the couch in the living room.

"I feel so lazy today," Abigail said.

"Me too. Do you want to stay lazy or do you want to do something?"

"What do you have in mind?"

"I was thinking that with the wedding and our honeymoon coming up we won't have much time for the horses. We haven't taken a ride in a long time."

Abigail pursed her lips and frowned for a moment and then said, "I think I'd like to lay down for a power nap for maybe ten or fifteen minutes and then take a ride." The post-lunch, summer-doldrums, Sunday-afternoon lethargy was washing over her.

"Sounds like a plan," Lee agreed. "I'll just stretch out here on the couch. Wake me when you're ready." Lee was breathing heavily within a few minutes.

Abigail willed her body to relax on her bed and kept her eyes closed while her mind whirred with all the details of the wedding and the move. She finally drifted into a not-quite-asleep-yet-not-quite-awake state and rested until her leg twitched and brought her fully awake again. Swinging her legs over the side of the bed, she sat up and stretched before walking out to the living room. Gazing on her husband-to-be, smiling contentedly, she softly approached him.

"Hey, babe. Are you going to sleep all day?"

He grunted and stirred with eyes half open. Suddenly his left hand shot out and grabbed the startled Abigail by the wrist and firmly pulled her down. Wrapping his arms around her, he said, "No, I'm not. I was just waiting for you." Planting a big kiss on her lips, caressing her face with his hand, he reluctantly released her, and said, "We better get moving now or I'll want to stay here the rest of the day."

Abigail sighed and agreed, "I know. We have just one more week."

Within a few minutes they were getting ready to go for their ride. Abigail grabbed her boots out of the utility room and poked her head out to see where Carrie Sue and Amy were. Locating them in their chairs under the shade of the trees, she called out, "Hey, Lee and I are going to go for a ride. We'll be back when we're back."

"You have fun with that."

Within thirty minutes Lee and Abigail had Misty and Buster saddled and heading down the trail. Lee wanted to see how Misty would do after her wound. Just as he thought, it was quickly evident that she did not appear to be affected by the bullet wound. The only reminder seemed to be the scar that was almost covered over by the new growth of hair.

"Where do you want to go today?" Lee asked.

"I'd kind of like to go out toward the bridge, but I'm curious about that rock in the field."

"Well, there's nothing saying that we can't do both."

"Let's check to see if the rock is still down there first and then head over to the bridge."

They followed the familiar trail along York Creek, splashed across it, and rejoined it as it traced the uneven edges of the corn and soy bean fields.

"Wow! Look at how tall that corn is!" The stalks were only a few inches tall the last time they rode this trail and now they were nearly four feet tall.

"That's better than the old knee-high-by-the-fourth-of-July standard," Lee agreed. He was looking beyond the corn field toward the soy bean field hoping to catch a glimpse of the rock. He was also surveying the area to be sure that there would be no surprises.

Abigail was doing the same thing as they rode side by side on the wider parts of the trail. Lee took the lead through the gap between the two fields.

"I think it's gone," Abigail said as she pointed ahead. "Wasn't it over there?"

"I think you're right. Those soy beans aren't tall enough to hide it. Someone must have moved it."

They nudged the horses to quicken the pace. Buster was tense. His ears were up and scanning. His nostrils were flared. He stepped more like an Arabian than a Quarter Horse when he sensed certain things. Abigail sensed his tension and stroked his neck. "You're all right, big boy. We'll be out of here soon."

The steed obediently responded to her firm but gentle commands as they reached the place where they had stopped on their previous ride, and drew up next to Lee and Misty. Neither of them spoke. It was obvious that the rock was no longer there. Some of the soy bean plants were trampled and it was evident that a large piece of equipment had been used to retrieve the pentagon shaped rock.

"So that must have been ritual traffic last night and not just night riders."

Turning the horses, lost in their own thoughts, they retraced their steps back toward the stream. The sounds of crickets and birds, hoof beats and swishing tails, saddle creaks and an occasional snort from the horses was all that was heard until they splashed through the creek.

"Well, let's head to the bridge," Lee said. "Are you, all right?"

"Yes. I'm just worrying a little bit about leaving the ladies up there alone while we're gone. There are a couple of rituals at the end of the week – Friday the thirteenth and a new moon and whatever else they come up with."

"They're not coming with us on our honeymoon!" Lee laughed.

"I know. No weapon formed against us, or them, will prosper."

"No weapon!" With that he kicked Misty and they exploded down the trail toward the road.

"Hey!" Abigail yelled as her heel touched Buster's flank. "Come on, Buster! Let's get 'em!"

It felt good to have the wind in their faces blowing hair and manes straight back. They galloped until they neared the road. Lee pulled up and waited briefly for Abigail to join him. Waiting for traffic to clear, they walked the horses across the pavement and angled down to the trail that they had followed months before when they searched for Carrie Sue. It seemed like such a long time ago. Neither one of them spoke of it, but the memory was triggered for each of them as they went down the same trail and passed the same tree where they found and rescued the beleaguered woman.

After crossing York Creek again, they picked up the trail that followed the edge of the field directly behind the York's property. They did not know that Martha York was watching them from her kitchen window.

"There go those horses again," she muttered mostly to herself.

"What did you say, Mom?" Richard asked. These days he was entirely not sure if she was commenting on something present or something from the past.

"Horses."

"Where?"

She impatiently waved her hand palm down as if she was shooing a bug. "Over there."

Richard joined her at the window and saw two figures disappearing around the bend. He returned to his conversation with his father as Lee and Abigail moved deeper into the woods.

It was a warm day so Lee and Abigail mostly walked the trails that followed the irregular contours of the fields. Heat shimmered off the lush crops and grasses. Pairs of hawks rose on the thermal drafts. The rhythmic steps of the horses barely interrupted the quiet afternoon.

"So," Lee interrupted the silence, "what did you think of the sermon this morning?"

"It was thought-provoking. It probably made a few people uncomfortable."

"What about you? Are you worried about a guy that you haven't known for a year who might make choices that hurt you?"

"Are you getting cold feet at the last minute?" Abigail looked over at him.

"Not at all. I just want to make sure that *you're* not having any second thoughts."

"I've been watching you and you seem to make very thoughtful decisions. If you have a vice, you've hidden it really well. I'm not worried. I've prayed. We've prayed. I have complete peace about marrying you."

"Thanks."

"Besides, like Peter said, I'm entrusting myself to the Shepherd and Guardian of my soul. I know we won't agree about every decision, but you're the head of the household, and that's your responsibility before God. Even if you make a mistake, He'll redeem it."

"Me?" Lee put his hand over his chest in mock shock. "Me make a mistake?"

"It could happen. I'm just sayin'." Abigail laughed and then sobered up. "You know that next week at this time we'll be married for about twenty-four hours? Where will we be?"

"At the beach, of course," Lee replied.

"Which beach?"

"*That's* a surprise."

Lee's cheesy grin and sparkling eyes let Abigail know that she would not be able to pry it out of him. *So what? We'll be at a beach!*

"What have you got going this week?" Lee asked.

"Well, there's the Ministerial Alliance meeting at noon tomorrow at Bluebrook. Robert Warrens is the pastor out there."

"Oh? What kind of church does he have?"

"It's non-denominational. He started out with a Bible study in his home and it grew. Now they meet in an old store on the main drag. Ooh, that reminds me, I'll be driving past that creepy lodge."

"Do you want me to go with you?"

"Only if you want to get involved in the ministry stuff. I don't think I need a body guard. And another thing – Carrie Sue's mother goes there; at least some religious part of hers does. I think I'll try to find out from Pastor Warrens. I'm curious."

"Okay. What about the rest of the week?"

"Aside from the Fourth of July Gospel sing that the Ministerial Alliance is putting on, I'll just be getting ready to move and get married. Sounds like a light week to me. No pressure."

"Right," Lee said. "What do you say we turn these critters around and head for home? We need to get some supper in us and get ready for our light week."

"Dad," Richard said, "I've accumulated lots of vacation and personal time. I haven't used it. I'm going to call Landrum tomorrow morning and put in for more time off. I agree that something's not right around here and I think we need to get to the bottom of it."

"I could use the help. It's one thing to have all the harassments and things going on next door, but this has turned deadly. I have some ideas, but I'm going to be laid up for a while so I won't be able to do any of the legwork. Besides, I need to keep a closer eye on your mother. I think she's been going downhill faster since the shooting."

"Just what I was thinking. She still has her lucid moments though. What does the doctor say?

"I haven't taken her to the doctor because I didn't think it was much of a problem until recently. I don't know what they can do but I'll get her there when I get squared away."

"I can do that if you want," Richard offered.

"Let's wait a bit. Maybe with me home she'll settle down. Meanwhile, I think we need to get together with the neighbors. We all have a piece of the puzzle and together we might be able to get to the bottom of it."

"What's your take on the sheriff's department?"

"Corrupt! Dishonest!" David snorted with disdain. "You should have heard the way those deputies talked about the very people they were supposed to serve and protect! Stuff was regularly taken from the evidence lockers or just plain stolen from the prisoners. Last fall they literally threw a kid in there who could hardly walk because someone smashed his knee and they wouldn't even let him have crutches."

"That's inexcusable."

"Sometimes they'd take a prisoner out and tell him there was a hearing. I know that the courts weren't meeting at that hour!"

"I wonder what they did with them."

"I don't know. They never came back."

"I hope you don't mind sharing your bathroom for a while," Carrie Sue said. "I put my stuff in those empty drawers on the left side."

"It's not exactly *my* bathroom. I'm a guest here, too." Amy smiled. "I can hardly believe how crazy-generous that woman is. I mean, she's saved my life. I'm a homeless, jobless, friendless, family-less..."

"You're not friendless." Carrie Sue interrupted. "We haven't known each other long, but I consider you my friend and since I'm pretty much in the same boat as far as family goes, I'm going to consider you my sister."

"Thanks. I feel the same way about you." Amy almost teared up so she changed the subject. "We need to do something special for Abigail and Lee."

"Yeah, but what?"

"Don't know. But we can think about it and surprise her someday. Meanwhile, we'll live here and get healed and maybe when we get rich and famous we can pay them back."

"Yeah. By the way, what are you wearing to their wedding? Any one of those maternity outfits would work, but if you want me to, I can keep my eye out at the thrift shop for something dressier."

"That would be nice. Thanks." After thinking for a minute, she added in a sarcasm-dripping tone, "But you know that if I get a fancier top, I'll need fancier shoes. And if I get fancier shoes and top, I'll have to get my hair and nails done. And if I get my..."

Carrie Sue giggled and interrupted her. "You'll be fine. Besides, Abigail will be so beautiful and Lee will be so handsome that everyone will be looking at them."

"You're right. What are you going to wear?"

Talking and bantering, laughing and misting up, the ladies moved from the porch to the kitchen and began to prepare a light supper. It was a ritual night but neither one of them seemed to notice.

7

Monday, July 2

The sun rose around five o'clock in the morning and by the time she got up, Abigail could tell that it would be a sultry day by the feel of the air that was being drawn into her room. It was moist and sweet with the lingering night aromas, but soon the sun would become a broiler and she would have to use the air conditioner.

Rolling out of bed, she mentally did a countdown and stuck a finger up for each day: *Tuesday, Wednesday, Thursday, Friday.* Dad and the rest of the family would arrive sometime on Friday and practically fill up the quaint little Kingston Inn. *I've got four more days after today to do stuff until the wedding. Yikes!* The thought energized her as she started her day.

All around the area, pastors and ministers, worship leaders, and prayer warriors were getting ready for the Ministerial Alliance meeting that would take place at Robert Warrens' storefront church in unincorporated Bluebrook. They had not anticipated the number of vehicles that would have to fit into their tiny parking lot behind the building so it became necessary for many of the cars to park on the shoulder of the narrow two-lane road.

"Welcome!" the lanky, towering ex-basketball player greeted his guests. "Just make yourselves comfortable in the big room." He jerked his thumb in the direction of the room that served as a sanctuary or a fellowship hall or whatever was needed for the occasion. It had one wall at the back of the building which separated the kitchen, restrooms, and an office from the big room.

By noon there were about forty people assembled. Abigail found Cindy and Paula and they sat down by Wanda where they got caught up on Paula's restaurant and Wanda's chickens, Cindy's children and Abigail's upcoming wedding.

Pastor Warrens got the attention of the group, opened with prayer, and directed them to the buffet-style lunch. "I thought we'd get in the mood for the Fourth of July. Help yourself to hotdogs, potato salad, slaw, baked beans, and watermelon. Drinks are on the other table."

Food was efficiently put onto plates and soon everyone settled down to business. Robert called on Pastor Spalding to give a quick summary of what had transpired previously as well as the current plans for the Gospel Sing on the Fourth of July. "Folks, I am just tickled at the report I'm hearing from my worship leader and I want to thank all those who will be playing instruments and singing for all the extra time that they've put into this project. Can someone give us a report?" He looked around the room and gave the nod to Kyle Scott who volunteered.

"Thank you," Kyle beamed. "I have got to say that this has been one of the most fun, satisfying projects I have ever worked on. We can sense the hand of the Lord in everything from the musicians and singers to the songs that we all know as well as some that are stretching some of us."

"Oh yeah!" one singer agreed with a chuckle.

"Amen!"

"We're becoming non-methbyterian-baptismatics," another contributed, bringing smiles and chuckles, rolled eyes and groans from the group. They were beginning to drop religious barriers and focus on unity as they rallied around the Gospel of Jesus Christ.

"By the way, that's not the name of our group."

More groans.

The territorial and geographic spirits howled their displeasure. Their golden rule was to kill, steal, and destroy; to divide and conquer. Just as God was displeased with those who unified to build the Tower of Babel because nothing evil that they purposed to do would be impossible for them, so the demons were displeased that the believers were gathering as a unified force. With their unity in the bond of peace empowered by the Holy Spirit, these mud mortals could undo all the evil that they had worked so diligently to preserve.

Urdang rocketed over his territory calling for destruction. "Plant lies!" "Stir up envy and jealousy!" "Distract them!" "Attack their families!" "Find a curse that will alight with cause!" He was incensed. Fear drove him. He was beginning to realize that he was powerless over these dedicated People of the Empty Tomb as he continued to eavesdrop on their meeting.

Newcomers included the Baptist pastor of the church on Kingston Road near the end of York Creek Road where Abigail had turned around after her brake lines had been cut the previous fall. When he was introduced, Abigail made it a point to introduce herself to him when the meeting was over.

The group finalized the plans for the Gospel Sing to be in the large parking lot of Pastor Spalding's Baptist church. It was on the main street that the parade would follow. The musicians and singers had been diligent to practice together over the past month. The other committee members reported that food and water was taken care of. There would be face painters and other activities for the children. Booths would be set up for people who wanted prayer. Ads had been put in the paper and on the local radio station. Flyers were ready to be stapled onto telephone poles.

Pastor Spalding asked Abigail to give an update on the York Creek Road shooting spree.

She assured them that the Milners were recovering nicely. She was not sure about her other neighbor, the Yorks, but the news reports indicated that Mr. York survived and was home from the hospital. She also mentioned that it was connected to the cult that infested that neighborhood. "The man that did the shooting is dead, and even though they have not released his name, I believe it is the cult member who shot at me a few months back."

She could hear breaths being sharply sucked in, but she continued. "That threat is gone, but I believe that the cult will try to escalate. We need to be vigilant; we need to pray. Above all, we must remember that the enemy is the enemy and not these people. We must remember that no weapon formed against us will prosper." After answering a few questions, she turned the meeting back over to Pastor Spalding.

He reminded the crowd that the next Ministerial Alliance meeting would be the first Monday of August at his own Springfield Baptist Church. Robert Warrens dismissed them with a prayer of blessing. "See you all at the Gospel Sing!" His exuberance was evident.

Abigail excused herself from the ladies at her table and made a beeline for Pastor Ryan Crenshaw. "Howdy, neighbor," she greeted him. "I live a couple miles down York Creek Road."

"Ah," he said with a smile and a handshake, "very nice to meet you. I have several parishioners who live down your road. You said you live next to the Yorks?"

"Yes, we're neighbors. They live to the south of me and I'm ashamed to say that we've never even met in all the years I've lived here. I've been thinking about visiting them, but with the shooting and getting ready for my wedding and all, I've put that on hold."

"Did you know that their son, Richard, has come home? He said he was taking a leave from the DOJ so he could help his dad. Apparently, his mom is starting to show some moderate signs of dementia."

"Oh, that's too bad. I will definitely make it a point to get over there after I'm back from my honeymoon. I'll just be moving kiddie-whoppus across the road so we'll still be neighbors."

"Yes, I noticed that that old place went up for sale. It looks like the new owner has been busy."

"He sure has. His name is Lee Norris. He used to live around here with his folks when he was a kid but moved to Montana at some point."

"Interesting. Did you know that there was a murder in that old mobile home years ago?"

"Seriously?" Abigail asked and dropped her jaw.

"It was never solved. They even had that Unsolved Murders show come here and do a piece on it."

"That must have been before I got here. I moved in about ten years ago after my husband and sons were killed in a wreck."

"Oh, my." It was his turn to drop a jaw. "I'm so sorry. I had no idea."

"God is the God of second chances. He brought Lee into my life at a good time."

"There sure have been a lot of murders and deaths in this little county," he mused. "Well, listen, it's been really nice meeting you today, but I have another appointment. I would love to talk again. This meeting has really opened my eyes."

Abigail spoke to Pastor Robert Warrens on her way out and remembered to ask if Susan Wagner had been coming to church lately.

"Yes, she's been here more regularly since her husband died. She doesn't look so great, though. I don't know if she just has a bad cold or if she's got some kind of lung condition."

"Interesting. Her daughter and I have been praying that she would be willing to get counseling and get out of the cult. It's a long shot, but there's always hope."

"I'll add my prayers to your prayers and maybe I can even sneak in a suggestion or two when I talk to her while I'm at it."

Abigail prayed in the spirit as she passed the windowless lodge on her way home. She continued to pray as she passed Charlie Fletcher's place as well. Driving past her own driveway, Abigail made the turn into Lee's driveway. She tooted twice to let him know she was there. He could be just about anywhere on the eighty acres at this time of day.

She noticed movement by the barn and saw him coming toward her with a big smile. Hopping out of the truck and into his arms, they hugged and kissed.

The intensity of their passion was increasing in anticipation of their wedding.

"I wasn't expecting you so soon," Lee said. "What's up?" His discernment and intuition allowed him to read people fairly accurately.

"I had an interesting conversation with the pastor from the Baptist Church at the end of our road." Abigail nodded toward the north. "His name is Ryan Crenshaw. He knows the Yorks. Apparently, they attend his church and he mentioned that their son is going to be here for a while helping with his mom. Well, I guess his dad is still recovering from the gunshot, too. She's got dementia setting in."

"Whoa, slow down." Lee chuckled at her rambling. "So why is that so interesting?"

"Well, their son, Richard, works for the DOJ. Isn't that the Department of Justice?"

"Yes."

"I think we need to visit them after we get back from our honeymoon. And he told me something even more interesting about this place."

"What?"

"He said that someone was murdered in that trailer that used to be here. The Unsolved Murders people came and did a program on it but the murder has never been solved."

"That *is* interesting. Very interesting."

"I think we need to pray another prayer over this property. Isn't the house built on the same place as the trailer was?"

"It sure is."

"Think about Billy getting killed. I mean, maybe they didn't kill him here, but his car was here and then they definitely tried to kill Carrie Sue when they nabbed her from here."

"There seems to be a lot of death associated with this place," Lee agreed as he thoughtfully stroked his chin. "Why don't you pray first and I'll pray in agreement."

"Just remember that you're the legal owner, so you can pray with more authority than me. At least until we're married," she added with a grin before she launched into her prayer. "Lord, we appeal to You as the God and Judge of all and ask that You would cleanse this land from the blood that was shed on it. Lord, we don't know the circumstances. We don't know if it was cult related, but we do ask that the strongholds that have been established here because of murder and other violence would be demolished and that all the related demonic entities that may still be hanging around here be sent to a place where they will never be able to oppress again. Heal and seal all these things and bring to justice any murderers associated with this land. I pray this in Jesus' name, amen."

"Lord, I certainly pray in agreement, and as the legal owner of this property, I renounce everything that has to do with the unsolved murder and any other attempts on life, both human and animal. Thank You for Your protection, amen."

"Oh, I hadn't thought about the critters, but there have been attempts at killing them, too."

"I guess the Holy Spirit quickened that thought to my mind because I was just thinking about people like you were."

"That's the cool thing about praying with someone else." Abigail beamed. *How wonderful to have a praying husband!*

"Do you have time to hang around for a little bit?"

"I have so much to do at the house, I really shouldn't. See you for supper?"

"I'll be there," Lee said and leaned over to kiss her. Opening the door of her truck, he whispered, "I love you, Abigail."

"Love you! I can't wait until Saturday!" With that, Abigail turned her truck around and headed for her own house. Pulling up in the driveway, she suddenly missed her old welcoming committee. Dude was dead, but at least Buster was reasonably safe in Lee's pasture. Sighing, she got out and started to think about all the things on her to-do list that still needed to be done.

"Hey, ladies, I'm home!"

"How was the meeting?"

"Good. I met the Baptist pastor from the church at the end of our road. Nice guy. He said that the Yorks attend that church and that their son, Richard, is home for a while. It seems that Martha York is starting to have trouble with dementia."

"Oh, that's so sad. I wonder if there's anything we can do to help."

"You know, I think that when Lee and I get back from our honeymoon, we should visit them and find out. I'd like to meet with them anyway because I feel responsible for the shooting somehow. But then, you never know if Charlie Fletcher had it in for them for some other reason."

"If it's anyone's fault, it's ours," Carrie Sue asserted.

"Yeah, if you weren't working with us, they'd leave you alone," Amy added.

"Yes and no. You *do* realize that I've been working with survivors since way before I met the two of you."

"Okay, so it's all of our faults." Amy pursued the argument a bit.

"There has been enmity between God's kingdom and Satan's kingdom from the very beginning. Some of us are assigned to the front lines. I guess we need to stop the blame game and keep following our Leader."

The ladies agreed and changed the subject. They discussed the week's schedule. Carrie Sue was working Tuesday and Thursday this week. Amy had another appointment with her doctor. Abigail had some packing she wanted to finish. She was planning to meet with Max and Pastor Spalding on Friday. Then there was the rehearsal and the rehearsal dinner and Saturday was the wedding.

"This week is going to fly by!" Abigail said.

"What can we do to help you?" Carrie Sue asked.

"Well, I have plenty in my office that needs to be packed. I've barely touched the book shelves. I should have enough boxes. I'll take care of my computer and all the junk on the top of the desk, but if you want to get the books done, that'd be great. Then maybe you could box up the stuff just from the two big bottom drawers of the desk and the stuff in the filing cabinet if you have the energy."

"We can do that," Amy volunteered.

"Promise me that you won't lift anything heavy."

"Promise."

"I can do the lifting," Carrie Sue said.

"All right, then. If you two want to get started on that, it'll free me up to get my clothes packed. I have a bunch of boxes in the upstairs closet and under the eaves that I need to clear out, too. There should be a marker on my desk to label the boxes."

"Oh," Amy said mischievously as she turned to Carrie Sue, "what do you think we should label them?"

"Well, we could come up with some good labels. We could label one box 'psychochondriac' and another one could be 'oppositionally compliant' and another one could be 'psychoceramic' and another one could be 'rectalopia'..."

"And just what is rectalopia?" Abigail had an idea but she wanted to hear it from them.

Carrie Sue looked mischievously at Amy before explaining, "It's when someone gets so stressed that their brain synapses mess up and the nerve to their rectum crosses the nerve to their eyes and they get a really crappy outlook."

"Aargh!" Abigail groaned. "And psychoceramic?"

"Oh, that's a crack pot."

Abigail playfully scolded them, "Okay, you two, you're having way too much fun with your psycho-babble. I'll be upstairs or in my room if you need me." Secretly she was delighted that these once helpless, hopeless victims of Satanism were well on the path to healing and wholeness.

Tuesday was another sultry July day. Carrie Sue left at nine-thirty so that she would be at her job in plenty of time. She enjoyed the work and was getting more and more comfortable with interacting with strangers, even irascible ones. Her supervisor, Barbara Peters, noticed and made it a habit to encourage and compliment her. She was also pleased that Carrie Sue was a whiz with a computer and had asked for her help when she got stuck processing files pertaining to various business aspects of The Thrift Shoppe.

Amy left shortly after Carrie Sue did and headed to the doctor's office. She did not pay attention to the SUV that followed her to town. Her mind was on her appointment. Today they were going to try to get a clear ultrasound picture to confirm the gender of the baby. Amy was very curious, but still not sure if she was ready to know. She had mixed feelings about the issue. Girls seemed to be more vulnerable and more likely to be victimized. Boys might escape some of the degrading abuse, but they were still abused and more likely to be groomed to rise in the cult to master level. *I won't let them get you, baby!*

Amy hated having to get into a patient gown for the examinations, but she managed to do what was necessary. She had called a "committee meeting" with her inside personalities, reminding them that she needed to stay in executive control today. The male personalities had no trouble with staying away from a gynecological exam.

"Well, are you ready to see if it's a boy or a girl?" the perky technician asked. "We should be able to tell today if the baby gives us the right pose."

"Yes and no."

"Well, if you want to, I can tell you when to look the other way and then we can print up the pictures and put them in an envelope. You can take them home and look at them whenever you're comfortable."

"Really? I'd like that. I still want to see the baby, but just not that part. At least not yet."

"I'll let you know." The technician expertly applied the cold gel and guided the cool transducer head over Amy's belly.

Amy heard a series of clicks and watched as lines appeared on the screen and measurements were taken. The baby no longer looked like a seahorse and was recognizable as a miniature human being. She saw the profile of the tiny face with the cute little nose. She watched arms and legs waving and kicking. She heard the rapid swooshing of the heartbeat.

"Wow! That's fast," she said in amazement.

"One hundred fifty-nine. That's pretty normal for this stage of the game. Your baby is about half a pound now and measures pretty close to six inches."

"It looks like a real baby!" Amy said in amazement. She felt a thrill as her maternal impulses surged. *I won't let anything happen to you, baby.*

"Okay, I'm going in for the gender shot right now if you want to look away. It looks like your baby is cooperating today."

Amy heard the clicks that indicated that pictures were being taken. It was not long before the images scrolled off the ultrasound machine. Folding them, the technician placed them in an envelope and handed it to Amy. "There you are," she said with a smile.

After meeting with the doctor, Amy headed back into the sweltering heat and got back into her baking car. Once again, she was tailed by the SUV. This time she noticed. The big black grill guard was distinctive as it hovered close to her back bumper. The glare of the sunlight did not allow her to see the driver clearly.

"Oh, Lord, I have a bad feeling about that guy. Please protect us." She was not sure what to do. She did not want to get out on the isolated roads that led home. "God, what shall I do?"

Instantly she had the idea that she should head to the church. It was only a couple blocks away and she had to pass it on her way out of Springfield anyway. Putting on her turn signal, slowing to make the turn into the parking lot, she felt a significant jolt as the SUV accelerated and grazed the back corner of her car causing her to spin out in the parking lot. It roared away as Amy regained control of the car. Not that long ago she would have gone after him. Today she was thinking about her baby.

Not knowing what else to do, she decided to go into the office to see if Pastor Spalding was there. She did not realize how shaken she was until she stepped out of the car. *Oh, Jesus, thank You for getting me here safely. Help me get home.* She took the time to walk on wobbly legs around the back of her car to look at the damage. Her heart sank when she saw the smashed taillight and a black mark on the dented bumper.

Making her way into the church, she followed the signs to the office. This was way out of her comfort zone, but being out there with that maniac was even more out of her comfort zone.

"Well, hello there." Ginny's automatic smile lit her face, but it quickly darkened with concern when she noticed Amy's distress. "What's the matter, honey, are you all right?" She came around the desk and ushered Amy to a chair.

"I'm so sorry to bother you. Some guy was tailing me and when I pulled into the parking lot he bumped into my car. I think it was on purpose. My taillight is smashed and the bumper is dented in."

"That's terrible! You come in here and sit down. You're no bother, honey. You did the exact right thing coming in here. Can I get you something to drink?" Ginny hovered over her like a mother hen.

"No, I'm okay. I'm just a little scared about driving back home. Do you think you can call Abigail?"

"I sure can and then we are going to pray. Pastor Spalding is out on a call right now, and if it's all right, I'll let him know what happened."

They prayed. Ginny called Abigail. Abigail called Lee. Together they drove to Springfield and followed Amy home after Lee determined that Amy's car was fit to drive. He thought they could pound out the dent and get a used taillight assembly from the junkyard. It would not be a good idea to risk being pulled over for having a taillight out in this county.

They fussed over Amy and made her rest. She vehemently protested, but lost that battle and took a nap until dinnertime. She was too tired to think about the close call. She was too tired to think about the gender of her baby. Today she was just too tired.

Checking the damage, taking another picture, Lee took a scraping of the black residue before he pounded out the bumper. It was still lumpy but at least it looked better. From Amy's description, the driver might have been trained in controlling fleeing vehicles. That might indicate a sheriff. Or it might have been a fluky hit.

"Hey, Amy. You hungry?"

"Yeah. I'll be right there." Amy felt better. At least she felt safer with her friends around her. *What's it going to be like when Abigail's gone?* She brushed away the thought as her eyes rested on the envelope that the ultrasound technician gave her earlier that day.

8

Wednesday, July 4

Amy seemed to be back to her old self by breakfast time. She and Carrie Sue were in the middle of an animated conversation by the time Abigail returned from letting the chickens out and wandering through her lush garden. The corn was shoulder high and would soon start to tassel. More tomatoes were getting close to ripening and green beans were ready to be picked again. She had staggered the planting so that she got beans all season long.

"What are you two so excited about?" Abigail asked as she joined them.

"Amy's too chicken to look in the envelope," Carrie Sue reported.

"I am not. I'm just waiting for the right time," Amy countered.

"What envelope?"

"The one she got yesterday from the ultrasound that tells the baby's gender."

"Well, that's cool," Abigail said lightly, "I guess we'll need to know if we have to paint my old office pink or blue." More seriously, she added, "Are you waiting because you want to be surprised or are you waiting because you're not sure if it's safer for your baby to be a boy or a girl?"

"That!" Amy said decisively and then added, "I guess it really doesn't matter. I have to trust that God made the right choice for this baby and I'll have to do the best I can whether I have a son or a daughter."

"I'm so proud of you," Abigail said. "You've come such a long way."

"Thanks."

"It seems like something else is bothering you. Do we need to have a session?"

Amy sighed deeply and looked from Abigail to Carrie Sue and back again. "No, I don't need a session, but I do want to say something." She looked down at the envelope that she pulled from her pocket. It was obvious that it was a serious matter for her. Finally, she shrugged her shoulders as if to indicate that she might as well just plunge in and get it said.

Looking at Carrie Sue, she said, "I know they took away your babies. You never got to hold them or love them or know if they were boys or girls."

"Amy," Carrie Sue started to interrupt.

"No, let me finish," Amy insisted. "I need to say this. I know how I'd feel if the roles were reversed. I know I'd be happy for you because they didn't win this time, but I also know that it'll remind you of what they stole from you. I don't want to add to your pain."

"Amy." Carrie Sue moved over to her friend, put an arm around her, and said, "I hate the losses, but God has taken the sting out of the memories and they're all safely with Him waiting for a family reunion. Me and my kids; you and your kids. They stole from you, too. I'm good. Really, I am. I'm just happy that they didn't win this time. This baby is going to be a mighty man or woman of God and not a Satanist, and I'm going to celebrate that with you every day of that kid's life."

Amy was visibly relieved. "Okay; thanks. I really appreciate both of you. I don't know how I'd ever get through this without you." She was on the verge tears, and that was just not her style. Abruptly she changed the subject and the mood. "I'm ready!" she announced. "Give me a drum roll."

Carrie Sue and Abigail broke into smiles and began drumming on the table like school girls as Amy made an elaborate show of opening the envelope and taking out the strip of images. With heads together, the three women carefully examined each image, oohing and aahing at the tiny features until they got to the last one. Then they hugged and cheered and celebrated.

Lee's toot-toot got Abigail's attention. "Are you two sure you don't want to come with us to town? I know it'll be hot as blazes, but I have a feeling that the Gospel Sing is going to be worth hearing."

"What time is the parade?"

"Noon. The singing is going to go on all afternoon. Our church is going to be the happening place!" Abigail tried to entice them.

"I'd rather not revisit the scene of the crime," Amy answered, "I feel a lot safer here." She was thinking of her recent harrowing ordeal that landed her in the church parking lot.

"I think I'll stay here, too. I'm not big on crowds. Or heat."

"Suit yourselves. We'll be back when we're back."

As Lee and Abigail made their way to Springfield they noticed that the traffic was heavier than normal. The parade, the carnival, and all the accompanying festivities drew people from the neighboring counties. They were able to find a good parking place at the back edge of the church parking lot and took their time wandering past the various booths. Abigail had signed up for one hour in the prayer booth, but told Cindy to call her on her cell phone if one of the teams ran into someone with deeper issues than they could handle.

Lee was a free agent, but he was on a mission. He intended to blend into the lively crowd and be as inconspicuous as possible as he wandered through parking lots and along the street looking for a dark SUV with a large black grill guard that was missing some paint. Amy described the grill guard as the kind that some people put on the front end to avert damage in case there was a collision with a deer or other large animals. She was not entirely sure about the color of the vehicle, but it was definitely dark.

Cindy headed the prayer booth project and made sure that each three-person team had a mix of men and women, and had different denominations represented. Abigail, Paula Archer, and Pastor Warrens were on the one o'clock team. They prayed together for their upcoming hour and then waited for folks to come by with prayer requests.

Lee figured that if he had just committed a hit-and-run and did not have time to repair any damage and was cocky enough to come to town, he would probably not park on the main road. Wandering down alleys and several side streets that ran parallel to the main road, Lee prayed silently, *Lord, would You give me favor and help me find this vehicle if it's here?* He walked for miles up and down the parade route, but he was in no hurry. He believed that if he needed to find it today, the Lord would guide his steps.

He was on his way back to the church to find Abigail when the sound of laughter caught his attention. He looked down the side street and noticed three young men leaning up against a forest green SUV that had a

111

large black grill guard. *Thank You, Lord!* Casually pulling the bill of his cap lower over his sunglasses, he crossed the street and passed them on the sidewalk while appearing to be interested in the display in the nearby store window. Finding a perfect angle, locating the license plate, Lee looked at the numbers and letters that appeared backward in the reflection. 1NG5050.

Lord, I need to memorize that plate. Ha! He almost laughed out loud. *One No Good So and So. I can surely remember that!*

The young men did not seem to notice him as he resumed his walk down the to side street where it intersected with another street that ran parallel to the main road. Having accomplished his mission, he broke into a satisfied smile and headed back around the block. Crossing to the far side, he prayed that the young men had moved away from the truck. His prayers were answered. Pulling out his cell phone, he took pictures of the tan paint from Amy's car that was smudged on the passenger side of the guard and got the license plate as well. Perfect. His smile was even bigger as he headed back to the church.

"Mission accomplished," he said, greeting Abigail with a kiss.

"What mission?"

"I found the SUV that knocked into Amy and I got some pictures."

"Nice work. I wonder who it belongs to."

"There were a bunch of young men hanging around it. It might have been one of them. We'll just add it to our evidence files for now. One of these days these bullies are going to get what's coming to them."

Carrie Sue and Amy decided that they would continue to work on packing up Abigail's office. Amy was more energized now that she knew the gender of her baby. Carrie Sue was equally excited and they set to work soon after Lee and Abigail left.

"Whew!" Amy exclaimed near noon, "I'm ready for a break. Let's do lunch."

"Good idea." They stopped packing and went into the kitchen where they continued their conversations. It always came back to the baby.

"You know, Amy, sometimes we get bedding and curtains and stuff like that at The Thrift Shoppe. If I see something you might like, I can hold it and let you take a look."

"Thanks. I'd really like that."

"Are you thinking about a more traditional color or something else?"

"You know," Amy said thoughtfully, "I've been a non-conformist all my life. I think this time I am going to go more traditional. Find me something blue."

"Do you want teddy bears or puppies or some kind of super-hero? I don't even know who's popular with kids these days."

"I've been thinking about a super-hero from the Bible. I want to have a David theme. He was a mighty man of God and that's what I want my son to be."

"Good for you. I like the way you're thinking." Carrie Sue voiced her approval and then asked curiously, "What female super-hero would you have chosen if it were a girl? I can't think of any off hand."

"I like the story of Abigail. She was pretty heroic like our Abigail."

"Oh yeah, and she ended up marrying King David."
"There ya go!"

They continued to plan and dream as they finished lunch and returned to work on packing the rest of the books. Sometimes they stopped to comment about a particular title or an author, but mostly they kept working steadily. They wanted to help their benefactor as much as possible, and by mid-afternoon they had completely finished boxing up the books.

"Didn't she say that if we finished with the books we could box up the stuff in the two big bottom drawers of the desk and the file cabinet?"

"Yes, she did."

"I'll go get another box," Carrie Sue volunteered and went to the living room to retrieve one.

Meanwhile, Amy opened the bottom drawers of the desk. When Carrie Sue returned with the box, she filled it with the contents of the two drawers, carefully labeling the box. She moved over to the four-drawer file cabinet and took a quick peek in the drawers.

"I feel kind of funny looking at her personal stuff," Amy said.

"She told us we should do it," Carrie Sue countered. Everything's in private files or envelopes anyway."

"Tax returns. Yuk!" Amy grunted.

"Why don't you sit here and I'll hand you the stuff. You shouldn't be getting up and down so much," Carrie Sue fussed.

"I won't argue."

They worked methodically down the four-drawer file cabinet, filling boxes and carefully labeling them. Carrie Sue triumphantly handed Amy the last handful of files. Too late she realized that she had grabbed a larger bundle than she should have. The open-ended files and envelopes slipped out of her hands before Amy could secure them.

"Oh no!" Carrie Sue exclaimed. "I can't believe I just did that!"

"Don't worry. Let me help you." Before Carrie Sue could protest, Amy knelt down beside her and started gathering files.

They were able to slide the right papers back into the right folders. Finally, Amy picked up the last manila envelope and triumphantly handed it to Carrie Sue. "There! See? No harm."

Carrie Sue did not respond. She kept staring at the envelope.

"What?" Amy was puzzled by Carrie Sue's lack of response and peered at the envelope.

Carrie Sue just pointed to the label: October 31, 1996 – Accident Report.

"What?" Amy did not understand the significance.

"It's got to be the accident that killed her family."

"So?"

"They died on the same day as my brother, Danny. He wrecked his truck on a curve because his brake lines were cut."

"I didn't know you had another brother."

"I had two of them. Billy and Danny. Danny died ten years ago on Halloween night. Go figure! Billy died last year."

"I don't know what to say." Amy puzzled at the information. *Billy. Could he be the same Billy?*

"I have a feeling about this. I know it would be really rude and nosy, I mean, she trusts us, but I just gotta know something." Carrie Sue was very tense.

115

"Do you think there was some connection between your brother's accident and Abigail's family? I mean, do you think it was the same accident or maybe something else?"

Carrie Sue looked thoughtfully at the floor and slowly said, "I had a little part of me come out one time and tell Abigail that she watched her father cut our brother's brake lines. It was on Halloween because the bio-dad said that he was going to trick Danny and if my little part kept it a secret, she would get a treat."

"Oh crap."

"Yeah." Carrie Sue said. "I really want to take a peek. I really want to know that my brother didn't kill Abigail's family and that I was a part of it."

"Whoa! Wait a minute! Let me pull an Abigail on you. You know that if one of your child parts was pulled into one of your father's tricks it was not *her* fault. It's *not* your fault."

"I know that logically, but…"

"Okay, so take a look."

Lee and Abigail decided that fresh burgers on the grill sounded better than the over-priced carnival fare that was being hawked at the park which had been taken over by the festivities. They had seen their share of fireworks over the years and did not particularly want to battle heavy traffic later in the evening.

"I guess we're showing our age," Lee said.

"It was a lot more fun with little kids." The thought momentarily saddened Abigail.

Lee wrapped his arm around her waist as they walked back to the truck. Let's go see how the critters are doing and then we can rustle up some supper."

"Sounds like a plan!"

They said little as Lee drove down the wildflower-lined country roads toward their farms. The summer sun was unimpeded by clouds and continued to send its heat. A quick check on the horses satisfied them that all was well on Lee's farm. Crunching up Abigail's winding driveway, they looked forward to a quiet evening in the air-conditioned house.

"Hey, ladies," Abigail called out, "we're home!"

"I'm in the kitchen," Amy called out. "Good timing. I'm starting a salad for supper."

"Excellent! We were thinking of doing some burgers on the grill, too. Where's Carrie Sue?"

"Oh, she wanted to take a little nap. She's upstairs."

Lee scrubbed the grill with the wire brush and got the fire going while Abigail and Amy continued to prepare things in the kitchen. Carrie Sue heard the commotion and soon joined them.

Abigail sensed that something was not quite right with Carrie Sue, but she did not say anything. As they got ready to eat their meal in the dining room, Lee also noticed a certain amount of awkwardness, but said nothing. Amy made up for it with her chatter.

"So, what did you do today?" Abigail tried to start a conversation.

"We got all your books packed up finally," Amy said brightly.

"We had time to get to those bottom desk drawers and your four-drawer file cabinet," Carrie Sue added.

"That's fantastic! I really appreciate your help."

"Well, maybe it was a little self-serving on my part," Amy confessed as she hung her head in mock shame. "I want to get started on the nursery now that I know that it's a boy."

"A boy!" Lee smiled broadly. "It's about time I got a little help around here. Congratulations!"

"Thanks." Amy blushed at the attention.

"I know you were looking at that name book," Abigail said, "have you narrowed down your choices yet?"

"I have one name. I'm not sure if I want it for his first or middle name."

"What name?"

"Well, while Carrie Sue and I were talking about decorating today, I thought that David would be a good super-hero. I don't want all those masked tight-wearing, flying guys they have these days, you know? David was a man after God's own heart and that's what I want my son to be."

"Very cool." Abigail was impressed that Amy was beginning to learn the Bible.

"David Bolton." Amy spoke the name aloud for the first time. "Yes, David should be his first name."

"I like it."

"Wouldn't Prinz have a fit?" Carrie Sue added. "His son – a man after God's own heart." Her mood finally lightened a shade.

Lee excused himself to man the grill and Abigail took the opportunity to ask Carrie Sue what was wrong with her.

"I'd rather not talk about it right now."

"After supper?"

"Actually, I'd prefer to never talk about it, but I suppose I need to."

"Sounds like one of those 'new normal' things, eh?" Abigail tried to lighten the mood.

"I guess so." Carrie Sue was clearly uncomfortable, but that, too, was progress.

They set the table for supper, put out condiments, and steamed a mound of fresh green beans. It was a quintessential summer meal which was oddly quiet until Lee spoke.

"I found the SUV today."

"Really?" Amy was all ears. "Where was it? Do you know who it belongs to? Was anyone in it? What did he look like?"

"Whoa, slow down." Lee smiled at her animation which reminded him of his daughter. He went on to describe his adventure that day and showed them the pictures he took.

"It doesn't look familiar."

"You know," Abigail said thoughtfully, "that Russ Ranson guy followed Carrie Sue and I, and when we busted him, he got a new vehicle."

"That's right," Carrie Sue affirmed, "he tailed us in a BMF, uh, what did you call it?"

"BFOMC. Big, fat, old man car like my dad drives."

"Yeah, that. You said he went from that to an SUV."

"He blocked me in at Rev. Griffin's Presbyterian church when we went up there to look at the blood and stuff that his janitor saw a few months back. Russ just *happened* to stop by and he just *happened* to park behind my truck in the empty lot," Abigail said grudgingly. "The jerk."

"Tell us how you really feel about him," Lee teased while Carrie Sue and Amy exchanged looks.

"Sorry. I sinned. Again! I really need to pray for his transformation even though I think it's a long shot. Anyway, he had a medium-gray SUV so it probably wasn't him."

"There were three younger men hanging around it. It probably belonged to one of them. They were just average-looking guys cutting up and having a little holiday fun."

Abigail picked up her thought trail again, "I confronted one guy who had that BLAZE license plate. Maybe he got a different vehicle after that."

"Okay, so what do we do? All we have is a file full of evidence that's getting fatter and no place to turn so far," Carrie Sue said.

"And," Abigail added, "I hate to say this, but you were probably followed to town from here. I think we all have to assume that the cult is aware that both of you live here now. We know that no weapon formed against us will prosper, but we still need to be wise as serpents and innocent as doves."

"I think it would be a good idea to create a couple of safe places in the house and on the property that the two of you can retreat to if someone were to have the nerve to come up here," Lee said.

The ladies looked at him quizzically. Finally, Amy said, "All right, I'll bite. What are you talking about?"

"Abigail, do you remember when Billy came in here and tried to kill you?" Lee asked.

"What! My brother? Billy?"

"Oops," Lee said apologetically as he looked from Abigail to Carrie Sue. "I thought you knew about that. I'm so sorry."

"Billy tried to kill you, too?" Carrie Sue looked with horror at Abigail as it dawned on her that Danny had probably killed Abigail's family and now she was saying that Billy definitely had tried to kill her. She was overwhelmed. Face in hands, shoulders hunched, she began to weep and shudder. "No, no, no."

"Too?" Abigail questioned. She caught the meaning behind that word.

Amy's eyes got big. She slowly leaned back in her chair and tried to make herself invisible. She was not comfortable with confrontation or emotions. Lee was equally uncomfortable but for different reasons. He felt responsible for opening this can of worms.

Carrie Sue wiped her eyes and sniffled. "Abigail, that's what I *didn't* want to talk to you about."

"What are you talking about?"

"When Amy and I were packing up your file cabinet, we kind of fumbled the last bundle and we saw an envelope that was labeled 'Accident Report' and it was the exact same day that my brother was killed and we did a session once with my child part that knew about Dad cutting Danny's brake lines and she wanted a treat but she didn't know the trick her dad was going to pull on Danny would..." she finally took a breath and tried not to start wailing again, "I just have a feeling that my brother killed your family and I was a part of it somehow, and now you say that Billy tried to kill you, too."

Abigail took a deep breath and placed her hand on Carrie Sue's forearm. "Carrie Sue, none of *any* of this is your fault. None of it. And yes, your brother Danny was in the accident with my family."

Carrie Sue was in agony, "How can you love me like you do? How can you let me live here?" None of her life experience prepared her for grace and mercy, love and acceptance.

"Let me go get the envelope and let's just get things out on the table." Abigail patted Carrie Sue's arm and went to her office to retrieve the envelope from the box at the base of the file cabinet. Returning to her place at the dining room table, opening the clasp, pulling out all the papers, she found the accident report and laid it on the table in front of Carrie Sue.

"Look," she said pointing to one of the lines, "the driver was under the influence. DUI. It didn't say anything about cut brake lines."

Carrie Sue looked at the report. "Daniel W. Wagner. It *was* Danny. My brother still killed your family. My little part saw Dad cut his brake lines. He said he needed to teach Danny a lesson for driving too fast."

"Okay. So, if we have to blame someone, we blame your father for cutting the lines and we blame your brother for driving too fast while intoxicated. Case closed. You are not at fault by any stretch of the imagination. You were a little kid. Even if you could have predicted the outcome, there is no way you could have stopped your father or your brother."

Carrie Sue still did not look convinced. She wanted to make it her fault somehow. Guilt by association. She wanted to fix it. She wanted to go back and do something different. She was trying to wriggle out from under the crushing boulder of her family history.

"What about Billy?" she asked flatly. "Lee said he tried to kill you, too."

"I'm so sorry, Abigail," Lee injected, "I didn't know you hadn't told Carrie Sue. I guess I assumed that since you showed her his car on my place that she knew about everything. I really blew it. I mean, and I guess that since Gary was a part of that whole deal, it was common knowledge."

"Gary?"

"Yeah, he was fixing her brake lines." Lee stopped abruptly as he realized that Carrie Sue would pick up on the "coincidence" of the brake lines, too. "Er, fixing her car that day at his shop."

"Brakes?"

"Well it looks like I took one foot out of my mouth and put the other one in," Lee drawled as he looked helplessly to Abigail to help him out of this mess.

Abigail would have laughed as he squirmed. It was so atypical of him. Instead she puffed out a breath and said, "Well, I suppose it would all have come out some time with all the crisscrossed and dual relationships we've got going here. Billy's car on Lee's property. Cousins and friends. You and Amy. Please forgive me for not guarding confidentiality better."

"Well, it happened to *you*. You can talk about your own stuff to anyone."

"Yes and no. I mean, I don't want to harm anyone in the process. I don't want you to think that I blab all your stuff to everyone, but Cindy is my prayer partner and she gets mostly general, dumbed-down requests so she doesn't know who she's praying for unless we get a particular crisis. And that's usually about me."

"Like Billy trying to kill you."

"Like Billy trying to kill me. He thought I wasn't home and he came in. I was in the basement. When he came down the steps, I tripped him. When he tried to use his knife, I took out his knee. Gary was here right after it happened."

"You! *You* took out his knee? He told me some crazy story about a fall."

"You're welcome," Abigail said dryly and smiled with mock pride. "He went to jail and never showed up for his court date." She tapped the file and added, "That's another folder."

"Billy's dead," Amy piped flatly as she tried to absorb the implications.

"We don't know for sure, but we have a good idea that he was taken out by the cult," Abigail concurred.

"He hasn't been home since he disappeared months ago. And Mom, or one of the moms, said that he was dead and that it was my fault," Carrie Sue said.

"What does he look like?" Amy asked.

Carrie Sue's face asked the question that she did not voice. Instead she went into a description of him and then threw out another thought, "He doesn't look like any of the rest of us. If you ask me, he looks more like Prinz than our dad."

"Do you happen to have a picture of him?"

"No. It's not like I want to be reminded of him."

"We do." Lee dared to speak up, and then answered the ladies' puzzled looks. "Don't you remember? Gary took a picture of his driver's license when he was in your basement."

"That's right. We transferred it to the computer file and downloaded a hard copy, too. I'll go get it. That file is in the part of my desk that hasn't been packed up yet." Abigail jumped up, hurried back to her office, and retrieved it.

"You sure have a lot of stuff in that file!" Carrie Sue exclaimed. "Is that all from Billy and Danny?"

"No. I've been documenting things for over a year now." She flipped through the folders in the file until she came to the one for William J. Wagner. She pulled out the slightly grainy picture and laid it on the table in front of Amy.

Pointing at his face, Amy exclaimed, "That's the guy! That's him."

"How do you know my brother?"

Looking at Abigail, Amy said, "Do you remember that session we did where that little girl part of me freaked out when she saw your stairs?"

"Wraithe."

"That's the one. She saw someone. That's him."

Carrie Sue and Lee were puzzled by this exchange and waited for a further explanation.

"She predicted his death last year. This year she predicted someone that we assumed was Prinz and Charlie Fletcher, too, because she saw them both on the stairs this year."

"Why would ..." Carrie Sue let the question dangle unfinished and then answered it herself. "Well, I guess it would make sense that we would know a lot of the same masters and people from the big regional rituals."

Lee was getting confused with all the connections that he was never apprised of. He remained silent as the ladies continued to flesh out some details that added to their understanding.

After several minutes, Abigail said, "Okay, since it seems that all the cats are out of their bags, let's see if we can make some sense of this. There are too many quirks that caused each of us to end up here together. I think it's a God-thing."

"So," Carrie Sue summarized, "Danny killed your family. Amy knew that Billy and Prinz were going to die. Billy is probably Prinz' son because he sure looks like him, and he tried to kill you, too."

"And, um," Amy added, "we're pretty sure that Prinz is the father of my son."

"Well, if that isn't weird! If Prinz is the father of my brother and your son, I don't even want to think about all the implications and how many others he sired."

Amy's humor bubbled up and broke the tension. "Well, I do! It makes us paternal second half-cousins twice removed." She paused dramatically, flung her hands up in triumph and exclaimed, "We're family!" and gave Carrie Sue a great big hug.

9

Friday, July 6

"I can't believe you're working today! You're getting married tomorrow," Pastor Spalding said to Abigail as he entered the counseling room.

"I'm all packed, I can finish moving when we get back from our honeymoon, I have to check with Ginny to see if there's any last-minute stuff, and my family won't get to the Kingston Inn until around noon."

Max was doubly ashamed for all the grief he had caused her just in the last year. How many times had he stalked her and threatened her? How many times had he tried to destroy her property or kill her horse? Now here she was trying to save his life. His thoughts were disrupted when she spoke to him.

"Yep. You're welcome to come. Wear something purple if you want to make the bride happy." She grinned. "Let's get started if you're ready."

"I sure am."

"How's it been internally since the last time? That was really big with General Maximillian defecting and his group getting healed and integrated."

"Things feel different, that's for sure. In some ways it's a lot calmer, but there's some kind of tension. I could feel the tug earlier this week, but I'm real sure that I didn't go anywhere."

"There were a couple of ritual nights so that would make sense. Let's ask God to start us where we need to start." She opened with prayer and saw the switch.

Max assumed a ramrod posture reflecting hostile body language. He cleared his throat.

"Brutuz?" Abigail ventured a guess.

Palpable silence and a malevolent glare greeted her. Whoever he was, he was not going to make it easy.

"Do you understand what I'm saying?" she asked.

Glare.

"Et tu, Brute?" Abigail blurted. It was the only Latin Abigail could remember and it seemed as if it might be appropriate here. She had not consciously planned on saying it, but having done so, she assumed that it was another nudge from the Holy Spirit because of the personality's visceral response.

He erupted in a colorful diatribe as he ranted about her, attacked her impudence for having the audacity to question him, and threatened to throw her to the lions.

"So, I take it that you're Brutuz and that you're assigned to be some kind of a traitor." Sometimes the only way to get a direct response was to be direct. Abigail always tried to make sure that she did not sound accusing or condescending. She was not always successful.

Her statement further inflamed him. His face turned a deep shade of red, and it was obvious that if he could have throttled her, he would have.

"Who are you supposed to betray?" Abigail pressed. She was getting the idea that he and his soldiers were the persecutors within the system.

"How would you know about that?" he demanded as he folded his arms across his chest.

"I must admit that I am making an educated guess that you are named for Brutus who lived a couple thousand years ago, and since he stabbed his Caesar in the back, you may have a similar role. So why do you want to kill Caesar? You both came from the same person and if you kill him, you kill yourself."

"You make no sense. I will kill Caesar in spite of the fact that you have alerted him."

"What does the other general think of this plan? Is he a traitor, too, or is he on the Caesar's side?"

"There is no other general other than the traitor that just defected."

"Okay; the Senate leader then." Abigail hazarded another educated guess. "Murkury?" For some reason she was thinking of Mercury, an ancient Roman god. It would make sense that it would have a cult-twisted pronunciation and spelling.

He was stunned by her accurate word of knowledge. He suddenly switched out and was displaced by yet another personality.

"Murkury?" Abigail acknowledged the switch.

"How did you know?"

"Good guess," Abigail said quietly. She was not sure if he was antagonistic or friendly. "How can I help you today?"

"Who says I need any help?"

"I have a feeling that you've been dancing between Caesar and the generals and trying to maintain your leadership in the senate. What have you got? Twelve or thirteen senators vying for your position?"

"How would you know all of this? Are you some sort of diviner?"

"No, that's from Satan's kingdom. I belong to the kingdom of the true God. His Holy Spirit often lets me know what I need to know so I can help you."

"I know nothing of other kingdoms. I serve Caesar."

"How do you serve him? What do you do?"

"That is privileged information."

"No problem." Abigail prayed for a different tack that would allow her to negotiate with this crucial part of Max's system of personalities. "Do you know about Brutuz' plan to kill Caesar?"

"It is my duty to be aware."

"Correct me if I'm wrong, but it seems as if his plans are imminent. It's as if he's always had this plan, but the time to implement it is close. Or perhaps he's late since the Ides of March are well past."

"That was when he was activated."

"Do you understand that if he succeeds in killing Caesar he will also kill the rest of you?"

"I was privy to the conversations of the last meeting. It was enlightening."

Abigail was encouraged that their prayer against the lie of multiplicity last week affected this leader, too. "Are you willing to consider doing something like General Maximillian did?"

"I shall confer with my senators." Having said that, he disappeared into his internal place.

Max reappeared and spoke up, "This all sounds like a history book gone crazy. *I've* gone crazy."

"No, you haven't. I've heard about all kinds of internal worlds. Just go with it. It seems that the senate leader is leaning toward following Maximillian's lead. That would be about two-thirds of your system."

Murkury suddenly displaced Max again. "We have conferred and we agree that it would be in our best interest to do as Maximillian and his legions did. However, we have one concern. If there is a reduction in the number of forces that are defected, as you say, then would we not be in more jeopardy?"

"No. You would actually be safer because the little ones and the wounded ones wouldn't be vulnerable any more. In fact, they would strengthen the ones that do remain. Strongholds would also be demolished and demons wouldn't have access. Besides, you would be empowered by the Holy Spirit of the Most High God."

"Okay, we're ready. Do what you need to do." Murkury sounded weary.

After Abigail prayed her comprehensive prayer for Murkury and the senate and anyone associated with them, she checked back with Murkury. He sensed that everyone was taken care of. He sounded relieved. They prayed again and felt sure that they should all be integrated. Once that was done, Max emerged again.

"That seemed a lot easier than some of the other groups," he remarked. "Now what?"

"How do you feel? Did you sense the integration?"

"Yeah, it was kind of weird," he said as he circled his hand over his belly, "it was like they came in and everyone had to scoot over to make room and then they all settled down together. I feel fuller. Stronger."

"Excellent! Now let's ask the Lord what we need to do about Brutuz and his gang."

After praying, Max said, "I'm sensing that we need to ask the Lord to put them in some kind of safe place where they can't do any harm."

"Go for it," Abigail encouraged him.

Max was getting less self-conscious about praying. When he finished and he was at peace, they made their next appointment for July twentieth. After debriefing with Pastor Spalding, Abigail accompanied him to his office. Ginny was her unofficial wedding planner. Actually, she was the go-to person for every occasion in the church. She seemed to know all of the gifts and talents of everybody in the church and could pull together a classy event in no time. They finalized a couple of points and went to the sanctuary to check on the decorations. Silver and purple. Perfect.

Hustling out to her truck, turning right at the main light, she soon pulled in at the Kingston Inn where her father's car was parked near the office. As she went in to inquire about his room number, she heard the sound of laughter and familiar voices coming from the breakfast area off the main lobby.

"You got here!" Abigail greeted her dad with a hug and a peck on the cheek. "Did you have a good trip?"

"Good trip, good trip. I got twenty-seven miles to the gallon," he reported.

Abigail should have known that she would have received a report about miles-per-gallon. He had done that all his life.

"Now don't you look all aglow? Where's that man of yours?" Junior asked. Abigail braced for his hug and then hugged her other brothers and their wives, nieces and nephews, and cousins.

"Lee's working on some last-minute projects at the house. I worked this morning and just wanted to make sure everyone knows how to get to the church. We're supposed to have rehearsal at five and we've got reservations at The Iron Skillet at six-thirty."

"That gives us about five hours to kill," Junior said.

"Would you like to come see the new house?"

"I'd love it," her father said. "How about if we follow you there? It's been so long since I've been in this area that I'm not sure if I'd miss that turn or not."

"In case we get separated, just go down Kingston Road a couple miles. There's that big dip where York Creek Road starts. If you pass the Kingston Road Baptist Church, you've just missed it. Go about one mile down York Creek Road and Lee's driveway is at the top of the hill on the left. He's got a big black mailbox mounted on an old metal wagon wheel."

It took a few minutes to round up the family and decide who would ride with whom. Abigail laughed with delight at all her nieces and nephews who cried out, "I want to ride with Grandpa!" Car seats and boosters were placed in Grandpa's spacious BFOMC. They were in a festive mood so when Junior suddenly jumped out of his car and yelled, "Fire drill!" car doors swung open and everyone except Grandpa and the children found a different seat in a different vehicle. Junior jumped in with Abigail, rolled down the window, and signaled that the parade should begin.

"I guess you're only young once, but ya can be immature forever," he quipped.

Abigail chuckled as she put the truck into drive. "I agree," she said and started singing, "I'll never grow up, never grow up. Not me!"

Abigail missed her family at times like this. They could be so much fun. They could turn just about any occasion into a party. She suspected that this weekend would be no exception.

Lee had been alerted so he was standing on the front porch when the seven-vehicle caravan pulled up to the house. Soon nearly thirty people poured out of the doors and looked with wonder at the barn and the house, the out-buildings and the pond, the pastures and woods.

"This is a beautiful place!"

"Do you have cows in the barn?"

"Wow! A tractor!"

"Oh, this is so peaceful."

"Well, come on in," Lee invited. "I'll give you the nickel tour. My daughter is inside right now. Lisa flew in earlier. I'll introduce you when we run into her."

The women oohed and aahed over the kitchen. The men loved the fireplace that was centered between the living room and the dining room. The kids made loops down the hall and around the stairs passing through the living room, dining room, and back through the kitchen again. They admired the master bedroom with the beautiful new bed and the office that was also downstairs before trooping upstairs to investigate the guest rooms up there. Lee was using one of them until after the wedding. Lisa was in the other guest room.

"This is my lovely daughter, Lisa. I'm afraid I haven't quite gotten everyone's name memorized yet, so Lisa, these fine folks are Abigail's brothers and their families with a few cousins thrown in the lot."

They laughed and introduced themselves and then moved on while Lisa continued to unpack. Lisa was going to spend the night in the guest room and visit with her father for a short day, but since Lee and Abigail were going to spend their first night at home, Lisa would be with her grandparents after that.

"Nice view from the balcony."

"Kind of empty, sis," Junior commented.

"I'm not all the way moved in yet. It'll get filled up eventually," she replied. He was always bordering on criticizing her, but he would act offended if he was confronted. She stopped confronting him a long time ago. *I'm not playing your games today, big brother.*

"What are you going to do with your place?" her other brother, Pete, asked.

"My roommates will still live there plus we've got the chickens and my garden and orchard and we might need the pasture one of these days," Abigail said somewhat evasively. She did not want to get into a long discussion about the need for a sanctuary house for Satanic Ritual Abuse survivors. Her family had no idea about how wild and crazy her life could be. They thought she was a reclusive widow quietly living on her little farm.

"Hey!" Lee called out to the kids, "Who wants to see the horses and cows?"

"I do!"

"Me!"

"Me, too!"

Lee was quickly surrounded. His soon-to-be nieces, nephews, and second cousins were excitedly jumping up and down. The adults looked interested as well. "Follow me," he said and took off at a slow pace as he caught the hands of a couple of three-year olds.

Points! Abigail smiled contentedly at the man that she would soon marry. The group meandered down the trail to see the horses. Lee was pointing to some things along the way and warning the children about the barbs on the barbed wire fencing. He told them to stay by the gate and to move slowly and talk softly to the horses. They were enthralled by the magnificent animals who pranced and paraded, whinnied and snorted as they came up to the gate tossing their proud heads and snuffling their warm breath onto extended little hands.

Junior hung back with Abigail who fervently prayed that he would not say something hurtful. So far, he had been fairly considerate, but there was always an edge, an angle, a criticism simmering beneath the surface.

"Hey, sis," Junior began, "I heard about a shooting somewhere around Kingston a couple weeks ago."

"You heard right."

"Did you know the guy who did it?"

"Not really."

"Where did it happen? Around here?"

"Considering how small a community this is, I guess you could say it was around here." Abigail laughed lightly as she avoided a direct answer and hoped that he would not press for more details. She was not about to tell him that the shooting was directed at her and her neighbors because Charlie Fletcher was trying to kill her. Again.

"Does this happen very often?" Junior asked with apparent concern. He lived in the suburbs, and in his world, shootings only occurred in the larger city.

"Oh yeah," Abigail responded as if it was no big deal, "practically everyone out here owns a gun. Someone's bound to get drunk and shoot up the town." Quickening her pace, she changed the subject and said, "Come on, let's catch up. I want to watch the kids with the horses."

Noticing their waning interest after about twenty minutes, leading them along another trail, the group trekked up the gentle slope and was able to see the cows grazing at the far end of the field. Unlike the horses, they merely looked up from their grazing and stared with big brown eyes. The children were getting rambunctious so they headed up to the barn to see the tractor and other equipment, and then finished with a quick look at some of the other out-buildings.

"I guess we ought to get back to town and start to get ready for the rehearsal," Janet remarked.

"I don't know why," Mitzi replied barely audibly, "Dad's the only one that has to do anything."

"Mitzi!" Jennifer hissed, "That's not nice. They're taking all of us out to dinner afterward. Besides, the guys are going to usher; that's important."

"Well," huffed the proud mother of a couple of the youngsters who were prime ring-bearer and flower-girl ages, "we don't have a part in the ceremony. Does anyone in your family?"

After the relatively relaxed pace of the morning and afternoon, it seemed that someone put a finger on the clock and gave it a spin. Time flew. It was going to be a fairly late evening and they would only have until about three o'clock to finish the myriad of details that suddenly seemed urgent.

"Don't you need to take a nap or something?" Amy asked as she watched Abigail's nervous, excited energy propel her around the house.

"I couldn't sleep right now if you hit me with a sledge hammer."

"Well, can't you just sit down and take a load off? You're making us tired just watching you," Carrie Sue added.

137

They were interrupted by the toot of Lee's horn. The ladies looked questioningly at Abigail.

"He has something for you."

"Us?" They looked at each other. Neither one was accustomed to receiving gifts – especially from a man. They trusted Lee, but they were automatically nervous.

"Yes. Let's go to the living room." Abigail led the way and by the time Lee knocked lightly and entered the living room, the ladies were settling into their seats.

"Hey there," Lee greeted them. It was obvious that he was in a really good mood. He had a bag in his hand that he set down on the floor in front of his chair. Reaching in, he pulled out three packages and handed one to each of the ladies.

"What's this?" Amy asked with a puzzled frown as she turned the package over.

"Pepper gel spray," Lee said. "We believe that God is going to protect you while we're gone, but after that guy bumped you and all the other things that have happened lately, it's just a good idea."

"Pepper gel? I've heard of pepper spray but not pepper gel." Carrie Sue was also intrigued.

"It still sprays, but the gel is better than the other kinds of sprays because it's easier to hit your target and less likely to blow back on you if there's a breeze."

"Ew, that would be bad," Amy commented.

"These are supposed to be good for ten to twelve feet which means you can pretty much get anyone who's in the same room with you."

"Ah." Carrie Sue was beginning to get the picture. "Thanks!"

"You can put those on your key chains and these," he reached into the bag again, "we'll place in strategic spots around the house in case you have to retreat to a safe place."

"We need to put one upstairs and one in the basement," Abigail added. "How many do you have?"

"I've got seven more. I think we also need to put one down in the barn in case you're outside."

"What about in that room over the barn?"

"Good idea."

"Another thing: do you know how to signal SOS in Morse code?"

"No," the ladies chimed together.

"It's dot-dot-dot, dash-dash-dash, dot-dot-dot. So, if you're in peril, you can blow a horn or tap a pipe or the iron porch rail. Both of your neighbors were military so they would recognize it, too. We'll let them know. Just make sure there aren't any false alarms."

"Hey Dad!" Abigail greeted her father with a smile and a peck on the cheek. Lee and his future father-in-law shook hands. Abigail had been excitedly watching for her family members to arrive at the church for the rehearsal. They arrived one after another. Adults with freshly scrubbed children trooped into the foyer and entered the auditorium.

Pastor Spalding had told them to allow an hour for the rehearsal. "Sometimes it's like herding chickens," he said with a laugh.

Introductions were made. Music was played so that the ushers, Gary and Cindy, Lee and Abigail, and her father, as well as Pastor Spalding would each know their cues.

"Ready?" Pastor Spalding asked after giving instructions to the participants. Abigail's brothers ushered their wives and children down the aisle. The older children laughed as they pretended to be adults. The younger ones followed along cluelessly. Pastor Spalding, Lee, and Gary walked to the front from the side door and looked expectantly toward the back. Cindy walked sedately down the aisle.

"I'm not giving you away, you know," John Rooze said as they walked toward the front. "I already did that once."

"I know, Dad." Abigail was not quite sure how to take that comment. "I'm just asking you to walk me down the aisle."

He held his elbow out and Abigail grasped it with her right hand. They walked calmly down the aisle where Lee met her and walked Abigail up to their marks in front of Pastor Spalding.

He efficiently walked them through the whole thing twice and then they all headed to The Iron Skillet for a light dinner.

10

Saturday, July 7

"You're riding with us!" Carrie Sue exclaimed.

"Yeah," Amy chimed in, "you can't let Lee see you in your wedding dress before the wedding."

"I won't be in my wedding dress. It's already there. I'm getting changed at the church."

"It ain't right."

"Not right!"

"Fine. I'll call Lee and let him know that I'll ride over to the church with you two. He'll have Lisa with him anyway." She continued to pepper them with last minute items. "Don't forget to tell Ginny to take any of the left-overs that she wants and whatever you two can't eat, put in the freezer."

"We've got it covered," Amy laughed. "And we'll call Earl if we need to. And we have Gary's home and work number. And we have pepper sprays all over the place. We'll be fine."

"We'll weed the garden and pick stuff. We won't forget the chickens, either."

"And we won't stay up past our bed time," Carrie Sue teased.

"And we'll do our chores," Amy added with a playful grin. She looked pretty in the flattering top that Carrie Sue had found for her at her thrift shop.

By two-thirty they were on the way with Carrie Sue driving. Amy and Carrie Sue were highly amused by their jittery counselor. *They* were cool and calm; *she* was a bundle of nerves.

The rest of the wedding party was already there so Ginny was watching for Abigail and led her to the restroom with the large powder room. It was designed for occasions such as this. Cindy was waiting in a lovely dark purple dress that nicely complimented Abigail's. Tearful smiles reflected her happiness for her best friend and soon-to-be cousin.

Abigail carefully took her simple but stunning lavender gown out of its bag and slipped it on. The sleeveless A-line style flowed around her as she moved. Silver sandals glistening on her feet, Mom's pearls gracing her neck, she touched up her make-up and hair. The sound of the muted music sent the butterflies swirling anew. It was time.

"Come on," Ginny urged as the purple-clad friends each lightly held a knot of their gowns to keep from tripping up the stairs. "The guys are up front and it's almost time for Cindy to join them. Ready? Oh! Yes! There's your cue."

Cindy's smiling lips trembled as her happiness for her friend nearly caused her to burst into tears of joy. Gliding down the aisle, she nodded to friends from church who were seated toward the back of the auditorium. Closer to the front she shot a discrete wink at Traci and Bryan who were sitting with their grandparents. Once she arrived at the front and turned around, the music changed.

Everyone stood up and turned to watch Abigail walk down the aisle with her father. Abigail was thrilled with the way the purple and silver decorations accented the room. She was elated that people took her seriously when she told them to wear something purple. Purple ties. Purple shirts. Purple dresses.

Purple, purple everywhere. Purple paled as her eyes sought and found Lee's moist brown eyes.

Lee could not take his eyes off of Abigail. Her graceful gait in the elegant gown made her appear to be floating down the aisle next to her father. Lee battled the slight tremor in his chin and the knot in his throat. It seemed that he could not swallow hard enough as his eyes were riveted on his bride-to-be. The ceremony was meaningful and mercifully brief. The special music was short and sweet. Lee was eager to begin the rest of his life with this woman at his side. Finally, he heard the words, "Ladies and gentlemen, I present to you Mr. and Mrs. Lee Norris!"

Smiles and claps, cheers and hallelujahs came from all over the room. Lee and Abigail were bursting with joy as they made their way up the aisle arm in arm. They went down to the fellowship hall where they were joined by Gary and Cindy so they could greet each guest. The ushers and other relatives would be introduced once everyone settled down for appetizers and hors d'oeuvers, cheese and crackers, fruits and vegetables, and other finger foods.

The fellowship hall was also decorated in purple and silver. Purple table cloths were decorated with silver doilies and silver candles. Guests trickling into the room in clusters, hugged and shook hands with the couple, filled plates with goodies, and found their places at tables. Happy chatter filled the room.

Ting! Ting! Ting! The sound of plastic utensils on plastic cups crescendoed as the crowd looked expectantly at the head table. Lee and Abigail happily obliged the group by standing and kissing. Adults smiled. Small children laughed and enthusiastically tapped their cups again.

Time whirled quickly by after introductions and speeches, posed photos and cake cutting. Lee and Abigail visited each table and opened gifts. Soon, the room began to empty except for Abigail's relatives, Lee's relatives, the Milners, and the Spaldings. They lingered until it was time to head over to The Steak House for the formal dinner reception.

After the delicious meal was finished and everyone was quieting down, Lee and Abigail thanked everyone, said their good-byes, and made their exit. Lee escorted Abigail to his freshly detailed truck and opened the door for her.

"You'd better check to see if anyone booby-trapped it," Abigail said.

"Good idea," Lee agreed. "Between my cousins and your brothers, we could be in trouble." He looked under the truck to see if there were cans tied to the bumpers and reported that they were free and clear.

"They wouldn't have had time to do anything at the house, would they?"

"Absolutely not. I told Gary that he needed to warn everyone that after the neighborhood shoot-out it wouldn't be a very good idea and he agreed. I think we're safe."

"Thanks for thinking of that."

They rode back through Springfield, down through Kingston, and out to York Creek Road.

"You look beautiful."

"You were the most handsome man there. I love the leather vest and purple tie. How did you get Pastor Spalding to wear a vest, too?"

"That was easy. He said he loved the idea of not having to wear what he called his 'marry 'em and bury 'em suit.' Besides, I bought it for him."

Turning left into Lee's long driveway felt strange to Abigail. "I can't believe how odd this feels. This is my home now. I love it!"

Lee smiled warmly at his new bride. Pulling up to the house, turning off the ignition, he kissed her lightly, walked around the truck, and opened the door. "No, no, no," he cautioned as she scooted toward the door, "I can't let your silver slippers touch this dusty earth."

Before she could protest, he scooped her up in his arms, kicked the door shut with a booted foot and carried her up the porch steps. Deftly unlocking the door, he pushed it open, and walked into their home with her in his arms. Closing the door with his foot, he carried her into their bedroom.

———

Abigail's eyes fluttered open in the dim early morning light. After a brief moment of disorientation, she remembered. *We're married!* She looked around the room and saw the evidence of an evening that was *not* focused on hanging up clothes or putting shoes away. She took a few minutes to watch Lee's brawny chest rhythmically rise and fall before she used the bathroom. Returning to the bed, she snuggled down next to the sleeping man and contentedly dozed off again. They were both tired from the marathon week that preceded their wedding. She was thankful that their flight was scheduled for the afternoon.

Lee stirred from his sleep and rolled toward Abigail. Taking her in his arms, he murmured, "Good morning, Mrs. Norris."

Abigail's response was muffled by warm, hungry lips over hers.

"I'm sure glad you're good at travel arrangements," Abigail said. "I've only been on planes twice and that was a long time ago."

"I've been all over the United States and a few foreign countries. It's not all that glamorous. For this trip I wanted to make it as easy as possible for both of us so I booked an all-inclusive trip. That's why we're going to the bigger airport. We have a direct flight."

"I'm not sure what all-inclusive means."

"It means that I got a package. The round-trip air fare, the shuttle to and from the resort..."

"Resort! We're going to a resort? Which one?"

The instant bubbling up of Abigail's child-like excitement caused Lee to chuckle delightedly as she bounced exuberantly for nearly a mile in the seat next to him.

"How does Cancun sound?"

"Mexico?"

"Yep."

"Wonderful!" Abigail paused as she did a mental inventory of her suitcase and said, "Oh, I hope my clothes are nice enough. It sounds so glamorous."

"Don't worry. You'll look classy in whatever you wear. Besides," he added with a double flick of his eyebrows, "we'll be in our swimsuits – or less – most of the time."

They caught the shuttle from the long-term parking lot. Check-in at the airport went smoothly. Security personnel were polite. The time before boarding was not excessively long. Soon they were settled in their seats with about a hundred other sun and sand seekers bound for various resorts.

Five hours after taking off, Lee and Abigail had the keys to their suite in hand. It was early evening and they were hungry so after they were settled in their room, they found one of several restaurants off of the main lobby.

"Look at the variety! I don't even know what some of these fruits are! It looks like a postcard."

"I'm absolutely starving!" the six-foot, four-inch man pronounced. "That cute little snack we had on the plane didn't quite cut it."

Lee took her arm and walked with her to the buffet line where they picked up a tray for their plates and utensils. Everything looked utterly scrumptious. They loaded their plates and found a comfortable booth by the windows where they could watch the waves curl and break on the shore. Couples were silhouetted against the ocean as they walked hand in hand. Runners took advantage of the empty beach. Parents were herding children back to the resort.

After going back for a light dessert, Lee and Abigail explored the spacious resort and found an exit that led directly to the beach. They meandered hand in hand through the fine sand before coming upon a huge swimming pool. There was a swim-up bar at the far end complete with underwater stools. A volleyball net was strung over the near end. They crossed a bridge that spanned the pool and headed to the ocean.

"I just want to stick my toes in and feel what it's like," Abigail said. "I was in the ocean off Rhode Island once, but the water was cold and dark, and the sand was coarse and rocky."

"This water will be warmer and clearer."

Removing their sandals, rolling up their pant legs, Lee and Abigail walked at a leisurely pace along the foamy edge of the water. The rhythmic sound of cascading waves, the balmy temperatures, and the briny aroma of the ocean were pleasant companions as they kicked through the white sand. Approaching the northern end of the beach, they finally turned and headed back to room 707 through a side entrance. The seventh-floor room was high enough and faced north and east so that they had a panoramic view of the ocean and some of the neighboring villas far down the shore line. The sun was beginning to set as they finished their long and happy day together.

Carrie Sue and Amy had breakfast together. Carrie Sue had gone down to let the chickens out despite Amy's protests about being perfectly able to do it. She felt protective of Amy and little David who was steadily developing within Amy's protective womb.

"You can let the chickens out on the days that I have to go in to work."

"Fine."

That led to another conversation about the division of labor for the various household chores. And that discussion led to chats about Abigail and Lee.

"I wonder if they're going to church today."

"They'll have a hard time choosing between Beach side Baptist, Pool side Presbyterian, and St. Mattress." Amy giggled at her own playful irreverence.

"I think they'll attend all three," Carrie Sue laughed.

"Speaking of church, do you want to drive, or shall I?"

"I will."

Neither one of them wanted to admit how much they missed Abigail's reassuring presence in the house and Lee's daily visits for meals. Neither one of them wanted to admit that they were nervous about the possibility of another attack by the cult. Amy did not want to think about being alone when Carrie Sue was at work. They were both grateful for the pepper gel and for being coached to think both defensively and offensively.

Evil forces were constantly prowling, constantly seeking whom they could devour. Urdang and his minions were delighted that the source of their consternation was not on the property. Perhaps they could devise some mischief. They still had to contend with the presence of warring angels who vigilantly stood watch, not only on her property, but also on the next hill and, more recently, on the property across the street. They were furious that more land was being wrested from their grip. They were incensed at their own impotence and inability to execute their tried-and-true tactics that had won many a battle and secured much of their territory.

Xerxes, the territorial master, had taken a special interest in the region that had once been ruled by Prinz.

Xerxes still smarted over the incident in which he and Prinz were pelted by hail stones as they drove past that detestable woman. A woman! The thought that a mere woman had superior powers infuriated the man.

Friday the thirteenth was coming up this week and there was a new moon the following night. As much as he despised the smaller venue, he would call for the regional rituals to be celebrated at the local gathering place one mile south of the woman's property. Perhaps the closer proximity would afford greater powers. He would call for several pre-ritual rituals every night this week to increase the potential if necessary.

Night after night they would sling arrows of curses at the cluster of houses a mile up the road. Night after night they would sacrifice the innocent or the not-so-innocent, and partake in counterfeit communion. Night after night they would embellish their powers through the orgies and covenants that were made at the expense of the weak and powerless; especially the women and children.

Zorroz felt the pressure both as a Satanist and as the sheriff. It fell to him to procure sacrifices if the breeders could not keep up with demand. Having been notified of the additional gatherings at Charlie Fletcher's place, he prowled the county for the unwary, unsuspecting public that he, as sheriff, pledged to serve and protect.

He knew all too well that his remaining daughter could also be demanded at any time. A paternal part of him was nauseated by the thought. The Satanist parts of him had no such reaction because the familial love that God designed within the male and female, the father and mother, was suppressed. There were no sweet touches, no loving eye contact, no soothing words. There was no natural drive to protect or to provide or to afford security. The biological child was a potential sacrifice or a bargaining chip used to obtain increased favor and power. At the very least, the child offered yet another means of self-gratification.

Richard York habitually slept lightly with trained senses that were attuned to every nuance of ordinary and unusual sounds. Keeping his bedroom door ajar in case his father or mother needed him, he heard his mother shuffling through the living room once again. He did not know if this was typical of dementia patients or if something was upsetting the confused woman. It was three o'clock in the morning.

"Mom," Richard said gently as he caught up with her in the kitchen, "are you, all right?"

"It's that horse," she said as she pointed toward the back of the property. "See it? There it goes again. There's going to be trouble."

"Mom, it's pitch black. I don't see a horse."

"It's over there. It's heading next door. It always goes next door."

Richard was baffled. How could his mother see a horse without her glasses? He had perfect vision and could see nothing in the inky night. "I'll go out and check, Mom. You go back to bed."

"Okay, honey. You be careful."

"I will." Richard went to his room and exchanged his sleeping shorts for a pair of denim jeans. He slipped into his shoulder holster and grabbed his night-vision goggles before he quietly slid the back door open. Moving to the side of the doorway to eliminate any possibility of his silhouette being seen, he stood silently and listened intently as his eyes adjusted to the darkness. Crickets and frogs were all that could be heard. Surveying the area with the night vision goggles revealed only the expected opossums and raccoons. An owl flew soundlessly over the stand of trees in the field.

Amy restlessly stirred in her bed shortly after three o'clock in the morning. She was feeling something peculiar and she did not like it. Not wanting to disturb Carrie Sue, she remained in her room and prayed. David was unusually active. It felt like he was doing acrobatics. It was becoming uncomfortable. The last time he did this, it was because of demonic activity.

"Oh, Lord, please protect my baby. Protect me. Please don't let those Satanists win. I plead the blood of Jesus Christ of Nazareth over us once again. Cover us and this property once more." She remembered how Abigail prayed and tried to include as many of the salient points as she could.

Amy began to feel pains – what she assumed were contractions. She had been pregnant before. She had been forced into pre-mature labor before. She was terrified. "No! Lord, it's too soon. He's only twenty weeks. Please, Lord, stop the contractions."

Carrie Sue woke up to use the bathroom downstairs. As she got to the bottom of the stairwell, she noticed that Amy's light was on. "Hey, A, are you, all right?"

"I don't know. I think I'm feeling contractions. I feel really weird and David's going crazy inside."

"What do you think we should do?"

"I don't know. If I call the doctor's office, I'll just get the answering service and they'll tell me to go to the emergency room."

"Do you think we need to go?"

"I don't know. I just don't know," Amy wailed as another bout of pain stabbed her belly. "Ouch!" This time she pointed to a very localized spot on the right side of her abdomen. "Right there."

"Are you sure it's labor?" Carrie Sue asked with growing concern. "I mean, aren't contractions all over and not just one spot?"

Amy thought a moment and then said, "Yes, maybe you're right. This reminds me of that time when the cult was trying to use David to torment me a couple of months ago."

"I think we ought to pray. I sure wish Abigail was here."

"Me too. We'll just have to muddle through it ourselves. I know both Jan and Cindy said we could call any time, but I don't want to bother anyone at this hour."

"Let's pray then."

The two women launched their fledgling prayers heavenward. Within minutes David calmed down and Amy reported that she was no longer feeling physical pain or the emotional and mental distress. After a triumphant high-five, Carrie Sue finished her business in the bathroom and returned to her bed. Amy was already settled down.

Thursday came too soon for Lee and Abigail, and yet they shared an urgency to get back to their new home to begin their married life together. As days passed, their conversations shifted more and more often to wondering how their horses and cows and chickens were faring. They mentioned concerns for how Carrie Sue and Amy were managing. They loved the ocean and the beach, the food and the unregimented schedule, but it was time to head home.

The shuttle to the airport was scheduled for noon so they had an early swim and an early breakfast so they could have a late brunch to hold them over until a late supper. Lee remembered the ultra-light airplane fare and determined to eat something at the airport even if it was over-priced.

They reversed their travels as they headed back home. Boarding the shuttle which brought them to the departure area of the airport, they checked their luggage and went through customs and security without a problem. Oblivious to time, they talked, sat quietly, or people-watched until it was time to board. Able to lightly doze snuggled next to each other, this flight seemed short.

They were tired, tanned, and wonderfully relaxed after their five glorious days in Cancun. Collecting their luggage, boarding the shuttle to the long-term parking, Lee soon had them heading back to the farm.

11

Friday, July 13

Lee slipped out of the bed leaving his bride to sleep a bit longer. He knew that she would not admit it, but she was tired after the non-stop flurry of the last couple of weeks and it did not look as if it would slow down any time soon. He smiled contentedly at her peaceful form, sighed a sigh of satisfaction, and headed out to check on the livestock.

Abigail was shocked to see that it was after nine o'clock when she rolled out of bed and that she never even noticed when her husband got up. Assuming that he was checking on the animals, she dressed and stepped onto the front porch. Lee was not in sight so she ducked back into the kitchen to see what she could rustle up for breakfast. *I definitely need to get to the grocery store!*

Across the road, Carrie Sue was already up and heading to work. Amy took her time going down to let the chickens out and then lingered near their coop. The normally bold young woman did not want to admit that she did not like to be alone. At least chickens were living creatures. Reluctantly, she plodded back up to the house noting that she was really feeling the effects of the pregnancy. *If I'm already waddling like a duck; what's it going to be like at forty weeks if this is only twenty?*

Shaking herself from her thoughts, she went back into the house. "Come on, David," she spoke aloud to her unborn son, "we've got things to do." She spent some time cleaning up the kitchen and planning supper for herself and Carrie Sue.

Earl Milner heard a vehicle crunch up his driveway and peeked out of the recently replaced front window to see an unfamiliar young man emerge from an equally unfamiliar SUV. Instantly wary, Earl picked up the handgun that he kept near the front door and held it behind his right leg as he cautiously opened the door.

"Hello, neighbor! I'm Richard, David and Martha York's son."

Earl cocked his head and took a closer look, "Well, so you are! I didn't recognize you. How long has it been? Come in, come in."

"Thanks. I don't want to bother you, but I came back after the shooting and I was wondering if you're up to talking about it."

"Sure, sure; come on in," Earl replied and called over his shoulder, "We've got company. It's Richard York."

"Why Richard!" Jan exclaimed when she saw him, "you're the spitting image of your father. How are you? And how are your folks doing? I'm so sorry, we've been so busy with our own mess that we haven't gotten down there to find out."

"No need to apologize. It's been crazy for everyone. I understand that both of you were shot, too. Dad's recovering nicely but Mom's going downhill fast with her dementia or Alzheimer's or whatever they call it these days."

"I'm so sorry to hear that. We will certainly keep them in our prayers. You be sure to let me know if we can do anything."

"Thanks; I will. If you've got the energy, I would like to talk about what's been going on around here. Do you have some time?"

"Definitely. Would you like a cup of coffee?"

"Definitely."

Coffee was poured and the three of them sat down in comfortable chairs in the living room. The Milners were aware that Richard worked in some government agency in DC, but did not know much more than that. Richard told them that he wanted to do some unofficial behind-the-scenes investigating of the events that led up to the shooting.

"You be careful," Earl warned. "The law is in on a lot of it. You need to talk to Abigail Steele who lives between our places." Earl jerked his thumb over his shoulder toward her place on the next hill.

"Abigail Norris. Across the street," Jan corrected him and pointed the other way. "She just got married to that fine young man who bought the property across the road from all of us. In fact, they just got home from their honeymoon yesterday."

An hour after Richard sat down, he left having been apprised of many more events that coincided with the things he and his father had discussed. Richard had taken the time to read his father's hand-written notes and the documents that had been down-loaded from the thumb drive onto his private computer. The Milners confirmed several things that his father reported. They confirmed that his mother was right about the big horse. He sat in amazement as Earl told him about the night he shot Charlie Fletcher in the hand just as Charlie was shooting at Abigail.

Richard was thoroughly puzzled by the events but after being told about the satanic cult that operated in the area, things started to make more sense. He had heard of such cases during his career, but was never directly involved in those investigations. There was a special division for such matters. Before he left, Jan had called Abigail and they arranged to have a neighborhood meeting the next day.

Bustling between the kitchen and the living room, Martha showed some signs of lucidity. Perhaps the familiarity of extending hospitality triggered the long-term memory that allowed her to be a gracious hostess once again. Richard kept an eye on her activities, making sure that she did not leave the refrigerator door open or a burner on again.

Walking gingerly, David insisted on greeting their guests. Gary McCord joined the group because he was another eye-witness and had evidence on his phone. Carrie Sue and Amy were not sure what to expect, but were willing to trust anyone that the others trusted. Abigail was prepared with her thumb drive and the file with hard copies.

"It looks like we have a fine neighborhood watch group," Earl said.

"We sure could use one," Abigail added.

"Let's get started," Richard suggested. "Mom's got hot coffee and iced tea for us."

Once everyone was settled around the dining room table, David cleared his throat and said, "I don't know if you know, but Richard and I both used to work for the FBI, so when I noticed the things that were going on around here, I started paying a little more attention at work. This old hound can still sniff out something fishy."

"Where did you work? I thought you were retired like me," Earl said. He was usually quite direct, often to the consternation of his wife.

"After I retired, I was a little bored around here so I picked up a part time job as a maintenance man for the county. I worked at the sheriff's office most of the time but I got called up to the courthouse, too. I started noticing some things and overheard some things as time went on. Before I get into that, would you folks be comfortable with sharing things from your perspective? I have a feeling that we might all be able to get a clearer picture when we start putting the odd pieces together."

Abigail started with the death of her family and moved through the attacks and threats, harassments and crimes. Breaking and entering by Billy and others. Trespassing. Arson – her woods and Amy's trailer. Assault. Vehicular damage. Stalking. Poisoned dog. Billy's disappearance and deserted car. Vandalism. Fence cutting. Blood in a church. Child abduction. Phone threats. Attempts to kill Buster. Kidnapping. Attempted murder. Buried baby skull. And these were just the things Abigail experienced or knew about.

Carrie Sue and Amy had given Abigail permission to speak for them about attacks against them, including the rape that brought about David's conception. She mentioned that there were things that came out in Carrie Sue's memories that could not be proven such as bodies buried in her mother's back yard. There had also been other counselees over the years that mentioned kidnapped and sacrificed people.

Gary gave his expert opinion about the cut brake lines which he kept at his shop. Lee attested to the matter of Charlie Fletcher's five-sided rock. Carrie Sue confirmed that there were rituals on Fletcher's property based on her harrowing escape. They allowed Richard to download pictures from the security cameras as well as their cell phones. He and his father would comb through their files and begin to make some plans.

"You ought to come to our Ministerial Alliance meeting. We're praying about the cult in this area but we aren't investigators or anything. It would be nice to battle this on both spiritual and legal fronts. I met your pastor at the last one," Abigail invited. "We meet on the first Monday of the month. It'll be at my church in August. First Baptist on the main drag in Springfield."

"I'd like that," Richard said.

"I'd love to come, but I'm not sure I can leave Martha alone safely these days," David said.

Martha brightened and smiled at David when he spoke her name.

"We can come sit with her," Carrie Sue offered as she looked to Amy for confirmation.

"That might just work. I'll let you know."

After exchanging phone numbers and email addresses, the neighbors left. Richard and David settled down for a long talk. They now had concrete proof about crimes, corruption, and the cult. They now had names and faces, driver's licenses and license plates, places and dates.

Richard called Landrum and briefed him on his father's recovery as well as the corruption in the area. Landrum, also a retired Marine, gave him an indefinite paid leave of absence with unrestricted access to DOJ resources. No one attacks a Marine, an FBI agent, or a DOJ family and gets away with it!

The days flew by relatively uneventfully. Abigail and Amy had a session and were able to integrate a few more of her personalities who managed to escape from Abaddon's section. Sherry Samuels did not show for her appointment which was scheduled right after Max's on the twentieth. Max called and cancelled.

Abigail was disappointed, but not surprised because it marked the beginning of the preparations for the Grand Climax ritual on July twenty-seventh. That would be followed by a full moon on the thirtieth and, of course, the ritual for the thirty-first. There was the Feast of the Sun God and another Sabbat on August first.

Amy and Carrie Sue cleaned the nursery, but only Carrie Sue painted it, and insisted that Amy stay clear of the fumes. It lacked furniture. She had no baby clothes. There were no diapers or shampoos or lotions. Amy looked at the barren room after it dried and wondered how she was going to take care of her little boy. Indeed, she doubted that she could reasonably support herself.

Lee and Abigail made countless small and large adjustments to married life. Without purposefully intending to, they studied each other. Lee was an early-to-bed, early-to-rise man. Abigail preferred to stay up later and get up a bit later. Lee could live with more clutter than Abigail could. They adjusted, they laughed, and at times they scratched their heads.

"Hey, Lee," Gary said, "I got a question for you."

"Shoot."

"Do you remember my mechanic?"

"Sure do. He's the big red head."

"That's the guy. Rusty. Anyway, his dog had a huge litter of pups a few months ago and he still has three left. He's looking for good homes. I told him I'd see if you and Abigail might be ready."

"What breed?"

"German Shepherd. Both parents are purebred, but he doesn't have papers on them. He's letting them go free to good homes."

"I'll check with Abigail. It was rough putting Bullet down, but I miss having a dog. It was really tough for Abigail when Dude was poisoned, but maybe she's ready by now. This place could use a dog. I'll get back to you."

Slipping his phone back into his pocket, Lee finished his project and headed to the house for supper.

"Something sure smells good!"

"Nothing fancy," Abigail replied with a smile, "just grilled burgers with fresh stir-fried zucchini and onions with garlic and spices."

"Yum!"

"Oh, yeah," she said as she pointed at the large pot on the stove top, "fresh sweet corn from the farm stand and fresh green beans from our garden."

"The garden is really putting out."

"It sure is. Tomorrow I'm going to teach Carrie Sue and Amy how to can. We're going to make tomato sauce from scratch and can it. That way they can learn two skills."

"What time will you head over there?"

"Sometime in the morning."

"What time will you be done?"

"Sometime in the afternoon. Why?"

"I was hoping we could take a ride to Rusty's place."

"Rusty?"

"Gary's mechanic."

"What for? You're being evasive tonight. What's going on?"

"I want to look at some German Shepherd pups. I'm hoping that you might be ready for another dog." Lee looked hopefully at Abigail for the long minute that it took for her to form her answer.

"Okay. I think that would work if it's the right dog. I mean, we're both around most of the time so it's not like he'll be unsupervised."

"Great!" Lee was relieved and began to get excited.

"One question first." Abigail eyed him, turned her head slightly, and raised her chin a little.

"What?"

"You let your dog inside your house; I never let Dude in. How are we going to negotiate this? If you're as adamant as I am about inside versus outside, we might have a problem. Why did you let Bullet in?"

Lee stroked his chin and huffed slightly before slowly saying, "Lisa's mom always had cats inside. I hated them but I tolerated them. Bullet just followed me everywhere. He was a good dog and never got into things. Actually, Bullet stayed outside until she left. Maybe it was my way of rebelling."

"Makes sense."

"Why don't you want a dog inside?"

"Because we have enough dust bunnies without adding a bunch of dog hair to the mix. It just seems unsanitary to me. I don't want to find a dog hair in my food, so it would mean the kitchen and dining areas would be off-limits. I don't like animals on furniture; not couches and especially not beds, so that means the living areas and bedrooms would be off-limits."

Lee knew that he was not going to win this one. Her rationale was sound. They had covered porches, outbuildings, and a huge barn. "I'll tell you what," Lee answered, "I'm okay with keeping the dog outside, but since it's just a puppy, I'd like to put a dog house on the porch so I can keep an eye on him at night."

"No problem! That's where I kept Dude. Maybe we can use his old dog house."

"I had no idea that you had to put so much work into making this stuff!" Amy exclaimed as she skinned and cored the tomatoes that had been dipped in boiling water and then dunked in cold water.

"Me either," said Carrie Sue as she diced onions and bell peppers and minced fresh garlic.

"It's so much easier when there's help," Abigail replied gratefully as she washed and sterilized nine quart jars and their lids. She had an assortment of gadgets that made canning easier, but it was still a labor-intensive project. "It's a lot more fun, too."

After using a blender and a seed-removing cone shaped colander on the tomatoes, they added Carrie Sue's bowl full of diced vegetables and spices.

"What do we do with all these seeds?" Carrie Sue asked.

"We take them to the chickens. They'll love 'em!"

"Cool. Now what?" Amy asked.

"Now we let it simmer for a while. Then we taste test it and then add more spices if we need to."

"Then what?"

"Then we fill the jars and let them boil in the canner for forty-five minutes."

"And that's it?"

"We have to take them out and make sure that the lids sealed. You'll hear a plink. That means that the jar is sealed. Don't ever eat anything that doesn't have a depressed lid." She continued to instruct these ladies who had virtually no instruction from their mothers. "And that's it," Abigail said with a quick nod of her head. "Except for the clean-up."

"We can do that."

"Yeah, let us do that."

"One more question," Amy said with a puzzled look on her face.

"What's that?"

"Why don't they call it jarring? These are glass jars, not cans."

Shaking her head, Abigail answered, "I don't know. I've wondered that myself."

The canning sequence went without incident and after being satisfied that all the cooled jars had sealed, Abigail returned home while Amy and Carrie Sue finished the kitchen clean-up and looked proudly at their picturesque finished product.

Lee had Rusty's address and Abigail knew how to get there. Rusty greeted them as they emerged from the truck and took them behind his three-car garage where he had the dog run. The sound of the truck doors got the dogs barking.

"They're real friendly," Rusty began, "I just need to get them to good homes." Turning to the dogs, he commanded, "Quiet!" They immediately quieted. One of them whined a high-pitched query.

"Oh, they're so beautiful!" Abigail was already hooked. "How do we choose one?"

"I like to let the dog choose me," Lee said.

"What do you mean?"

Turning to Rusty, he asked, "Will they run off if you let them out?"

"Nope. They just stay near their momma and she stays close."

"Would it be all right if we sat down on your back porch and when you let them out, we'll see how they interact?"

"No problem." Rusty opened the gate and let the rambunctious puppies out. They were close to thirty pounds already and looked to be almost half grown. Simulating life-and-death fights, snarling fierce puppy snarls, they tumbled in the yard and burned off their pent-up energy.

Lee and Abigail discussed possibilities as they laughed at the antics. There were two males and one female. Which one would it be? One seemed too aggressive. Another one had a beautiful saddle that blended with its sable shoulders and hips. Abigail liked the lighter colors of yet another puppy's face.

After some time, the female flopped down as if to say, "I'm ready for a nap." The other two continued their muzzle duels. Each round became quieter and less aggressive. Finally, the dark-faced one settled down next to his sister leaving the light-faced one looking lost.

"What's the matter, big guy? No one to play with?" Lee said softly.

Ears perking up, eyes scanning for the source of the words, becoming fully aware of the two strangers, the puppy wagged his tail enthusiastically and trotted over to Lee and Abigail. They sat still and let him sniff the unfamiliar scents on their hands and clothing. Finally, he dropped down in front of them ready for a nap.

"I think we have a winner," Lee announced.

"He's perfect," Abigail agreed.

"He's yours," Rusty said. "I like the way you let him pick you. Most folks do it the other way around. I'll have to remember that. Why don't you hang on to him while I put the others back?"

The other puppies readily followed Queenie back into their dog run. The remaining puppy happily followed Lee and Abigail back to their truck. It was as if he knew that he belonged.

"What do you want to name him?" Lee asked.

"This is going to sound weird, but when I was a little girl, my grandparents lived next door to a magnificent German Shepherd named Reno. I remember thinking that when I grew up, I was going to get a Shepherd and name him Reno."

The sleepy pup lifted his nose and looked at Abigail.

"Reno? Like Nevada?"

"I don't know; maybe it was spelled R-E-N-N-O-E or maybe it was spelled like Reno, Nevada."

The pup whined a high-pitched whine and looked at Abigail through his big brown eyes.

167

"Is your name Reno?" Lee took his eyes off the road momentarily. "You react every time we say Reno."

The pup looked at Lee, yipped a puppy yip, and then settled back down onto the floorboard under Abigail's legs.

"Reno, it is." Lee shook his head and laughed at the newest member of their household.

12

Friday, July 27, Grand Climax

Abigail wound her way down the county roads on her way to work while mentally reviewing her day. She and Pastor Spalding would meet with Max and then she would meet with Sherry Samuels, that is, if she remembered, or was not sabotaged by an internal or external force. Sherry had called to reschedule her appointment and used one of the standard excuses that Abigail had become accustomed to hearing from her ritual abuse survivors. Abigail graciously accepted her apologies and fervently hoped that Sherry would become another success story.

"It's good to get back with you and Max again," Pastor Spalding said when he entered the office.

"It's good to get back into the saddle again."

Max came in a few minutes later and apologized for being late. He was not limping as much these days but he still wore the leg brace. He looked healthy after his long journey back from the ICU. No longer going to physical therapy, he worked full time at his father's dealership. Max actually worked this time.

"Let's open with prayer and then you can tell me how things are going both inside and out." Abigail said as she settled into her chair. She led the prayer and then looked expectantly at Max.

"Well, you know how I wanted to start some kind of internship at the dealership for teens at risk? Dad thought it was a great idea so I recruited a couple of high school guys that used to hang out at the park."

"Great!" Pastor Spalding could not restrain himself from responding. He was even more excited when Max filled them in on how the guys were responding to the positive intervention.

"How are things going inside?" Abigail probed. It had been a couple of weeks and the last time they met there had been significant healing and integration for Murkury and his senate, but there was a stalemate with other leaders. Caesar and Brutuz and their followers would not budge. They had their agenda. Maximillian could not convince them that they were wrong. They called him a traitor. Max was frustrated and Abigail was disappointed.

"Pretty much the same," Max said with a sigh. It was clear that he expected more of the same today.

"Let's pray and ask the Lord to give us a strategy to break this dissociative hold on you. Remember that dissociation is necessary when there is an intolerable conflict still present."

"I remember the words, but I'm not sure exactly what you mean by them."

"Okay, let me give you an example from my life. I had horribly crooked teeth when I was a kid. When I was a junior in high school, my brother, Junior, was a senior. He saw me with a group of girls and I was smiling because I wanted to seem friendly so I could maybe have friends. At supper that night he said, 'You should keep your mouth shut so your ugly teeth don't hang out.' I felt so hurt and embarrassed and ashamed. I was ready to throw my glass of milk at him but I was afraid Dad would kill me so I ran upstairs bawling."

"Ouch," Pastor Spalding said.

"I'm not looking for sympathy. God used that painful incident to get my parents to allow me to get my front teeth capped. Anyway, my point is this: my brother did not tell me anything I did not know about my teeth. One intolerable conflict in that very minor trauma was because my deep desire to have friends was in conflict with having ugly teeth – something that I had no control over. I believed the lie that said that if I couldn't or shouldn't smile, I would never have friends. So, I felt hopeless and gave up, and became a loner for the rest of my high school years. I believed a bunch of lies and made a boat-load of vows. Another part of the intolerable conflict was that if my own brother was ashamed of me, who would accept me? And then there was the resentment toward my parents because it took that crisis to motivate them to do something about my teeth – yet another intolerable conflict. My well-being was not important to them. At least that was how I processed it. There was presence of trauma – although, comparatively speaking, my issues were trivial – *and* the absence of good."

"Okay, I think I see."

"So, we need to pray and ask the Lord to highlight the intolerable conflict or conflicts that have you locked into opposing agendas that came from your relationship issues or early traumas with the leukemia which subsequently escalated in your high school years with the ritual traumas. We need to find the lies and vows that keep things locked in place."

Max bowed his head while Abigail prayed. When she was finished he looked up and said sadly, "I didn't fit in either. Levi was the only one who befriended me in high school."

"So, what is the conflict?"

"Back then I was scrawny and sickly and alone. Nobody wanted me. Actually, I was bullied. I was just a bother to my parents. I'm not important to anyone."

"Most conflicts seem to have a root in acceptance and rejection issues. Keep talking, I think you're onto something."

"I guess I felt accepted and powerful and important when I was doing cult stuff or when I was roaring around in a big truck or flashing Dad's money around and promising kids that I could get them a job."

"That makes sense with what's going on with Caesar and the rest who want to stay connected to the cult and their demonic powers. They don't know that they're accepted in Christ Jesus and have the power of the Holy Spirit available to them."

"How do we get that through to them?"

"What is the deception that you're still believing about yourself?"

Surprising himself, Max blurted, "That God allowed the leukemia and made me that way."

"What way?"

"Unimportant. Unwanted. Unacceptable. Weak. Powerless."

"So, is there resentment toward God?"

Max's face twisted into a frown. "I thought we took care of that, but maybe there is some. Maybe I think that He's not going to help me so I have to figure it out myself or find someone else who will. I mean, I do resent Him in some ways, but in most ways, I don't."

"That's a conflict. What would it mean if you were not strong and powerful?"

"It would mean that I would be vulnerable. Not accepted. Not perfect. Not good enough."

"And if that were true?" Abigail prompted.

Barely audibly, Max whispered, "My parents really didn't want me. They just tolerated me. They act nice, but they really wish I had never been born. I was so much trouble and cost them so much money."

That was his deepest conflict, his deepest fear. Hearing the words come out of his own mouth impacted him deeply. Max collapsed in tears with his hands over his face.

Both Abigail and Pastor Spalding resisted their parental urges to hug the despondent young man. "Can we ask the Lord to bring His truth to you about those thoughts?"

A muffled assent was followed by a shuddering sob.

"Lord, we come before Your throne of grace. Would You speak to Max, to all the parts of Max about these thoughts and fears that he was never wanted by his own parents?"

There was no need for an elaborate prayer. Abigail and Pastor Spalding waited long minutes silently and prayerfully while Max waited for Truth.

Slowly Max straightened and plucked a handful of tissues from the box. Mopping his face, he looked relieved as he softly said, "I think I heard Jesus say, 'Your parents wanted you and *I* wanted you. You have searched for strength and significance in ways that have hurt you. Seek Me. When you are weak, then you are strong if you turn to Me as your source.'"

"Wow! That's beautiful. Do you believe Him?"

"Yeah. I do. I feel peaceful. I mean, I was feeling pretty good before, but this is a really deep peace."

"I can see why. Jesus ministered to a core issue. How are Caesar, Brutuz, and the others doing?"

"They don't seem to be quite as agitated, but they still don't want to talk to you."

"Okay then, let's ask the Lord to continue to minister this truth to them and pick up there next week."

Max left after they finished praying. Pastor Spalding and Abigail debriefed as usual. He noted that they seemed to be going after deeper layers of the same issues. Abigail was pleased with how much the man was absorbing as he sat in on the sessions. They prayed together that Sherry Samuels would show up for her appointment that day.

"Are you sure you'll be safe down here with her?"

"I've got her knife," Abigail teased with a straight face.

"Oh, my!"

"I'll be fine!" Abigail assured him with a light-hearted laugh. "I hear the door; maybe that's her."

Indeed, it was. Meeting her in the hallway, Pastor Spalding paused and introduced himself. Noting that she was as tall as he, confused by her wall-eyed glance, he was further disconcerted by the uncertainty of which eye upon which to focus as she switched from eye to eye. He was unnerved by more than just her eyes, and involuntarily shivered as he made his way back to his office.

"I'm so glad you made it this week."

"Me too," an amiable part of Sherry replied, "I'm really sorry about missing last time. I'm sorry about the other times too." She shouldered her enormous bag as if she bore the weight of the world.

"No problem. I'm curious though; what's changed? Why did you decide to come back?"

Taking her seat, Sherry sighed as she placed the bulging burden beside her chair. "Well, one thing is that my grandmother died. I'm all alone now. Besides that, I keep thinking about what you said last time about helping me get out of the cult."

"Was your grandmother a Satanist too?"

Blinking hard in response to the blunt question, Sherry paused before she answered. "Yeah. Yeah, I think she was. She spent the last ten or fifteen years mostly just staring at that old television. She muttered some really weird stuff sometimes. It creeped me out when she'd stand up and point at me and screech something like, 'You did it!' and then she'd settle down for a long time."

"What do you think she meant by that?" Abigail rarely dismissed anything a survivor said and tucked that bit of information away for later. They often were keys that percolated up from some exhausted internal source. Unable to hold the pain and conflict down, bubbles of clues eventually escaped to the surface.

"I don't know," Sherry answered very softly and very sadly.

"Was your mother a Satanist?"

"Yes. No. I, I don't know. She died a long time ago and I never knew my dad. Grandma raised me."

Taking a slightly different tack, Abigail asked another blunt question. "Do you sense that her demons passed to you when she died?"

"And how would you know about that?" Another part switched in and challenged Abigail.

"It happens. Who are you, if you don't mind my asking?"

"What? Don't you recognize me?"

"Damon?"

He gave her a snotty teenage-style sneer. "Yeah."

"Thanks for coming back. How much trouble did you and Abaddon get into for failing to kill me last time?"

"Not much."

"That's unusual," Abigail mused and also filed that information away before getting back to her first question. "You inherited your grandmother's familial demons then."

"Yeah, what of it?" Damon was suspicious of this woman and his defensiveness was quite evident. He wanted to play the tough guy, but after their encounter last fall that culminated with the loss of his favorite knife, he was more cautious of this woman with the superior powers.

"Just curious. Are they helping you or are they going to take you down, too?"

Damon reacted to the unexpected question. "They help me!" he exploded. "They'll always help me," he added with less conviction.

"Can I ask you another question?"

"Uh, sure."

"You saw the way my God protects me. I don't have to pay a price for His protection. Are you interested in trading up?"

"No way!"

"Are you saying that because you'll be in trouble, or are you truly convinced that all of Satan's promises are as good as the promises of the likes of Prinz and the other masters?" Abigail went straight for the jugular once again. The goal was not to antagonize or to "win" an argument; she wanted to challenge the personality to think.

"I can't say."

"Fair enough. I just want you to know that you do have a choice now. You didn't before. You do now."

"I choose Satan."

"Okay. I respect that. I can't and won't force anything on you like they did. Thanks for talking to me. If you don't have anything else, I wonder if I can touch base with Abaddon."

Abigail noted the switch in personalities. Abaddon was older and more imposing. He was also rattled after their last meeting and he could still visualize the armor that protected Abigail. Somewhat subdued, and yet emanating tension, he warily said, "I'm here. What do you want?"

"I just wanted to talk if you're okay with that."

"Talk," he commanded brusquely. He, too, was trying to maintain a fierce façade.

"I want to help you and Sherry and all the others. I don't want to add to your problems and I know that you're just being here is enough to endanger you so I want to be as careful as I can. Please know that. I'm not your enemy and you are not mine, but your god is the enemy of my God."

"So how do you think you can help me and why would you give a rip about me?" Abaddon restrained himself from giving vent to the demon-fueled anger that simmered within him.

"In my own power, in my own flesh, I'm just like any other person walking on the face of this planet – I

177

want what I want when I want it. But just like Satan and his followers want to kill, steal, and destroy, I follow the Christ and want to bring life, to help restore, to build people up. It blesses me and glorifies God."

"Humph!"

"Do you mind if I keep talking and ask you a few more questions?"

"Whatever floats your boat." He feigned disinterest.

"I find that there is reluctance to make changes for several reasons. One is fear of punishment. Another is fear of having to admit that one has gotten to the top of the ladder and realized that it was leaning against the wrong building. Another of the biggest fears is having to admit that one was totally rejected and unwanted by one's own family."

"What does any of that have to do with me?" Abaddon contested. She was striking very close to issues about which he did not want to think.

"Or maybe," she continued, "it's too overwhelming to have to think about what your grandmother accused you of." Abigail had no idea of the specifics of the grandmother's accusations, but apparently it was significant enough to rouse an elderly woman out of her hazy mental stupor.

"How do you know it was me?" he challenged and squirmed in his seat. "She was out of her mind! She was just ranting! It could have been anyone."

His heated disputes reminded Abigail of the times when her sons protested the most vehemently because they were the most guilty. "Abaddon," Abigail said gently, "I know for a fact that anything that she accused you of was orchestrated by someone within the cult –

178

maybe even her. I *know* for a fact that you were put into a double-bind and it was probably do or die."

"How would you know? You weren't even there."

"No, but I've heard variations on this theme for a long time from every one of my other ritual abuse survivors. Whatever it was; it's not your fault. Now, if you choose to do it again today, it would be on you."

"Whatever."

Abigail had a thought pop into her head at that moment and sensed that it was from the Holy Spirit. "Did they make you kill your mother?"

He looked like a fish that had been hooked, drawn through murky waters, and flung onto a rocky shore. He had nothing to say and just glared at Abigail.

Emphasizing each word, Abigail said, "It's not your fault."

Abaddon disappeared and another Sherry showed up looking confused. Abigail had identified several of Sherry's personalities in their previous session – the poised one and the pious one, Damon and Abaddon. There were many more beneath the surface. There were functional parts. There were parts who denied everything and others who felt all the pain. There were those who were closely connected to the cult and demons and gave them actual or feigned loyalty. There was no indication of how Sherry Samuel's system was configured. Abigail needed to find an internal ally.

"Are you, all right?" Abigail asked.

"Uh, yeah. I'm not sure what just happened but my insides feel all twisted up."

"I think we touched on a key issue with Abaddon. Do you know him?"

"I've heard of him. He's mean and everyone tries to steer clear of him."

Knowing that Abaddon was probably listening in, Abigail said, "There are no bad parts, just parts that have bad jobs. The rest of you should be grateful to him for carrying whatever load he's carrying because that means that you guys don't have to."

"We never thought about it like that."

"Can I pray for you before we finish up?"

"I'd like that."

She must be Pious. "True Lord Jesus, thank You for giving us an opportunity today to start working together to bring peace and healing to Sherry. Lord, I ask that You would soothe those parts that are upset as they wrestle with the things that we discussed today. Amen."

"Amen."

After setting up an appointment for the following week, Abigail heaved a sigh of relief. She also went up to Pastor Spalding's office to assure him that she was alive and well. Stopping at the store, purchasing her usual staples plus some of Lee's staples, she reflected on how much her life had changed and yet how much remained the same. Life. Oh, the wonder and mystery of life!

She still thought of it as Lee's driveway but Abigail was getting accustomed to pulling into it. Never knowing what she'd find when she got there, she peered around the gentle bends hoping to glimpse the love of her life. Today he was out front with Reno.

Lee held his collar until Abigail called out, "Reno! Come here, boy!"

Rapidly covering the ground, stopping at Abigail's feet, Reno sat expectantly at her command with his tongue hanging out and his tail wagging. "Sorry, I don't have a treat. Ask Lee." Abigail pointed to Lee.

Laughing at the retreating pup, Abigail walked around to the passenger side to retrieve her groceries.

"Let me help you with that," Lee offered as he hustled over to greet her with a kiss.

"Thanks. If you could take that stuff in, I can get over to the old place and work with Amy before supper."

About the same time that Abigail arrived at her former residence, Zorroz arrived at Charlie Fletcher's place. Other participants arrived and began to set up for tonight's ritual. The Grand Climax ritual would be graced by the presence of Xerxes as well as many masters from surrounding areas. Blood would flow; powers would be transferred; curses would be sent out. The main targets were conveniently located within a mile – not that distance mattered much to the menacing messengers. They were swift and they were enraged at their ineffective forays against those particular enemies thus far.

Settling into her favorite comfortable chair in the living room, Amy gently massaged her swelling belly and waited for Abigail to get her notebook ready. "How's life on the *other* farm?" she asked. "How's Reno?"

"I'm still getting used to it all, but so far it's great. Lee built us a beautiful house and he's working hard training Reno and he seems to be catching on. Reno, that is. He seems to know our property lines. Mostly he follows Lee everywhere. It's good for both of them."

"What about you? Is Reno good for you?" Amy would never have thought to ask a question like that even six months before. Her healing was becoming evident in more areas than just the trauma of satanic ritual abuse.

"Hey! I thought I was supposed to be doing the counseling." Abigail laughed delightedly. "Seriously, though, I'm fine. I miss Dude but I really like Reno. It doesn't hurt if that's what you mean."

"I'm so glad. And, by the way, I don't know how to thank you for everything you're doing for me and David. I mean, I lost pretty much everything."

"Like I told you," Abigail said with a cheesy smile, "I have a long, long, long list of chores. Don't worry, you're good. And when little David gets bigger, he can help out too. We'll make a little farmer or rancher out of him. And just how is the little guy?"

"Well, he's not ready to slay any giants yet, but he sure is making his presence known." Amy proudly patted her belly.

"Very good. Are you ready to get started? It seems like months since we met last."

"I know what you mean, but it's only been weeks. I'll open us," Amy stated, and then launched into one of her simple yet direct prayers. "God, here we are again. Thanks for meeting with us. We really need a bunch of help from Your Holy Spirit today to figure out what to do about Apollyon and all the ones that are still attached to the cult and stuff. Thanks, amen."

Noting a shift after a moment of silence, Abigail asked, "What are you sensing?"

"It's me, Original Amy." Fuchsya Amy Bolton. Sometimes she preferred to use Amy instead of Fuchsya. It was another indication that the key personalities were coming together.

"Hi there. How are you and where do you think God's leading us today?"

"I think it's time to confront Apollyon and all the ones on the dark side." It was obvious that she was not looking forward to the battle that would inevitably ensue. All the leaders of the second through the sixth levels – Achan, Beor, Jonah, Judas, and Apollyon – were still sealed in one area. Their numbers were dwindling and their powers appeared to be as well. At least it seemed quieter over there lately according to Original Amy's report.

"What about the ones that were left over on the light side?"

"Oh, we took care of them. They're all completely healed and integrated."

"Woo hoo! I'm so proud of you! That's amazing! Of course, I've always said that I like to work myself out of a job. Are you ready to pray and ask the Lord to bring out the highest-level leader of the ones that are still attached to the cult and the demons?"

"Sure. Uh, would you mind leading? I'm not sure exactly how I should pray."

"I'm winging it too," Abigail said and winked at the surprised Amy. "Lord, we surely need Your wisdom and leading right now. Apollyon and the others have been given tough assignments within the system and it is our desire that they, too, would be set free from cult control. We ask once again for a fresh anointing, fresh oil, fresh manna, Your healing balm, and plenty of Your warring angels. We ask that You would not allow the enemy to interfere in any way, shape, or form. We also ask that You would compel anyone who shows up today to speak and receive truth and only truth. Holy Spirit, we ask that You would continue to intercede according to the will of the Father and complete and correct anything we pray inadequately, amen."

"Now what do you want!" an angry personality demanded.

"Apollyon?" Abigail guessed.

"What do you want?"

"Talk."

"There's nothing to discuss."

"So, you're still convinced that you will be highly honored and empowered if you continue to do the bidding of Satan and the cult."

"Yes."

"What exactly did they promise you?"

"I can't say."

"All right. But here's the problem as I see it," Abigail said, sounding like a lawyer, "they have given you some promises about honor and power. I believe that you have gotten a bit of that, but I really don't think they'll keep their promises."

"They will!" he asserted through clenched teeth.

"Hang with me. I want to share one observation with you. I know that everyone's different, but based on years of working with survivors, I think they might just be playing you for a fool. Satan despises women. You know that. You're in a woman's body. Your authentic identity is female. I'm sorry, but you will never, never, never rise in power or position. Never."

"I will too! I have power! I'll kill you! I'll kill her! I'll kill David!" Having been slapped in the face with truth, Apollyon was furious and exasperated beyond words. He struggled against gravity, but could not rise out of the chair to do the harm that he envisioned.

The murderous look in his eyes was unnerving, but Abigail continued in an even tone, "I know that you have a measure of power, but you cannot contend with the Most High God and win. I can't. No one can, not even Satan." Abigail continued carefully so as to not further inflame him, "Power gives you a sense of control. Control makes you feel safe. What if I were to show you a way that you could be out from under the control of the cult and still feel safe?"

"I don't want to be controlled by your God either. Besides, I'm not scared of anything or anybody!"

"That's not the point. What I'm saying is that you have never been given a real choice before. Today you do have a choice. You've seen the demonstrations of God's powers. It's available to you, too. You've had to spend your time and energy in keeping the cult-traumatized parts from spilling their guts so that the whole system isn't overwhelmed."

"You're the one that's been pulling them out and getting them to talk!"

"Look, Amy's in her early thirty's. Neurologically, the dissociation is breaking down. Even before you met me, flashbacks were happening. Memories were bubbling up. There's no way you or anyone else can keep all of this a secret anymore. The original Fuchsya Amy Bolton has emerged and she's a strong woman.

But she needs for everyone to be on board. Would you just listen to her again for a few minutes?"

He said nothing, but nodded his assent and disappeared inside.

Original Amy emerged again. "I'm sensing that he's thinking about what you said about them playing him for a fool. I kind of think he wants to change but his ego won't let him admit that he might have been wrong. I'll talk to him. Can you ask God to put us in a private bubble?"

Abigail was hoping that she would hear a report about the conversation between the original Amy and Apollyon but the host Amy returned to executive control. "They're talking. I think it's going to be good but it's probably going to take a while."

They closed the session and made plans for meeting again the following week. Abigail packed up her office-in-a-bag and stowed it in her truck. Walking down to the chicken coop to see the young hens, strolling back up through the orchard and garden, picking some vegetables for her and Lee, Abigail turned and surveyed the little farm before heading home to Lee.

13

Friday, August 3, Demon Revels

"Reno, go find Lee," Abigail commanded. Smiling at the retreating puppy, Abigail got into her truck and headed to town for her appointments.

Anticipating a breakthrough session, Abigail, Max, and Pastor Spalding settled down quickly and opened with prayer. Soon it was evident that Max had been displaced by another personality.

"Hello," Abigail greeted the newcomer.

"Hello," came a gruff reply.

"May I ask who you are?"

"Caesar."

"Very good to meet you. How can I help you?" He was not as hostile as Abigail had expected. Something had changed.

Maintaining a dignified posture and full eye contact, Caesar replied, "We've been listening to what you've been telling Max. Maximillian explained much to us. We now understand that there is more at stake than what we had previously thought." He was clearly uncomfortable.

"It takes a strong and confident man to reevaluate his life and make appropriate changes if necessary. What do you want to do?"

"I, uh, we are ready to change our allegiance and pledge our fidelity to the King of the Jews that we thought we had crucified."

"Excellent!" Abigail exclaimed. Having another thought pop into her mind, she added, "Who do you think was actually crucified in that ritual?"

"I think you'd better talk to Maximillian. He was there."

"I'll check with him once you've done some business with the King of kings and Lord of lords."

Caesar humbled himself and relinquished his throne. He then ordered those under him to change their allegiances as well. Looking to Abigail for further guidance, he accepted the prayers for healing and integration for all those under his jurisdiction except for Maximillian who needed to address his unfinished business.

"Maximillian?"

"Yes. I have neglected to convey a detail that may prove helpful in some manner."

"Okay." Abigail was intrigued.

"I am loath to bring up the crucifixion in which I participated, however, I believe that the King of kings would have me mention it to you."

"I'm listening," Abigail prompted once again.

"It's about the man that was crucified. I don't know why he wasn't subdued like the others. He kept shouting things."

"Like what?"

"I already told you that he identified Zorroz as the sheriff and said that he wouldn't get away with this. At one point he screamed at the rest of us... pleading with us to stop this charade. He looked me in the eye and said, 'My name is Barry Romanowski. Please! Contact my wife! Tell her what happened!' He kept screaming other things until they stopped him."

"Barry Romanowski," Abigail repeated flatly as she wrote the name down. "Is there anything else you think our King wants you to disclose before you integrate?"

"No. I believe that is all."

"Are you ready for integration?"

"I am ready."

Abigail prayed for this critical part of Max Berryman and he was integrated. Waiting for Max to open his eyes, Abigail wondered if Max might now be fully integrated. "How do you feel?"

"I'm not sure how to describe it," Max began uncertainly. "I feel full. Complete. Whole." He gave her a half-smile and described what had just transpired internally. "It was as if someone opened a gate and a whole herd of them came thundering in. It, it was like being in a wind tunnel. Whoosh!" Max began to laugh as tears of relief, tear of joy, tears of gratitude coursed down his cheeks.

Pastor Spalding was dabbing at his eyes with his large white handkerchief. "Praise the Lord," he whispered softly.

"Am I done? Is this it?"

"Hallelujah!" Abigail rejoiced with the men. "I don't know if you're done or not. Time will tell on that, but you sure took a giant step forward today."

"What would be left?"

"I'm not sure. I usually tell my survivors to give it one calendar year to see if any hidden stragglers get triggered and show up, but your system is different than most. We've dealt with the young ones from the leukemia days and we seem to have dealt with all the ones created by the Satanists. Why don't we pray and ask the Lord?"

"Sure. Would you?"

"Lord, we are so grateful for the breakthrough today. We bless You for Your faithfulness. Would You give Max peace about whether or not he's fully integrated and what's left for us to work on? Amen."

After a long minute Max lifted his head and said, "I just heard one word: Rest. What does that mean?"

"Lord, what does that mean for Max?"

Max blinked hard and then said, "Rest. That's all I heard."

"May I?" Pastor Spalding asked looking at Abigail. Getting a nod, he looked at Max and said, "I think this would be a good time for you to do a word study on what the Bible says about rest. If it's all right with you, why don't you start by writing out verses that speak about rest and we can get together and brain-storm about what you find."

"I'd like that. Thanks."

"Okay, you get started with your concordance and let me know when you can meet with me next week."

"Will do. What about more counseling here?" Max asked Abigail.

"I want to make sure that you're okay, but if you think you're all right, we can meet every other week and see how it goes. Or we can play it by ear and if something comes up you can give me a call."

"Let's do that."

Abigail was comfortable with that option. They prayed together before Max left and then she and Pastor Spalding debriefed before her next appointment.

"I have a legal-ethical question," Pastor Spalding said. "What do we do about the murder?"

"That's a good question," Abigail answered. "I wrote down the guy's name and I'm going to research missing person's. This is the first time I've ever gotten the name of a victim."

"But if what Maximillian said was true, then Max murdered the man."

"Yes and no. If a jury had no idea about Satanism, they'd probably convict him in a heartbeat. But Max was drugged, dissociated, coerced, manipulated, and more. How can you hold him liable when it was a set-up? Where's the body? Where's the proof one way or the other? For all we know he was programmed and hypnotized into believing that he did it."

"This is complicated. I mean, I, as a pastor, and you, as a counselor, have a legal obligation to report certain things."

"Yes, we are. All of the survivors I've worked with have reported murders and sacrifices. If I go running to the police every time I hear something in session, I'd be looked at like I'm some kind of a paranoid kook."

"I see what you mean."

"Besides, if a counselee is not endangering others or self, I can't report something that would be considered hearsay. They would have to report it themselves and most of them want to stay under the radar."

"So, what can we do?"

"There's no proof. No bodies. No evidence. It's their word against someone else's word. Report it to whom? Sheriff Bynum? He's the one that put Max into the double-bind."

"We'll have to pray about this."

"Definitely, but I think God has provided another resource for us."

"Oh?"

"My neighbors. The Yorks. Both the father and the son are former FBI agents and they're doing an unofficial investigation of all the cult corruption since David, the father, was shot too. Actually, we've already reported it to them."

"Really!"

"Yes. I invited them to the Ministerial Alliance meeting on Monday. They were interested, especially after hearing that their pastor was there last time."

"God is at work. I just know it. This is not a coincidence. Praise the Lord!"

"I think it might be a good idea to ask them about what we should do with this information. Something still doesn't seem right to me and I can't put my finger on it."

"Let's pray about it." This time Pastor Spalding led the prayer.

"Wait a minute," Abigail said as she started flipping back through her notes. "When did Max get back home from the hospital?"

"What are you getting at?"

"Here it is. We had our first session here on April thirty. You had prayed with him before that at his house." She stabbed her finger on a page and said, "He got home right after that Good Friday weekend. We're *assuming* that Barry Romanowski was sacrificed at the Good Friday ritual. If he was, it's unlikely that Max would have been there so Maximillian couldn't have killed him."

"But how would he know what happened? How would he know the guy's name if he wasn't there?"

"Humph! Good question." Abigail pondered that for a bit. "It could be programming. Remember that he was at that Pentecost ritual and had his hair burned. They could have done something with someone else at that ritual and then programed it in as Romanowski. Or they could have killed Romanowski at the Pentecost ritual and we're just assuming it was at the Good Friday one. We're also assuming that Max was only at one ritual since he got out of the hospital. For all I know, they could have dragged him out of the hospital. There's all kinds of possibilities."

"But why would they risk letting him know the guy's name and all that stuff about Sheriff Bynum?"

"I don't know. They could be just that cocky and believe that their programing was solid and that Max was loyal. Or maybe Max got a demon introjected into him from someone who *was* there when they tortured him and they didn't count on Max getting all the demon's info."

"That can happen?" Pastor Spalding asked. He was being stretched in so many ways.

"Do you want to hear a weird one?"

"I'm game."

"I was talking with the sister of a guy who believed in reincarnation. He said that he has memories of reincarnating into different people starting several hundred years ago in India. He knew his names and particulars about his so-called life as those other people. He said that he did research and actually found the historic men."

"Really! How could that be?"

"My guess is that when that guy started reading the Bhagavad Gita and the Vedic scriptures and started practicing that religion, he opened himself up to demons. It would make sense that the demons – whose job it is to deceive – would give him thoughts and so-called memories of all the people that they previously inhabited."

"That makes sense."

"Yeah, she said that she sent him a birthday card one year and he reamed her out because he didn't have birthdays since he reincarnated. The next year she decided to send him a happy re-birthday card."

Pastor Spalding shook his head and chuckled as he replied, "I don't know if you're pulling my leg or not half the time."

"No! It's true. I think I'm just going to have to write a novel about my life because no one will ever believe it if it was a memoir."

"Well," he said, getting back to the subject at hand, "I'd better scoot, so why don't we do like you said and have the Yorks look into it. If it's a real guy and it really happened, they might be able to figure it out."

They were both at peace with that strategy. Pastor Spalding went back upstairs to his office while Abigail waited for Sherry to show up for her appointment.

"Hello?"

"Come in. You're right on time," Abigail invited some part of Sherry. "How have you been since our last meeting?"

"I guess I've been kind of jittery."

"Last week was packed with rituals. Do you think it was because of that or because of what came up with

Abaddon?" *Why did every survivor seem to have a personality named Abaddon or Apollyon?*

"Maybe both."

"How much time have you lost?" This personality seemed to function as the host personality when she was with Abigail, but it was not yet clear to Abigail if she was assigned to handle just the counseling or if she was indeed the usual host and handled other aspects of her life.

"Er, uh, lost time?"

"Are there minutes or hours or even days that you cannot account for?"

"Huh. Oh, that," she half-smiled ruefully, "that would be my whole life."

"What about this past week?"

"Almost every night."

"Do you think you might have gone to rituals? Were you sore in your private areas? Do you have unexplained bruising or anything?" Abigail noticed that she was rubbing her wrists.

"You're awfully nosy, lady!" another personality injected as she displaced the host.

"Yes, I am," Abigail agreed with a pleasant smile. "Have we met?"

"I've been around. I've been watching you. I know what you want. I've met people like you."

"I'm Abigail. Who are you?" Abigail chose not to address the thinly veiled accusations of this somewhat nervous protector.

"You can call me Frankie."

"I take it that you're a protector." It was more like an inquiry than a statement. "Did your people get accessed recently? Maybe tied down?" Abigail asked as she clasped her own left wrist with her right hand.

"How would you know about that?" she demanded.

"Good guess. I saw someone rubbing your wrists earlier. Your people are vulnerable. They can be accessed easily."

Frankie pursed her lips and tried to decide how to retort. Nothing came.

"Look, I know you don't know me from Eve and you certainly don't know if you can trust me. I just want to help you keep your people safe. You've had to do an impossible job with both hands tied behind your back, so to speak. Can I at least talk to you about some possible options?"

"Sure."

"Thanks," Abigail said with relief. She was hoping that she would not need to have a huge negotiation session. "I don't know all the details of Sherry's life, but apparently you have been raised by Satanists, or at least your grandmother was one so your mother was probably one as well. That tells me that you've been accessed since before birth."

"How would you know anything about that?" Frankie was uneasy because of the directness and accuracy of Abigail's opening statements.

"Let me finish, please. I know that it makes you nervous to think that someone knows stuff about you. I don't know many specifics about you, but I do know a lot of generalities about SRA and a lot of specifics about the local cult. Okay?"

"Go on," she answered warily; wearily.

"The cult programs and assigns demons to each of the personalities they create. They use trauma to create them. Usually sexual trauma. It's the most effective way to cause dissociation – the splitting off of new personalities that they know and control. Then they assign demons to those parts. I usually say that STD stands for Sexually Transmitted Demons." Abigail paused to be sure that Frankie was following her.

"So, whether or not you are cult-loyal, you probably resent your little ones being accessed, as well as being accessed and programmed yourself."

Frankie was thinking. Deeply. Desperately. "What do you want from me?"

"Nothing. What do you want for yourself and those you're supposed to protect?"

Shoulders sagging, cheeks puffing out with her sigh, Frankie confessed, "I'm tired. I'm so blasted tired."

"Are you allowed to make a decision for yourself or is there someone over you that we need to consult?"

"We make our own decisions," a deeper voice declared. Frankie's wilted posture changed as she sat taller and squared her shoulders.

"And you are?"

"Franky."

"A different Frankie?"

"Me and her are together."

"Together? Like co-workers?"

"It's hard to explain. It's like we're the same person but she's a female and I'm a guy."

"A he-she," Abigail blurted. Abigail had run into other survivors who had he-she personalities in their systems. It was rare. It seemed that the situation that created these personalities involved a combination of simultaneous heterosexual and homosexual trauma. It was a way of accommodating the perverseness of the

197

confusing sexual encounter by creating personalities that countered the sexual trauma that went against their instinctive core values. They created a male to deal with the female perpetrators and a female to deal with the males.

"That would describe us."

"I'll ask you the same question: What do you want? What do you need?"

"We're tired, but we have to protect the others."

"What if I could show you a way to protect them once and for all?"

Abigail spent the next fifteen minutes explaining about the true Lord Jesus Christ and how He could save, heal, deliver, deprogram, and integrate or reassign all of those in this sector. They were ready and agreed to have Abigail pray. When all of the parts that were under their jurisdiction were healed, Franky and Frankie remained. They sensed that the Lord wanted them to remain dissociated for the time being so they could help with the healing process. Abigail was jubilant. She had found her internal allies.

Once again Urdang and his allies screamed in horror as the warrior of the Great Enemy gained another foothold in his territory. He had never encountered a dust puppet like this one. Confounded by Abigail's success, Urdang took his pent-up frustrations out on his underlings with vicious attacks. The natural skies roiled and churned as the spirits clashed and shook in response to the supernatural conflicts.

"Whew! Lord, where did this storm come from?" Abigail was pelted with raindrops driven by gusts of wind as she hustled out to her truck. Driving cautiously, she went directly to her former residence so she could work with Amy. Abigail loved her six-day weekends, so she saw all her counselees on the same day whenever possible.

Winding up the familiar driveway, she tooted to let Amy know that she had arrived.

"Hey there!" Amy greeted her enthusiastically from the porch.

Abigail gathered her bag and ran to the shelter of the front porch. "I wasn't expecting a storm today."

"It came up suddenly. I hope we don't lose our electricity."

"Well, if we do, you and Carrie Sue can come down by us."

"We'll be all right."

After settling into their chairs and praying, Abigail asked her standard questions: "What are you sensing? Where do we need to start today?"

"It's me, Original Amy."

"I am so curious about your conversation with Apollyon."

"It was intense; that's for sure. Here's the bottom line: he realizes that he's out-numbered and that the other leaders have lost their confidence in him and the whole big satanic agenda. They were listening when you were talking last time about the cult playing them for fools and all the stuff about being in a woman's body and all."

"Okay," Abigail replied. She was fervently praying that Apollyon was ready to surrender once and for all.

"He has a couple more questions."

"I'll be glad to answer them and if I don't know, I'll just make up some facts," Abigail said with a wink and a grin.

"You!"

"Seriously, I'll answer as honestly as I know how."

Amy shifted into the background and Apollyon switched into executive control. It was apparent that he was uncomfortable. He tried to maintain his dignity but it was obvious that he was deflated.

"Hi. What's on your mind?"

"Some of the guys want to know something about being in this woman's body. Humph! This *pregnant* woman's body," he added with disdain.

"I'll do the best I can to help them figure things out."

"How did we do what we did as guys?" he asked bluntly.

Abigail had heard several other female survivors with male personalities question their ability to function as a male, so she was not surprised by the question. There was very little that surprised or shocked her any more. They claimed that they used the toilet like a man and they also raped and sodomized others as a male would. Not wanting to assume anything, she asked, "What are you referring to in particular?"

"I mean, we did everything like all guys do. We see ourselves with male parts and without female parts, if you know what I mean."

"I understand. You have to remember that they can do some very sophisticated things with programming and hypnotism."

"But how? I mean we really did those things!" he asserted.

"Let me tell you about what the Lord revealed to one of the ladies I worked with a long time ago. She had the same issue and one day after one of the male personalities showed up during a session, he had to use the toilet. When he came back, he discovered that he couldn't stand up to pee any more. He was furious and accused me of all kinds of sorcery, but when he calmed down he consented to pray for truth. The Lord showed him that the cult had strapped a dildo on him and the rest was programming. I'm not sure how they did the toilet thing. It's got to be programming, too."

Abaddon was quiet for several long minutes. Finally, he sighed and said, "Okay, suppose you're right and I'm wrong. Why would they do that?"

"Can you think of a better way to confuse someone? Can you think of a better way to mock the Creator? I mean, if God created us to be biologically male or female, wouldn't Satan want to screw up His design? Wouldn't Satan want to mess with all of you in there? Remember that he hates women."

"Why?"

"It goes back to the curse-prophecy in Genesis. Her seed, that is, Eve's seed, and Mary's seed, was going to bruise Satan's head. There was a near and a far fulfillment of prophecy with Cain and Jesus which I won't go into now, but basically, Satan has had it out for women from the start because he didn't know which woman was going to be the Messiah-bearer. Apparently, he still has it out for us."

"I'm confused."

"What do you want to do?"

201

"I'm just done. I, that is, me and the other leaders are ready to do like Nicholai and all the others did." He was sad. Defeated.

"I'm sorry for everything they put you through. Like I always say, there are no bad parts, just parts with bad jobs. You had one of the worst jobs and I know that the others are grateful that they didn't have to carry the load that you did."

"I don't know about that; I just know I'm tired."

"Are you and all the others ready to defect into Jesus' kingdom?"

"Yes," he said gratefully, "and we'd all like to disappear, too."

"Well, you won't exactly disappear, but we can ask the Lord about that once we pray for healing."

Abigail prayed while Apollyon bowed his head. When she finished, they prayed about integration and they both sensed that the Lord wanted to give them time to rest before integration.

"Wow!" Amy exclaimed as she popped back out. "I can hardly believe what just happened! Pinch me! Did the entire bad-guy section get saved, healed, and delivered?"

"It sure looks like it." Abigail glowed with joy and relief for her friend.

"Now what?"

"I guess we just wait for the Lord to give them their rest. He might spontaneously integrate them at some point or we might have to check back with Him about them next time."

"Or maybe," Amy added with a grin, "Original Amy will get in there and make them integrate. She's in a hurry to get us all in."

"What about you?" Abigail asked the one she knew as Host Amy. "When are you going to integrate?"

"Me?" Host Amy was taken aback. "I don't like to think about it that much. I guess me and Original Amy will need to have a talk."

High in the second heavens, the temporary domain of the kingdom of darkness, there was a reaction to the flow of the prayers of the saints which ascended to the throne of grace. They could not thwart the ribbons of incense that soared past them. This was a day of great defeat as they watched their captured comrades go to the place the Risen One reserved for them until they were cast into the lake of fire. They had become the latest POWs in this eternal war. All the remaining ones could do was dodge and curse, shriek and clash against one another.

Urdang and his minions were joined by many others who were drawn to this territory by the presence of the various dignitaries who would attend the Demon Revel that would be hosted by Xerxes and other high-ranking human agents at Charlie Fletcher's farm. The updrafts of the quarrels and downdrafts of the collisions once again stirred up fierce natural storms in the area.

14

Saturday, August 4

It was scarcely past midnight when the storm front assaulted the dwellings just north of the ritual site. It rattled windows and lifted loose shingles. Rain and hail strafed everything in the path of the storm. Horses headed for shelters and birds tucked their heads deeper under their wings. A large tree was twisted off of its trunk and thrown into a transformer along the road. The loud cannon-like boom awakened those who resided near it. Any lights that remained on at that hour were extinguished for lack of electricity.

Carrie Sue was awakened by the urgent clatter of the blinds in the open windows. Amy had long been tossing and turning while little David somersaulted in her womb. Strange noises and thumps had both of them on edge.

"Amy?" Carrie Sue called out softly as she crept down the stairs by the light of her little flashlight. "Are you awake? The power is out."

"Yeah. I guess we'd better close up some of these windows." Amy reached into the top drawer of the nightstand and found her flashlight.

Together they checked all the windows and lowered the ones facing south.

"I want to step outside to see if there's been any damage to the cars. I thought I heard something hit one of them," Amy said. "I don't see the yard lights on at the Milner's or the York's either. It must affect more than just our house."

"You'll need that monster flashlight that Abigail keeps at the top of the basement stairs. Wait! I'll get it for you." Carrie Sue abruptly turned back to the kitchen, opened the basement door, and found the hefty flashlight.

"Good idea. That solar powered light should get triggered when I go out," Amy said, "but it won't shine out far enough to see if anything was damaged."

Handing the flashlight to Amy, Carrie Sue walked back into the kitchen to wait for her friend's report. She thought a cup of chamomile tea might be a good idea. She heard the clacks and metallic rattles of the locks and the doorknob as Amy ventured out onto the front porch and triggered the light.

Suddenly, Amy was aware of movement coming up the steps. Directly at her. Letting out a scream, she lashed out at the charging target with the flashlight. It connected with a thud and her would-be assailant was momentarily stunned.

Shrieking a blood-curdling scream, retreating into the house, Amy tried to slam the door shut against the second intruder. "Run! Carrie Sue! Run!"

She was not strong enough to hold them out and stumbled backward as two men put their shoulders into the door and crashed into the house. Launching into the living room with the thrashing, wriggling Amy in their arms, they fought to subdue her.

Carrie Sue quickly took in the chaotic scene and froze for half a second. "Jesus, help us!" she breathed. Instantly, she was mobilized. Jerking the basement door open again, focusing her little flashlight on the shelf, grabbing the pepper gel, she flipped the cap and held it in front of her as she took short, uncertain steps toward the three people who were grappling in front of her on the floor.

Both men were wearing ski masks. One of them had a trickle of blood coursing down from above his eye. He was livid.

"Get 'em! Get 'em!" Amy shouted as she caught a glimpse of Carrie Sue.

"I don't want to hit you!"

"Do it! Just do it!" Amy pleaded as they started to pummel her. One of them landed a glancing blow to her extended belly.

As Carrie Sue stepped closer, she caught the attention of one of the men. She shot a direct spray of pepper gel full in his face as he turned toward her.

Releasing Amy, snatching the mask off of his head, he began to scream as he rubbed at the gel. His efforts only smeared the gel deeper into the delicate tissues of his eyes and nostrils. Thrashing around and bellowing obscenities, he groped his way to the front door and lurched out onto the porch. Stumbling down the steps, pawing at his face, he sprawled in the cool, rain-drenched grass.

The second man had gotten a spattering from that first shot and quickly turned his head just as Carrie Sue released another shot. It hit the back of his neck. Reacting with a vengeance, he came around with a punch that landed squarely in Amy's face snapping her head back. Knees buckling, she slumped to the floor. He let her sagging body go and hastily followed his companion out the door. Together they hustled down the front lawn; one howling and the other trying to quiet him.

"Amy! Oh, God! Help us Jesus!" Carrie Sue cried out as she rushed to her fallen friend. "Amy! Amy!"

Amy moaned, opened her eyes, and reached for her rapidly swelling cheek. "Are they gone?"

"I think so. I just heard a car peel out from the bottom of the drive."

Amy grunted and tried to sit up.

"No! Lay still! You might really be hurt. David might be hurt."

Amy gingerly explored her right cheek with the fingertips of her right hand while holding her side with her left. "I hope they didn't hurt David. I don't feel him moving right now."

"Oh, Lord Jesus!" Carrie Sue prayed as she laid her hand over Amy's, "we speak life and health to David. Come and heal this little guy from all the trauma. Please heal both of them."

"Amen," Amy finished softly as tears seeped from her eyes. "What do we do now? I wish Abigail and Lee were here."

"I'll try to call her," Carrie Sue said as she picked up the phone. "It's dead. Wait; let me get my cell phone and try to call hers. It's a long shot because she doesn't usually keep it on." She hurried into the kitchen and got an ice pack and a clean dish cloth for Amy's cheek as she listened to the robot informing her that the call could not be completed.

"What do we do? I don't want to leave you here alone and I don't think it's a good idea to move you until we're sure about David. I don't think we should call 911 either. They'd send a sheriff and I don't like that idea at all."

"Lord, please give us wisdom," Amy prayed and then removed her ice pack for a second and looked with astonishment at Carrie Sue. "I think you need to go to your car and do that SOS thing."

"Great idea! Dot-dot-dot, dash-dash-dash, dot-dot-dot. You're a genius."

"Give God the credit for that one."

Jumping up from her friend's side, grabbing the large flashlight, shining it in a careful arc around the property, Carrie Sue hurriedly went out to her car. Sliding into the front seat she tapped out the signal with the horn three times before she came back inside.

Within minutes they heard the soft toot-toot of Lee's truck. Lee went into paramedic mode as he checked Amy's face. Abigail and Carrie Sue waited. After praying together, they agreed that it would be safe to transport Amy to the hospital. It would be prudent to check David, too.

Soon after that, Richard York rapped lightly on the door. "I heard the SOS and a lot of commotion on the road and I wondered if something was going on up here again," he said as he went into his investigator's mode. After listening to the ladies' account of the attack, he played his flashlight around the room and noticed the bloodied ski mask. "Don't touch anything. I'll get an evidence bag from my truck. It looks like someone was kind enough to leave evidence behind."

His mind was racing as his eyes were surveying the crime scene. He was fully into his FBI investigator mode. "Do you mind if I take a picture of your face?"

"Just don't ask me to smile," Amy quipped.

Richard took the picture with a ruler placed next to it. He also asked them not to touch the outside of the door or the hand railings just in case one of the men touched those surfaces. He informed them that he'd be back in the morning to take some fingerprints and tire tread evidence.

By late afternoon the linemen had cut away the tree, replaced the transformer, and stabilized the pole. Electricity was restored and the storm was forgotten by most of the area residents. Amy spent the rest of the night in the emergency department under observation. Carrie Sue, Lee, and Abigail remained with her. The ultrasound confirmed that David was fine. The placenta remained intact. There was no bleeding.

Her doctor came in early, checked Amy and David, and pronounced them fit to go home. She was concerned about the glaring shiner that Amy was now sporting. "I have a legal obligation to report suspected abuse or crime, you know."

"Yes. We've already contacted the appropriate law enforcement officer and made a report," Amy said. "It's being investigated." She did not mind that the doctor believed that it was the local sheriff.

The others in the room nodded their affirmation.

Not entirely convinced, but not willing to call Amy a liar, she said, "I want to see you for a follow-up on Friday. Rest. Any bleeding and you call me right away or get back to the emergency room. Sometimes things show up a little later. Kind of like your shiner. It'll be a beauty in a couple of days. Keep some ice on it."

"Yes ma'am," Amy replied and then added with a hint of humor, "and if I forget, one of my watchdogs will remind me."

"What do you make of it?" David York asked his son when they chatted over their early breakfast.

"It's suspicious all right. They said something about it being another ritual night. I think I'm going to have to do some research into cults."

"Good idea. Meanwhile, you have some evidence to collect and process."

"Yes, I do. I called Landrum and he arranged for me to get it over to the FBI lab in the capitol. No questions asked. I'm going to meet my contact there this afternoon. I'll be gone for a few hours. Oh, yeah," Richard added an afterthought, "one of the guys is probably a southpaw. Her right cheek and eye and temple are all swollen."

"I'll check my notes to see if any of the deputies are left-handed," the elder York answered.

"Will you and Mom be okay? Do you need anything while I'm gone?"

"We're fine, you go on ahead with that. I can always call you if something comes up."

"This would be a good day to tackle those tomatoes," Abigail said. She used canning as her excuse to hang out with Amy and Carrie Sue. Still rattled by the events of the previous night, they were both grateful for her presence and wanted to help. Bell peppers, fresh thyme and oregano were picked and added to the buckets of tomatoes that had been picked over the last week and stored in the refrigerator.

They repeated all the steps from their first canning experience except this time Carrie Sue scalded and peeled the tomatoes while Amy diced up the other ingredients. She was relegated to tasks that she could do while sitting. Carrie Sue and Abigail did the brunt of the more strenuous work. They talked and joked, rehashed the attack, or just thought pensively for the next several hours.

"I'm so proud of you for your quick thinking," Abigail remarked.

"It was Carrie Sue mostly. I was a bit preoccupied."

"It was God. I mean, we were both praying and I know God put those ideas in my head. I think He must have had one of His angels kick me into action, too. I mean, I never thought I'd ever have to shoot someone with that pepper gel."

"Thank God that Lee thought of getting it."

"And I'm really glad you guys heard our SOS from here." Carrie Sue added. "I didn't want to think about driving with all those maniacs out there or leaving Amy here alone while I went to get someone. And I sure wasn't going to call the sheriff!"

"Okay, so the next question is," Abigail pursued the subject, "are the two of you safe enough up here? Do we need to add more security measures?"

"Well, I have to admit that I'm a bit rattled, but that's been the story of my life," Amy admitted.

"Me, too," Carrie Sue added. "This is actually the safest place I've ever lived. I'm surrounded by good neighbors and Amy's a tiger. You should have seen her fight those guys!"

They paused and chuckled as Amy scowled and did some mock shadow-boxing from her perch by the counter. "Ow! My cheek!"

"Why don't you stop for now and put some more ice on it?" Abigail suggested.

"Good idea."

"But, back to the security issue. What would you think of a dog? Maybe one of Reno's litter-mates are still available."

Carrie Sue was transported back in her mind to the previous year when she last encountered a dog as she fought to get away from the ritual. "That big dog protected me. Well, I mean, my little girl part that showed up. I think it might be a good idea. What do you think Amy?"

"I love dogs. I just never could afford to have one and I'd love for David to grow up with a dog."

"I'll get Lee to work on that."

Levi was not at all happy. He was surly and took it out on everything and everybody around him. Snaking down the highway in his dark SUV, he vented his anger in a steady stream of curses. He called upon the rulers, the powers, the world forces of darkness, the spiritual forces of wickedness in the heavenly places. Failure and humiliation filled him with fears that drove his anger. He vowed vengeance. He vowed retaliation. This was not the first time that that scrawny woman bested him. And pregnant, too! He was satisfied with one blow that connected with her belly and hoped that he gave her a headache to remember too.

Richard interrupted their canning session to collect fingerprints from the front door and the door frame. There were bloody fingerprints on the wall next to the door where the man had blindly groped for the opening as well as a smudged set on the outside of the door. Richard also took prints from Abigail, Amy, and Carrie Sue for comparisons.

Abigail called Lee on his cell phone. "Lee, Richard is taking fingerprints of all of us. Can you take a break and come up here?"

"Sure, no problem. I'll be right up." He was inspecting fence lines on the far side of one of the fields that he planned to move his heifers into next. The grass was getting poor in the field that they were in, so he rotated them as needed. August was hot and mostly dry in spite of the recent rains. Firing up the four-wheeler, he took the trail that went directly to the foot of Abigail's old driveway.

Reno happily romped alongside of him until they reached the road. "Reno! Sit!"

The dog sat until his master returned. He whined, but he sat.

Richard soon had his samples and then went to the end of the driveway where it was evident that a vehicle had parked and then peeled out recently. Taking his kit out of the back of his Suburban, Richard positioned his L-shaped ruler and snapped pictures before mixing the quick-setting plaster-like concoction. After pouring it into the depression, he scanned the area for other evidence while waiting for it to harden. A partial shoe print was dug into the soft dirt and gravel surface. He photographed it with the ruler as well. Satisfied that he

213

had all the evidence he could find, he settled into his vehicle for the three-hour trip to the capitol.

After presenting his identification, Richard was soon in the lobby where his FBI contact was waiting. Introductions and handshakes were exchanged as they made their way to the laboratory where the evidence was logged in.

"We'll put a rush on this evidence. DNA will still take about three weeks minimum," the lab technician said, "but we can get the tire information sooner and maybe get you a lead on the shoe print. That one's a long shot, but we'll see what we can do. We've got some pretty sharp people working here."

"I appreciate anything you can do. It gets real personal when these dogs go after pregnant women and old folks."

"I understand your father was shot," Agent Steven Diblassio said. "Is he, all right?"

"Yes, he's coming along all right. He's itching to get in on the action again."

"Once a marine, always a marine," Steven Diblassio chuckled.

"Yes, and once an agent," Richard started but did not need to finish. The man understood. They were always brothers and would have each other's back.

"We'll take her," Lee said decisively. "How much do you want?"

"I'll charge you the same for her as I did for yours. It's one less mouth for me to feed and I know she'll be going to a good home."

"Thanks. Is it all right if I pick her up later on this afternoon?"

"Perfect. Your slave-master cousin actually gave us the day off today so I'll be home," Rusty joked.

Once Abigail returned home from another successful canning session, she and Lee hopped into the truck and headed to town.

"I think we should get a good starter kit for their new dog. What do you think they'll need?"

Lee thought for a moment and then said, "Let's swing by the feed store and pick up the puppy chow. We could use some more for Reno. He's growing so fast!"

"Tell me about it!"

"We might as well pick up some sweet feed for the horses while we're at it."

After picking up their feed, they went to the hardware store and picked up a collar and leash, a sturdy bowl for food, and one for water.

"Are you going to let them keep her inside the house?" Lee asked.

"You know," Abigail sighed, "I've been thinking about that. I mean, if I was still living there, I'd say no. But if they want to live with her inside, I think it'll be okay. But if she chews up my furniture or woodwork, I think I'll have to insist that she be kept outside."

"That's reasonable."

They hummed down the road in companionable silence until they got to Rusty's house. With the windows rolled down they could hear the warning barks of Queenie and her unnamed female pup.

Rusty greeted them with a big smile and a hearty handshake. "Here she is," he said as the pup wiggled her way to his side. It was as if her energetic tail made her whole body wag.

"She's so pretty," Abigail said.

"I can't believe someone hasn't snatched her up by now," Lee added.

"How's your dog working out?"

"Oh, he's great. He's settled right in to farm life," Lee said as he squatted down and let the pup get acquainted with him and the unfamiliar scents that he carried.

Rusty noticed that Abigail was getting the tags off of the collar and leash. "Why don't you let me put those on her? She's used to me."

"I think you'll miss each other when she's gone," Lee commented.

"Yep, you're right, but we still have Queenie. Oh, here," Rusty said, extending a well-worn, somewhat torn comforter, "this is what's left of her blankey. You might need it.

The puppy offered no resistance to walking away with Lee and Abigail and settled down in the front seat between Abigail's knees much like Reno did not all that long ago. Driving down the road, they talked and laughed, held hands and enjoyed watching the big pup sniff at the air through the partially opened window.

Amy and Carrie Sue were sitting on the front porch in anticipation of their arrival and rushed to the side of the truck much like little girls on a Christmas morning. Squealing with delight they peered into the partially open window at the curious puppy.

"Oh, she's so pretty!"

"She's a beauty. What's her name?"

"I guess whatever you name her," Abigail said as she slowly opened the door. "Let's just sit like this for a bit until she gets used to the two of you."

"Hey, girl," Amy said as she extended her hand.

The pup stretched toward her, eagerly sniffed and licked, and then started her full-body wag. She quickly showed her friendliness with these strangers.

"Pretty girl," Carrie Sue crooned as she gave the puppy an opportunity to sniff her hand too.

Abigail handed the leash to Carrie Sue and with very little effort the dog jumped down to the gravel and shook herself off. Lifting her nose and eagerly sniffing the air, it was as if she knew she was home and wanted to explore every bit of it. Now.

Lee unloaded the puppy chow and the bowls and then they all settled down on chairs in the shade of the front porch. The puppy contentedly flopped down on her comforter between Amy and Carrie Sue.

Lee told them that they would need to keep her on leash while they walked the boundary lines of the property. "Don't be afraid to jerk hard on the leash and say, 'No!' if she crosses the line or if she makes a move for one of the chickens or the garden. Eventually she can be let loose."

They also talked about whether or not she would be an outside dog or be allowed inside the house. Abigail expressed her worries about woodwork being chewed up, but left it up to them. "Remember, she's used to being outside in a kennel so she isn't potty trained."

Carrie Sue and Amy bantered about several names. Banshee sounded too fierce and Daisy was too mild.

"I had a friend who named his dog Pooper. His mom refused to call the dog in."

"Well," Amy finally said after some serious thought, "if her mother is Queenie, then I think that makes her a princess."

"I like that!" Carrie Sue exclaimed. "We should name her Princess."

15

Monday, August 6

"I heard you got the papers ready," Sheriff Bynum said with a wicked smirk.

"They're right here," Ed Jeffers, the prosecuting attorney, answered as he picked them off the corner of his desk and handed them to the sheriff. "Judge Roberts approved it and signed off first thing this morning." Daggett and Herrak had worked quickly that morning to complete their part in the evil plan.

"Very good. I'm on my way." Malice and glee were apparent as Zorroz tucked the documents away. He wanted to vindicate himself. He wanted revenge.

Cruising past the Berryman's house, Sheriff Bynum noted that Max's truck was not there. He headed directly to the dealership where he was sure to find the young man.

Ted looked up from his desk when a mechanic ran in. "Mr. Berryman! The sheriff just arrested Max!"

"What?"

"He just went into the garage, handcuffed him, and threw him in the back of the squad car. He said he had a warrant for his arrest."

Jumping up from his desk with alarm, Ted said, "I'll see about this!" Putting on his sport coat, he rushed to his car speed-dialing Barbara as he went.

Carrie Sue had gone off to work leaving Amy and Princess. Amy did not want to admit how much she

Lynda L. Irons

appreciated having Princess with her. She was not a trained attack dog, but she would definitely sound an alarm if anyone came near. That alone gave her peace of mind. Her biggest worry now was what she should do with Princess while she sat with Martha York next door so that both David and Richard could attend the Ministerial Alliance meeting. She finally settled on tying Princess to a length of chain on the front porch steps where she would have access to shade, water, and the front lawn. And her ratty old blankey.

Abigail was one of the first to arrive at the Baptist church in Springfield for the monthly meeting of the Ministerial Alliance. Pastor Spalding was already there and Ginny had recruited a couple of ladies to prepare a variety of salads. It was a hot day and cold salads would hit the spot. Tuna salad and chicken salad, garden salads and fruit salads graced the serving table. Breads and rolls, crackers and chips embellished the meal. Homemade cookies and brownies, iced tea, and hot coffee completed the luncheon.

It was not long before the room began to fill. The Ministerial Alliance had grown from a handful of pastors to this group of nearly fifty. Introductions and chatter filled the fellowship hall until Pastor Spalding called for their attention. After opening with prayer, he directed them to the buffet line. Soon they were settled back down in their places and the conversations began to flow anew.

"May I have your attention?" Pastor Spalding asked in his outside voice. The group quieted and looked at him expectantly. "Welcome to the monthly Ministerial Alliance meeting everyone, and a special welcome to the new faces I see here. Would you mind introducing yourselves – let us know where you live and where you attend church, and please let us know what brought you here."

"I live out near the county line past our church. I came with Pastor Clara Bardwell," Janice stated. "I'm here because I'm excited about all the different churches coming together and I'm interested in praying for this area."

She was followed by two other ladies who gave similar answers. David York stood up next and said, "I'm David York. I attend the Kingston Road Baptist Church with Pastor Crenshaw. I was one of the ones who was shot back in June. You might say I have a personal interest in putting that group out of business. I'd prefer that they all get saved, but if not, they need to be stopped."

"I'm his son, Richard, I'm here for the same reason as my father. We can work on this issue from a legal standpoint and would welcome any information that any of you may have."

That got the room buzzing. These people had been praying for relief, for transformation, for justice. They believed that the Lord was answering their prayers. God was bringing in prayer warriors, ministry leaders, para-church organizations, business leaders, and now someone who could give them practical help on a judicial front.

After the introductions, Pastor Spalding praised all the workers, musicians, and the men and women who took care of a myriad of tasks that made the Fourth of July event successful. Cindy reported that there were several salvations and at least five people that she knew of who received physical healings.

"In fact," she said excitedly, "one of the people who got healed wasn't saved. When we prayed, he said that his shoulder got hot. Really hot. We could feel it, too. Then he whooped and hollered and started raising his arm over his head. He said he couldn't do that before. The best part is that he said that he wanted to meet and serve this Jesus who had just healed him."

The group clapped and cheered at the report.

"I think we need to keep doing community events," Pastor Dennis Walsh added enthusiastically. "We can't let up. We need to be a united presence for Christ in this whole area."

"Amen, brother!"

"That's right."

"Does anyone have any ideas for August? There are no holidays that I'm aware of." Pastor Spalding threw the challenge out to the group.

One of the new ladies raised a timid hand and was recognized. "Well, the children will be going back to school at the end of August. We could do something to help the families who need school supplies or new clothes for their kids. Maybe there's a hairdresser who could do free haircuts."

"Oh, that's such a good idea," Pastor Clara Bardwell added. "We have so many who would benefit from that. We might think of doing a free gently-used clothing giveaway."

"You know," Rev. George Bordman said, "I have a friend who owns a good-sized department store. I can contact him today and see if he could make a corporate donation. There may be other stores that would do that if we ask the right person."

That got the room buzzing with excitement. In the middle of it, Ginny came bustling into the room and made a beeline for Pastor Spalding.

Whispering urgently into his ear, she said, "Max got arrested and Ted is in your office. Can you break away? He said they wouldn't let him even see Max. He's afraid of what they might do."

"Oh, my," Pastor Spalding gasped as he bent near the diminutive woman. "Of course. I'll be right there." After straightening back up he cleared his throat and announced, "Folks, I'm sorry, but I have an emergency that I need to attend to. Don, could you step in here for me? I need Abigail and the Yorks to come as well."

Surprise and curiosity registered on many faces but as soon as the four left the room, Don Wilmore refocused their attention and they got busy with their plans. Within an hour they had the who-what-when-where-why questions covered. They had volunteers and committees. Notices would be put in the church bulletins asking for donations, supplies, and workers.

Having hurried through long hallways and up the stairs, the four reached the pastor's office and found a very distraught couple. Ted was agitated and pacing; Barbara was in tears. Ginny hovered near her.

Seeing the pastor, Ted blurted, "They arrested Max. They just came into the dealership and arrested him. They won't talk to us. They won't tell us what he's done. Nothing!"

"When did this happen?" Pastor Spalding asked.

"About two hours ago. I've been trying to get in there to see Max ever since. They just kept telling me that he's being processed and that they'll let us know if and when we can visit him."

"I asked about bail and they said that the judge hadn't set any bail. We're just getting the run-around and being stonewalled."

"I just know they're going to do something awful to my Max," Barbara wailed.

"Now, who's Max?" Richard asked.

"He's our son," Ted answered.

"Help me understand why you've asked us here," Richard addressed Pastor Spalding.

"Abigail, maybe you could fill them in a bit better."

"Sure. Oh, boy! How do I do this without breaking confidentiality?"

"As his father, I can guarantee that Max wouldn't care what you told the world right now. Please say whatever you have to if you think it would be helpful. Max will not sue you. I can assure you of that."

"Me too," Barbara sniffled, but brightened at the slim glimmer of hope.

"Okay, then," Abigail took a breath and plunged in. "Max got recruited into the cult when he was in high school. He's the guy I was telling you about who said that he was at the ritual where that man... what was his name again?" she asked Pastor Spalding.

"Roman something. It sounded Polish or Italian."

"Romanowski. Thanks. Anyway, Max said that he was the one that used a sword or killing dagger to kill the man, but before they silenced him Romanowski looked at Max and told him to contact his wife and he also pointed at Zorroz, er, Sheriff Bynum, and told him that he wouldn't get away with it."

Barbara gasped. Ted stood dumbfounded. What had their son gotten himself into?

"Sheriff Bynum, and probably the judge and a few others at the courthouse, are cult members. Anyway, Max was in a terrible wreck a few months back and turned his life around. Pastor Spalding and I have been working with him since then, so I would guess that this is their way of getting back at him or getting him back into the cult. I mean, there are a couple of rituals next week and if they can grab him now..." Her voice trailed off.

"Do you have any idea of what the charges might be?" David York asked Ted.

"No. They won't tell me anything."

"Do you think anyone at your shop might have overheard anything when they arrested him?" Richard asked.

"I don't know. Let me call and see." Ted stepped out of the office, speed-dialed his office and asked to be transferred to the shop foreman immediately.

"Uh, huh. Uh, huh. Okay. Thanks."

Everyone looked expectantly at Ted as he reentered the office. "One of the guys said that he thought he heard 'battery' and another one said that he heard something about criminal trespassing."

"Oh, my!" Abigail blurted out as she made the connection. "I'll bet they suddenly *found* all those lost complaints I've been filing for the last year and are using them against him now. Can they do that if I don't want to prosecute him?" She was incredulous as she looked from Richard to David and back again.

"I'm afraid they can. If a prosecuting attorney wants to push it, he certainly can. If you ever get charged it's always the name of the jurisdiction vs. the offender. It's the state or county's job to get criminals off of the streets. If the original complainant is not cooperative, they don't usually pursue it unless they have an airtight case."

"Well, I certainly won't be very cooperative. I'll drop the charges."

"But meanwhile, he's in their hands," Ted said gravely. He had no idea that his son had harassed Abigail. He tried to sweep away the wave of guilt that threatened to wash over him. He'd have to deal with his own crime of neglecting his son too much for the sake of building his business.

"Yes, he is," David agreed. "I was a maintenance man for the county courthouse and sheriff's complex for a couple of years. I retired recently. There were some suspicious things going on there and now I know why. I think you're justified in being alarmed about Max being at their mercy in there. Richard, what do you think?"

"You're sure he said that he participated in killing Romanowski?" Richard was thinking about finding a valid legal approach.

"Yes. I have it written in my notes. Oh, now I remember that his first name is Barry."

"Barry Romanowski. Okay, then. We might have an angle we can work. I think I can call in a favor. If you'll excuse me, I need to make a couple of calls." Richard strode into the hallway and dialed Landrum's personal number.

A few minutes later Richard poked his head into the office and asked, "Do you have a fax machine here?"

"Yes," Pastor Spalding answered and pointed behind him, "Check with Ginny, she has the number."

Max was curled up against the cold concrete wall trying to protect his head from further damage. He could feel the warm ooze of blood coming from his scalp. He lost count of the number of blows and kicks he had received. *Oh God, please don't let them break my back again. Help me, Jesus!* The deputies delighted in pummeling the young man.

"Traitor!"

"Where's your Jesus now?"

"You belong to Satan. You belong to us."

"Did you think you could get away from us?"

"We ought to take *you* out to the wood shed."

They taunted and tormented the young man until Sheriff Bynum came down the corridor and stopped them. He barked out his stern order, "That's enough! We want him alive. Get him onto that bunk."

It was nearly an hour after Richard's phone call that the church's fax machine began to click and pierce the air with its shrill signals and buzzes. Paper was slowly fed through the rollers and finally spit out into waiting hands.

"This is what I need," Richard said as he quickly scanned the pages. "I'm afraid we'll have to wait until the FBI agents get here from the capitol. It took me three hours the other day, but I have a hunch that they'll get here a bit sooner." He glanced at his watch and noted the time.

Barbara heaved a huge sigh of relief as the tears started flowing again. She did not know what all of it meant, but she was sure that Max would soon be safe. However, she was well aware that Sheriff Bynum and his callous deputies could still do much damage.

227

"I'll go down there and serve this warrant. At least it will keep them honest until the agents arrive. I'd guess it'll take them at least another hour or two."

"I'll go with you, son," David York said.

"Is that a good idea?"

"I would *not* miss it," he said with a glint in his eyes that was reminiscent of his younger years. "I feel fine, and besides, the gig's up. When they find out that a former FBI agent was under their noses, they'll start doing some fancy back-pedaling and I'd kinda like to see that."

"Let's go."

Ted and Barbara looked like lost school children. Normally decisive and assertive, they were both subdued. They had had some time to ponder some of the things Abigail said about Max's involvement in the cult. *Murder? Criminal trespassing? Battery?*

Ginny kept Barbara supplied with tissues and pats on her shoulder between phone calls and other church business. Ted continued to pace.

Pastor Spalding broke the heavy silence. "Let's pray."

"Good idea," Abigail agreed. "We need to pray for favor and protection for the Yorks and for Max."

Bowing their heads, the four of them took turns imploring the Most High God to protect the men. They prayed for Max and for Ted and Barbara. They prayed that the FBI agents would get there quickly. They appealed to the throne of grace and to God's Heavenly Council for justice.

Richard was driving his black Suburban with the heavily tinted windows. Unlocking his glovebox, he retrieved his shield and his weapon. After chambering a round and holstering his weapon, he clipped his official badge onto his belt. The elder York reviewed the warrant on the short drive to the sheriff's complex.

The slow-moving, overweight deputy briefly looked up with disinterest when the two men entered the lobby. Feigning the need to attend to something urgent, he deliberately ignored them.

"Ahem." Richard cleared his throat loudly.

"I'll be with you in a minute."

"You'll be with me right now," Richard asserted.

That got the deputy's attention. He looked more closely at the gentleman who was extending his hand with the distinctive shiny badge in it. "Yes, sir. I'm sorry, sir. I was just finishing up this report here."

"I'm with the DOJ. I have a warrant that pertains to Max Berryman. I believe he recently arrived here."

"Uh, er," the unsure deputy stammered, "I'll have to get the sheriff."

"Well get him! Make it snappy!" Richard ordered. "I don't have time to play your little games."

"Yes sir."

The thoroughly alarmed deputy nervously scuttled through the back doors that led to the jail cells. He found Sheriff Bynum and three other deputies outside of Max's jail cell.

"Sir, there's a DOJ officer out front. He says he has a warrant for Max Berryman."

Bynum was clearly alarmed by this unexpected turn of events. He fought the panic that dried his mouth so quickly that his tongue filled his mouth like a gag. Hastily swallowing and regaining his composure, he barked out orders, "Clean him up! Find another shirt for him! I'll see about this." He wanted to be prepared in case there was something to the warrant.

The deputies scattered to do his bidding while he strode to the front of the building appearing more confident than he actually was. *Why is everything going wrong?* He burst through the doors with an air of authority and hoped to intimidate the man from the superior jurisdiction by his bluff.

"I'm Sheriff Bynum," he announced. His icy glare connected with Richard's confident glance.

"I'm Richard York. I'm with the Criminal Division of the Department of Justice. Agents from the FBI are en route and will be taking custody of Max Berryman when they arrive. I need for you to get the prisoner ready for transport."

"You wait one minute," Sheriff Bynum protested, "I need to take a look at this. I'm going to have to call our prosecuting attorney and maybe the judge."

"You do just that," Richard replied evenly. "They'll understand the legal precedent and order you to comply immediately."

"On what grounds?" he demanded sharply.

"We're investigating the murder of an out-of-state person. That makes this a federal case."

"I'll be right back." Sheriff Bynum disappeared through the back doors once again. His deputies had Max looking half-way decent, but it was obvious by his swollen face and dazed expression that he had been beaten. The blood had been wiped away and he was wearing a wrinkled, over-sized shirt.

"Get him something to eat and drink."

"Should we take him out of here?" They were all starting to feel the tension.

"No. That would make us look like we're guilty of something. This man resisted arrest and we had to subdue him."

"Right."

Bynum walked further down the hall and speed-dialed a number as he went. Judge Roberts was in his chambers and answered immediately. After being apprised of the situation, he swore under his breath. He suddenly had the feeling that he, too, was up against something that he could not control. His little fiefdom was coming apart bit by bit. The unexpected deaths of key cult members and their inability to neutralize anything that had to do with that woman in particular were weighing on his mind.

"Stall him!"

Sheriff Bynum was an expert at run-arounds and delays. He told the Yorks that he had to complete his paperwork for the local charges before the prisoner could be released. He informed them that he would do it himself. Promptly seating himself at the desk in his own office, he officiously ignored them. In the solitude of his office, it finally registered that David York was that spooky-quiet maintenance man. *What is he doing here? What in the blazes is going on?* Alarm bells were ringing loudly in his mind.

The oafish deputy was relieved since he had no idea about what was going on. He took an extraordinarily long time to use the restroom. Looking into the cell where Max was being held, he had a sinking feeling and wanted to walk out the back door and never return. The other deputies had similar thoughts, but none were voiced out loud.

It took two hours and seven minutes for the two FBI agents to make the trip to Springfield. Richard saw their black vehicle pull up next to his and stepped outside to greet the men with his father.

"Diblassio! Good to see you. You made good time."

"Yes, we did. This is my partner, James Stockton. We're glad to help. I'm curious about what you have on your hands here."

"This is my father, David York, former Marine, former FBI agent."

"Honored to meet you, sir," Steven said as he shook his hand.

Richard handed over the warrant, debriefed Steven and James, and then they walked into the building together. Diblassio was a large, no-nonsense agent. As large as Bynum was, he seemed diminished by the size and authority of the men who now faced him. He was accustomed to being the proverbial big fish in a small pond. He now found things reversed.

"You have had time to review the warrant," Agent Diblassio said in a no-nonsense tone. "You will hand over the prisoner immediately." He slapped a form onto the counter causing Bynum to flinch. "We'll sign this after we assess the condition of the prisoner. You can make a copy if you like."

Bynum's spirit shrunk and no matter how much he called upon his diabolical powers, he did not feel as invincible as he once did. He nodded his assent and walked to the back.

"Bring him out!" he growled through clenched teeth. It took whatever remaining energy he had left to keep up his bravado.

Max was assisted out of the cell and down the hall to the front. Hoping to see his father, he was shocked by the sight of the men in the lobby. *Oh, God! Now what?* He could discern nothing from the expressions on the stern faces. *Were they Satanists, too?*

"May I see the prisoner's identification?" Diblassio asked politely. It was actually a command.

"This is everything he had on him." Sheriff Bynum spilled the contents of a small metal box onto the counter. "Go on," he ordered Max, "show him what he wants to see."

Max fumbled with his wallet, withdrew his driver's license, and handed it to the imposing man who looked from the picture to Max and back again.

"What happened to your face, son?"

It became so quiet in the room that the sound of a bug bumping its way back and forth across the ceiling seemed loud. Max was still standing next to Sheriff Bynum and was not sure how to answer. He did not want to cross the man who had the power to kill him.

Bynum hastily injected, "He resisted arrest and we had to subdue him."

"We'll investigate that statement, sheriff. Please sign this form and we'll get him out of your way."

Reluctantly signing the form, making a copy for his own records, Bynum transferred Max to the custody of the agents. He watched them walk out of the lobby and then he slunk into his office and closed the door. He did not want to make the call to Judge Roberts.

"Max, I'm Richard York. My father, David York," he nodded toward his father, "is a neighbor of Abigail

Norris. I work for the Department of Justice. These gentlemen are FBI agents."

"Am I under arrest?" Max gasped.

"No, not exactly. We'll explain later. Don't worry, you're safe now. But first I need to know if you're all right. It looks like they worked you over pretty good."

"I wasn't resisting arrest. Honest, I wasn't. My ribs are killing me. They kicked me and it feels like they're broken. I just kept praying that they wouldn't break my back. I've got a rod in there."

"Let's get you checked out at the hospital and then we'll go from there."

Agent Stockton remained with Max the entire time he was in the emergency department. Richard, David, and Steven huddled in an isolated corner of the waiting room where they debriefed one another. Ted and Barbara met them there and hovered as close to Max as they were allowed.

"I followed up on that Barry Romanowski fellow like you asked," Agent Diblassio said quietly. "His wife filed a missing person's report this past April. He used his credit card to fill up at a gas station on Route 1950 just south of Hawville. There was no more card activity after that. He seems to have just disappeared."

"He really could have been abducted and sacrificed at the ritual that Abigail and Pastor Spalding heard this kid talk about."

"I checked with one of our cult specialists. He said it's consistent with things he's investigated all over the country. He did say that it was unusual for the victim to be coherent enough to fight back. Dumb luck."

"Or maybe the hand of God giving us the break we need," David York muttered.

16

Friday, August 10

There was a flurry of natural and supernatural, legal and interpersonal activity all week. Wicked forces – evil men and fallen angels – were shocked at the recent turn of events. How do the People of the Book keep slipping away from their clutches? Who was to blame? Who was responsible? Who would take the fall?

Daggett and Herrak, as the judge and prosecuting attorney, examined the warrant that had freed Max Berryman. It did not matter what it said since the young man was now free to talk. What would he say?

They decided that it was worth the risk of contacting John Davidson who was known as Xerxes in their "real" life. He would be furious to find out about this most recent fiasco, but his fury would be incalculable if he found out about the debacle later. They made the phone call.

Pastor Spalding contacted Don Wilmore, pastor of the Hillsdale Baptist Church, and got caught up on the part of the Ministerial Alliance meeting that he missed. Rev. Benjamin Morgan had volunteered his centrally located Kingston United Methodist Church facility for the back-to-school event on Saturday, August twenty-five, just before the schools would be back in session. The September meeting would be hosted by Rev. George Bordman at his Hawville Presbyterian Church on Tuesday instead of Monday because of Labor Day.

Pastor Spalding had the permission of the Berryman family to put out an urgent prayer request through the

Ministerial Alliance regarding Max's safety. They also prayed for spiritual forces of darkness to be subdued in their region. More fervent prayers went up and further inflamed the occupants of the second heavens.

Agent Diblassio followed up on the missing person's report for Barry Romanowski and began to widen and deepen his investigation. Keeping in contact with Richard York, they began to see an obvious pattern of corruption and the probability of several other so-called missing persons who were last seen in this area. David York supplied him with more leads from his notes. He had kept a list of every person who passed through the jail. Abigail's downloads were added to a thickening pile of evidence. They needed something solid to justify a full-scale investigation of the sheriff's office as well as the county court system.

Landrum apprised Richard York that he was being pressured from Congressman John Davidson. "Keep going on your end and I'll do what I can to deflect the heat from this end."

There were many leads on which to follow up. They interviewed Lee and Abigail, Carrie Sue and Amy, Max and Jason, Earl and Jan, Pastor Spalding and Rev. Griffin. Each one added more pieces to the puzzle. Kidnapping, rape, arson, buried bodies, blood in the sanctuary, fender-benders, assaults, missing persons, vandalism, poisonings, and more.

Meanwhile, Amy and Carrie Sue diligently and happily started training Princess. She was a quick learner, but after scattering the entire flock of flapping, squawking chickens one time, Princess discovered that they and the coop were off-limits. She stayed out of the garden and kept away from the road unless she accompanied one of the ladies down to the mail box. She would sit impatiently at the edge of the road while they crossed the road, collected the mail, and returned.

Lee was content with his mini-ranch. It was nothing like the hundreds of acres he once owned in Montana, but this was good. Meandering up the trail from the cow pasture, he was satisfied with their growth. In about two months they would be ready to breed. He was looking forward to seeing his little herd grow. Lee chuckled as he remembered the last time his cousin Gary visited with his family. Little Bryan was disappointed when he learned that the calves would not arrive until he was out of school next year.

Max stuck close to his father. He rode to and from the dealership with him. He was shaken by the recent events, but he was determined to continue to become the authentic person God had intended for him to be.

"Will you be all right driving to your counseling session today?" Ted asked.

"Yeah. I guess I need to get out there on my own sooner or later. My ribs are still sore but I can handle driving." Max sounded surer than he felt. It was only a short drive to the church but anything could happen. It seemed like everything had.

He met Abigail and Pastor Spalding at their usual time and received a gentle hug from the pastor.

"It's so good to see you, Max."

"Thanks. It's good to be seen," Max said with a hint of humor. "I wasn't sure if I was going to get out of that last predicament alive."

"That's what we were thinking," Abigail added. "I'm glad you called. Are you ready to get started?"

They settled into their chairs and prayed together for the Lord's leading. Max reported that nothing was coming up right away.

"Let me ask you a couple of questions then," Abigail started. "Is there any sense that the trauma in the jail caused any new splitting? Is there anyone in there that knows anything about that?"

Max's face registered surprise. "I heard a voice say, 'I do.' It sounded like a kid. Is that going to happen every time I get beat up?"

"It might. I worked with a sixty-some year-old lady once who got beat up by her daughter-in-law and she split out a new personality. But once we went back to the trauma and processed it, she got integrated right away."

"Let's do that." Max was eager to get whole and stay whole.

They prayed about several aspects of that terrifying day and it was not long before Max reported that the little guy was okay and integrated.

"Can we ask you a few more questions about Barry Romanowski? Something's bothering me about it."

"Sure."

"We're kind of confused about the time line. Maximillian said that he killed him. We assumed that it was at the Good Friday ritual, but I was under the impression that you didn't get home from the hospital until the week after that."

Max tilted his head as he pondered that. "Just a minute," he said as an idea came to him, "let me call Mom. She has the date circled in red with a smiley face on the kitchen calendar." He fished his phone out of his pocket and called home. She confirmed that he got home after Easter.

"So how could I, er, Maximillian be so sure that he killed the guy?"

"I'm guessing that it might be programing and/or demonic deception," Abigail replied. "Thinking back on it, does it seem real?"

"Actually, I can hardly even remember it. All I do remember is that I saw him pointing at Zorroz and heard him tell me to tell his wife. It's surrealistic – kind of like it happened but it didn't. I don't know how to explain it."

"That sounds like programing. I mean, you can't be in two places at one time." Abigail was instantly stunned with another thought. "Humph. I wonder if they did some of that astral projection or astral travel stuff with you."

"Astral projection? Astral travel?"

"I think it's a colossal demonic deception, but there are some people that believe that they can transport themselves or have others transport them to other places. It's a counterfeit of what the Holy Spirit had Philip do when He wanted Philip to meet with the Ethiopian eunuch."

"I remember that story!" Pastor Spalding injected excitedly. "It's in the Book of Acts. Philip baptized the Ethiopian eunuch and then the Holy Spirit snatched him away and he found himself in Azotus."

"Well it's nice to think that I didn't kill the guy," Max said with relief. Then he thought about all the other rituals he had attended. *What would the legal ramifications be? Would the FBI prosecute me for what I did do?* Worry descended upon him and it showed plainly on his face.

"Max, I don't know how all of this is going to turn out, but the Yorks and their DOJ and FBI buddies understand. Trust the Lord. He's got it."

"Well, I don't even care. I do believe that Jesus hasn't gotten me out for *no* reason. If they decide I need to be in prison for my part in all of it, I'll do my time. All I want is for the truth to come out and spare other guys from having to go through what I did."

"We're in your corner, Max. There are a lot of folks in our county praying specifically for you and this whole situation," Pastor Spalding encouraged. "By the way, did you find time to finish your study on rest?"

"I did some of it," Max said.

They ended the session by praying about all of these concerns and especially for Max's safety. There was no telling what kind of mischief the cult would cook up now that they were being exposed. Max and Pastor Spalding arranged for their meeting before Max left and then he and Abigail spent a few minutes debriefing before he went to up to his office. Abigail waited for Sherry Samuels.

Hearing the outside door click and clunk, Abigail was relieved that Sherry showed up this week. She hoped that she would be able to connect with Franky and Frankie again.

"Hello! Come in. I'm glad you made it this week."

"Thanks. I almost didn't make it, but someone in there told us that we needed to come today," the host Sherry said. "Or else!"

Abigail barely suppressed a smile and said, "It sounds like someone thinks this is helpful."

"Not me, lady!" a voice growled and changed the pleasant demeanor into something quite the opposite.

"Damon? Or are you Abaddon?"

"Abaddon. What's it to ya?"

"Good to see you again. Have you been thinking about some of the stuff we've talked about before?"

"No. Why would I?"

"I just thought you might have been interested in finding out that you were set up and put into double-binds that forced you into lose-lose situations."

"Humph!" Abaddon sat there with folded arms.

The fact that he was still there gave Abigail some indication that he was interested in the subject. Either his pride kept him from pursuing things or he was being intimidated by demons. Probably both. "Would you be willing to have a private conversation with me? No outside critters allowed to eavesdrop?"

Almost imperceptibly Abaddon nodded.

Demonic intimidation. "Lord, I ask that You would put this room, me, and everything that pertains to it, as well as all the human parts of Sherry into a protective bubble so that nothing we say or do is detectible by the demons. And would You also keep the demons from detecting time gaps as a result of this meeting? Amen."

Abaddon relaxed slightly, but he remained highly suspicious of this woman. She demonstrated many of the tricks and powers that he had seen in the Satanists. "What do you want to talk to me about?"

"We talked a bit last time about your grandmother's accusation and I suspected that it had something to do with your role in your mother's death. Are you willing to talk about it?"

He looked around the room suspiciously, and said, "Are you sure we won't be heard?"

"Absolutely."

"I didn't do it myself, but it seems like all the three-year-old little girls in here had some part in it."

"May I ask how many of them there are?"

"Why is that important?"

"It just gives me an indication of how devastating the trauma was."

Abaddon weighed his options. He stared at Abigail as if boring a hole through her would help him to decide if he should trust her or not. Finally, he heaved a sigh and said, "Hundreds."

"And each one of them likely has others who picked up when they dropped out."

"Yeah. There's hundreds of them, too."

"I'm so sorry. I've been doing this for a long time and it seems like the cult does something horrific at age three. I'm not sure why, but whatever happened severely impacts their life. But the good news is that when there is healing in that memory, much of the battle is over because a lot of key issues are resolved. I'm not saying it's easy, but it's doable, and survivors all say it's worth it. Do you want to keep going?"

After a long minute, Abaddon agreed. He spoke slowly, weighing his words carefully. Trust was a big issue. "We were there. We were at a ritual. Mom was there and so was Grandma and a bunch of other people."

"I mentioned earlier that healing comes by going back to the memory and allowing the true Lord Jesus Christ to bring healing," Abigail said noticing that Abaddon was irritated by the mention of His name.

She hurriedly added, "I know that you are not a fan of Jesus because they likely told you lies about Him or presented a false Jesus to you."

Abaddon just glared.

"Can you tell me if you've ever encountered the true Jesus the Christ?"

"He was the jerk that told them what to do."

"I suspect that it was a false Jesus. The true Jesus would do nothing to counter His own word. If the Bible says, 'You shall not murder' and *that* Jesus said you should, then it wasn't the real Jesus."

"But he said that I needed to honor my mother."

"One law does not trump another law. Something's wrong here. If you'd be willing to walk me through the ritual and allow the true Lord Jesus Christ into the memory, I guarantee that you'll find relief. Truth will set you free and something isn't quite right here."

"Are you calling me a liar?" he challenged.

"Absolutely not. I'm saying that there's a deception somewhere that seemed logical at the time, but the Satanists are good at blocking out critical details and messing with reality." She let that sink in and then asked once again for some information on the ritual.

"Fine!" he huffed. "Here's what happened: Me and Mom and Grandma were sitting at one end of a circle of people around the fire. They all had hoods on. There were thirteen of them. I don't know why, but Grandma had to choose Mom or me to die. If she chose Mom, I'd have to kill her. If she chose me, Mom would have to kill me."

"That's a cruel double-bind," Abigail commented.

"Mom begged her to choose her and let me live. So she did."

243

"You had to kill your mother to 'honor' her word and all of you got left holding the guilt and grief bag."

"Not to mention the hatred and anger bag."

"Would you be willing to ask the true Jesus to bring all of you truth in that memory?"

"I told you that He was there."

"I don't think it was the real Jesus. What have you got to lose?"

"Fine!" he spat reluctantly. He was putting up a front of bravado and he knew that Abigail knew it.

"I'm going to pray. You let me know what's going on." Hearing no protest, she prayed, "Lord Jesus the Christ, You were at that ritual, would You take off any blinders, any deceptions, any tricks that keep Abaddon and all of the parts, especially the three-year olds, from seeing You with their spiritual eyes, hearing You with their spiritual ears, or sensing Your presence? We ask that as the Light of the World, You would illuminate that event and allow them to see everything clearly today. Please remove any masks or disguises, amen."

Abaddon sat looking at the floor. His eyes sweeping back and forth as he scrutinized some internal scene. Finally, he looked up at Abigail and said, "Okay, so the guy that we thought was Jesus was that guy with the snake tattooed up his leg."

Prinz! "I believe that Prinz is dead," Abigail said as a chill went up her spine. Of course, it would make sense that Prinz and Sherry would attend many of the same rituals. She was from the same territory as Amy and Carrie Sue who had each independently described the man's unique tattoo.

"And how would you know about that?" It was Abaddon's turn to be startled. *Who is this woman?*

244

"I have other survivors who have described that snake tattoo to me and we believe that he died a few months back. I think that's part of the reason you're willing to come see me. There's not as much pressure."

"Look, lady; you're spooking us. How do we know that you're not in on it too?"

"You don't. I know they set you up over the years with supposedly good Christians who turned on you just so that if you happen to meet a genuine believer who can actually help you, you won't trust him or her."

"We don't trust anyone."

"Good," Abigail said. "You haven't met very many trust-worthy people. You should test everyone, even me. I'll probably make mistakes along the way, but I assure you that I am not a Satanist."

"Fair enough."

"Do you want to keep going?"

"I think we've had enough for now."

"Thanks. I'm proud of all of you. I know that this can't be easy. Let me pray you outta here and then we can set up our next appointment."

Sherry switched back into her host personality, gathered up her over-sized tote, and swept out of the room. Abigail finished her notes and then grabbed a quick snack while she waited for the new lady.

Grace Jackson was a stunning brunette with light brown eyes. Her make-up was flawless. She could have been a model. She hesitantly poked her head into the waiting area and asked in a barely audible voice, "Am I in the right place?"

"If you're Grace Jackson, you sure are," Abigail welcomed the timid woman. "I'm Abigail Norris.

Come in and let me get you to fill out this form before we get started."

Grace accepted the pen and clipboard and filled out the form. Handing it back to Abigail, she scanned the office as if she were not sure which of the two empty chairs she should claim.

"Just make yourself comfortable and we can get started. What brings you here today?"

Grace began her rambling narrative by saying that her pastor, Mike Griffin, recommended that she see Abigail to address her self-esteem issues. "I just always felt like I didn't belong. I never really had friends and I wasn't close to my older brother." She paused and took a breath before plunging into more of her scattered thoughts. "Actually, I'm not close to my mom or dad, either. They say they love me, but I just feel distant. My brother was out-going and had a ton of friends. He was a valedictorian and star athlete in high school and was Phi Beta Kappa in college. He has a very successful business, a great marriage, and some amazing kids. He was the golden boy and I just grew up in his shadow. Sometimes I wondered if I was their step-child even though everyone says my brother and I are like two peas in a pod."

Abigail listened and took a few notes as Grace continued with her personal story. Sometimes she stopped her to clarify a point, but mostly she listened until Grace exhausted herself and looked hopefully at Abigail.

"Let me ask you a couple of questions," Abigail began. "First of all, what is your relationship with Jesus?"

"Well, um, I got saved when I was a little girl. My mother and father took us to church every week."

"I'm glad to hear that you're saved, but what's your relationship like with God? Do you feel close to Him? Do you feel like He answers your prayers?"

Grace hung her head and picked a dot of lint off the cuff of her immaculate blouse. "I don't know. I mean, I guess I think He just tolerates me. Sometimes my prayers get answered, but mostly I don't pray because I feel like it's a waste of time."

"Is that what it feels like when you try to interact with your family?"

Grace looked like she had been slapped. "Yes. I never really thought about it before, but that's exactly what it feels like. I mean, I know in my head that God accepts me, but it just feels like I'm His step-child, like I'm a second-class Christian, like it's for everyone else but me."

"What emotions come up when you think about being the step-child and growing up in the shadow of a golden boy and just being tolerated and not measuring up?"

"Oh my," she said sadly and then rattled off a number of feelings. "I feel rejected, left out, not good enough, neglected, unworthy..."

"Can you tell me about the circumstances of your birth? You said had an older brother. Are there any other siblings?"

"Oh no!" Grace reacted strongly. "My dad's family mostly believed in having only one child. He was an only child but Mom had some brothers. He said that I was an accident."

"Seriously? Your own father said that you were an accident?"

Abigail's reaction seemed to awaken something in Grace, as if she was finally receiving an inkling of validation for her existence. "Mother said that she knew about his family's beliefs and hid her pregnancy with me until she started really showing in the sixth month."

"No kidding."

"She said that my father dropped her off at the hospital and wasn't even there for my birth."

"I guess I can understand why you have all those feelings," Abigail said sympathetically. "Let me talk to you about one spiritual principle and one physiological principle." Abigail went on to tell Grace about how God intended our fathers and mothers to give us a tangible image of what God is like. They are supposed to supply nurturing, physical contact, security, provision, eye contact, and verbal connections. If parents fail to do so, the child will perceive God in the same way – abusive, absent, rejecting, neglectful, or any number of negative feelings.

"Oh, wow! I never knew that, but it makes so much sense."

"It's very common; believe me. Let me pray with you about this issue and then we'll go on to the physiological issue."

"Okay, but I'm not good at praying out loud."

"I'll lead and you can just say, 'What she said, amen.' We don't want the legalistic enemy to say, 'Abigail prayed but Grace didn't so we're not budging.' They're legalists and squatters," Abigail said with a wink and a grin.

Getting the nod, Abigail prayed, "Holy Father, we come to Your throne of grace in the name of Jesus to obtain mercy and grace in Grace's time of need. Father, we have come to realize that Grace's father and mother have failed to provide the positive affirmations, the acceptance, the blessings, and nurturing that You intended for them to supply to her all her life. Lord, Your word says that if my father or my mother have forsaken me or let me down that You will take me up. Lord we ask that You would now go through Grace's history from the moment of conception to the present and bless her with everything that her parents failed to give her. We ask that You would demolish any and all strongholds that were established in her life because of her parents' short-comings and send any and all demons who have been tormenting her to a place where they will never afflict anyone ever again. We ask that You would heal and seal all the broken places and fill her with Your Holy Spirit, blessings, and all the goodness that You have stored up for those who fear You. We pray this in the name of Jesus, amen."

"Um, yes, God, I pray what she prayed, amen."

"Are you sensing anything?"

"Yes. I feel lighter, like something lifted off of me." Her countenance reflected the change.

"Good. Now let's talk about the physiological issues. Emotions are chemically based and cross the placental lines. So, if your mother was feeling afraid and ashamed because she was pregnant with you, you would receive those feelings as well. You wouldn't know what they meant until later in life, but the groundwork was laid in the womb."

"I had no idea. No wonder I always felt like I had to hide. I mean, when we were out as a family, I was always walking a few steps behind the rest of them. Mother just said that I was painfully shy."

"I think you're starting to connect the dots," Abigail said delightedly. "We need to pray about your womb experience."

"Yes! Let's do."

"Holy Father, we come to Your throne of grace once again in the name of Jesus. You are the same yesterday, today, and forever. We ask that You would go into Grace's past, all the way to the womb and cover her with Your healing balm and sooth those painful feelings. We ask You to release her from the strongholds that were created by all the negative words that were spoken or thought by her father and her mother and any grandparents. We ask that You would neutralize the negative emotions that were chemically based which transferred to her from her mother. We ask that You would release her from oppressing spirits and fill her with Your Holy Spirit, blessings, the fruit of the Spirit, and activate the gifts of the Holy Spirit in her so she can minister to others who have suffered similar things. We pray this in the name of Jesus, amen."

"Amen! Yes, Lord, I fully agree," Grace said with a dazzling smile that enhanced her beauty ten-fold.

"How do you feel?"

"So much lighter. I can't believe it. I feel like my insides have been scrubbed clean. I had no idea that I was carrying so much weight."

"What do you think of yourself and what do you think God thinks of you?"

"I'm okay. I'm not an accident. I'm here because God wants me here. I feel like I can look the world in the eye and not feel like I have to make an excuse for taking up space and breathing the air."

"One more question. Do you harbor any anger or resentment toward your parents, grandparents, or even your brother?"

"Well, maybe a smidge," Grace confessed.

"Let's save that for next time. We got a lot of work done today and I've got a sneaking hunch that you're going to get some good ripples."

They closed the session with prayer and set up their next appointment for the following Friday. Abigail did not stop smiling until she got well down the road. It was a good day so far and she still needed to see Amy.

Amy and Princess were waiting for her on the front porch. The sight of Princess brought back bitter-sweet memories of Dude. Yes, she still missed him, but she had grieved and moved on.

"Hey, girl!" Abigail greeted Amy as she emerged from her truck. "You are really looking maternal these days!" She noted that the swelling had gone down by her eye, but there was still some evidence of bruising on the side of her face.

"Thanks. I feel great. That attack last week didn't hurt me or David."

"Praise God!" Abigail said as she walked up the familiar steps.

"In or out?" Amy addressed Princess. Carrie Sue and Amy decided that they felt safer with the dog inside the house with them after last week's assault. They were glad that Princess was a quick learner and was now fully trained to do her duty outside.

251

With Princess curled beside her chair, Amy was ready to begin their session. She brought Abigail up to speed on the internal status. Apollyon and the remainder of that group was still resting. That usually indicated that intentional integration might be in order.

After opening with prayer, Abigail asked, "What are you sensing?"

"I think they're all ready to integrate, but Apollyon wants to talk to you first."

"All right." Abigail was intrigued as she waited for the personalities to switch.

"Ahem," Apollyon cleared his voice softly. "I, um, that is, we all want to apologize to you for giving you such a rough time."

Princess woke and sat up. Looking at Apollyon, she cocked her head and gave a high-pitched whine. Somehow, she sensed the switch. It did not surprise Abigail since she had seen similar responses from the pets of other counselees. She had seen pets run from or snarl at personalities that were still demonized. It was an intriguing phenomenon.

"You are all forgiven. I know that you had little choice at the time and I don't hold anything against anyone."

"Thanks," the humble personality said gratefully. "I guess that's all. We've been resting with Jesus and He took care of integrating a bunch of the little ones already."

"Very cool. Do you mind if I ask how He did it?"

Apollyon assumed that Abigail would know because he assumed that all integrations went down the same way for all survivors. "Sure. He put us in this really peaceful green pasture. There was a little babbling brook meandering through the middle of it and He was sitting on a white rock. He would call the little ones over to sit on His lap. They were really hurting. Some were deformed and could hardly move. I mean, He'd just hold them until they fell asleep in His arms and then it was like they sunk into Him for a minute and when they came back out, they were healed and happy and would run off and play."

"That is very cool! I've had several others who described scenes like that. It reminds me of Psalm 23: *'He makes me lie down in green pastures, He leads me beside quiet waters. He restores my soul.'*"

"Yeah! Like that!"

"Are you ready to integrate now?"

"We sure are. We want to be a part of Amy the right way, the way God designed us to be."

"Let's pray!" Abigail prayed for Apollyon, Judas, Jonah, Beor, Achan, and all the personalities that were originally in the subterranean levels under the prison. How far they had come! Thousands upon thousands of personalities had been split off intentionally. Just as many split off spontaneously because of year after year and decade after decade of ritual trauma.

Original Amy surfaced with a satisfied smile on her face. "That was huge!"

"It sure was. What's next?"

"Well, it's pretty empty in here now. I can't see them, but I know there's still some stragglers hiding around somewhere wherever they hide. And then there's the host Amy."

"Are you up for more, or is that enough for today?"

"I think we should call it a day."

They closed the session and then walked down to the chicken coop together. Abigail eyed the garden on the way down and picked half a gallon of green beans and some tomatoes and peppers on the way back up. "You guys need to pick more stuff."

"We're out here every day. It's too much stuff."

"We've got that neighborhood meeting tomorrow, why don't you bring a bunch with you? We can give it away. I'm sure everyone will appreciate fresh vegies."

17

Saturday, August 11

Saturday marked one week since Amy and Carrie Sue had been attacked by the unknown thugs. Since the Norris' house was larger and several more people had been invited, the meeting was moved over there to accommodate the growing group. Even though Rev. Mike Griffin had not formally met the Yorks, he recognized them from the Ministerial Alliance meetings and greeted them warmly. Pastor Spalding came with a very nervous Max Berryman. The Millers and the McCords were there as well.

Abigail served a light luncheon and refreshments for the eleven o'clock meeting. It featured many of their home grown produce. Reno eagerly greeted each guest and was especially taken with little Ariel Miller, much to the child's delight.

"Hey, everyone, why don't we gather in the great room and we'll get started," Lee said. Bryan and Traci McCord were shooed outside to play with Ariel and Reno on the front porch. As soon as the adults were comfortably settled, he nodded at Abigail.

"I guess we should open with prayer," she said. "Would you do the honors, Rev. Griffin?"

"I'd be honored," he answered and got right to business with his prayer. "Holy God and Father, we come together today to seek justice for those who have been treated unfairly and illegally. We ask for wisdom and guidance, protection and discernment. We pray for verifiable facts to come to the surface. Lord, we thank You for each one who is here and ask that You would continue to heal what has been broken and restore whatever has been stolen. We pray in Jesus' name, amen."

"Amen!"

Abigail looked at Richard and said, "Since you bring the legal and criminal investigation element to our group, would you mind letting us know what kinds of information that we might have that you can use?"

"Why don't we go around the room and each of you can give us what you know in your own particular case?" Richard suggested.

"I'd like to start," Max blurted. "I feel like I'm responsible for most of it. I tried to recruit Jason here," he nodded toward Jason, "and that's probably why they went after Ariel, and I'm the one that harassed Abigail." He hung his head and confessed, "I cut your brake lines while your truck was parked at the church."

"I figured it was you, but it doesn't matter, Max. You're forgiven."

"I threatened you in that grocery store parking lot, I cut your gate so the horses got loose, and was going to poison your horse with arsenic."

"Until me and Gary convinced you to change your mind. While we're on the subject of forgiveness – Max, will you forgive me for beating you?"

"Absolutely! I deserved that and worse."

"I owe you an apology, too," Gary added. "It was wrong for us to threaten you and beat you like that. Will you forgive me?"

"No problem. I healed up just fine. I think God's been trying to get my attention and I didn't listen very well. He had to nearly kill me to get the message through my thick skull." He grinned sheepishly at Pastor Spalding.

Max continued to fill in details about locations of ritual sites and the baby skull that was buried in the river bottoms. He gave them additional information about Levi Blevins.

"Levi Blevins?" Richard interrupted. He began flipping through his notebook.

"Yes. He's the guy that recruited me when I was in high school."

Pointing at his notes, Richard said, "He's the one that owns the vehicle with the license plate number 1NG 5050."

"That's the guy that clipped me!" Amy exclaimed.

"That's the guy that followed me when I left Amy's burned out trailer. He used to have a slick sports car with plates that said BLAZE. He must have changed cars and plates after I pulled over and confronted him that day," Abigail said with satisfaction.

"Like Russ Ranson did after you busted him," Mike Griffin said. "He acted so suspicious when he just *happened* to show up that day my janitor found the blood in the baptismal font."

"Who's this Ranson guy?" Richard asked.

"Sorry," Mike answered. "He's an elder in my church. Russell Ranson. The Springfield Presbyterian Church. Anyway, we're quite certain that he's also a Satanist. He's kept a very low profile lately."

Richard took more notes and then looked back at Max. "What did you mean about someone going after Jason's little sister?"

"I don't have proof, but I ..." Max hung his head again. This was not easy. "I recruited Jason and his friend Nathan. One night we were going to go destroy Carrie Sue's Bible and, um ..." he hung his head again, wishing mightily that he did not have to utter the next words. But he lifted his head and looked at Carrie Sue, "um, we were going to rape you and then do the same to Abigail here." After a palpable moment of silence, he heaved another deep sigh, looked at the remains of the burn scars on his palms, and said, "I'm so sorry. Both of you. I'm so sorry."

"You're forgiven," they said in unison.

"What does that have to do with Jason's sister?" Richard brought the focus back.

"Oh, well, um, Jason walked away. He quit his job at Dad's dealership and Nathan was killed in a freak accident right after we left Carrie Sue's place. The cult punishes traitors and loves to sacrifice blonde-haired, blue-eyed little girls. We needed one for a certain ritual and Ariel fit the description. But I don't know who botched the kidnapping. It was a woman."

"Do you think Ariel could give us a description?"

Cassie and Paul glanced at each other. "We brought her to Abigail for healing and she's been great after that. She hasn't talked about it since then." Looking at Abigail, Paul asked, "Do you think she'd be re-traumatized by bringing it back up?"

"No. I believe that when the Lord brings healing, it's complete. Why don't you ask her?"

Ariel was called in and sat snugly between her parents. Looking wide-eyed around the room at all the adults who were looking at her, she asked, "Am I in trouble?"

"No, sweetie, we were just wondering if you remember what happened in the store when we were shopping for socks and that lady took you. This nice man," Cassie extended a hand toward Richard, "is trying to help us catch the bad guys but he needs to know what she looked like. Guess what? You're the only one who can help him. You can be a super-hero!"

Ariel smiled broadly displaying the gap from her missing tooth. "Okay."

Richard addressed her gently, "Ariel, let's start at the top with her hair. What do you remember about her hair? Do you remember what color it was? Or how long it was?"

"Well, I don't really think it was her hair," Ariel said as she wrinkled her nose. "It looked like she was wearing a wig like my Grandma does sometimes."

"Oh, that's interesting. What was the wig like?"

"It was just brown hair and a little bit curly."

"That's good. Do you remember what color her eyes were?"

"Brown. I didn't like them. They looked mean. She talked mean and she didn't cover her mouth when she coughed."

"Was she taller than your mom or shorter?"

"Shorter."

"Was she fat or skinny or something in-between?"

"Skinny."

"You're doing great," Richard encouraged. He continued to ask open-ended questions about her other facial features, scars, marks, build, foot size, and more. He finished by praising her and letting her go back out with Reno and the other children.

Carrie Sue was deep in thought and startled visibly when Abigail asked, "Carrie Sue?"

Carrie Sue replied slowly, flatly, "My mother fits that description. She has a personality that has a bunch of wigs. She's the one that dressed up if Dad ever took her out for dinner. Me and my brothers would joke about our 'wigged-out' mom 'cause she was kind of a space cadet. And she's got a chronic cough now and has been losing weight since the bio-dad died."

"Would you happen to have a picture of her?" Richard asked.

"Nothing recent. I could take one with my phone the next time she drops in at my work." Carrie Sue was clearly not excited about having an encounter with her mother. She was also ambivalent about the prospect of nailing her mother with a crime. On one hand, she wanted the evil Dorkas part of her mother to pay dearly, but on the other hand, she understood that her mother was programed and also a pitiful victim on some level which elicited a measure of sympathy. This was not a black and white issue.

"If you can do that and get it to me, we can get Ariel to confirm or deny that it's her. What's your mother's name?"

"Susan Wagner."

"Is there anything else that we might investigate?"

"Well, maybe," Carrie Sue hesitated and looked at Abigail.

"Tell him about the bodies that your father buried in the rose beds and him cutting your brother's brake lines and tell him about your kidnapping and how you punched out Sheriff Bynum."

That really got the discussion rolling. Carrie Sue filled all of them in on what she could remember from the day that she took a walk to this very property to take another look at Billy's car, and the kidnapping, and the escape from the ritual site located on Charlie Fletcher's property. She mentioned the windowless building and felt sure that she was taken there by her mother. Lee filled him in on some of Charlie's offenses from cutting fence lines to trying to ambush Abigail to shooting out her back door. Earl took up the narrative and verified that it was Charlie Fletcher.

Looking at his notes to refresh his memory, he asked Max to tell him more about Levi. They covered some of the things they did together as well as some of the things that Levi boasted about to Max. Once again Max apologized to Abigail – this time for his role in setting the woods on fire and once again he was forgiven.

"I have a feeling that he was responsible for burning down your trailer," Max said as he looked at Amy.

"I wouldn't put it past him. I can't tell you how many times he and his buddies broke into my house and beat the crap out of me. And more," she added ruefully.

Continuing to scribble notes, asking more pointed questions, Richard was finally satisfied that he had enough solid leads upon which he and his father could follow up.

Lunch was a light-hearted affair, especially with Lee and his cousin, Gary, bantering back and forth. Martha had been quietly sitting next to David on the couch during the discussions, but something stirred in her foggy mind with the familiarity of a luncheon that allowed her to function as if she were the hostess. Bryan would have filled his plate with only cherry tomatoes until Cindy reminded him that he needed some other colors on his plate, too.

Richard was curious about the baby skull buried in the river bottoms. "Is there any chance we can exhume it?"

Max told him that he was sure he could still find it, but it was a couple miles out. He neglected to mention that he had dug it up once to show it to Jason.

"No problem," Lee injected, "We have horses. We can cover that in a short time. Abigail brought me out there once. Sorry, but we found the spot and dug it up and then covered it back up. I hope that doesn't mess up your investigation. Are you up for a ride?"

"I'm up for it," Richard eagerly answered. It had been ages since he was on a horse. "Let me change clothes and bring some equipment with me."

"What about you, Max? Can you ride with that rod in your back and your sore ribs?"

"I guess so. As long as we just walk the horses."

"Can I go? Can I go? Can I go?" Bryan begged as he jumped up and down in front of Gary.

"What do you think?" Gary asked Abigail.

"We have enough horses. Why not?"

After the luncheon was finished, Cindy and Traci went with Carrie Sue and Amy to their place. Traci wanted to meet Princess and see how the chickens were growing. The Yorks went home where David got Martha settled and Richard got ready for his ride. Pastor Spalding left once he was assured that Max could get a ride back to town with the McCords. Mike Griffin left with more questions than answers.

Bryan felt like a king riding in front of Gary on Lady. She was the tallest of all the horses. Of course, Abigail rode Buster. Lee saddled Misty for himself, Sparkles for Max, and Sassy for Richard. This was going to be a good test for Reno. Lee had gone for short rides and Reno responded well to commands and kept close but he wanted to test the young dog with a group.

Holding Sassy's lead, Lee led the group down the trail that would take them out to the road right next to York Creek where they could cross directly onto the York's property. Richard was ready and waiting by the time they arrived. Handing his backpack to Lee, he mounted Sassy and then slid the backpack onto his back.

"Abigail, why don't you lead? You know the trails better than I do," Lee said.

Nudging Buster, she headed toward the field that ran all the way from York Creek to just past the Milner's place. Passing the tree-filled bog where Charlie Fletcher used to spy on her property, and then turning west, they walked the edge of the field. Entering the cool of the woods, Abigail found the trail that connected with the trail that led to the clearing. Buster wanted to run, but she kept him at a walk for Max's sake. Bryan wanted to gallop as well.

"Can you tell me how you know about the baby skull?" Richard asked Max once they arrived in the clearing.

"I buried it there a couple years ago. At least it seems like a long time ago. After one ritual, they handed it to me and said that it was my responsibility to make sure it was never found. They gave other bones to some of the others." Max was clearly uncomfortable. With his renewed mind, he was seeing clearly now. He was appalled at who he was and what he might have become had the Lord not intervened.

"Why here? Don't you live in town?"

Wondering if he was about to hang himself, Max gulped, "Well, um, that guy, um, Charlie Fletcher, brought me here once a couple years ago. He let me use one of his horses whenever I needed to, uh, to do something." Max knew that Abigail knew exactly what he was talking about.

Soon after they arrived in the clearing Richard took pictures and expertly uncovered the skull with his trowel. Placing the L-shaped ruler on the ground, he snapped more pictures. "What about that shack?" Looking over his shoulder he noted that Reno was enthusiastically sniffing the ground around the edge of the shack as he was circling it.

"Charlie said it was his hunting shack. His getaway. If the key is still in the hiding place, I can open it up for you," Max said as he started across the clearing. Tugging the aged corner board out about an inch, he snagged a key ring with his little finger and pulled out the key. Twisting the key in the padlock, he opened the creaky door, and stepped aside so Richard could look.

Richard snapped some pictures prior to stepping further inside. He took out his measuring tape and asked Lee to get the length and width of the outside of the building while he continued to search inside. He noted that a rusted shovel and an old pickax leaned against one corner. A corroded hand saw, rusty nails, and a rusty hammer sat under a layer of dust and dirt. Dust laden cobwebs hung like drapes from the ceiling. Empty bags were thrown into another corner. After taking pictures, Richard used his gloved hand to pick up a corner of one of the bags. It had been filled with lime at one time. Several of the bags had been repositioned at some point as evidenced by a thinner layer of dust and dirt on the bags underneath them.

"I've got four feet by six feet," Lee reported as he looked in over Richard's shoulder.

"Interesting measurements," Richard mused. "One could bury a coffin under here."

"Why would you say that?" Lee asked.

"Digging tools. Building tools. Lime."

"Are you thinking what I'm thinking?"

"Who owns this land?"

"Good question." Lee turned around and called to Gary who had been walking Lady around the clearing with a thoroughly delighted Bryan on her back, "Hey, Gary, do you know who might own this land?"

"I don't know for sure, but I would guess that it's county property since it's just river bottoms."

"Let's close this up and head back. I think I need to make a couple more phone calls," Richard said.

There would be the new moon ritual on Sunday and then Monday would be a ritual simply because it was the thirteenth. Satanists have used every pretext or justification for a ritual – month in and month out, year in and year out for centuries and millennia. Most of the Satanists in this area were born into Satanism as were their predecessors for many generations. It was all they knew. It was all they were permitted to know.

Unless.

"How do you propose to stop them?" Xerxes pressed. He made it very clear that this was a local problem. Local problems generated regional effects. Regional effects produced territorial consequences.

"We have assaulted each of them physically. We've gone after their vehicles. We tried to shoot that woman more than once. We've burned one of them out. We're trying to go after Mot through the legal system," Zorroz stated as he used Max's cult name, "but something's going on higher up."

"Excuses! All I'm hearing is excuses! Excuses and blame! Do I have to bring in someone who can actually do something around here? None of you seem capable of filling Prinz' shoes," Xerxes railed. He omitted the fact that his own powerlessness was demonstrated not all that long ago in that freak hail storm. He just could not let that one go.

"Those Yorks are up to something. They have pull in Washington," Daggett growled as respectfully as he could. "We got the end-around and had to let Mot go. It was something about the FBI and the DOJ having a federal case against him that takes precedent over our local misdemeanor charges."

"Leave that up to me. I'll take care of Landrum. He'll buckle."

Landrum hung up his secure line and kicked back in his chair, interlocking his fingers behind his head, he looked at the ceiling of his well-appointed office. *Lord, we're going to need natural and supernatural favor.* His ultra-analytical mind sifted through Richard York's verbal report.

Xerxes headed back to his home after hearing a report from his campaign manager. He cursed the distraction.

His congressional seat had been secure for many elections, but this year John Davidson was facing a serious contender. A popular entrepreneur, James Jackson Jennings, was making a serious bid for his office. November was not that far off and it looked like he needed to do some focused campaigning. The Davidson men had occupied that seat for generations. They expected that when John retired, his son would assume the helm.

18

Tuesday, August 14

Landrum had the feeling that he needed to move quickly on his end. His intuition had served him well in the past. Having both personal and professional relationships with several key personnel higher on the organizational chart than he, Landrum called in some favors. Red tape was removed, search warrants were generated, and various legal documents were created. Richard would be able to proceed.

By Tuesday Richard received the federal permit on his secure computer to investigate the shack in the clearing. Landrum was able to locate it via satellite photography. He confirmed that it was on county property so that Richard did not have to search for records in the courthouse. It would raise already suspicious eyebrows. He, too, was becoming a marked man in this county.

Driving down the road less than a mile, Richard turned onto the Norris' property. Crunching up the tree-lined gravel lane, Richard was greeted by an exuberant Reno. His friendly yaps alerted Lee.

Poking his head out of the barn, Lee hailed Richard with a big smile. "Hello there! What brings you here today?"

"A little follow-up business that I hope you can help me with."

"I'll do whatever I can."

"I have the search warrant for the shack and the area around it. Would you be able to provide me with a horse and your company while I investigate?"

Lee felt a surge of adrenaline. He was up for an adventure. "Absolutely!" Lee's child-like enthusiasm quickly bubbled up.

"Today if you can."

"I certainly can!"

"Say, Dad doesn't have a shovel anymore and I'd rather not use the one in the shack. Would you happen to have one?"

"We sure do. Between Abigail and me, we should have just about anything you'd need."

"I'd kind of like to get right on it. What's the soonest you can join me?"

"Right now. Just let me check with Abigail and make sure that there's nothing I might have forgotten."

Just then, Abigail walked out onto the front porch. "Hello! I thought that was you."

"Hello. Yep, it's me again. I wonder if I can borrow your husband for a few hours."

"I don't see why not."

"We're going to check out the shack again," Lee said. "Richard could use an extra man and a horse."

"Sounds glamorous. The mystery shack."

"Well, investigations aren't as glamorous as they sound. There's a lot of sweat involved. Then there's the paperwork," Richard said with a chuckle. "But it is satisfying, especially when we nail the bad guys. We might not find anything useful, but ya never know."

"Will you need an extra horse as a pack animal?"

"That's not a bad idea. I stowed everything I thought I might need in the back of my vehicle just in case we could get right on it."

Lee sent Abigail to the shed to procure their best shovel and a pickax while he and Richard went down to the pasture to bring up the horses. Lady, Misty, and Sassy were soon stamping their feet near the barn as they each waited their turn to be brushed and saddled. Lee expertly lashed the tools onto Sassy's saddle. Richard's backpack hung off one side and another large rucksack with an assortment of items for his field investigation hung off of the other.

"I'll be praying," Abigail said as she filled Lee's saddlebag with bottles of water, apples, and granola bars.

The sun was promising to scorch them later, but it was not uncomfortably hot by the time they headed out. Lee only knew one way to get the shack so they followed the same route that they had a few days earlier. It was a quiet ride. Both men were alert and wary of their surroundings. Lee remembered Abigail's remark about tattle-tale demons who could alert the Satanists. They were prepared.

They did not talk much on the ride and soon they arrived in the clearing. Dismounting, Lee tethered the horses while Richard retrieved the key and unlocked the shack. Normally Lee could just drop the reins and the horses would stay close, but he did not want to take any chances today.

"Let me know what I should and should not do," Lee said as he approached the shack.

"I think I'll let you be my camera man if you don't mind. We'll see if there's anything else later. I want to be careful about contamination of evidence and transfer of evidence if we happen to come across something."

"What made you want to dig a little further?"

"See those lime bags?" he asked as he pointed to the floor at the far end. "Everything here looks like it hasn't been moved since it was originally dropped except for some of those bags."

"I would never have noticed."

"Look at the shovel. It's been used fairly recently based on the shiny end. Now I don't know if they dug out there somewhere," he jerked his thumb toward the clearing, "or if there's something under this floor. Plus, Reno was mighty curious about this shack."

"Interesting."

Richard unpacked the large rucksack and found disposable coveralls and booties. He kept his FBI cap in place and donned gloves. Removing a soft case that was filled with plastic bags, he readied a large plastic bag in which to place the lime bags. Stepping to the side, he had Lee snap some pictures.

He carefully swept the floor. Gently tapping and listening, looking from one angle and then another, Richard finally applied the pry bar and lifted the entire middle section of the floor in one piece. "Here we go!" Richard exclaimed. "This is what I was looking for."

It took a well-trained eye to see that the middle of the floor was actually a large trap door. The rusty hinges on the underside groaned and squeaked as he began to slowly fold it back toward the shelf on the back wall.

Urdang wheeled and circled high above the woods and the clearing. Shrieking curses, ordering his underlings to notify their human charges, he felt his territory slipping from his grasp. He was infuriated and once again rallied his accomplices. "Find a curse that will alight!" "Thwart their plans!" "Attack those women!" *Aargh! Those damnable she-creatures!* How he despised them.

Susan Wagner suddenly had an inexplicable urge to go visit Carrie Sue at The Thrift Shoppe. The normally docile personality did not know that the demon-driven Dorkas was putting the thought into her mind. Finding her purse and keys, Susan walked out to the full-sized pickup truck that better suited her deceased husband than her. The coughing started up again with the minimal effort that she exerted with just walking to the truck. She spat the phlegm onto the driveway, but did not notice or did not care that it was tinged with bright crimson blood.

"Either I'm shrinking or this truck is growing," she muttered as she climbed into the driver's seat. Susan Wagner was in her late fifties, but she looked much older. Her health had also steadily deteriorated since Carrie Sue started her healing process. Parts of her understood the connection and wanted to destroy her remaining off-spring.

Driving at least ten miles per hour under the posted speed limit, Susan had a parade of vehicles lined up behind her by the time she reached town. Spotting two open spaces just down the street from The Thrift Shoppe, Susan pulled in leaving a wide space between her driver's side and the next vehicle. Unfortunately for other shoppers, the truck also stood over the line and ruined the parking place next to her. She was oblivious to all but her own mission.

"Carrie Sue!" Amanda whispered loudly as she looked up from the counter, "Isn't that your mother?"

Carrie Sue had been straightening racks and did not pay attention to the jingling bells that announced customers entering or leaving the store. Leaning back so she could see down the aisle, she groaned, "Yeah, it's the mom."

Amanda was amused by Carrie Sue's labels of her mother. Sometimes she called her the bio-mom or the egg-donor which only made Amanda more curious. *Someday she'll let me know what's up between them.* Many mother-daughter relationships were strained, but Carrie Sue and her mother took it to a whole different level. Amanda knew nothing about dissociation and multiple personalities, she only knew that sometimes Mrs. Wagner was sad and pitiful and sometimes she was angry and caustic. On the same visit!

Carrie Sue moved to intercept her mother before she could get to Amanda and inform Amanda about her wretched daughter or perhaps, enlist her sympathy. She never knew which mother was going to show up and whether or not that mother would stay in executive control.

"What brings you to town today?" Carrie Sue asked carefully. She did not want to step on a landmine or crack the egg shells that her mother scattered before her as she approached. Carrie Sue could handle it much better now that she was whole, but she did not want a scene. Not here. Not now. Not ever.

"I need you to help me buy a car," the whiny mother began. "I can't handle your father's truck anymore. It's so big and it guzzles gas. I want a car." Switching into a more aggressive and knowledgeable personality, she continued, "What did you do with Billy's car? I could use it now that he's gone. He ain't gonna need it where he is."

"I didn't take Billy's car. The sheriff probably found it and impounded it somewhere."

"Well, you should be thinking about your mother and not just about yourself. You've always been so self-centered."

"Mom!" Carrie Sue said, "Can we discuss this some other time? I'm at work."

"See what I mean? It's all about you all the time."

"Do you need anything from the store today?" Carrie Sue hoped to refocus the attention.

"Why, as a matter-of-fact, I do," Susan sniffed and walked imperiously to the back of the store leaving her daughter in her wake.

Oh, Lord! Help me. I wish You could get through to her. Suddenly Carrie Sue remembered that she needed a picture of her mother for Richard York. *Oh! That's why You brought her in here! Thank You, Lord.* Carrie Sue quickly reached into her back pocket and scrolled down to the camera feature. Positioning herself, steadying her hand, Carrie Sue snapped the picture. Checking to be sure that it was a good one, she hastily pocketed the phone just as her mother blew past her without another word.

"Oh!" Susan Wagner suddenly stopped and whirled around. "I forgot to give you this," she said in a gentler tone. "I had my will revised. Here," she said as she handed Carrie Sue an official-looking document. "Since you're my sole heir, I'm just signing it all over to you. I'm only asking that you let my sisters have some of the family heirlooms." The effort of speaking those sentences put her into another coughing fit.

"Sure, uh, they can have whatever they want." Carrie Sue was fairly sure that she had never met this personality before. She seemed so sensible.

"Good-bye." With that, Susan Wagner turned and left the store. She left Carrie Sue stunned.

Amanda came up to Carrie Sue and giggled. "Do you think she shop-lifted again?"

Carrie Sue rolled her eyes and replied, "Probably. Let me know if you can figure out what's missing and I'll pay for it."

Amy heard the phone ring and moved into the living room. Abigail kept the phone in her name and neither Amy nor Carrie Sue had changed the answering machine recording. Once she heard that it was David York, she picked up. "Hello?"

"This is David York, next door. Is this Amy?"

"Yes." Amy was comfortable speaking with the man since she had sat with Martha a couple of times when David had to leave the house to run errands.

"Let me get right to the point," he said. "I know you're pregnant right now, but are you able to do light housekeeping?"

"Yes. I'm not on any restrictions these days. I've still got about three months to go."

"Would you be interested in coming down here once a week and doing some cleaning and maybe some

275

laundry? Nothing heavy, mind you, it's just that Martha doesn't do anything much anymore and I'm just not good at it. I'm afraid Richard and I have turned this place into a bachelor pad of sorts."

"Yes, yes!" Amy answered excitedly. "What's the best day for you?"

"How about Mondays, say about ten o'clock?"

"Perfect."

"What do you charge?"

"Oh. I hadn't really thought about that. I'm not sure what the going rate is, but I'm sure that whatever you pay me will be fine."

Amy was overjoyed and spoke to her unborn son after she hung up, "Did you hear that, David? We have a job!" Amy had been careful with what was left of her tax refunds, but her savings account was steadily dwindling. *Thank you, Lord!*

Richard stepped back as a puff of dust was stirred up when he repositioned the two-foot by five-foot trap door. Removing his cap and wiping his brow, he huffed, "Whew! It's getting hotter."

"Are you talking about the weather or the case?"

"I think both. Shine that light in here and we'll see what we've got."

From just outside the door, Lee managed to hold the powerful flashlight at an angle that went around Richard and illuminated the hole under the closet-like shack.

"Well! What do you know? It's even gift-wrapped!" Richard was gratified that his hunch was correct. Actually, his well-trained nose had detected the faint odor of decomposition when he was here last. He also remembered that Reno had been quite inquisitive about the shack.

"What are we looking at?" All Lee could see was a dirt-covered gray plastic tarp of some kind.

"I believe that we have a body bag here. If we have a body bag, we have a body," Richard said, starting to sound more like an instructor. What he did not say out loud was that where there was a body bag, there was someone who had access to a body bag. *The coroner? A funeral director? The sheriff?*

"Before we go any further it would be a good idea to get you suited up."

Locating another set of disposable coveralls and booties, he gave them to Lee and showed him how to glove up as well. While Lee was donning the very unfamiliar gear, Richard made a call to his FBI friend, Steven Diblassio, and asked him to come down with a transport.

After taking as many pictures from as many angles as possible the two men carefully slid the body bag onto the grass in front of the shack and took a break. They were grateful for the water and the snacks. Lee sensed the horses' restlessness and attributed it to the heat and flies as well as the unusual setting and the scents that they were picking up from the unzipped body bag. He scanned the woods and saw nothing.

"There's not much left of him. My guess is that someone wanted this body to deteriorate quickly," Richard processed aloud as he carefully pulled back the edge and watched beetles and other insects scurry away from the light.

"Well, the bugs and other critters would definitely take care of that. So, would the lime," Lee added as he continued to document the process with the camera. *We could be here a long time!* He was starting to be concerned that Abigail would be worried about him.

"I'm going to have to zip this up and put it in another bag so we can transport it and keep it uncontaminated. Diblassio is on his way with a transport. He should be at Dad's house in a couple of hours. Let's see what else might be in here."

They worked together methodically. By the time the space under the shack was emptied, Richard had another body bag partially filled with an assortment of bones and skulls. He was mystified because it was apparent that the bones had come from dozens of different skeletons. Some were charred and some were clean. Some were delicate and some were thick. At long last they shed their protective wear and loaded the equipment and the body bags onto Sassy's already sweaty back.

The ride home was very quiet. It was as if the birds, tree frogs, and crickets were paying respect to those in the funeral procession who had never been properly mourned. Lee was thinking that Carrie Sue's bones might well have been added to the ossuary had she not escaped from that ritual. Richard was trying to find the logic behind the mismatched bones.

The procession made its way back through the woods, along the edge of the fields, and next to York Creek. Taking a diagonal, they arrived at the back of David and Martha's home hot and sweaty, hungry and tired. But satisfied.

"Well, what have we here?" David greeted the two men as they dismounted.

"We have a lot of evidence. Diblassio is coming with a transport," Richard stated in his debriefing tone, "he should be here within the hour. Maybe sooner, if I know him."

Turning to Lee, he said, "I really appreciate your help in this. Do you mind helping me unload the bags?"

"No problem."

The two men worked efficiently as a team for which Sassy was grateful. She was anxious to shed that saddle and roll in the pasture.

"In order to maintain a proper chain of possession, I need to stay here with the evidence until Diblassio gets here. Lee, I've been asking you for favors all day, but if you could bring the horses back and drive my car here, I'd really appreciate it."

"Glad to help. I've been itching to do something to help take these Satanists down."

Leaving Lady with the Yorks, Lee mounted Misty and grabbed Sassy's lead. They rounded the creek side of the house, crossed the road, and followed the faint trail up to the barn.

"Hey! You're back! How did it go? Did you find anything? Where's Richard? Where's Lady?"

"Slow down," Lee laughed, "I'll answer everything in due time, but yes, we found something."

Together they groomed the horses while Lee filled in as many details as he could remember with Abigail continuing to pepper him with questions. After walking the animals down to their pasture, Lee and

Abigail got into Richard's SUV and drove the short distance to the York residence.

"Wow! He made good time!" Lee exclaimed as he pointed out Steven Diblassio's black vehicle.

Parking Richard's vehicle in front of the garage, they walked around to the back of the house. Lady was impatiently stamping her feet, but tolerantly allowed the strangers to approach her while they waited for Lee to return. She was tied in the shade, but she wanted to go home.

"Steve, this is Lee Norris, the man who helped me this morning, and this is his wife, Abigail. She's the counselor who's been working with some of the victims and has been attacked in the process herself."

"It's nice to meet both of you," Steven said as he shook their hands.

"She might be able to answer the questions we have about all the different bones in that second bag," Richard said.

Abigail had been apprised of their find so she was prepared with a possible explanation. "After the rituals where there has been a human sacrifice, they have to dispose of any evidence that they don't burn or eat. I've heard from several of the survivors that they distribute bones to some of the participants and each one is responsible to destroy or hide them. I've heard of some using garbage disposals and others just find a remote burial place. Carrie Sue's father probably used his rose beds. I would guess that the shack might have been Charlie Fletchers' dumping ground."

"Why would he dump them out there when he has all that acreage on his farm?" Lee puzzled.

"Maybe he's just being careful. I mean, he's got so much evidence on that property already with that five-sided rock. Dude went nuts around it when we went up there once."

"Five-sided rock?" Steven asked the question for the others who were out of the loop.

"It's a rock about this high," Abigail said and indicated its height with her hand near her hip. "They use it in the rituals. I'm sure a lot of blood has been shed on it."

Steven and Richard exchanged looks but they said nothing. Wheels were turning in their minds and more questions were forming.

"Any idea about the body?" Richard asked, thinking that she might have heard a rumor or had an inkling of some kind.

"They do human sacrifices at all the rituals around here as far as I know. The only recent deaths I know of are Barry Romanowski that Max told us about and Charlie Fletcher who just kind of disappeared after the shooting spree back in June." Abigail frowned as she processed the possibilities.

"What are you thinking?" Lee asked. He knew that look.

"Well, it's probably *not* Romanowski because they don't usually dump a whole body like that and especially not in a body bag. They'd be more likely to burn and distribute the leftovers. Charlie is one of them and he *could* have been sacrificed, but not if he was already dead."

"Didn't Sheriff Bynum say that Charlie had been shot?" Lee asked.

"He sure did," Richard affirmed. "I was there that day at the press conference. He said that he wasn't sure who shot him."

"I remember that. We were afraid that they'd try to pin it on Earl or one of us," Lee added.

"If that's Charlie," Abigail jerked her head toward the bag, "and he was shot, that might be why they didn't sacrifice him at a ritual. He was already dead."

"Our M.E. will be able to either rule out or identify him," Steven said confidently. "If we need to, we can request his medical or dental records." Looking at the bags, Steven added, "Well, I guess I'd better get this mess on the road."

"Let me help you load these bags and download the pictures we took. I have a couple other things for you in my bag," Richard said as he walked toward his backpack. He wanted to be sure that the chain of custody was maintained so that nothing could be questioned when they brought their cases before a judge.

19

Friday, August 17

"What have you got going today?" Abigail asked Lee as they finished their breakfast.

"I guess Reno and I will make our morning rounds. If something needs attention, we'll take care of it. Otherwise, I think I'll head to town to pick up some hay. The last time we were in the feed store I got some numbers off of the bulletin board. One of the guys has some hay for sale and he said he'd be around today. It's not too early to start filling up that barn for winter."

"Sounds like a lot of hot, sweaty work."

"Yeah," Lee said, and added playfully, "and the best part is when the wind starts blowing all the hay dust around and it blows down the back of my shirt and I get nice and itchy."

"Can't you wait until tomorrow? I could help you."

"Nope. I want to do it today so you don't have to."

Abigail was nearly brought to tears since she was accustomed to having to fend for herself. Ever since Darryl was killed over ten years ago, she learned to be very independent of necessity. "Thanks, babe, I really appreciate you. Have I told you today that I love you?"

"Why, no!" he said with simulated shock. "As a matter of fact, I believe that you have not."

"Well I love you, Lee Norris."

Leaning over, Lee kissed his bride of almost six weeks. "I love you, too, sweet. I'll see you later on this afternoon, right?"

"Right. I have a couple people to see at the church starting at noon so I'll work with Amy this morning."

Finishing the dishes, pulling some meat out of the freezer, Abigail finally made her way out to her truck. Amy was waiting on the front porch holding Princess back until Abigail was parked. Princess exuberantly waggled her way to Abigail. Everyone was her new best friend.

"She's a beauty! I'm so glad she's up here with you two, er, you three."

"We are too. It seems like I have a debt of gratitude so big that I can't express it adequately."

"A simple thanks will suffice. You don't know how long I've wanted to have a sanctuary for my survivors and look what God did! He's the One we need to be thankful to."

"Amen to that," Amy agreed as they got settled in the living room. "Oh! More good news! I have a job!"

"A job? Where? When did that happen?"

"Next door. Mr. York called me Saturday and asked if I could come down there at least once a week and do some light cleaning and some laundry."

"How cool is that!"

"I started Monday already. He's paying me twenty dollars an hour! Do you believe it? I only work a couple hours, but he said that he might need me for special projects sometimes, you know, like cleaning closets and stuff like that."

"Praise God! Well, are you ready to get started with the internal stuff?"

"Let's do it." Original Fuchsya Amy Bolton quickly displaced the host personality and greeted Abigail.

"Well, what are you sensing that the Lord wants us to address today?"

"I think we need to call in the stragglers first and then we need to see if this is the day that Host Amy integrates or not."

"How do you feel about that?"

"I'm a little nervous, but kinda excited at the same time. I mean, this has been the goal all along, right?"

"Saved, healed, delivered, and integrated. You are taking back your life," Abigail said with a triumphant expression. She reached forward with both hands as if she had grabbed an invisible object and pulled it back to herself.

"Host Amy is feeling about the same."

"Well, why don't we go after the stragglers first and then I can talk with her."

They spent a few minutes praying for the Lord to minister to any remaining personalities who were hidden or who might have hidden themselves for any number of reasons. Some were afraid, others were programed, and many were too little or too hurt to help themselves. Original Amy was amazed at the number of personalities that she was unaware of. When they were healed and integrated, she reported feeling fuller and more complete. She also reported having more bits of her history of which she had no prior knowledge.

"Wow! I had no idea what a screwed-up life I had. How did I survive it? Why didn't I die? The stuff that they went through should have killed us."

"That's the beauty of dissociation," Abigail said. She, too, marveled at the tenaciousness of these remarkable survivors. "God has a plan and a purpose for you; that's for sure."

"I guess so." She was not entirely sure about that. "Do you want to talk to Host Amy now?"

"If you think we're done with this."

Host Amy answered, "I'm here." The switch between the two principal personalities was almost imperceptible even to an expert like Abigail. That was a good sign. The final integration between them would not be like slam-dancing.

"You've been thinking about integration for some time now. How do you feel about it today?"

"I'm like Original. I'm anxious for it all to be done, and I know in my head," she tapped the right side of her head, "that it's going to be good, but this is all I've ever known."

"Would you consider doing a trial integration for a set period of time?"

"Yeah. I think that's less intimidating."

"Starting now?"

She gulped as she considered it. "Uh, sure. I mean, if Original is up for it, I'm good."

"Let's ask the Lord if there's anything that needs to be addressed in either one of you first. If we get the all-clear, then you two can let me know what you're comfortable with."

"Okay," she replied with obvious relief. "Lord, here we are again. Could You please do a check on me and Original and let us know if we're good to go? Amen."

Abigail waited several minutes before she asked, "What are you sensing?"

"I, er, we're sensing that we're supposed to do a trial integration for seven days."

"Great! The number seven represents completeness, maturity. Do you two want to pray, or do you want me to do the honors?"

"You!"

"I'm going to customize verses from the end of Ephesians two. Lord we are so pleased to ask You to knit these two amazing parts of Amy together for this trial period. Lord, I thank You for bringing these together who have been at one time separate from Christ, excluded, without hope, and without You for so long. Thank you that all those who were far off have been brought near because You are their peace and You made both groups into one and broke down the barrier of the dividing walls and have established peace by reconciling them in one body. Thank You that they have access through Your Holy Spirit to the Father and that they are no longer strangers and aliens but fellow-citizens with the saints and are of God's household. Thank You for fitting them together into a holy temple where Your holy presence can dwell. Bless them in this trial integration in the name of Jesus the Christ, amen."

Amy sat there in peaceful silence soaking in the enormity of the moment. "Thank You, Jesus. Thank You, Jesus. Thank You, Jesus."

Abigail's eyes were misting up as she, too, savored the significance of what had just transpired. Both of them had worked so hard and so long against a very determined foe who was not about to give up.

Embracing the baby in her womb, Amy whispered, "We're going to make it, David. We're going to make it."

"Yes, you will. This is huge!" They relished the moment and then Abigail glanced at her watch, stood and said, "Well, I've got to get rolling. I'm so proud of you. I can't wait to hear about your week."

This was a special day to celebrate a major turning point in Amy's life. The women embraced before Abigail packed up her bag and left for the church. Praising the Lord all the way there, she wished she could shout Amy's good news to the world. Pulling into the parking lot, she noted that Sherry Samuels was already there. Excellent! This was promising to be a great day.

Sherry Samuels had been struggling externally and internally. Unfortunately, her internal system was dominated by programed cult and demon-loyal parts. Despite Franky and Frankie's best efforts she ended up being lured to the ritual on the thirteenth just four days earlier. Because the cult had created most of the personalities within her system, Sherry hardly stood a chance. She was the focus of much of the masters' displaced anger.

The masters were infuriated at Abigail for freeing Carrie Sue and Amy and Max from their grasp and so they took it out on Sherry. No! They could not let another one of theirs be wrested from their grasp. They were frustrated beyond description.

Sherry's body was still stiff and sore. Franky and Frankie had been blocked from trying to prevent anything. Pious One was as well. Abaddon celebrated what he thought was a victory, but afterward he was dissatisfied. This was something new for him. *What's going on? It has to be that counselor!* He had strapped a knife to his forearm underneath Sherry's blouse prior to coming to the session.

Poised one seemed to be the host personality and usually greeted Abigail. Pious One seemed to switch in whenever Abigail opened with prayer. It would make sense that any spiritual activity or setting would trigger her presence. Abigail finished her prayer by asking the Lord to start them where they needed to start.

It was obvious that a young personality was present. Sherry's face rounded and wrinkles seemed to have disappeared.

"Hello. I'm Abigail. Who are you?"

"Sammy," replied a precocious child personality.

"Why are you here?"

"They call me the Narc."

"Really?" Abigail knew about observers. Many systems had three or four-year-old observers who stealthily moved around the internal system. They knew a lot, but often did not have the mental capacity to process what they saw or heard very well. Observers were some of the best allies to have.

"Is there something that you saw or heard that you think I might need to know about?"

"Yep." The Narc leaned forward and whispered, "That bad guy put a knife up his sleeve." He pointed to his left forearm and continued, "He said he wants to try to kill you again."

Abigail leaned forward and replied in hushed tones, "Oh, that is important. Thank you. I'm really glad that you're brave enough to tell me. Do you want to give it to me so no one gets hurt?"

"Uh, huh," he said quietly as he slipped the razor-sharp weapon from its sheath and handed it to Abigail. He disappeared as quickly as he had appeared.

Thank You, Lord! Abigail slid the weapon into her drawer and continued as if nothing had happened, "Would Franky or Frankie be available today?"

After shifting in her chair uncomfortably, the internal switch was made and Franky answered, "I'm here. Franky with a Y."

"I think your voice is slightly huskier than Frankie's, but I'm glad you told me because I'm not real used to the cast of characters in there yet," Abigail said light-heartedly. "I always joke that y'all need a rolodex because y'all look alike."

That elicited a slight but momentary half-smile from Franky. "It's been a rough week."

"I'm sorry. What can you tell me?"

"All I know is that somehow we got taken to a ritual. The one on the thirteenth. Monday, I think. Sorry, but we lose track of days."

"Understandable," Abigail sympathized. "Do you know how you got accessed? Is there someone inside that covers rituals that land on the thirteenth?"

Sherry's eyes briefly looked up at the ceiling and when they came down, one of them made contact with Abigail's eyes. Another personality had switched in. "I'm here," a tiny voice came out of the towering woman.

Ah, a classic switch. The majority of people with multiple personalities seemed to indicate a switch by some kind of eye movement, blinking, or fluttering. Many also changed their posture, while others might sigh or yawn.

"I'm Abigail. Who are you?" Abigail sensed that it was a child or young teen.

"Thirteen."

"Is that your name or your age?"

"Both."

"I guess that would make sense. Can I assume that you or one of the other thirteens got accessed and taken to the ritual?"

She startled noticeably at Abigail's insightfulness but answered, "Yeah, uh, yes. There were a bunch of us there this time."

Abigail had another Holy Spirit hunch, did a quick mental calculation and said, "I'm not trying to upset you, but I have a feeling that there might be at least four hundred of you."

"Who do you think you are trying to intimidate her like that?" an older, gruffer voice demanded.

"I'm sorry. I tried not to do that. May I assume that you are her protector?"

"I don't like your assumptions, lady."

"Please. I'm not your enemy. I'm just trying to help. I was told by Franky that you were at a ritual on Monday. From what I learned by working with others like you, that was a reasonable question."

The imposing personality settled down slightly.

On another Holy Spirit hunch, Abigail asked, "Are you Thirty-one?"

She was greeted with an icy glare from Sherry's right eye while the left one gazed at the wall. The personality was furiously thinking about how to respond. Finally, he said, "Yes. You're freaking me out. How did you know?"

Thank You Lord. She's softening. "It was what I call a Holy Spirit hunch. I haven't run into a lot of he/she's, but when I do, there are usually more than one in the system. I figured that since the thirteenth and the

291

thirty-first of each month are ritual days, and the numbers are reverses of each other, it might be another he/she situation."

"You're right," Thirty-one conceded with a defeated sigh. "There are about twice as many thirteens, but we're their protectors."

"And probably frustrated because you can't really figure out a way to keep them protected."

"Yeah, and every month we get another one to take care of."

"I really appreciate you being up front with me. I realize that it's not easy or safe for you. Please know that I get that, and I want to be as careful as I can so that there's no retaliation. It may be too late for that. I know that the cult is really ticked at me for trying to help Sherry and probably took it out on you."

"Yeah, it was particularly vicious this time," Thirty-one admitted. "They're really hurting. We saw what happened with Franky and Frankie and their group and we want help. I'm sorry I was so rude, it's just that I don't know who I can trust anymore – including myself."

"No problem. I totally get it. Let's see if we can get some relief to all the thirteens and thirty-ones. Are you familiar with the true Lord Jesus the Christ?"

"Yeah. We were listening in. Us he/she parts kinda stick together. By the way, all the thirteens are girls and all the thirty-ones are guys."

"I figured. If I needed a protector, I'd want a big, strong guy." Abigail half smiled briefly. "Are you up for starting with getting everyone healed, saved, and delivered? We'll decide about integration later."

"That sounds good, but I'm not sure what to do."

"No problem, I'll lead and you can pray in agreement as their representative leader."

"Oh no you don't lady!" a deep, angry voice cut in. In one menacing movement while Sherry leaped up from her chair, Abaddon reached for the hidden knife. "Wha-at!" Perturbed, he searched frantically for the missing knife.

"It's not there," Abigail said evenly. "In the name of Jesus the Christ, sit down."

"Who do you think you are? I can just as easily throttle you as stab you!"

"Calm down, Abaddon. Why are you so angry today? I thought we made some progress last time with the three-year olds getting healed."

"You were there! I saw you with my own eyes! You can't deny it. All this nice talk that you're doing and you're just as bad as the worst of them. At least they're honest about being Satanists."

"What in the world are you talking about? I was *where*?"

"At the ritual! You were at the ritual and you were telling them what to do to those kids."

"I can guarantee you that I was *not* at any ritual. Not on the thirteenth and not ever."

"It was you! It was you. You can't talk yourself out of this. I'm going to kill you one of these days for being such a hypocrite."

"If it was true, I'd want to kill me, too. But I promise you, I was not there and there *is* an explanation for what you saw."

"Well, I'd like to hear it. I know what I saw."

"Are *you* willing to give me truthful answers?"

"I always have."

"Were you co-conscious with Sherry on Monday when one of the thirteens got accessed?"

"I was around."

"Did the phone ring? Was there a visitor? How did someone contact Sherry and get a programed part to cooperate with them?"

"The phone rang."

"What happened then? Did anyone say anything?"

"No. Just some beeps and then the kid came out," Abaddon said flatly, but then he flared up again. "What's that got to do with you being there?"

"Maybe nothing, but I think it's important to find out what else you saw. Can you please tell me what happened next? How did you get to the ritual site?"

"Nothing happened. She was just, um, like in a trance. After dark, someone came to the door. He said a couple of words and she got in the car with the guy."

"Then what? Did he give her anything to eat or drink?"

"Not until after we got there."

"Do you remember feeling woozy and disoriented or was your focus sharp?"

He sighed a short sigh of concession. "It felt a bit surrealistic. I just wanted to sleep."

"Okay. You know that they use drugs to enhance their programing. Don't you think it's probable that they would want to kill two birds with one stone? They could mess with you and discredit me at the same time."

He reluctantly agreed that it was possible.

"Would you be willing to go back to the memory of that night and let me ask the true Lord Jesus the Christ to reveal the true identity of the woman who you think was me? If it was me, you're justified. If it wasn't, then you have a chance to be free. It's a win-win for you."

"Fine!" he snarled and folded his arms. "You do that."

"Thanks. You just focus on that memory and I'll pray a little and then shut up. You look around in the memory and let me know what you see, hear, or sense."

Getting no verbal response from Abaddon, Abigail prayed as succinct a prayer as she could manage with this hostile skeptic glaring at her through one dagger-throwing eye. Soon Sherry's eyes began to sweep back and forth across the floor in front of her. Her wall-eyed condition made it appear very jerky.

After a short while, Abaddon fixed his left eye on her and slowly said, "I saw your Jesus, or at least some guy in a white robe that I never noticed before, take a wig off of you, er, that woman. She had long, black hair underneath."

"Do you believe they did that to set us up?"

"Yeah, yeah. I do now." Abaddon was very close to sounding penitent. "But how do I know that *this* isn't a set up, too?"

"How does it feel? What's your gut telling you?"

"I don't know. I'm so confused. It makes sense both ways."

"Maybe it's hard to face the probability that darn near everything they said or did was twisted in some way. Maybe you're wondering if you can trust your own judgment about anything you saw or heard or did. Maybe that makes you think that you might want to jump ship. But maybe you're not so sure that you won't be jumping from the frying pan into the fire."

"Yeah, something like that."

"It's what they do," Abigail said gently. "Abaddon, I'm guessing that because of your name you were privy to all the pain-side events. That's a huge burden to bear and a lot of injustice to process. I don't blame you for being angry. Anyone would be."

Abaddon sat there silently. It was apparent that he was thinking as deeply and as freely as he was ever permitted to think.

"Is it all right if I lay out some possibilities for you?"

"Sure."

"I have a feeling that you can't ever go back after today. If you do, they'll know something's changed and you'll be a target."

"They already did. I mean, something's changed since that last time we met. If I killed you, I would have been restored to my former status. If not..."

"So, you now know where they stand. They will punish you and you might not survive this time. Are you interested in having the true Lord Jesus sequester you and Damon and some of the others in a safe place?"

"Yeah. I, er, we'd like that."

Abigail prayed for a much humbler Abaddon and whoever else the Lord might include. When they disappeared into some internal safe haven, Thirty-one resurfaced. They resumed their disrupted prayer session. When the system seemed as stable as it could be considering all the unfinished work ahead of them, they set up their next appointment, and Abigail took a short break.

Grace Jackson looked even more stunning than she had at their first meeting. She reported that she felt like a new woman. She made unapologetic eye contact and carried herself with a confidence that was not previously there.

"It's amazing," Grace reported, "people have been treating me differently all week. They ask what's different and wonder if I lost weight or changed my hair or something." She was anxious to work on her forgiveness issues so they launched right into it. After a successful session, Abigail set her next one up for two weeks out.

———————————

"So, how was your day?" Lee asked as they settled down to supper.

"I'd say it was pretty good. There were lots of break-throughs for everyone. I wish I could tell you everything, but I can't. I even got another knife to add to my collection."

"Abigail!"

20

Sunday, August 19

Amy went down to let the chickens out today. After the fluttering flock settled down to their cracked corn, she went inside to check the nests as usual. Sucking her breath in sharply, she exclaimed out loud, "an egg!" She blinked and did a double-take just to make sure that her wishful thinking had not tricked her. Abigail told them that they should start laying eggs soon. Approaching the nest, carefully picking it up, Amy carried her warm brown treasure almost reverently in cupped hands up the hill to the house.

"Carrie Sue! Carrie Sue! Come look at this!"

Thinking that her friend was calling her to look at something dangerous, Carrie Sue grabbed her pepper gel from the hook at the top of the stairs and quickly came down to the kitchen. "What? Are you all right?"

"Look! An egg! We have our first egg!"

"Oh! It's so pretty. I wasn't expecting a brown egg."

"Me either. Oh, we have to tell Abigail. She'll be so excited."

"She should get the first one," Carrie Sue added.

The ladies continued to talk about the newest preoccupation on the farm. At last some blessings and favor were manifesting in the lives of these survivors. They were finally beginning to cease looking over their shoulders for inevitable backlash. Nothing had ever been free. Nothing had ever been easy. Nothing came without a price.

Riding together, they went to church as usual. Sliding into the pew next to Lee and Abigail, Amy leaned over and whispered, "We have a surprise for you."

"Oh really?"

"You'll have to come up to the house after church. It's something you have to see."

"Okay." Abigail was intrigued, but she knew that the ladies were having fun with the surprise so she did not press them to tell her immediately. "We'll swing by right after church," she said as she looked to Lee for confirmation.

"Works for me," Lee said.

"We haven't had a get-together in a long time," Abigail added, "why don't we invite Gary's family over and have a cook out at your place, that is, if you don't mind. We have that package of frozen burgers and there are plenty of things in the garden we can scrounge up."

"That would be fun. A surprise party."

"Yeah, let's do it."

Gary and Cindy were on board. A little spontaneity never hurts.

The musicians were starting the first song and the congregation rose as one for a time of praise and worship. It was soothing to God's ears. It was a cacophony to the demons' ears.

"Good morning! It's so good to see everyone here today! I know that some are out on vacation but I see some visitors. We welcome each and every one of you," Pastor Spalding said with his characteristic enthusiasm. "Hey, why don't we do that awkward church thing and spend a few minutes greeting one another? And let's make our visitors feel welcome while I make one last announcement: Don't forget the back-to-school event Saturday at the Kingston United Methodist Church. Check your bulletins for details."

There was a low buzz as people moved around in their pews or stepped into the aisles to greet someone with a hug or a handshake. The congregation had been steadily growing over the last few months and Pastor Spalding attributed it to the work of the Ministerial Alliance. More unchurched believers were starting to attend church again. The other pastors noted the same in their congregations.

"This morning I'm going to be preaching out of Ephesians six. We'll start with the tenth verse." Pastor Spalding took a few minutes to read verses ten through eighteen. "Let me start with the first word that Paul says here – *'finally'*. He's at the end of his letter and he wants to make sure that the church at Ephesus gets this important teaching about being strong in the Lord. I think most of us are very familiar with this passage which features the armor of God. I know that there are some who say that Jesus took care of all the demons when He died on the cross and we don't need to battle them. Others say that demons don't bother Christians. Others see demons under every bush and think that they have to put their armor on every day. I mean they literally go through the motions of setting a helmet on their head, and slipping shoes onto their feet every morning." He mimed the actions of someone dressing up in armor, drawing chuckles from the congregation.

"We may have a wide variety of responses to this passage, but I want to focus on one question: If we have put on our armor as Paul instructs, how does it come off?" He peered intently into the faces of his beloved congregation and saw some puzzled looks.

"Let's dig in! The reason we put on the full armor of God is so that we can resist and stand firm against the schemes of the devil. He's the enemy, not the people that he and his demons use against us. Remember that! The enemy is the enemy." He paused to make sure they were catching this important point.

"Notice that each piece of armor is linked to a spiritual value. Loins girded with truth. Breastplate of righteousness. Feet shod with the gospel of peace. Shield of faith. Helmet of salvation." Pastor Spalding went on to point out that Paul was quoting Old Testament passages in his descriptions and that each one of them was an attribute of Jesus Christ. "He's Truth. He's Righteousness. He's the Prince of Peace. He grants us faith. He's our salvation." Seeing nods as people connected the dots, he moved on.

"Okay, are you ready to talk about how you lose your armor?" he asked as he leaned over the pulpit. "It doesn't evaporate overnight. It doesn't just disappear. How do you take your armor off? And, might I add, *why* would you take it off? Let me suggest that when you walk in deception and not truth, your loins are no longer girded. When you walk in unrighteousness, you blow holes in your breastplate. When you live in chaos and turmoil, you're not walking in peace. When you live in unbelief, your shield is down. If you don't have salvation, or perhaps, if you doubt your salvation, you've removed your helmet."

Moving down to the front of the auditorium, he concluded, "Folks, we have a fellow-believer in this congregation who does a lot of spiritual warfare and I'd like to quote her right now. She says, 'I never take my armor off; I wear it under my jammies.' I'd like to challenge you to consider any attitude or behavior that would make you more vulnerable. We are in a battle. Jesus has promised us that in this world we will have tribulation, but we are not to fear because He has overcome the world."

He invited the prayer team down to pray with anyone who wanted to do business with the Lord about this or any other issue. Musicians played softly as most of the congregation headed out into the steamy August afternoon.

The McCord's were the last to arrive at the farm, having swung by their home to get some play clothes for Traci and Bryan. As they piled out of the van they were greeted by Carrie Sue, Abigail, and Princess.

"You have a dog!" Traci squealed with delight.

"What's his name?" Bryan asked.

"Her. It's a girl dog. Her name is Princess," Carrie Sue corrected him with a laugh.

Princess was excited by the presence of the children. She yipped as she playfully knelt with her front legs down and her rear end up, tail wagging furiously. Hopping back and forth between Bryan and Traci as they ran in large circles around the back yard, Princess released her pent-up puppy energy in bursts of speed.

Gary and Lee manned the grill and talked about Gary's business and Lee's farm. Abigail and Cindy, Carrie Sue and Amy got caught up on their lives as they wandered through the garden and picked tomatoes and green beans. As they were setting the table, Amy told them about her new job next door and

Carrie Sue related the story of her mother coming into The Thrift Shoppe.

Gathering around the table, the chatter continued after Lee prayed over the meal.

"You two have been busy. How are you adjusting to living up here? And how are you after that awful attack?" Cindy asked.

"I'm okay. I was a bit worried about David, but he's great," Amy said with a big smile as she patted her growing belly.

"I'm just thankful that Lee thought about that pepper gel," Carrie Sue said. "You should have seen that one guy after he got a shot in the face!"

"I just hope they bring them to justice."

"Well, the Yorks are working on a bunch of evidence with their FBI friends," Lee said. "I got to meet one of them when I helped Richard haul in some evidence."

"Evidence?" Gary asked. He voiced the question that the rest of them also had.

"Are we supposed to talk about this stuff?" Lee asked Abigail, remembering the last time he had broken confidentiality.

"I don't see why not. All of us are involved in one way or another. I'm just worried about the little ears."

"Good idea. We'll wait."

"I won't tell," Bryan protested. He knew they were talking about him.

"I know you won't, buddy," Lee said as he reached over to tousle his hair. "Hey, why don't you ask Amy what her big surprise is?"

Eyes widening, Bryan sucked in his breath in anticipation. "You have a surprise?"

"I do. Do you want to come with me to get it so we can show everybody?"

"Me too! Can I come? I want to come too!" Traci added enthusiastically.

"Come on." Amy led the way to the kitchen leaving the others waiting. Opening the refrigerator, putting one finger to her mouth to remind them to keep it a secret, she brought out the egg carton with the lone brown egg.

"Ooh!"

"Can I touch it?"

"Sure. It feels just like all the other ones."

"Mommy will think it's pretty."

"Let's show them." Amy led her little parade back to the dining room where the curious adults were waiting for the big surprise. Setting the carton in front of Abigail, she said, "Open it."

Abigail eagerly opened the carton. She had been waiting for those chickens to earn their keep. "It's so cute. Look! Our first egg," she said as she turned the carton for the McCords to see.

"Well, what do you know?"

"How many chickens do you have?"

"Twenty."

"You are going to have all the eggs you need."

"Works for me!" Abigail said and looked at Lee. "Egg salad, boiled eggs, 'angeled' eggs, omelets, quiche, shall I go on?"

"Absolutely!" He joined in the big celebration for the small brown egg and the promises it held.

"Well," Gary said after a few more minutes, "I think it's time we head down the road."

"But we haven't seen the chickens yet," Traci protested.

"Okay. Let's walk down there and you can take a quick look and then we have to head back home."

Princess was exuberant as she romped alongside the six adults and two children until they got close to the chickens.

"Sit!" Amy commanded.

"Wow!" Lee said as he observed Princess' instant response. "I'm impressed. Good job training her."

"She's a really quick learner," Carrie Sue said.

"Actually, I think she needs to make an appointment with Abigail because she's kind of a co-dependent people-pleaser."

"Go slow, now," Cindy cautioned her children as they approached the wary chickens. "You don't want to scare them. They're not used to you."

Abigail peeked into the coop before she invited the children to follow her. Carrie Sue and Amy kept the coop as clean as could be expected with twenty birds. "Let's check the nests to see if there are any more eggs."

Bryan and Traci carefully stepped behind her and approached the nesting boxes. Bryan was too short to see inside, but Traci could see if she stood on tip-toes.

"Look!" she pointed excitedly. "I see one! Can I have it?"

Abigail looked at Amy and Carrie Sue. Who could resist a child's request?

"I see another one in the next box," Abigail said.

"Three? We got three eggs?" Amy was as excited as the children.

"Well, they're all the same age. They should all start laying this week," Abigail said. "I think that God loves

305

it when we share our blessings. We'll be getting more, so we'll send two home with you and keep the other ones for Amy and Carrie Sue."

"But you get the first one," Carrie Sue insisted.

While the ladies and children were fussing over the chickens and the eggs, Lee filled Gary in on what he and Richard found at the shack. They discussed the possible pressures that might come from the county judicial system as well as their spiritual foes.

"That sure was a timely sermon this morning," Gary remarked.

"No weapon formed against us will prosper," Lee responded.

"No weapon!"

Xerxes was weary of making the long drive to the fringes of his territory. Daggett and Darod were wary of his long drives into this region. Prinz' position had not yet been filled and they feared that an outsider would be brought in to manage things. They feared the retribution that was sure to come if they did not reclaim lost ground.

Xerxes was stymied by his inability to intimidate Landrum. *What is going on?* He was a man who was accustomed to getting pretty much whatever he wanted whenever he wanted it. This was new to him. Calling upon his upper echelon demons, he implored them for superior power and strategies with which to defeat those inferior trouble makers.

The men met in the windowless building and had their own worship service. Afterward they schemed as only master Satanists could. St. Barthowmew's Day and a Great Sabbat and Fire Festival was coming up on Friday. They plotted as only politicians and judges, prosecutors and sheriffs could. There would be future opportunities to disrupt the lives of Max Berryman and the York Creek Road neighbors.

Zorroz was exceptionally eager to wreak havoc on these people. But first he had to see something for himself. Rather than going through Kingston on his way back to Springfield, he turned down the back road that connected to York Creek Road. Calling his deputy, he questioned him closely about exactly how the man had disposed of Charlie.

"I don't think anyone will ever find him, boss. He's way off in the bottoms."

"I don't care what you think! Things have had a way of going south lately in case you haven't noticed!" Sheriff Bynum let a stream of curses fly and demanded, "I just need to know one thing: What did you do with the bag?"

21

Monday, August 20

Both Amy and Carrie Sue were up early to prepare for work. Amy was particularly excited about her new job. Carrie Sue was excited about her added responsibilities in the office which came with a small raise. They both wanted to let the chickens out that morning. The novelty of collecting eggs was yet another positive aspect of life for each of them. The novelty of living in a relatively safe and care-free situation was something that neither of them took for granted.

"Abigail's book says that they usually lay eggs every twenty-five hours at their peak of production."

"That's weird."

"Yeah, and that means that they'll start to lay later in the day. I think we'll probably need to check for eggs a couple times a day."

"Good idea."

"I'm going to have to read that chicken book she bought."

They were delighted to find another egg in one of the nesting boxes and one hen sitting in another box.

"Hoo, boy! It's a good thing we've been saving egg cartons! I have a feeling that we're going to need them."

They stowed their treasure in the refrigerator and then made their final preparations to get ready to go to work. Carrie Sue dressed up a little bit and Amy dressed down a little bit.

"See ya tonight." Carrie Sue called as she waved to Amy and headed down the driveway.

Although it always put her on edge, Carrie Sue was accustomed to seeing the sheriff or one of the deputies driving in the downtown area. Making the final turn around the one-way streets that circled the courthouse in the town square, Carrie Sue was distracted from looking for a parking place by flashing blue lights in her rear-view mirror. Panic grabbed her heart like a hawk pouncing on its unsuspecting prey.

"Oh, Lord! Help me!" It was the only prayer she had time to utter as she pulled into a parking place and reached for her wallet. Dropping from her heart to her stomach, dread struck like a hammer as thoughts registered about her precarious situation.

Sheriff Bynum blocked her in and took his sweet time sauntering up to her window. "Good morning, ma'am," he said politely with a barely disguised venomous undercurrent. "May I see your license and registration please?"

"Yes sir." Carrie Sue's stomach was about to empty its contents. *Surely, he wouldn't do something in broad daylight. Lord!* Handing the documents to the sheriff with visibly trembling hands she dared to ask, "Did I do something wrong?"

"You failed to use your turn signal at that last corner. Is this your correct address?"

Carrie Sue's heart sank. "No sir. I'm so sorry, I just moved recently and haven't gotten it changed yet." After giving him her new address, her heart sank even more. He definitely knew exactly where she lived. She looked miserable. Pitiful.

Passersby did not see the malevolent gleam in his eye. This man knew very little of compassion. He only knew what served him best. "I'll be right back."

Carrie Sue continued to pray under her breath. *God, I need help here. This guy's up to no good. Please don't let him throw me in jail... or worse.* The minutes were interminably long while she awaited her fate. She knew that he recognized her. How could he forget that she broke his hyoid bone on the night she escaped from the ritual?

Smiling his winsome political smile, Sheriff Bynum returned to her car and handed her documents through her open window along with a warning ticket. "I want you to have a very nice day, ma'am. You just be sure to update your license and other documents real soon. If you were ever to be in an accident, we wouldn't know how to contact your friend."

Carrie Sue sat in stunned silence for a couple of minutes as she processed the last ten minutes. *What is he up to? Was that a threat? My friend? Not my family? I've got to call Abigail.*

Carrie Sue called Abigail as soon as she got inside The Thrift Shoppe. Abigail called Pastor Spalding who called the Ministerial Alliance prayer chain. Abigail also called Cindy who told Gary. Finally, she told Lee and they prayed too.

Streamers of incense began to flow toward the throne of grace and the Heavenly Council. They prayed for protection. They prayed for justice. They prayed for the enemy's plans to be thwarted. Just like the messenger angel who immediately left heaven with an answer for Daniel, so angels were directed to the area. Just as Daniel's messenger was thwarted, so these warring angels encountered resistance. The Sovereign God dispatched His angels, mighty in strength to perform His word.

"Well, Princess," Amy said, "that leaves you and me for now. Do I need to tie you up today, or will you stay home like a good girl?"

Princess cocked her head and whined as if to say, "You shouldn't even have to ask me that since I'm an exemplary dog." She trotted around to the back deck and flopped down in its shade as if to emphasize her point.

"Fine. I'll leave you off the chain, but if you mess up, you know the consequences." Amy laughed at herself as the thoughts came up: *I used to talk to my inside personalities and felt normal. Now I talk to a dog as if she can talk back, I have conversations with my unborn baby, and I pray to an invisible God. And I'm supposed to be normal now?*

Amy was in a good mood as she finished tidying up the kitchen, got into her car, and drove next door. It seemed silly to take her car half of a mile to get one tenth of a mile to her neighbor's house. However, there was the matter of the hilly stand of woods and the barbed wire fencing that stood between their homes.

Ringing the doorbell, Amy waited a minute. David still walked somewhat guardedly these days and he moved carefully up to the door, peered through the little viewer, and unlocked it. "Come in. How are you today?" David York greeted her cordially. Martha got up from the couch and shuffled up behind him.

"Real good. We just got our first eggs yesterday," she announced since it was fresh on her mind.

"Oh?"

"Yeah. Abigail bought twenty chicks about four months ago. They're finally starting to lay."

"Oh, I remember my grandmother's chickens. Those eggs were the best! Deep yellow yolks! You can't beat 'em with those store-bought eggs. If you ever get too many to handle, we'd be glad to buy some off of you."

"I'll remember to tell Abigail," Amy said and then changed the subject. "So, what do you need for me to do today?"

"The same as last week except there might be extra laundry this week. You did a real good job and I just want to let you know that we appreciate it."

"Oh, you're welcome. I think it's a God-thing. I, um, well, I lost my job after I got pregnant and had to be on bed rest so the extra income really helps me." Amy was amazed at how she handled herself these days. There was no lost time. There were no voices inside her head. There were no other personalities switching in. *This must be what if feels like to be normal.* She relished the thought as she went through her cleaning routine.

Martha followed Amy around and scolded her as if she were her guest. "Now, honey, you don't have to do that. Come sit in the living room and I'll get you a cup of coffee."

Richard had been in the back bedroom all morning. He and his father had turned it into a command center of sorts. They had a large bulletin board on one wall with a number of items tacked onto it. They had large one-year calendar posters on another wall. One was for

2006 and the other was for 2007. Sticky tabs were used for uncertain dates. Documented events were written in color-coded ink.

Amy knocked lightly on the open bedroom door and asked, "Do you want me to vacuum the floor in here real quick?"

"Sure, I need to refill my coffee anyway. I'll be right back and then if you don't mind, I'd like to ask you some questions about some of this stuff."

"Sure." Amy efficiently vacuumed the room and felt the butterflies starting to flutter.

Turning off the switch and setting the vacuum in the hallway, Amy was ready to talk with Richard. This would have been a daunting encounter before full integration, but today Amy felt an unexpected amount of composure. She would have had difficulty making full eye contact before. Not today. Amy was relishing the positive changes. Normal.

"Mom said something about that big horse again yesterday. Did you have any trouble up there?"

"Not that we noticed. I think Princess would have alerted us, but then, we were at church in the morning. I can check the cameras after I get home and let you know if anything shows up."

"Thanks. I never know if it's the dementia or if she's really seeing things. It's kind of spooky; like she can see stuff in the spiritual realm or something."

"It wouldn't surprise me, but you'll have to ask Abigail about stuff like that," Amy replied thoughtfully and then added another quick thought. "You might check with Lee if anything ever shows up. He's a good tracker and can find hoof prints if there are any. I guess he got lots of experience when he had that big ranch in Montana."

"I might just do that. Let me know if you find anything and we'll go from there."

Richard enjoyed Lee's company and admired his character. Richard had few friends since he had been so immersed in his career. He hated to admit that he was lonely. Most of his romantic pursuits ended rather quickly because he was so involved in his work.

"What can you tell me about this Levi character?" he asked, looking at his notes. "Levi Blevins."

"He and I were from the same local area as far as I can tell. At least he always seemed to be at the same rituals I was. He's broken into my house, I mean, the trailer I used to live in before someone – probably him – burned it down. He and his buddies have beaten and raped me a couple of times. I'm pretty sure that he's trying to work his way up to be a master instead of some creep they call Herrak."

"Is that his last name?"

"Sorry. No. It's his cult name. I don't know what his street name is but I get the idea that he's pretty influential in government or politics or something. Abigail says that most of the upper level masters are."

"Go on."

"There's another master above him that they call Darod. I know they don't like each other. Actually, there's really no love lost between any of them. I think they all want to take over as the regional master since Prinz died."

"Prince?"

"P-r-i-n-z," Amy spelled. "I have no idea who he was except that he was sadistically vicious." Amy shuddered involuntarily. "I cringed whenever I went to one of the big rituals where he was in charge."

"Are you sure he's dead?"

"As sure as I can be about anything. They say he was way over one hundred years old. You probably need to talk to Abigail about the master levels and people living long and how they start dying after their victims start getting healed."

"I'll be sure to do that. I had no idea," Richard said as he scribbled more notes. "Is there anything else you can tell me about that Levi character? Max said they went to school together so I assume he lived around here at one time. Did you go to school with him, too?"

"No, I'm from northern Indiana originally. We moved a county over when I was a little kid."

"Do you have any way to prove that Levi attacked you? Would you happen to remember dates?"

"Sorry, I guess it would be my word against his. Abigail had me document stuff on a calendar but that got burned up with the trailer. I used to work at The Pizza Palace out there and he'd access me from there a lot. Abigail and Lee were with me at the hospital and saw him and his buddy when they were in the parking lot waiting for me to come out. I can get you a date on that night."

"Thanks, every little bit helps. It's the details that build a case."

"Well, I'd better get that last load out of the dryer and be on my way. I'll call you one way or the other on what I find on the cameras."

Amy stowed the vacuum cleaner in the hall closet and went to the laundry room. Martha followed her into the room and folded clothes alongside of Amy.

Martha either prattled on about things that made no sense to Amy or else lapsed into a hazy silence.

"I'll see you next week, Mrs. York," Amy said cheerily as she gave the elderly woman a brief hug.

David thanked her and placed an envelope in her hand as he walked her to the door. "Be careful, now."

Amy was pleased to see Princess shoot across the front lawn in a gloriously happy blur as she sped from wherever she had been sitting in the back. *So, you were a good girl.* Parking the car, opening the door, she vigorously scratched Princess behind the ears, "You're such a good girl! Are you ready to take a walk?"

Princess would agree to anything and yipped her affirmation.

"Let's go." Amy walked down the trail to the end of the pasture. She would have called it waddling at twenty-six weeks pregnant. Deftly removing the SD card, Amy pocketed it and then made the rounds to all the other cameras. Princess kept her inquisitive nose to the ground and broke away from Amy's side to chase down various scents and one hapless squirrel.

Settling down in front of the computer, Amy found the proper slot and inserted one of the SD cards. Scrolling through the first one that covered the parking area, she giggled as she saw images of Princess greeting anyone and everyone who came up to the house. "Wait! What's this?" Amy paused and looked closely at the image before her. A man was squatted down at the post across the driveway. "That's the phone box! What's he doing there?"

Several frames later he was looking surreptitiously around before he walked back down the driveway. The range and angle limitations of the camera did not permit Amy to see if he walked to a vehicle or not. I need to copy this and get it to Abigail. And Richard. *Dang! What was the date?* Amy scrolled through the images and found July 29, 2007 11:06 a.m. on the bottom. Looking at the calendar, she ascertained that it was a Sunday. *Humph! He knew we'd be at church.*

Amy's stomach lurched. "We've got to call Abigail!" Amy declared emphatically to David. Without looking at any more frames or any of the other SD cards, Amy rushed to the phone and tapped out Abigail's number. *Ooh! Answer the phone!* After the third ring, Amy hung up and searched for Lee's cell phone number.

"What's up?"

"Oh, Lee, I'm so glad I got you. Can you and Abigail come up here?" Amy stopped abruptly as she realized that if the phone line was tapped, she would alert the eavesdroppers. "I, uh, well, I really need help with something right now. I don't want to risk hurting myself or David."

"Sure. I'll find Abigail and we'll be right up." Lee caught on to her need for secrecy and wondered if she were in danger or trying to speak in code for some other reason. He'd be ready either way.

"Thanks." Amy hung up and heaved a great sigh of relief and then breathed a frustrated, "Oh, God! Just when I start to feel safe and normal!"

Lee and Abigail were soon looking at the SD card images with Amy.

"Why did you decide to pull the cards today?" Abigail asked.

"Oh, I was cleaning at the Yorks this morning and Richard asked if we had any trouble up here yesterday because his mom was talking about that big horse again. I told him that I'd check the cameras and let him know if I saw something."

"Good thing you did."

"Sorry I didn't think of doing it sooner. I mean, someone probably has the house phone tapped."

"I'm sorry. I should have either done it or reminded you. We're all responsible. It looks like we have a new chore to add to the list, eh?"

"Let's see what shows up on the other cards," Lee said. "Do you mind if I take over?"

"Please do!" Amy gladly relinquished her seat.

"While he's doing that, why don't you show me how the nursery is coming along?"

Amy was grateful for the diversion. "Well, not much has changed since the last time, but Carrie Sue has been bringing home some really cute clothes from The Thrift Shoppe." Opening the closet, Amy carefully pulled out a number of little blue plastic hangers with mostly blue outfits on them.

They oohed and aahed over tiny shirts and miniature coveralls as they envisioned David wearing them in about three months. Abigail momentarily flashed back to those happy days when she did the same thing in anticipation of the birth of each of her sons. Quickly doing the math, she realized that they would have been twenty, eighteen, and sixteen this year. They would probably have had sons of their own in a couple of years. *I would have been a grandmother.* That thought momentarily jolted her and brought her back to the present with Amy.

"Hey! Come see this!" Lee shouted from the front bedroom-turned-office.

Looking over his shoulders, Amy and Abigail said in unison, "The big horse!"

"Who's riding it?"

"What's the date and time?"

"11:02 a.m. on August 19, 2007."

"Yesterday!" Amy gasped. She was surprised, but knew that she should not be. "Go figure! While we were at church."

"Well, at least he didn't come onto the property; he was heading out to the woods. I'll keep scrolling in case he came back the same way," Lee said.

"Maybe we'll be able to figure out who he is."

"I'll bet Richard or his FBI buddy has equipment that can do that."

Lee did not find any images of the returning rider. None of the other SD cards had anything suspicious on them. After copying the pertinent images onto a thumb drive, Lee asked, "Do you want me to put these back into the cameras for you?"

"I'll do it. But first I need to call Richard and let him know that we found something."

"How about if I do that from my cell while you take care of the cameras up here? I'll take care of the one down there. I'd like to chat with Richard again, so why don't you just let us take it from here?"

"Works for me!" Amy was beginning to feel a little bit safe again. Protected. Cared for.

"I'll help you, Amy," Abigail offered, "and then I'll go with Lee down to the Yorks'. We'll let you know if anything comes of it."

"Sounds like a plan."

Amy and Abigail replaced the SD cards around the house which gave them an opportunity to talk some more about the pregnancy and the latest ultrasound.

Princess was torn between going with Lee or Amy, but finally opted for romping in the pasture. After Abigail took care of the cameras she strolled over to the faded gray casing that held the phone wires. She noted that it had an official looking seal on it. There were some wires that went from the bottom of the box into the disturbed ground.

The ladies also took the time to stop by the chicken coop where Amy happily collected more eggs. "Oh, I forgot to tell you – Mr. York said that if we ever get too many eggs to handle, he'd love to buy some off of us."

"You know, I never really considered selling eggs, but I think that if we have twenty chickens laying eggs nearly every day, eventually we'll have about ten dozen eggs a week. That's plenty for all of us to eat with enough to give some away and some to sell, too. That way they'll at least pay for their feed."

"Ready?" Lee asked Abigail as they met up by the truck. The new and intriguing scents kept Princess busily circling and sniffing everything. "Richard is expecting us."

"I sure am. Catch you later, Amy."

Following the same half mile route that Amy had driven earlier, they were greeted by Richard who was standing on the front porch waiting for them. Ushering them into the back bedroom, Richard explained what he and his father had been working on. The pair were amazed at the organization and the extensiveness of the project.

"Well, we have another piece of evidence here," Lee said as he dangled the lanyard holding the thumb drive from his thumb and index finger. "Your mother was right. Someone rode that big horse behind your place and headed out to the river bottoms yesterday."

"11:02 while we were all in church," Abigail added. "Tell him about the phone box."

"Oh?" Richard took the thumb drive. "Let's have a quick look."

"It looks like someone came up there a couple weeks ago – on a Sunday morning again – and tampered with the phone wires in that box by the driveway."

"Hm." Richard was thoughtfully processing the new items. "It sounds like they're not letting up. I'm not sure what they're up to, but we can sure find out."

"Oh, that reminds me!" Abigail blurted, "Carrie Sue called and said that Sheriff Bynum pulled her over this morning and gave her a warning ticket for failure to use her turn signal and for not updating her license with her new address."

"He also gave her some kind of a veiled threat," Lee added. "She's pretty shaken up and not really looking forward to her drive back home."

Richard took in the recent report about Carrie Sue and then turned to the subject at hand. "I've got some software that can clarify those images. We can ID these guys. If you don't recognize them, I'll forward it to Diblassio." Richard busied himself with pulling up the images of the man on the large horse. After tweaking them with his software, the three of them found themselves staring into the face of none other than Sheriff Bynum.

"Well, I'll be.   I wonder what he's doing riding Charlie Fletcher's horse," Lee mused.

"I don't know if he's desperate and careless or if he's pompous and over-confident."   David York said. He had stepped into the room in the middle of their conversation.

Richard had a hunch.   His hunches were usually accurate.   "I don't suppose you want to saddle up again and see what we can find out," Richard asked Lee. *I'll bet he goes right to the shack.*   "It hasn't rained so the tracks should be fairly easy to follow today. Amy said you're an experienced tracker."

"I've done my share of tracking."   Looking at Abigail, he said, "Are you up for an adventure?"

"Wouldn't miss it! That is, if it's okay with Richard. I don't want to get in the way or anything."

"You'll be fine.   Besides, you know the trails better than we do. That might come in handy. We can look at the phone box on our way back in."

It took less than an hour for Lee and Abigail to drive home, change into riding clothes, update Amy, grab water and snacks, groom and saddle three horses and get back to the York residence. Lee was riding Lady and Abigail was on her beloved Buster. Richard had his backpack ready and easily climbed onto Misty's broad back.

Lee led the way and easily picked up the large-hoofed horse's tracks at the edge of York Creek. Richard and Abigail kept a twenty-foot distance between themselves and Lee in case he lost the trail and had to back-track. Lee picked up the pace once they hit the well-worn trail that skirted around the tree-filled bog and followed the edge of the field. Entering the woods at the far end of the field, he slowed down again. There was more debris on the trail and there had also been some four-wheelers on the trail very recently.

Patiently following the leads and noting that the tracks went both ways on this section of the trail, Lee brought them through a couple of muddy stream beds and down the trail that headed west. He had been down this trail before; one time with Abigail and his daughter and several more times to see the shack.

"Wait right here," he instructed as they approached the clearing. "I want to walk the perimeter just to make sure that he didn't keep going."

"What happened to the shack?" Abigail asked as she looked toward its place. "It looks like someone broke into it."

"It sure does," Richard agreed.

"This is where he came," Lee announced. "He was here for some time. Look at all the horse droppings. I would guess that he was here at least an hour." He pointed to a place where it was obvious that a horse had been grazing and left droppings.

Richard dismounted and handed his reins to Abigail. Opening his backpack, he pulled out his camera and snapped a number of pictures from several angles. Once he was satisfied that he had enough of them, he moved closer and looked for footprints or any other tell-tale evidence. Finding only some boot prints, he photographed them before he extended a collapsible spade and lifted the trap door in the floor once again.

Using his flashlight, he confirmed that the now empty space was virtually the same as it was when he and Lee left with the body and the bag of bones.

Peering over his shoulder, Lee said, "I'll bet he's in a bit of a panic right about now."

"No doubt. Maybe that's why he put the pressure on Carrie Sue this morning," Abigail surmised.

"We better warn the Milners and make sure that we're all watching our backs," Lee responded.

"And each other's," Richard added.

They bunched up on the ride back and talked about the case. Richard had not gotten DNA test results back from the FBI lab yet. He had kept in touch with Agent Diblassio and had a few more pieces of the puzzle confirmed. Finding the spot at which Bynum veered off the out-bound trail, Lee stopped and studied the hoof prints.

"I think these tracks will just lead back to Charlie Fletcher's place. Is there any reason we should make sure?"

"None that I can think of. It was important just to know that he went out there. That ties him to the evidence." Richard had taken the time on the way out to photograph hoof prints. It would not really prove anything, but it might establish the pattern that his mother had detected: the large horse in the vicinity meant trouble.

Riding up through Abigail's pasture and past the farmhouse, the trio made their way to the telephone box. Princess had raced down excitedly to greet them and escorted them all the way up to the house. The clomping of the hoofs made a rhythmic sound as the hot, sweaty horses plodded along.

Once again Richard unpacked his camera and took pictures. The seal had been broken. "If it was a legitimate lineman, he would have sealed it back up again. I'd suggest that you notify the phone company." Pointing at the wires coming out of the bottom of the box, he stated, "I believe that there's only supposed to be one ground wire. You've got two coming out. I'd say your phone is bugged."

22

Wednesday, August 22

Carrie Sue's nerves jangled just thinking about going to work each morning. There always seemed to be a deputy or Sheriff Bynum lurking around the square. She had taken a lunch hour to update her documents so she had no concerns about the warning ticket, but she never knew when they would pull her over for some other real or contrived reason. It was more than just a warning ticket. It was an intentional warning delivered by Zorroz himself.

"I'll tell you what I'd do," Amy suggested. "They know your routine. Why don't you park somewhere else for a while? There are plenty of public parking lots all around there."

"Good idea, A," Carrie Sue replied, using her nickname. "I don't know why I didn't think of that. It's so simple. Duh!" She smacked her forehead with the heel of her hand. "Maybe I can go in a bit early some days, too."

"Yeah. You start messing with them for a change!" Amy's infectious mischievousness prevailed and she pulled a reluctant smile from her friend.

Amy puttered around the house cleaning the already immaculate home. Her cleaning habits were quite a change from the days in which all the internal characters kept her home in chaos.

It was hot enough that they left the air conditioner on all the time now. Being pregnant in August was not very comfortable, but Amy was so grateful that she was carrying David and that he was mature enough to survive even if there was another threat to the pregnancy. Noting that her feet were beginning to swell toward the afternoon, Amy made it a habit to elevate them when she took a nap.

Abigail made it a habit to leave her cell phone turned on just in case Amy or Carrie Sue needed her. Feeling the vibration in her pocket, Abigail fished it out and answered the call. "What's up?"

"Oh, nothing urgent," Amy said. "I just wanted to use up some of these eggs and I wonder if you can teach me how to make a squash quiche. We're getting about half a dozen a day! Eggs, that is. Do you believe it? Oh, and we have a bunch of squash coming in, too."

"What a wonderful problem," Abigail said as she looked at the time. "We have enough time to do it right now if you want. Lee and I are planning on going to church tonight."

"Works. Carrie Sue and I are going to be heathens tonight. She's still a bit leery about going to town and my feet are swollen."

"No problem," Abigail laughed. "Making a baby is hard work. Listen to your body and don't worry about being at church every time the doors are open."

Abigail brought her own casserole dish so they baked both of them at the same time. It was rewarding to see Amy's progress in so many areas of her life. Bantering and chatting in the midst of their parallel chopping and grating, mixing and layering, they soon had two dinners made in one easy cooking lesson.

Lee and Abigail enjoyed their quiche and then headed to church together. Sliding into their usual Wednesday night pew situated closer to the front of the church, Lee and Abigail anticipated the devotional and subsequent prayer time.

"Good evening, folks," Pastor Spalding welcomed the small but growing Wednesday night group. "I'm so glad to see so many of you make it out here on this hot August night." After opening with prayer, he had them turn to Genesis. "I'm just fascinated with this book and I want to follow up with some random thoughts about Adam and Eve. How many of you are maybe a little miffed that the first two people on this planet managed to screw it up for the rest of us?"

Noting the smiles and nods, he continued, "How many of us think that we might have done any better?" He gave them a minute to process their thoughts and then laughed when he saw no raised hands. "Yeah, me neither. Let's take a closer look at the circumstances surrounding the fall both from Adam's point of view and from Eve's."

He read from the end of Genesis two and the beginning of Genesis three, pointing out some of the salient points which got people thinking. "So, we have Adam who just named all the animals for God and realized that there was no mate, no helper, no female who was suitable for him. He was lonely. I don't know about you, but I think God set him up. God didn't make a mistake. He didn't say, 'Whoops! I forgot to make a woman to go with the man.' I believe that He wanted Adam to realize his need. I mean, sometimes we guys need to be smacked up-side the head to get something!"

After drawing a few nods and light laughs, Pastor Spalding continued, "Let's look at what Eve did. I have to believe that the couple was pretty much inseparable and it does say that Adam was with her when she ate the fruit. It was the tree of the knowledge of good *and* evil. Is it possible that Eve thought that she was picking a fruit of the knowledge of good without realizing that the knowledge of evil was intrinsically linked to it? I mean, how many of us have justified a bad choice by pointing out the good that came with it? Like the guy who cheats on his taxes and justifies it by giving a larger tithe, or the person who skips church so he can spend quality time with his family."

Again, the congregation puzzled over questions that many of them had not thought to ask. "I've mulled over this since our last study and my biggest question is still this: Why didn't Adam smack that piece of fruit out of her hand? Why didn't he stop her? Why didn't he send the serpent packing? *He* was not deceived; she was. Could it be that she just made an impulsive decision and quickly took a bite? How long was the gap between the time she ate and the time he ate?"

Again, he paused before he asked another question. "Remember that Adam knew that in the day they ate of it, they would surely die. After she ate, he may have thought, 'Oh, great! I finally get a suitable mate and now she's going to die. I might as well join her.' He didn't know if it would be an instant death or not. Folks, we weren't there so we don't know for sure. I just know that ever since the Fall, men have failed in similar ways and women have failed in similar ways. We can't point fingers, but we can continue to take dominion in our areas of jurisdiction as men and women, husbands and wives. Without stereotyping anyone, let's pray for men to be the providers and protective leaders in the family and for the women to be submissive and discerning nurturers."

Pastor Spalding brought up one more issue for them to contemplate. "Folks, when it said that their eyes were opened, it didn't mean that they were closed before. It means that their pupils enlarged. They were walking in light so the pupils were constricted. Now they were walking in darkness and their pupils had to dilate just like when we walk from the light to the dark in a natural setting."

"I always wondered what that meant," Maggie commented.

"That makes sense," another remarked.

Pastor Spalding opened the floor for more questions and comments before they broke up into small groups and prayed for the individual needs within each respective group. Afterward, Lee and Abigail found Pastor Spalding and apprised him of the latest developments including Ariel's positive identification of Susan Wagner as the lady who had abducted her.

"What's going to happen with that?" Pastor Spalding asked.

"We're not sure. Richard says that he has a plan in the works, but that the timing of things might get a bit tricky. He doesn't want to tip his hand if the rest of the evidence isn't ready yet. He's trying to coordinate things with Agent Diblassio."

"That makes sense. I just wish these evil people would get saved. If they can't," he hesitated over the difficult words that he did not want to utter, "then I wish that God would remove them from the face of the earth so they can't do any more damage."

"Same here," Lee agreed emphatically.

"It's sad, but they get to choose. Amy and Carrie Sue were raised in it and they made their way out. Max got out. We'll keep praying and working with the ones who try to escape," Abigail added. "And I know Carrie Sue has been praying for her mother. She was hoping that without her father around to program her and keep her involved with the cult, she would have softened by now."

"We'll keep praying for all of them. That's all we can do. Well, you folks have a blessed evening and I'll see you Sunday." Pastor Spalding shook Lee's hand and turned his attention to another couple who approached him.

Lee and Abigail headed home with the windows open with the slightly cooler air blowing around the cab of the truck. They discussed the devotional. "What if Adam never took a bite and Eve was lost?"

"Good question," Lee answered. "Would God have had to create another wife for him? How many ribs can a guy stand to lose?"

———————

Carrie Sue answered the phone when she saw the Springfield Hospital identification.

"Is this Carrie Sue Wagner?" the professional-sounding voice asked.

"Yes."

"I'm calling from the Springfield Hospital. We found your name in Susan Wagner's wallet."

"That's my mother." Carrie Sue's senses were on high alert. "Is she okay?"

"Would you be able to come to the emergency department? She was asking for you. She asked me to call you."

"Uh, sure. It might take me a little while to get there, but I'll be over as soon as I can." Carrie Sue punched the red button that ended the call. *Oh, Lord, is this a trick? Is this a set up? What's going on? Is she dying or did she finally total that stupid truck?* She sat and prayed for a few moments longer because she was so reluctant to go to her mother. *Humph! Which mother?*

"Amy?" Carrie Sue called out from her room.

"Yeah. What's up?"

"I just got a call from the Springfield Hospital. Someone said that my mother's in there and they wanted me to go there because they found my name and number in her wallet."

"Why would your mother have your name in her wallet? Did you give her your number?"

"I don't know. It sounds fishy because she also said that my mother asked for me; but then, she has that other personality that got the new will made. I don't know; it just didn't sound right to me. I'm not sure what to do."

"Call Abigail."

"Of course." Carrie Sue looked at her watch and noted that it was getting close to eleven o'clock. "It's kind of late."

"She won't mind. If you don't call her, I will. You can't go there alone."

"You're right. I'll call."

Abigail insisted that she and Lee pick Carrie Sue up and take her there. Her spiritual antennae were also on high alert and probing. Within fifteen minutes they were rolling up the driveway to the old farmhouse. Carrie Sue was waiting on the front porch with Amy and Princess.

Scooting in next to Abigail, Carrie Sue buckled up and started to chatter nervously. "They didn't say what was wrong with her. I don't know if she wrecked that monster truck or if there's something really wrong. The last time I saw her, she looked awful. She's been going downhill with her health. It sure isn't because she's grieving dad."

"Well, your father went downhill after you got significant healing. Maybe that's what's going on with your mother. The time frame jives."

"I hadn't thought of that since bio-dad was one of my main perps. It makes sense that he died, but now, well, maybe I have to rethink her role in all of this. Maybe she was as evil as Dad." Carrie Sue was deep in thought as she pondered this development. Lee's voice jarred her back to the present situation.

"If you don't mind, I think we all need to go in there together," Lee said as he parked the truck in the partially filled lot near the emergency entrance. They walked into the nearly empty waiting area together.

Carrie Sue's jitters were obvious as she nervously approached the desk.

"May I help you?"

"Someone called me here because of my mother. Susan Wagner. She told me to come to the emergency department."

Jutting her head forward as she scrolled down a computer screen, she said, "I'm sorry, I don't have a Susan Wagner listed here. W-a-g-n-e-r?" she confirmed as she spelled it out.

"Yes. Okay, I, um, maybe I'm at the wrong hospital. Sorry to bother you." Carrie Sue backed away from the desk, partially shocked and fully perplexed. Turning and looking with wide eyes at Abigail and Lee who were standing a short way back, she shrugged her shoulders and held her empty hands out in an I-don't-know-what's-going-on-here gesture.

"She's not here?"

"Call Amy!" Lee ordered Abigail as they walked out to the parking lot. "This might be a set up for her. I'm calling Richard."

"Something's fishy!"

They each punched in numbers as they rushed to the truck. Carrie Sue could catch bits of each conversation. Amy had called Princess inside because she had been barking at something in the front yard. Amy assumed that it was just a raccoon or an opossum.

Richard responded on the first ring, "Hello!"

"Sorry to bother you, but we think Amy might be in danger. She's up there alone. I'll tell you more when we get there, but could you go up and make sure that she's okay? She knows we've called you. We should be there within twenty minutes."

"Not a problem." Richard was already pulling on his bullet proof vest and fastening the tabs. Throwing a shirt on over it, he checked his weapon and finished dressing in efficient, practiced moves.

Rapping lightly on his parents' bedroom door, he whispered, "Dad, I'm going next door. Something might be up."

"Be careful, son."

Amy had turned off the inside lights so she would not be silhouetted as she peered out into the darkness.

Walking carefully from window to window, she peeked out and saw nothing. None of the motion sensor lights were triggered. Nothing was visible within the arc of the yard light out back.

Greatly relieved by the double toot of Richard's vehicle, Amy dared to relax. He triggered motion sensor lights and cameras and he, too, saw nothing obvious with his headlights as he drove up. Directing his powerful flashlight all around the edges of the property as he walked around the house, he managed to scare up an owl. Nothing.

Amy had cracked the front door and set off the porch lights. "Richard, thanks for coming. I haven't seen anything, but Princess was going nuts earlier."

"Well, it might have been a raccoon. I scared up an owl just now."

"Sorry to drag you out in the middle of the night."

Chuckling lightly, he replied, "You didn't; Lee did. They should be here pretty soon."

Just as Lee predicted, they rolled up the driveway within twenty minutes. They congregated on the front porch and rehashed the phone call and the time line of the evening's events. Richard and Lee paired up and walked the path around the perimeter of the property with Princess. Flashlights probing and crisscrossing the front yard, the pasture, and the woods, they returned satisfied that it was a false alarm.

"Well, better safe than sorry," Lee said.

"Absolutely," Richard agreed. "Call me any time."

The ladies were much calmer and assured everyone that they would be fine. They'd either call or use the SOS signal if necessary. Lee and Abigail turned around and went home. Richard did the same.

335

"Where's Reno?" Lee asked as they rolled up their driveway. Normally the dog would greet them. The porch light and the yard light revealed nothing.

"Something's not right. We would have awakened him if he was sleeping."

"You stay in here and lock the truck. I'm going to check around."

Abigail could hardly restrain herself but she knew that Lee was right. If something was amiss, it would be wiser to stay here where she could call for help or provide back up. *Good thinking!* Abigail slid Walther from her holster, chambered a round, and carefully replaced it. She pulled Richard's number up and had it ready to speed dial just in case.

"Reno! Reno! Where are you, buddy?" Lee called out as he shined his flashlight around the property.

Hearing a faint barking and some scratching sounds coming from one of the weathered old sheds, walking toward it, senses on high alert, Lee focused on the door as he scanned his surroundings. "How'd you manage to get yourself locked up in there?"

As Abigail followed Lee, faint movement at the periphery of her vision caught her attention. Two men suddenly rushed out of the shadowy darkness. They went after Lee. Reno barked and clawed frantically. Unknown to Abigail, another man had slipped behind the truck.

"Lee!" Abigail screamed through the partly opened window. "Oh Jesus! Help!" Remembering to punch in Richard's number, she impulsively jumped out of the truck.

Having sensed their presence, Lee quickly whirled and caught the first man in the side of his neck with a high side-kick. The attacker went down in a stunned heap. The second man hesitated at the unexpected counter-attack, but his impetus carried him into Lee. Deftly side-stepping the weak punch, grabbing the man's forearm, pivoting, bending sharply at the waist, Lee flipped the man over his shoulder. He wryly noted that his martial arts training was coming back.

Hearing a satisfying grunt as the wind was knocked out of the man, Lee dropped onto his chest and smashed his jaw with a powerful punch. Making sure that the first man was still incapacitated, he caught movement at the side of the truck.

"Abigail!"

The third man had managed to grab Abigail. Her shouts were muffled by his gloved hand. Kicking and punching, elbowing and clawing, Abigail slowed her would-be abductor down. Lee easily caught up with them as they neared the edge of the tree line.

Shoving Abigail roughly to the ground in front of the charging Lee, the man turned and ran toward his four-wheeler. Lee hurdled Abigail, tackled the man, and drove him into the ground. Slipping a quick and effective choke hold on the man, Lee efficiently subdued him just as Richard York arrived and rapidly assessed the situation.

"Watch this guy!" Lee shouted. "Two more over there!" Lee pointed toward the shed as he ran back to Abigail.

Richard secured the semi-conscious man who had been tackled and then moved to the shed area. Their shocked bodies and numbed brains were still able to register the fact that Richard's weapon was at the ready. They had just enough sense to remain on the ground.

Lee lifted the now trembling woman up and wrapped her in a huge hug. Planting a kiss on her forehead, he said, "So it *was* a set up. They were setting *you* up."

Abigail's knees went weak as she absorbed the thought. They were going to abduct her and without a doubt, do unspeakable things to her at the next ritual. She probably would not have survived. "Oh God," Abigail breathed as she grasped the reality of the situation.

"Come here and sit in the truck," Lee insisted. Walking her over to the truck, he helped her into the passenger seat. Noticing her phone on the ground, he picked it up and handed it to her. "Nice work."

"Team Norris!" Abigail grinned at Lee who was reassured by her returning spunk. "I would have taken that guy out, you know."

"Right!" Lee chuckled with relief. "Let me get Reno and then see what we need to do with those guys."

Unlatching the creaky old shed door, Lee quickly determined that Reno was unscathed. He released him and wondered why they didn't kill him. Perhaps he was used as a decoy to separate Lee and Abigail. It almost worked. Hearing Abigail's call, Reno shot over to the truck where the two of them commiserated about their ill-treatment.

Richard had all three miserable and somewhat damaged men handcuffed where they had gone down. Moving out of ear shot of the three men, he walked back up to the truck. "What happened here?" Richard assessed the damage to the three men and noted that

Lee was barely ruffled. *Who are these people?* "By the way, nice tackle. How'd you get those two?"

Pointing at the man near the four-wheelers, Lee said, "That was college football coming back. My martial arts training kicked in for the first two guys. Maybe I'm not as rusty as I thought."

"I'd say not."

Lee gave his initial assessment. "I guess Abigail was the target. *That* was the set up. They knew we'd go with Carrie Sue. That gave them time to get positioned down here. They jumped us when we got back."

"Interesting. Amy said Princess had been barking at something out this way earlier. It must have been them. Let me get a hold of Diblassio and Landrum," Richard said as he moved slowly to his SUV speed-dialing as he went. After lengthy phone conversations, Richard rejoined Lee and Abigail and Reno.

"Diblassio is on his way. He said that he's going to start charging me by the mile." Richard provided them with much needed comic relief.

"What do we do with this mess?" Lee asked as he gestured with his palm up, in an arc that included the three men and the three four-wheelers.

"Let me get my kit and I'll do some preliminary processing. I have a feeling that Diblassio will want to do a turn around."

A few hours later, Steven Diblassio and his partner rolled up the driveway in an unmarked full-sized van. "You remember James?" Steven asked Richard.

"Sure do! Thanks for coming."

The three men huddled over the information that Richard had obtained from the driver's licenses. Steven tapped into his high-level data base and was astounded to discover that two of the men were deputy sheriffs. James took official statements from Lee and Abigail. Richard would interview Carrie Sue and Amy, and follow up on the call from the hospital.

"We'll take these men into custody and charge them with several felonies in connection with our federal investigation. When one person does it, it's a crime. When someone joins him, we've got a conspiracy. They're making it easier for us to prove our case."

"What about the four-wheelers?" Lee asked.

Steven contemplated his options and asked, "Is there some place around here that might rent a trailer? I'd hate to have to wait until they open in the morning, but if we have to, we will."

"I have a trailer sitting behind the barn. I won't need it right away," Lee offered.

23

Friday, August 24, Fire Festival

Satanists world-wide were priming their diabolical weapons for the triple unholy day. Not only was it a Sabbat – a witches Sabbath, it was a Fire Festival which celebrated the old Celtic May Day and it coincided with St. Bartholomew's Day.

St. Bartholomew's Day was tarnished by death. It stood as a black mark in the French Wars of Religion in 1572. The Huguenots were lulled into a false sense of security just prior to a treacherous wave of anti-Protestant mob violence. It unleashed its brutality and thousands of Huguenots were assassinated.

Territorial, regional, area-wide, and local covens and cult groups anticipated a steamy night of revelry. Xerxes and all those who fell under his jurisdiction were no different – with one major exception. Xerxes was losing control of a part of his portion of Satan's kingdom. The People of the Empty Tomb were now exerting dominion.

Xerxes was under pressure. He had been contacted by the current antichrist-in-waiting. Satan had peered over the shoulders of the prophets and scribes, but even he did not know the day nor the hour in which the Christ would return. Down through the ages he was compelled to groom an evil man who could step in when the birth pangs loomed. Some men were more notorious than others. Ancient Antiochus Epiphanes and the more modern Adolph Hitler were among those rumored to be *the* antichrist in their day.

Sheriff Bynum was beside himself trying to figure out what had happened to Andy Lockman and Don Barnhart. The third man was just a callow muscle man. He was disposable, but posed a distinct danger to the local cult if he opened his mouth. Charging around his small office, looking at his watch, he finally burst into the reception area. "Where are they?"

The hapless man at the front desk tried to shrink his sloppy frame deeper into his chair. "I don't know, sir. They've never missed work without calling in," he offered. "Their wives keep calling and asking."

Ignoring the man, Sheriff Bynum snatched his hat off of his desk, slapped it on his head, and stalked out of the office. Remembering to look as if he were on urgent official business, he trudged heavily into the courthouse. Punching the elevator button, pacing agitatedly, he abruptly turned toward the elevator when he heard the ping of the bell and the sound of the slow-motion door gliding open. Doffing his hat in a pseudo-polite gesture to the exiting couple, he entered the elevator alone and cursed himself for not taking the twenty steps to the second floor.

Daggett and Darod were seated uncomfortably in overstuffed chairs. Xerxes was imperiously seated at Daggett's desk. Jeff Roberts was not functioning as a judge today any more than Xerxes feigned being a congressman or Ed Jeffers assumed his service as a prosecuting attorney. They all looked up as the door swung open and Sheriff Bynum switched into his role as Zorroz.

"Where are they?"

"They haven't checked in, sir," Zorroz reported.

"Such a simple operation! How could they botch it? You used two trained men plus another capable man against a middle-aged couple!"

"I don't know, sir." Zorroz could sense the palpable tension in the room. None of them had answers and when that happened, the low man on the totem pole usually paid the price. Zorroz was that low man. "All I know is that they haven't shown up at work for two days. Their wives have been calling so I told them that they were on a special assignment. Their trucks are still at Charlie's place. Their last known whereabouts is that Norris place."

"Well, find out if they're still there!" he ordered.

"Yes sir." Zorroz responded. "Do you want me to go low key or do we want a search warrant?" Zorroz desperately wanted to please this man. He saw too many heads roll. Literally. This was too important to risk aggravating Xerxes and the other higher-level masters. Subconsciously rubbing the tell-tale scar on his throat, Zorroz waited for his orders.

———————

The first thing Tuesday morning Lee purchased motion sensor cameras and installed them in strategic positions all around the property. Having back-tracked the four-wheelers, he confirmed their suspicions that they had come from Charlie Fletcher's place. Later, he and Richard had boldly driven up Charlie's driveway and photographed license plates on the three trucks that were parked near the barn. Charlie's pickup truck remained where he had left it months ago. The yard was overgrown and layers of dust had settled on everything. It was obvious that someone was still caring for the large-hoofed horse.

The camera near Lee's mailbox that captured images of anyone entering the property was activated as Sheriff Bynum's vehicle slowly rolled up the long driveway. Another one documented his arrival at the house. Looking all around for any overt evidence of the four-wheelers, Sheriff Bynum picked his hat off the seat as he exited his vehicle and walked toward the house. He stopped when Reno burst out of his napping place with his hackles up and teeth bared.

Abigail was in the house getting ready for her appointment with Sherry Samuels. Stepping onto the porch she commanded, "Reno! Stay!" *Good instincts, buddy.*

The obedient dog's feet stopped immediately but the low rumble in his chest did not. He was sensing more than mere flesh and blood. Most of the man's demons had dropped off at the edge of the property. They saw the warring angels that the mortal only sensed as he felt his strength wane. He cursed under his breath.

Lee was in the barn looking at his phone. His motion sensors alerted his smart phone any time they were activated and he was able to watch the sheriff's approach. Sauntering over to the man, Lee greeted him amiably, "Morning, sheriff. What brings you here on a hot August day?"

The prickly man was startled by the voice coming from slightly behind him. "Good morning, Mr. Norris. I'll get right to the point. I'm following up on a report of some stolen four-wheelers. The owners said they had been riding in this area so I'm stopping by all the good folks up and down this section of the road. We can't let criminals ruin this fine community." He made a feeble attempt to cover his malice.

Lee choked down a sarcastic laugh and used Abigail's approach to cover it as he turned away momentarily. "I haven't seen anyone riding on our property. We hear wheelers practically any time of day or night around here. Everybody owns one."

"True, true," Sheriff Bynum agreed with a congenial tone that scarcely covered his simmering hatred. He automatically doffed his hat as Abigail joined Lee and said, "Morning, ma'am." Clearing his throat, he looked at Lee and continued, "Do you mind if I take a look around? You have a fair piece of land here and they could have been ditched anywhere." The unmistakable accusation was clear.

"I cover my whole spread practically every day and I haven't come across four-wheelers," Lee countered.

"I could get a warrant."

"Oh, that's not necessary, Sheriff, I'd be glad to walk the property with you."

Having had his bluff called, Bynum trapped himself into a long, hot walk on a sultry August day in his stuffy uniform and shoes that were more suited for pavement than for trails.

"I'll wait here for you," Abigail called out cheerily as she watched the two men and one attentive dog disappear down the trail toward the road. She laughed as she realized that Lee was going to take the sheriff on the most over-grown, muddy, hilly terrain on the property. *He'll probably take him straight through that thorny blackberry patch.* She giggled and then she prayed for protection.

Forty-five minutes later, Abigail saw the trio emerge from behind the barn. She greeted the two men with large glasses of ice water. "I thought you might have worked up a thirst," she said graciously as they each gratefully accepted the icy liquid.

"If you're planning on walking the property across the road, I'll be glad to go with you," Lee offered. What he wanted to say was, "You're not stepping a foot on that property unless I'm with you!"

"No, no, not today," Sheriff Bynum answered as he looked at his watch. "I'm afraid I have other business to attend to right now. Thanks for your time." He took a final gulp of the water, handed her the glass, and thanked Abigail before he returned to his car and left.

The two of them dissolved in laughter as the car disappeared down the lane. Lee checked his phone alert and noted that Bynum turned to the right. He was not going to their other farm. "Well, what do you think?"

"I think he knows that they were here. He won't search anyone else's property."

"I think you're right," Lee agreed and added after a thoughtful frown. "I wonder if he left finger prints on the glass. I'll check with Richard. Of course, being in law enforcement, his prints will be readily available."

"Good idea. I hate that he got to walk our property, but I saw the scratches on his arms."

"Oh, you gotta love the places that we walked. You should have seen the look on his face when he didn't see the cow pie."

"No!" Abigail squealed with delight as she covered her mouth and whispered, "Sorry, Lord, I'm sinning."

"And He wasn't very pleased when his shirt got hooked on the barbed wire when I decided to cut through the fields."
"You didn't!"
"Did."
"Lee Norris!"

Abigail felt less apprehensive in some ways, but more unsettled in other ways. They made one attempt to nab her. Would they try again? Had they tried before and she did not know it? She kept her cell phone on and was extra vigilant on her trip to the church. Sherry Samuels was her only appointment today, that is, if she showed up. Amy was doing great and Grace Jackson was skipping a week. Max was fine. Abigail was working herself out of a job again. It was usually slow in the summer anyway.

Pulling into her usual parking spot, Abigail was delighted to see that Sherry's car was already there. Noticing that the trunk was open and the hazards were flashing, Abigail was curious as she grabbed her office-in-a-bag and emerged from her truck.

Sherry sprang out of her car and whirled to face Abigail. "Look!" she exclaimed as she pointed a long finger at her hair. "Look at what those kids did!"

Abigail could hardly keep from grinning as she put her hand over her mouth and said, "Oh, my!" Some child personality had evidently gotten a hold of a pair of scissors.

Noticing the open trunk, Sherry stalked to the back of her car and slammed it shut. "Those kids are driving me nuts! They get into everything! They push every stinking button in the car!"

"Check your hazards," Abigail cautioned.

"Thanks."

Sherry got her car in order and followed Abigail into the church. They settled in, opened with prayer and soon Abaddon was switched into executive control and talking. He was agitated. Nervous.

"How was your week? Were you able to sort some things out while you were in seclusion?"

"Yeah," the reluctant near-convert, near-defector answered begrudgingly.

"What is the intolerable conflict?"

"What do you mean?"

"There's always at least one key issue that hangs everyone up. It's usually something that is difficult to face, to speak, to acknowledge because if you do, you'll have to admit something that you don't want to admit about yourself. It's not what you did or did not do. It's deeper. It probably involves rejection, neglect, and/or abandonment issues."

Abaddon reacted as if he'd been sucker-punched. Grimacing, he replied, "I gotta admit you know your stuff."

"Can you talk about it? I have a hunch, but it's better coming from you."

"It's about Mom and Grandma and that ritual where Grandma had to choose between us."

"Do you know what kind of double-bind they put your grandmother in?"

"What do you mean?"

"Like, what kind of threat was hanging over her head if she didn't choose?"

Abaddon thought for a few moments and then said, "They made some promises to her about becoming the first female master in this region."

"Why her?"

"She was a witch, too. That might have something to do with it. They said something about a double honor because she was a witch and a Satanist."

"So, what's the deep pain? What does her decision say about you? What have you been thinking about yourself because of it?"

Abaddon hung his head. "No one cared about me. Mom said…"

Ah, it's not the grandmother, it's the mom. Abigail knew that this would be a key statement and waited in the heavy silence.

"She said that it was a win-win situation for her. Either she would be out of her misery and Grandma would be stuck with me or she'd be alive and free of me."

"Ouch!" Abigail exclaimed as she stabbed her fist to her heart and twisted it twice. "I thought you said that she begged her mother to kill her and let you live."

"She did." Abaddon thoughtfully cocked his head as he considered the apparent contradiction. "But that was before Grandma made the decision."

"I think it only makes sense if your mother also had multiple personalities. One was a mean and vindictive Satanist and the other one might have actually been a caring mother."

"What difference does that make now? I still had to look into her eyes when I killed her. *I* still did it. I'm a murderer. I murdered my own mother. What kind of person does that?"

"Who are you?" Abigail asked after she perceived another switch. The voice and mannerisms were the same, but the content of the speech was definitely not typical of Abaddon.

"They call me Baddy. I'm bad." This personality was obviously closely associated with Abaddon.

"Guilt?"

"Big time," she whispered as she hung her head.

Abigail spent several minutes explaining the cult's effective use of double-binds and duplicity to control and manipulate their victims. She introduced her to the true Lord Jesus. She talked about dissociation and the cult's programming to create controllable multiple personalities. Baddy finally settled down, allowed Jesus to minister to her, and accepted her new name: Virtue.

Abaddon switched back in. "Thanks."

"You're welcome. What about you?"

"It still hurts that they said and did that. I mean, my father definitely abandoned me and Mom never loved me."

"So, the intolerable conflict comes from being unwanted, unworthy, unneeded, and so on. Therefore, if you can please the masters, if you can please your grandmother somehow by being at least as evil as they are, you are accepted. Loved. Desired."

"Yeah, something like that."

"It's not only the presence of evil and trauma in your life, it's the absence of the good that you have to face."

"Exactly. So, what do we do about it?"

"I love Psalm 27:10. It says that if my father or mother forsake or let me down, the Lord will lift me up. Why don't we ask the Lord to re-parent you in those areas where your family let you down?"

"We'd like that."

Abigail prayed a comprehensive prayer for Damon and all the others in Abaddon's sector. Then they went back to the memory where she was forced to kill her mother and they received more healing. Finally, they consolidated the sector. All the pre-borns, infants, toddlers, children, teens, and young adults were healed and integrated into some of the leaders who were under Abaddon.

Damon said that he was not pleased, but reluctantly consented to the integration. He was very weary and was secretly grateful for the change in status. Abaddon reported feeling lighter and freer.

"One more prayer," Abigail announced. "Tonight is a big ritual night. We need to ask the Lord to block all communications that would summon any susceptible personality to the ritual tonight."

"Good idea!" Sherry agreed. She had switched in shortly after Abaddon's last report.

They prayed and closed the session. After making an appointment for the following Friday, they made their way out to the parking lot. Sherry shouldered her giant tote bag and Abigail slipped her office-in-a-bag over her shoulder.

"I guess I need to find a beautician," Sherry remarked ruefully as she ran her fingers through her butchered hair. "I probably need to cut this mess anyway. I look too much like a witch with this long black stuff. Maybe it's time."

"I'll look forward to the new look," Abigail said with a smile. *Yes! Thank You, Lord!* She got into her truck and rejoiced all the way home.

Abigail did not know that several cars had come into the church parking lot while she and Sherry were having their session. As dedicated as that church property was to the Lord, the evil men and women boldly approached their vehicles and breathed curses. The curses were carried to Satan's throne of disgrace where he dispatched messengers of cruelty and malice.

Driving homeward as vigilantly as she had driven to town, Abigail was relieved when she made the final turn that brought her safely home. She rolled up the window and closed the door with a mild nudge.

The sudden popping and crackling, splintering and tinkling of glass startled her. She momentarily flashed back to the memory of Charlie Fletcher's gunshot to her back door and instinctively squatted down as she screamed for Lee.

"Abigail!" Lee looked all around as he and Reno ran toward her. "What happened? Are you all right?"

"I don't know. I just shut the door and the back window exploded."

Lee helped his trembling wife up and opened the door. Looking into the cab, they saw a jagged hole in the back window. There was not a square inch of the window that was not crazed like a giant irregular spider-web. Crumbles of safety glass were all over the seat and behind it. Some had bounced back into the bed of the truck or rattled to the ground in the space between the cab and the bed.

"What in the world?" Lee was mystified.

"Is that from a gunshot? I didn't hear anything."

"I don't think so. Let me check inside. If it was, the windshield would be blown out or the dash would have a hole in it."

They looked uneasily down their driveway, hoping that this was not another ambush.

Abigail was rattled and still not sure if someone had shot the glass out. Someone might have a silencer.

Lee inspected the cab and reported, "Nothing. I don't see a thing. This is really weird. It *im*ploded, not exploded."

"I'm going to call the church to see if they saw anything unusual and then I'm calling Cindy. We need to pray about this one."

"You do that. I'll call Richard and see if he has any ideas. He's going to start charging us by the mile, too," he said, hoping to inject a little humor into the tension.

Ginny recognized the number and answered, "Hi Abigail. How are you today?"

"I'm pretty good, but I need to ask if you or pastor noticed anything or anybody unusual in the church parking lot today around noon while I was there."

"No, no," Ginny said slowly as she thought. "Wait! There was something. Right around lunch time I went for my walk around the block and when I came back I did see a car near your back entrance. It was just stopped there and the passenger was holding his hand out toward your truck."

"Thanks Ginny. That helps."

"They took off when they saw me. It seemed weird but I thought it might be a new client or something. Is something wrong?"

"The back window of my truck imploded when I got home. It's hot enough but Lee said that if it was a heat thing it would have exploded, not imploded. Besides I had just driven it with the window open. It wasn't that hot inside the cab."

"Oh my! Do you think those people had something to do with it?"

"I'm not sure. Well, I won't keep you. Thanks for the info."

"You're welcome. I hope you get this sorted out okay. See you Sunday."

Abigail called Cindy as soon as she finished her call to Ginny. "Cindy, have you got a couple of minutes?"

"Sure do, my friend. What's up?"

"Well, I was just at church working with one of the SRA survivors. When I got back home, I shut my door like usual and the back window imploded. Ginny said that someone was in the parking lot with their hand extended toward my truck. She thought it was weird but dismissed it as maybe being a new client. Lee says it wasn't shot out, er, or in. He's going to call Richard. I'd like to pray."

"Let's do it!"

They took turns praying short prayers, leaving silences so they could receive impressions or words from the Lord.

"Are you getting anything?" Abigail asked.

"Curses."

"Curses?"

"That's the word."

"Imagine that! And on a triple ritual day. Oh! I forgot to tell you something. Sheriff Bynum was here this morning looking for some four-wheelers that were supposedly stolen. Maybe he left something behind. But Lee and I prayed over the whole property again, so it shouldn't be that."

"Interesting. Can demons do that? Break windows? Aren't you scared?"

"Well, if that's the best they can do, I don't think I'll worry. I'll just have to figure out how I'm going to tell the insurance company that a demon did it."

Having been confident that the flurry of curses and spells would counter anything that Sherry was subjected to by her counselor, Sherry's handler was furious. She did not answer the phone. Something was changing. Previously, she was an easy assignment. Compliant. Clueless. Her diabolical cult personalities were completely in charge. *Why weren't they sabotaging the sessions with that counselor? Why hadn't they killed that woman yet? Why didn't she answer the phone?* Disturbing questions bubbled up as he drove to her house. He was concerned for his own welfare.

Rapping on the front door of the bungalow, the man waited for Sherry to show. Not wanting to cause a scene, he flashed the goat sign and used her cult name and whispered hoarsely, "Sheol! It's time!"

Abaddon tried his best to keep that cult-loyal personality from surfacing. He was unsuccessful. He was furious. *I thought that Abigail's Jesus was supposed to keep this from happening!* He was helpless as the now docile Sherry followed the man out to the car with Abaddon and everyone else was included.

Like all the original St. Bartholomew's Day victims who thought they were safe, Abaddon was ambushed by this development. *I knew I shouldn't trust her! I knew she was conning us! She's just like all the other so-called Christians!* His futile fury was spewed out in curses.

The only redeeming thing in the otherwise horrific night was the fact that no matter how hard they tried, the masters were unsuccessful in drawing out Abaddon or any of those in his sector. This further inflamed the desperate and frustrated masters. Sherry could barely move by the time she woke up the next morning.

Zorroz was much relieved that he was able to keep a relatively low profile at the large regional gathering. His two deputies were still mysteriously absent along with the third man. Fortunately, Xerxes appeared to have other things on his mind. Daggett and Darod put up as gracious a front as they could muster when a master who ruled another area under Xerxes' territory was named as the replacement for Prinz.

Amalek was not quite as imposing as Prinz, but his coyote-like personality was evident. He was an opportunist. He picked off the weak, the stragglers, and the disadvantaged without regard to anything but fulfilling his own self-serving goals. A quick study, he rose in the ranks of the masters with record speed. He even had Xerxes looking over his shoulder.

24

Tuesday, August 28, Full Moon

The Saturday Ministerial Alliance back-to-school event had been a huge success and many needy families received the much-needed school supplies that they could scarcely afford. It was a timely event since school would be starting on Monday. Refreshments and a variety of music lifted everyone's spirits.

Many unchurched people of the community were exposed to church people who broke their stereotypes of religious people. They took up invitations to attend various churches in the community. Those who were affiliated with a church were somewhat mystified at the mix of denominations represented. Signs and posters intentionally made it very evident that the universal Church of Jesus Christ came from many local churches and denominations.

Richard York finally felt comfortable leaving his parents' home for the week that he would be working with Steven Diblassio. His father was almost back to his old self. Amy agreed to sit with his mother if his father needed to run errands without Martha. Richard squeezed in a quick trip back to Eldersburg so he could check on the house, hire the neighbor's son to mow his lawn, empty the post office box, and pick up more clothes, supplies, and equipment.

His visit with Landrum was also very productive. They had the beginnings of a sweeping case that should change the political and spiritual landscape of that county. Landrum apprised him of the pressure that he was getting from Congressman Davidson as well as the support he was getting from influential godly men and women who also wielded power in congress.

"The problem is that the people who we can prove directly shot or violated my father and his neighbors are dead or gone. Charlie Fletcher did the shooting. He's dead. William Wagner attacked Abigail and he's missing and presumed dead. His sister, Carrie Sue, said that their father killed a neighbor and buried him in the rose garden. He's dead. Their mother abducted that little girl, but she looks like death warmed over right now. I saw a recent picture."

"We have those three men," Landrum reminded Richard. "Why don't you see if they'll talk to you? They might be willing to point a finger at the sheriff or the judge or the other county officials. Let me know what Diblassio finds."

Richard visited the three men who were being held in the federal detention facility. They continued to remain uncooperative. They were demanding. They did not know with whom they were dealing. Richard and Steven had linked the two deputies to Max's jail house beating. He linked one of them to the prints on the body bag that held Charlie Fletcher's remains. They maintained their silence. After all, who was more intimidating, federal agents or Satanists? Richard or Xerxes?

The team was also looking at a number of unsolved disappearances. Barry Romanowski's case held the most promising leads, but there had been a number of teenagers who had disappeared as well. Carrie Sue provided a possible burial site for the Wagner's missing neighbor and others, but the biggest problem remained the lack of bodies. According to the survivors of the rituals, what was not consumed was buried or burned.

The various search warrants might turn up some evidence. There would have to be a quick-strike task force for the various locations. Levi was looking good for arson, assault, and a hit and run with Amy. The greedy owner of the junkyard had left a sloppy paper trail. His clandestine chop shop would likely yield something useful. If nothing else, the man would probably point fingers. David York's documentation of irregularities in the jail should connect the sheriff with the court system.

"I'm outta here!" Carrie Sue called out to Amy as she headed out the door.

"Have a great day!" Amy called back.

"You too!"

Carrie Sue was relieved that Sheriff Bynum seemed to have called off his daily harassment and intimidation duties. Perhaps it was because he was distracted by the disappearance of two of his deputies. She laughed as she resumed her previous routine. Joy was becoming a more consistent companion. Life was worth living.

Unlocking the door to The Thrift Shoppe, Carrie Sue flipped on the lights and made sure that the store was ready for customers. Shortly afterward, Amanda came in closely followed by Barbara Peters.

"Good morning, ladies," Barbara greeted her fellow-employees with a smile. "I'm glad the place is empty this morning. I need to talk with the two of you."

Carrie Sue fought the automatic sinking feeling in her stomach. Life had been filled with ambushes. It felt like she was being called into the principal's office. *Uh, oh, what's up? I hope Mom didn't shoplift again.* She walked into the tiny office and waited with Amanda.

"I've finally decided that it's time for me to retire."

"Oh no," Amanda warbled. "What are we going to do without you?"

"You'll manage just fine," Barbara continued. "You know this old hip of mine has been giving me fits and walking around on this concrete floor isn't helping. I'm almost sixty-four and my doctor said that it's time to replace it. I agree. My husband wants to travel, and so, I decided that since this place has someone who is capable of managing it, I'm going to take advantage of the situation and retire."

Amanda and Carrie Sue turned their heads and looked at each other, but did not voice their question.

"Amanda, I know that you've been here a little bit longer, but I'm going to ask Carrie Sue to take over as the manager."

"No problem!" Amanda sighed her relief. "I don't want to hassle with all that stuff you guys do in this office. I'd rather be out there on the floor."

"That's what I thought." Barbara turned and said, "Carrie Sue, will you step in?"

When Carrie Sue was able to get the words out, she said, "Yes! Oh, yes! Thank you. I'd be honored. But will you let me call you if I get stuck on something? I mean, I don't know everything you do yet."

"Of course you can call me any time, but you'll do fine. You're a whiz with the budget and payroll and taxes. You might even be able to hire another person to help with intake and such. Amanda can cover the floor. You'll both do great!"

Carrie Sue floated through her day on adrenaline and joy. She was excited. Manager! She could not wait to tell Amy and Abigail. Closing the shop that evening, she looked back through the store with new eyes. Maybe she could gradually implement some of her ideas.

Pulling into her parking place by the old farmhouse, Carrie Sue laughed as Princess greeted her. "Guess what, Princess. I got promoted today! I'm a manager!"

Princess barked and wagged at her news, but then, she barked and wagged at everything.

"You're not going to believe what happened at work today," Carrie Sue declared as she stepped briskly into the kitchen.

"Must be something good. You look happy," Amy replied as she turned from the counter where she was putting the finishing touches on their dinner.

"It is. Barbara is retiring and I'm going to be the new manager starting in September!"

"That's fantastic! Wait a sec. That's just a couple of days away."

"Saturday."

The two of them celebrated as they settled into their comfortable evening routine. Most of the time they sat out on the front porch or the back deck after dinner and talked unless the heat or the bugs drove them back inside. Sometimes they weeded the garden; sometimes they just watched the inane antics of the chickens. Tonight, they talked about how blessed they were and what their lives might have looked like if not for Lee and Abigail's generosity.

Sherry would not have been able to relate to their conversation if she had been with them. She was grappling with hope, wrestling with faith. She was still on the fence about totally defecting to Christianity. There were too many cult-loyal personalities who had not even heard about the possibility of defection. There were many who knew that there was an option, but having been traumatized once again at Friday's ritual, she had been fragmented and programed again.

Abaddon was confused. He knew that he could never resume his duties as a cult-loyal personality. They would kill him. It was traitorous to have had conversations with that woman. Something changed in him and they knew it. He knew it. Tonight was another ritual night. If they got dragged off again, and he was to be accessed, it was all over. He considered the transformation of Baddy to Virtue and the healings in his own vast section in the last session with Abigail, but what was that compared to the big picture? There were other sectors just as extensive as his once was.

Having the freedom to take executive control once again, Abaddon made a decision. Decisively tapping out the digits, he waited as the phone rang three times before it was answered.

"Hello?" Abigail said as she recognized Sherry Samuel's number. She had taken the time to look at the screen to make sure that it was a familiar number.

"Hey, it's me, Abaddon."

"Trouble?"

"Yeah, you could say that. They accessed us and we ended up at a ritual. I thought your God was going to protect us," he accused in a somewhat controlled tone.

"What happened?"

"They somehow got a hold of a part named Sheol. I couldn't stay out to keep it from happening. I thought we prayed about all the parts that might have been programed for that night."

"We did. Unfortunately, we can't always cover every part and we can't always thwart their will."

"Well, why not? I thought your God was bigger, better, stronger, and smarter than Satan." Abaddon was heating up with the thoughts that were spilling out of his mouth.

"Abaddon, I'm sorry. All I can say is that my other survivors have experienced the same frustration. There always seem to be parts who squirt out from under the protective prayers. I would bet you that Sheol has no idea about her options."

"I don't know what to do," Abaddon confessed. It was humbling to admit that he was powerless and clueless. Humility was brand new territory for him.

"I'll tell you what," Abigail said as she made a decision and quickly consulted the clock. "Let's meet at the church. Lee and I can get there in about thirty minutes. I'm going to have my husband come with since it's already after seven."

"We'll be there." Abaddon was relieved. He could feel familiar stirrings inside and hoped that this meeting would take care of things. He really did not want to go to another ritual, but he was not entirely sure about that Jesus character.

Lee did not hesitate when Abigail told him about the situation. They hastily changed into clean clothes and got into Abigail's recently repaired truck. Sherry's beat-up car was in the parking lot already. It was an old full-sized Chevrolet that had had its share of fender-benders. It looked as if someone had used several cans of black rust-proofing spray paint to cover the entire car.

Lee walked around the parking lot while Abigail and Sherry went into her office. The church seemed very dark and very quiet at this time of the evening.

After opening with prayer, Abigail asked for the personality that Abaddon identified as Sheol.

"Who the blazes are you, and what right do you have calling me out?" Sheol exploded.

"Sorry," Abigail said as she looked intently into her eyes. "Abaddon was concerned about getting pulled into another ritual tonight."

"Abaddon! That weenie traitor! He deserves every stinking thing they give him."

"So, I guess that your job is to get everybody to the ritual so you can sit back and enjoy watching all those little kids in there getting abused."

"Watch it, lady! I don't get off on any of that. It doesn't affect me. It's just the way things are."

"*Why* is that the way things are? Why do you get raped and tortured and those men get to do it to you?"

"They're not doing it to me."

"Really?" Abigail questioned gently. "You happen to occupy the same body, so when they rape a little girl, you're getting raped too."

"Am not!" she protested.

"You're not a bunch of different people who happen to occupy the same body."

"I don't have anything to do with them."

"Then why do you give a rip if Abaddon decides that Satanism isn't for him?"

Caught off guard, Sheol cut off her first retort and glared at Abigail. She had never been challenged in this way. It sounded lame as she answered, "Because I have to do my job."

"Who gave you that job?"

"You're mighty nosey, lady!"

"So, you just woke up one morning and decided that you ought to be a Satanist like your grandmother and your mother."

"No! I'm not like them. This is the way I've always been."

"Which means you're programed just like the rest of them in there."

"I am not!"

"Why would you be the only one that's not? Does that make any sense? Look at what they do to all the other victims at all the rituals. They intentionally create new personalities and program them so they can control them and access them any time they want. Just like they did last week and got you to surface so they could do more damage."

"That's not my problem. I just do my job so no one bothers me."

"And if you don't do your job, you'd be in as much trouble as Abaddon is in. Right?"

"Yes. No!" Sheol was not accustomed to having to think about her circumstances, her history, her life.

"I know you have an assignment from the masters. They want you to believe that you have no choices. I want you to know that you do have options."

"I do what I want."

"Really?" Abigail purposely tinged that reply with a bit of sarcasm. "They let you do whatever you want."

"Yes."

365

"So that means that you want to see little kids hurt and maimed, and traumatized for life."

"Yes. No!"

"So, you're telling me that if you had a choice, you would not want kids to be hurt."

"Yes."

"Then why do you do it? Why do you set them up?"

Pressing her lips together as if to keep words from pouring out, Sheol finally said, "It's my job."

"And now we've come full circle. You have a job. Whether or not you're programed or just trying to avoid nasty consequences, you do your job for the Satanists. I mean, I don't see any benefit for you."

"We get rewarded."

"What kind of rewards?" *We. It was not unusual for someone with multiple personalities, but maybe she's not alone.* Abigail quickly processed the subtle hints and nuances of these complex survivors.

"We get more power. We get promoted."

"And how many times have they said, 'Oh, sorry, but you missed this or failed there, so we can't promote you'?" Abigail really wanted Sheol to think.

Sheol once again sat with lips pressed together. A vein began to stick out in her forehead as her anger and frustration rose.

"How high can a female go?" Abigail continued to challenge her paradigm.

"What do you mean?"

"Are there any female masters? Aren't the victims predominantly female? You know how much Satan hates women."

"We have guys in here," she said defensively.

Abigail had another Holy Spirit hunch. "Would you happen to be a he-she? Maybe paired up with a guy named Hades?"

Sheol's immense frame leaped up and towered over Abigail who was grateful that there was a desk between them. "I ought to strangle you, woman!"

Abigail shot back, "You can't do anything the true Lord Jesus doesn't permit. Please sit down. I'm not your enemy."

Reluctantly, the menacing part sat down. Glaring.

"I assume that you've been listening in?"

No answer.

"I won't bore you with a repetition of the conversation that I had with Sheol then. What I would like to do is lay out a challenge to both of you. If you accept it and still want to keep doing the same old things then I won't bother you anymore. I want you to know that you do have options that the cult has been keeping from you." Abigail briefly thought about the challenge that Satan had presented to Eve. It, too, had been framed in the idea that something good was being withheld. *God, I don't want to manipulate. Let this be pure and good from You.*

Hades thought for a long moment as he looked disdainfully with one eye down his nose at the woman. *Was she right? Had they kept anything from them?* "What do you have in mind?"

"I'd like to ask my God to remove any programing from you and Sheol."

"Ain't happening!"

"Why not?" Abigail challenged. She had challenged so many other survivors in the past with a similar line of questioning. "If you're not programed then nothing will happen. If something changes, then you'll know they messed with you. Wouldn't you want to know?"

"Fine! Just know that if you pull something, you're dead meat."

"I'll do just as I said." Abigail maintained the staring contest and prayed, "True Lord Jesus Christ of Nazareth, we're asking You to neutralize programing and anything that keeps it in place that may have been put on Sheol and Hades." She remained silent and waited for Hades to respond. Noting the barely hidden look of shock, Abigail knew that the Lord had revealed something to him.

"What did you do?"

"I prayed. You heard what I said. What changed?"

"I don't know. We don't feel as angry right now."

"Did you have any thoughts or memories come up?"

Hades hesitated. His pride made him reluctant to admit that he might be wrong about what he would have staked his life on just minutes before. "I'm remembering something that I overheard at a ritual. They must have thought I was unconscious after everything they did to us that night. Maybe I was, but I remember hearing the head master tell my immediate master that he'd done an excellent job with me. He said something like I was his big horse and that I'd keep doing what he wanted as long as he kept the carrots dangling in front of me."

"Ouch," Abigail said sympathetically. "What does that mean for you today?"

Taking in a deep breath, adjusting his position in the chair, he puffed out his cheeks as he slowly let the air out of his lungs and the prideful wind drained out of his satanic sails. "They're using me."

"I'm sorry. You don't deserve that. No one does."

"I don't need your pity!" he retorted, but not quite as fiercely as he would have earlier.

"That's not what I'm doing. I'm just saying that I hate it when someone intentionally grooms someone else to do their bidding. They get everything and you get nothing."

"I got something," he snapped. He was trying to maintain some level of dignity.

"All I'm saying is that you got the short end of the stick. They control every aspect of your life and didn't ask you what you wanted. That's what Satanists do. They emulate Satan: kill, steal, and destroy. He's the father of lies and he is a murderer from the beginning. You're not his first victim and you won't be the last."

"It's all I know."

"I know that. I hate that for you. But today you have a chance to change your history. You don't have to be like your parents and grandparents and great-grandparents."

"It's all I know. They'll kill me."

"I realize that this is a lot to consider, and yes, they'll try to kill you. God, my God, the true creator God, may permit it, but I don't think so. I've heard the same stuff from my other survivors and they're still living and breathing in spite of their past and in spite of the threats against their lives. Each one of them should have been dead a hundred times by now, but God brought them through it."

"Yeah, well, where was He for me?"

"He was there. He is here. He won't force Himself on you like Satan does."

"Well if He's stronger than Satan, why didn't He stop him? Why didn't He stop the Satanists? Why did He put me into that family?"

"There are answers. Are you willing to give this God a chance now that you know that you have a choice?"

"We're already in trouble. Me and Sheol and all the Little Hellions will be busted just like Abaddon and his group."

"What do you want to do?"

"I don't know. I just know that if we go to the ritual tonight, we're in for big trouble."

"We can ask the true God to do for you like He's done for Abaddon. Are you okay with having Him provide a safe place inside? We can pray again and ask Him to block attempts to trigger anyone inside."

"What guarantee do we have that we won't get accessed again?"

"I don't have a guarantee. He didn't violate your will and He won't violate the others' either. I would guess that there are other leaders and other sectors inside of you who aren't on board yet. We could repeat history here until everyone is safe. And until everyone is safe, that is, saved, healed, delivered, and integrated, there will be a risk. I've been praying for a one-size-fits-all, one-time, all-encompassing prayer that will fix everything in one session. For whatever reason, we're still stuck with a process. God's shown me some short cuts, but it's still a process."

Sherry slumped in the chair and sat staring at the space in front of her for several minutes. It was obvious to Abigail that there was a mighty internal conference taking place. Finally, she looked up and resumed her one-eyed stare at Abigail. "Fine. We talked to Abaddon and he said that it was the only way to go. He'd keep a lookout while we hunker down."

"I'm glad. I don't want to see you guys hurt anymore. Healing isn't simple, but it is possible. I'm not perfect and I might make some mistakes along the way, but please know that I don't ever want to add to your problems."

"I'm beginning to believe you," Hades said softly, puckering his right cheek as he briefly drew the right side of his closed lips back. It was the closest thing to a smile that he could achieve at this point.

"How about if I pray and ask the true Lord Jesus to bring you and your group into a safe place and then I'll ask Him to keep anyone else from being accessed for tonight's ritual."

Abigail prayed as extensive a prayer as she dared. She was not entirely sure that some more superior personality might stop the whole process. When they were finished, Abigail packed up her office-in-a-bag and led the way back out to the parking lot. The sun was already down.

Lee was on the far side of the lot but covered the distance swiftly with his long legs. "Well! That must have been quite a session!"

"Sure was. Thanks for coming with me. I just know that she would have been taken to a ritual tonight without this meeting, but there's still enough cult-loyal ones in there that it still might happen. I hate this part of the healing journey for them. It's so up and down."

"One of these days, you'll find a way to help folks like her. Isn't that why we have that haven of a farm across the road?"

"Yes. Now I'm wondering what we can do for Sherry. I mean, with Carrie Sue and Amy pretty well healed, what would it do to throw someone like Sherry into the mix? Amy's going to have that baby in a couple of months."

"You don't even know if that's a possibility or a necessity right now."

"I suppose so. Sherry still has a house to live in. I assume that she inherited it from her grandmother. I don't know anything about her finances, but I think she's on disability and gets food stamps."

Hours passed. Sherry Samuels experienced extreme restlessness. The phone rang.

25

Friday, August 31

The brief nightly respite from the baking August sun did little to remove the heaviness from the morning air. It would be another sultry, windless, slightly overcast day with empty promises of rain.

Lee was still acclimating to the weather conditions here. Having lived in Montana, he was accustomed to the drier mountain climate. Temperatures might climb as high out there, but it did not seem quite so hot. He had to look after his livestock as carefully in the hot weather as he did during the most frigid winter. Arms folded over the large red metal gate with one foot on the second bar, he stood quietly with Reno at his side just observing his heifers. "It won't be long, Reno. This time next year we'll be looking at a bunch of frisky calves."

Reno yipped when Lee asked him if he had any herding instincts left in him.

They finished their morning rounds at a leisurely pace. Abigail had breakfast ready and they began their day in an unhurried manner. She knew that the rest of her day might not be so relaxed with Grace Jackson at ten-thirty and Sherry at noon.

"I'm going to stop up at the house to see Amy. She seems to be doing great, but I just want to make sure. It's the thirty-first and another ritual night."

Lee rolled his eyes and shook his head. "It never ends, does it? I mean, those Satanists just keep the pressure on."

"It would be nice if they were saying the same thing about us Christians."

After reading their morning devotional together, they held hands across the table and prayed for their day. Lee prayed for an exceptional anointing and protection for Abigail. Abigail prayed for Lee's safety and success in his latest projects.

Carrie Sue and Amanda planned an impromptu retirement party for Barbara. They made posters and placed them prominently in the show windows with all the pertinent information as well as an offer for one free item with any purchase or donation.

Another empty poster was on the counter for people to sign. Practically everyone in town knew Barbara Peters. She attended the large Methodist church and had been at The Thrift Shoppe since its beginning.

"Are we crazy?" Amanda asked. "We could get cleaned out today if enough people show up."

"Yeah. We're certifiable."

"Well, what if that happens?"

"It'll be fine. I think there'll be as many givers as takers. We might just have a back log of stuff to process next week. Besides, it's Labor Day weekend. Lots of people will be out of town."

Amy was nearly twenty-seven weeks along in her pregnancy. David was kicking and dancing. After letting the chickens out, Amy prepared for her routine check-up. She was so excited every time she got to see David. The ultra-sounds were able to clearly show his features and his tiny fingers and toes. Oh, how she longed to hold him in her arms! And yet, the prospect of being the provider and protector of this helpless little guy terrified her. Focusing so intently on keeping him alive in her womb, she had not given as much thought about how to raise a son.

Grace Jackson was punctual as expected. They quickly got settled in the office. Grace was animated as she described the positive changes in her life just from the two previous sessions. "I'm not sure what's left. I mean, my life is good right now. My husband and I are getting along better than ever. In fact, we're even talking about having another child."

"Wonderful! Remind me. How many children do you have now?" Abigail had that information in her file, but she was not absolutely certain about it.

"Just one," Grace said with a tight close-lipped smile that reflected no humor. "Family rule!"

"Oh. That's right. Those lovely family rules. How old is your child now?"

"Craig's eleven. Almost twelve. He's been begging me for a brother forever."

"Craig Jackson?" Abigail queried with a furrow. "That name sounds familiar."

Grace momentarily hung her head in shame and then defiantly looked up. "You're probably thinking of my cousin – the guy that murdered his girlfriend in The Taco Tower. He's my youngest uncle's only son."

"O-oh." Abigail replied quietly. "That must have been a shock to the whole family."

"We don't like to talk about it. It was a shock, but we could see it coming once he got in with that bad crowd." It was obvious that Grace needed to talk about this issue.

"What in particular bothers you about it, I mean, besides the obvious?"

"I'm worried that my Craig will turn out to be just like him. They're only about eight years apart and my Craig looked up to him. In fact, Craig is really his middle name. When his older cousin was so cool with driving and girlfriends and smoking and stuff, my Phillip told everyone that he wanted to be called Craig, too. He looked up to him so much."

"How is he now that Craig is in prison for murder?"

"He won't talk about him. Actually, he won't talk about anything with me anymore. I just chalked it up to puberty. I'm his mom and I guess I'm just not cool."

"Does he talk with his father?"

"Not really. Maybe I need to have him see you."

"I'd be glad to see him."

"Oh, would you? I never even thought of that."

"Absolutely. If you don't mind, I'd like to have my husband sit in on the session. Lee is an intercessor and I think your son might be more comfortable with a man here, too. Meanwhile, let's pray about your worry and whatever other fallout has come from that tragedy. Your whole family must be shaken up."

"Yep. Only one egg in the basket and it was rotten."

They prayed and processed Grace's issues and set an appointment for Craig for the following week. Grace left with a lighter heart and more hope.

Sherry drove up a few minutes later. Abigail had been watching for her through the small window in the heavy outside door. *Lord, please let her come today. Please set her free! Grant me favor with those hostile ones.* Abigail prayed continually until she saw the black beater roll up next to her truck.

Opening the door, Abigail greeted Sherry with a hearty, "Come in. I'm so glad you made it." She wasn't entirely sure which personality was in executive control at the moment, but she received a cordial reply and assumed that it was the usual host.

They quickly settled down in their respective chairs. Sherry dropped her bulging tote bag next to her as usual. Odd rustlings and clunks made Abigail curious about what this woman carried with her in that bag.

"How has it been since Tuesday? Did you get accessed?" Abigail hoped that Sherry had been spared more damage. She was still making educated guesses about the extent of Sherry's internal system. She had very few clues about how her internal world had been constructed since Sherry had the influences of both witchcraft and Satanism.

"I don't know anything about that, you'll have to talk to someone else."

"Okay. Can I talk to someone who knows what went on since Tuesday?"

A smiling, head-bobbing, foot-tapping personality emerged.

"Sammy?"

"Yep. How'd ya know?"

"I could just tell." Abigail smiled at the three-year-old observer. *This should be interesting.* Child alters usually displayed understanding far beyond their tender years. "What can you tell me?"

"Well, the bad guys tried to get us, but they couldn't so they're really, really mad."

"How do you know they're mad?"

He lowered his voice to a whisper as he revealed his secret. "Because Seimers is mad. He wants to know who's responsible."

"Who's Seimers?" This was a new name.

"Oh, he's the guy in charge of the hospital."

"Is this an inside guy or an outside guy?"

"Inside."

"What hospital?"

"Our hospital, silly. It's where we live."

"Oh. I didn't know."

Suddenly he had a panicked look on his face and said, "I gotta go now."

Sammy disappeared and Sherry's face hardened as an adult personality switched in. "What are you doing meddling in our business again?"

"Are you Seimers?"

"What if I am?" he challenged.

"I'd like to talk with you if you don't mind."

"Everyone who talks with you either disappears or changes. I don't like it. You're getting us in trouble and I won't stand for your trickery anymore."

"It's not my intention to put you into danger. But you're hooked up with Satanists. They're trouble by definition."

"You're trouble. You and your Jesus! I saw how He messed with Sheol's group."

Abruptly changing the conversation back to the matter at hand, Abigail stated, "So, I guess you didn't make it to the ritual Tuesday night."

"Nope! But we'll make it tonight, no thanks to you."

"Why do you want to go to the ritual? What's in it for you? What happens if you don't go?"

"It's what I do."

"Were you listening in when I was talking with Sheol and Hades the other day? I really don't want to waste your time with a repeat of that conversation. But I would like to know what they have hanging over your head. What kind of leverage do they have?"

His jaw jutted out and Abigail could hear him breathing heavily. His mind was churning. He really did not have a good answer and he really did not understand why he was thinking about some of the things that were rolling through his mind. This was his life. This is the way it always was. He had a job to do like all the others. That was that.

"Are you really a die-hard Satanist with a twist of witchcraft thrown in or are you someone who, deep down, despises what's been going on?"

His lips tightened. He was debating. An internal war was raging. To lose a battle, a skirmish, would mean the eventual loss of the war. Seimers did not want to lose. He knew all the threats. He'd seen them viciously carried out on other traitors. It would have to be all or nothing. Anything in between would be painfully disastrous. His own personal tale was similar to those personalities within other survivors who chose to be victor over victim.

"Can you tell me about the hospital?" Abigail boldly pressed.

"You'll just use anything I say against me. I'm not telling you anything."

"Was someone in your family in the medical field?"

"How would you know about that?" he demanded. Her questions were unnerving, but he did not want to relinquish executive control to someone else who might supply her with too much information.

"I'm just connecting some of the dots. I'm sorry. I know that you're in a tricky spot right now. You don't know who you can trust. Please let me help you. I have a feeling that the things that they do – especially to little girls – sickens you. Maybe that's why you built the hospital."

There was a slight softening of the glare that came from Seimers' left eye even though he was alarmed by her uncanny insights. It was as if he had held so much in for so long that he could not help but let bursts of information escape. "My mother was a nurse. She kept taking me to the doctor. I spent a lot of time in the hospital. I had lots of surgeries. Some were not very successful as you can see," he said as he pointed to his divergent eyes with his index and middle fingers.

"Do you really want to go to the ritual tonight?"

"I don't have a choice."

"That's not what I asked you. Do you *want* to go?"

"I've already said too much."

"Let me ask God to put us in a private bubble so the demons can't listen in," Abigail offered.

"Not today."

"Will you talk with me again some time?"

It was too late. He disappeared into his internal abode and was replaced by the business-like one who lifted her chin and looked down her nose at Abigail, sniffed her disdain, and gathered her bag as she stood up. "Next week, I presume?" she asked as if it were her office and she was dismissing Abigail at the conclusion of a corporate meeting.

"I would like to pray for protection before you leave so that you can hopefully avoid the ritual tonight."

"That won't be necessary. I'll see you next week at the same time."

The imposing figure walked briskly out of the room and left Abigail pondering Sherry's situation. "Oh, Lord, please don't let them get accessed tonight. Please keep them safe. Oh, God, they've been through hell and back already. Mercy!"

She packed up her office and felt a little bit comforted by the thought that the he-she personalities named for rituals that occurred on the thirteenth and the thirty-first had been taken care of. Perhaps they would be safe after all.

Sitting in his office, Zorroz was relieved that the rituals tonight would be smaller gatherings of locals only. His little group would meet at Charlie Fletcher's place as usual. He did not want to admit just how nervous he felt in the presence of Xerxes. Indeed, prior to the death of Prinz, he had only heard of the master and his respected family that boasted of roots that went to the ancient days of Nimrod.

Nimrod's reputation as a mighty hunter before the Great Enemy was not meant to be a compliment. The ancient languages would more rightly state that Nimrod was a mighty hunter *against* the Great Enemy. Nimrod rebelled. His false religion was an affront to the Great Enemy.

Zorroz was more familiar with Xerxes in his role as Congressman John Davidson. He voted for him. He campaigned for him. He fulfilled his financial duty to support him despite the fact that the congressman had inherited much of the family wealth that had been accumulated through shrewd investments and insider information. They had made a killing in the stock market during the Great Depression while others jumped out of windows in despair.

It did not matter. Cult members in the lower levels never seemed to be able to accumulate wealth despite landing good jobs. Sheriff Bynum's wife constantly complained that they were living from paycheck to paycheck. He dared not deny any demand placed upon him by those above him.

Zorroz ruefully thought about Mastiff who recently died. Ron Wagner was a foreman in a fairly big plant. He made great money compared to most who lived in this county, but his family lived in an average house and Mastiff left his widow impoverished. The Parkers who owned the appliance store had a similar issue. Reflecting on the poverty and scarcity, Zorroz shook his head but continued to faithfully execute his duties.

The gathering tonight would be even smaller with his two missing deputies and their accomplice. Where were Lockman and Barnhart? Their wives received a phone call each, but all they knew was that the men were being held in a federal facility. The other deputies were making comments and asking how long they would have to put in extra shifts. Pretty soon the general public would start wondering about the sheriff's department.

The jangle of the phone jerked his mind out of the dark valley in which he had been wandering. "Bynum."

A barely audible voice on the other end of the line snapped orders.

"Yes sir." Sheriff Bynum knew the voice. He knew what the request meant. Hanging up the phone, blowing out a weary breath, Sheriff Bynum finally pressed his lips together in resolve as he slapped his hat on his head and headed for the door.

"Sheriff," the hapless desk jockey said, "I need your signature on this report."

Pausing to scrawl his signature at the bottom of the report, Sheriff Bynum slapped the pen onto the paper and left wordlessly.

"What's got his goat?" the man muttered out loud after the front door slammed behind the sheriff.

Locals covertly began to arrive at Charlie Fletcher's place on horseback and four-wheelers, pickup trucks and cars. Surveying his gathering, Zorroz reflected on the fact that several key people were missing from his group. All the Wagner men were dead. Susan seemed to be dying as well. Carrie Sue! His anger flared as he thought of her escape and continued elusiveness. Rubbing the scar on his neck, he thought of Charlie's death as well as the sacrifice of his own young daughter. She would have been more beautiful than her mother. Wrenching his thoughts away from that dark subject, he fully switched back into Zorroz, the ruthless master.

Directing others to do the duties that his deputies normally did, he gave himself to his sinister powers. Imbibing in the intoxicating fluids, participating in the wanton orgy, he abandoned himself to the rhythms of unrestrained debauchery.

All over the state, the region, the country, and the world, Satan worshipers brought their frenzied obeisance to their cruel master. Living beings were given in a vain attempt to satiate the insatiable appetite of the most blood-thirsty being in the universe. His mockery of the supreme sacrifice by the Holy Lamb fueled his counterfeit religion. His worshipers believed the promises of status and power and they would do the unthinkable to attain them.

Bible readers are universally horrified to read Old Testament accounts of mothers in cities under siege bargaining with one another. "Today we will eat my child. Tomorrow we will eat yours." They would be astounded at what went on in their own communities month after month. There is no sanctity of life. Not in this kingdom.

At what point on the continuum does the dividing line slash a distinction between these unabashed Satan followers whose credo is to kill, steal, and destroy, and those who attend Christian churches and allow an unplanned pregnancy to be terminated for the sake of pride or convenience? Perhaps the king of the second heavens had a greater hold on these communities than they might have imagined.

Was the land crying out because it had to drink the blood of the innocent? Could *that* be the cause of those cataclysmic atmospheric clashes? Floods. Tsunamis. Earthquakes. Droughts. Famines. Cyclones. Wild fires.   Infestations.   Viruses.   The whole creation groaned and suffered as with pangs of childbirth.

This was a good weekend for the Satanists. Tomorrow was the first of the month, another ritual day.   Monday was the third, yet another ritual day. Friday was the Marriage to the Beast of Satan.   Yes, it would be a good week.   Indeed, the whole month was filled with rituals.   Ember days, the new moon, and the thirteenth all were warm ups that would crescendo on the autumnal equinox.

26

Monday, September 3, Labor Day

For once the weather was cooperating for Labor Day celebrations. It would not be too hot or too cool. And there was no rain in the forecast. Lee and Abigail were excited. This was the first big family gathering that they would be able to host. Practically everyone would be there from Grandpa and Grandma McVeigh down to the fourth generation. They also invited the Yorks and the Milners, as well as Carrie Sue and Amy.

"I'm so glad you were able to make it in again, Lisa!" Abigail exclaimed with genuine delight. She was tickled to be able to get to know her step-daughter better. Working side by side in the kitchen as they prepared food for their guests provided the perfect opportunity to chit chat.

"Well, I'm glad I'm here, too. Mom's not very pleased, but that's not my problem." Lisa gave a half smile as she washed the vegetables. They had raided Abigail's garden across the road earlier and brought back tomatoes, squash, and peppers.

"I'm just glad you and your dad can make up for some lost time," Abigail said as she formed another hamburger patty and added it to the growing pile.

"Me too," Lisa said softly as her head drooped. "I kinda bought Mom's take on everything and poor Dad got vilified. I really do need to make it up to him."

"I think you already have. Just being here and hanging with his side of the family means so much to him. He was tickled that you were at our wedding and he still talks about it."

"Good." Lisa's smile reflected relief. "I sure hope you have a big grill. This is a lot of stuff!"

"We'll be feeding a small army today. We're just supplying burgers and some veges. Those vegetables will taste great grilled. Everyone else will be bringing in beans and potato salad and enough desert to make us all hyper for a week!"

Across the road Carrie Sue and Amy were preparing their contribution to the feast: "angeled" eggs.

"I sure hope these taste as good as Abigail's."

"They will. We're using her recipe. It can't go wrong." Amy was becoming a bit of an optimist lately.

"How many shall we make?"

"Well, she said that Lee's entire family is coming plus all the neighbors. There'll be around twenty of us if everyone shows."

"So, if we make double that, we should have enough. Some people might not like them."

They used eighteen fresh eggs. Amy had been bringing a dozen eggs down to the Yorks every Monday morning when she went in to work. They still had plenty of eggs even after Lee and Abigail and the Milners were supplied. They solved their excess egg problem by putting up a sign at the end of the driveway: FRESH EGGS. $2.50/dozen. PARK HERE and call 448-3877. Bring cartons to exchange.

They had purchased an inexpensive cell phone on sale and only needed to add minutes when they got low. Amy would take the order and walk down to the end of the driveway with Princess to deliver the eggs. She would exchange a full carton for an empty one.

They felt much safer knowing that someone with an ulterior motive would not be able to come up to the house posing as an egg customer.

By the time Amy and Carrie Sue arrived, there were vehicles parked all along the driveway. A Frisbee was floating in soft arcs across the front lawn between the younger cousins and their friends. Reno liked the new game and nearly exhausted himself chasing it back and forth between the players. Abigail was on the front porch with some of the ladies while the men seemed drawn to the grill. They shifted with the breezes as plumes of smoke rose from the fire. The tantalizing aroma of char-broiled burgers and hot dogs set their stomachs rumbling.

Tables were ready in the dining room. Card tables were set up on the front porch for those who preferred the outdoors. Benches and chairs and stairs and grass provided plenty of options for everyone.

"Abigail, I believe we're ready here," Lee yelled over the hubbub and got everyone's attention. Those were the words they had been waiting for.

Abigail stood at the center of the front porch steps and called out, "Okay, everyone! Let's gather around! We've got all the food lined up on the counter inside. Grab a plate and find a place to eat. Lee, would you ask a blessing on the food?"

"I would rather defer to Grandpa." Lee smiled and nodded at the revered head of this clan.

"Thank you, son." The elderly man bowed his head and as he did, everyone else followed suit. Caps were respectfully snatched off of heads while the beloved man intoned a prayer that was familiar to most of them. They finished the prayer with him as they echoed, "Amen!"

"Let's eat!

"Yum! Hey, Grandma did you make your special brownies?"

"Desert goes last!" she commanded with a twinkle.

"But Gram, life is short, we should eat dessert first," the teenaged Shane protested.

"If you eat desert first, *I'll* shorten your life! You get on in there and eat a proper meal for a growing boy," she happily chided him. Elsa McVeigh loved her great-grandchildren and doted on every one of them. She was a prayer warrior and prayed for each one by name every day.

"Richard! I'm so glad you could make it," Lee said as he joined him in the line. "How are your folks doing these days?"

"Thanks for inviting us. It's good to be out. I wish the folks were up to this," he replied. Lowering his voice, he added with a wry grin, "It's nice that we're not facing some kind of crisis for once."

"You can say that again. Be sure to bring some food back for them." Changing the subject, he asked, "How long are you going to be able to stay in the area?"

"Thanks," he replied to Lee's first statement. "I've accrued a lot of vacation and personal days. I never used them. I guess I've been married to my job. I'm not used to relaxing."

"You call this relaxing?" Lee asked. "I'd hate to see what the rest of your life is like."

"This is just one case. It's complicated – they all seem to be – but I usually have to juggle several at one time. I've got Dad to bounce things off of. He's been a great help and thinks outside of the box a lot."

Just then Bryan McCord came bounding up to Lee and Richard. Tugging on Lee's pant leg, he begged, "Can I ride a horse today?"

"I don't see why not," Lee laughed as he tousled Bryan's hair. "Let's wait until everyone's finished eating and we'll see if anyone else wants to ride."

"Okay!" With that, Bryan scampered over to Traci and gave her the good news.

It was not long before Lee and Gary, Bryan and Traci, Shane and his friend, Joel, walked down to the horse pasture with halter ropes and Reno tagging along. Shannon had a secret crush on Joel and shyly walked down with them. Quickly catching all five horses, they brought them up to the barn where they were groomed and saddled.

Lee put Bryan in front of him on Lady and took the lead while Gary put Traci in front of him on Misty and took up the rear. Shannon rode Buster. That left Sassy and Sparkles for Shane and Joel. Leading the parade down the faint trail, Lee was ever vigilant for two-footed, four-footed, and slithering dangers. He took them across the road, followed York Creek until they got into the fields, and headed west toward the river bottoms.

"Can we gallop?" Bryan asked eagerly.

Turning around, Lee asked, "Is everyone okay with a gallop to the tree line?"

"Yes!"

"Let's do it!"

"Giddy-up," Traci squealed in a shrill voice.

Nudging Lady, Lee set the pace for the enthusiastic group. No one was more excited than Bryan who was flapping his legs like a rodeo rider. Soon they were near the tree line and Lee slowed them down to a walk once again. Reno was quick but he did not have the stamina to run that far with the horses. He eventually caught up and then followed random scents as they crossed his path.

The breezes and shade were just enough to keep them comfortable. The horses bobbed their heads rhythmically, swished their tails incessantly, and snorted out of their flared nostrils from time to time as if they were disgusted or impatient, but they were happy to be out of the confines of the pasture for a change. Connecting with the trail that wound through the pine tree stand, Lee led them back to the lane that came out at York Creek Road. They stayed on the shoulder until reaching Lee's driveway and finished their adventure about an hour after they started.

Lee and Gary attended to the horses while the others scooted over to the dessert table. It was filled with melons and fruits, brownies and pies, cookies and ice cream, making it difficult to choose. Between bites of cookie, Bryan was describing his grand adventure to Grandpa McVeigh who delighted in the boy's lively reenactment of galloping along the trails.

After a rich afternoon of visiting and relaxing, playing horseshoes and croquet, the various families began to gather their empty serving dishes and headed home to face another work week. Lee had stacked some wood near the fire pit and began to build a fire. Gathering lawn chairs into a cozy circle, Gary and Cindy, Lee and Abigail, Carrie Sue and Amy, were joined by Richard and Lisa. Bryan and Traci were eyeing the bag of marshmallows.

"If anyone's still hungry, there are plenty of leftovers in the fridge," Abigail offered.

She was met by a chorus of groans. Everyone seemed to be in a post-feeding lethargy and were content to slouch in the lawn chairs with legs comfortably stretched toward the fire. There was something calming about watching the spiral tongues of orange and amber flames flicker and flare. The soft hissing and crackling of the burning wood with an occasional pop that sent out a few brief sparks was mesmerizing.

"We've got another Ministerial Alliance meeting tomorrow," Cindy remarked.

"Oh, that's right," Abigail responded. "It's at Rev. Bordman's church this month."

"Are you and your father going to be able to make it?" Cindy asked Richard.

"We're planning on it. Amy's going to stay with Mom," Richard replied and then turned to Amy. "You might as well do your cleaning while you're with her if you want."

"Oh, good idea. I'll do that, er, *we'll* do that. Your mom always helps and scolds me for doing anything. She's so sweet. What time do you need me?"

"Yes, she is." Turning to Abigail, he asked, "Where is the church and about how much time will it take for us to get there?"

"Hawville Pres is north of Springfield right on route 1950 almost to the county border. I usually allow a minimum of thirty minutes to get there."

Turning back to Amy, Richard said, "Why don't you be at the house by eleven fifteen?"

"Works."

"I wonder if it'll be as crazy as the last meeting. It's hard to believe that it's already a month since Max got arrested," Abigail mused.

"What's going to happen to him?" Lee asked as he absent-mindedly stroked Reno's glossy coat. The over-stimulated dog had flopped down next to him and fell asleep.

Richard answered with his tongue firmly planted in his cheek. "Nothing much. We're taking a chapter out of Bynum's book, and somehow, we can't find any files. No files; no charges."

"What about those three thugs you hauled out of here?" Lee asked.

"Oh, we didn't lose any of those files. In fact, those files are getting thicker by the week according to Agent Diblassio."

That brought a chuckle from everyone who had been apprised of the local situation. Lisa said nothing, but kept listening and turning from one person to another as if she were watching a tennis match. *Thugs? Hauled out of here? Here? As in Dad's place?* She made a mental note to ask more later if it did not come up before then.

"I wish we could nail Bynum. He's the ringleader around here," Carrie Sue added ruefully.

"I wish we could round all of them up," Abigail asserted. "Then maybe their victims could get healed up quicker when they're not accessed over and over again." She was thinking about Sherry Samuels at the moment.

"What about my mom?" Carrie Sue finally got up the courage to ask the question that she was not entirely sure she wanted to have answered.

Richard looked sympathetically at Carrie Sue. He was beginning to understand the tension that existed in these victims after having had extensive conversations with Amy on her cleaning days. "I think that we're going to go slow in her case. Even though Ariel identified her, it's apparent that she's just following someone else's orders. Besides, if that latest picture of her isn't lying, she looks like she's in rough shape."

Carrie Sue heaved a sigh thick with impatience, sadness, and frustration driven by anger. She would be glad when it was all over. She mostly prayed that her mother was saved enough to make it to heaven despite having demonized personalities – she was not entirely sure about her theology in this matter. Sometimes she wished that her mother would pay for her cruelty over the years. She was definitely conflicted.

"Yes, she's deteriorating. She came into the store again last week and she looked awful. I thought she was going to cough up a lung. And she keeps on smoking!" She exchanged a meaningful glance with Abigail. They did not have to say that Carrie Sue's healing and the reversal of all things demonic were contributing to her mother's decline just as it had for her father. That he died more quickly only indicated that he had made more spiritual exchanges using Carrie Sue than her mother did.

Bryan's marshmallow suddenly erupted into a flame. Gary quickly snatched the stick from his hand and blew it out leaving a blackened, gooey blob at the end of the stick. "Aw," Bryan moaned.

"Let me get you another one," Gary said patiently as he knocked the mess off the end of the stick and into the fire. "This time watch how close you put it."

"I will, Daddy. I can do it," he said with all the confidence of a four-year-old.

The little diversion put a halt into the flow of the conversation and the group lapsed into a comfortable silence as they enjoyed their quintessential summer evening. Stars and planets began to make their presence known as the last vestiges of daylight faded. The chatter turned to more mundane things. Lee talked about the farm. Gary talked about his business. Their usual banter amused Lisa.

Richard finally stretched and yawned. "Folks, this has been a wonderful day. I haven't had such good down-home food in forever! Thanks for inviting me, but I should probably get home. I'm a grown man, but Mom and Dad will be wondering about me."

The men rose together and shook hands. Lee said, "You're welcome here any time."

"If you need an oil change or anything while you're here, I'll take care of you," Gary invited.

"I'm glad you mentioned that. I'm overdue. I'll take you up on that and be by this week." Richard was beginning to feel like he had come home and was nestling into a community. He did not realize how much he missed this kind of comradery and fellowship.

"Yeah, we should get going, too," Amy spoke for Carrie Sue who started to rise at the same time.

"Ooh! We need to lock up the chickens!" Carrie Sue remembered with alarm. She was envisioning an opportunistic fox or raccoon or opossum raiding the hen house.

"Work tomorrow," Gary announced. "We'd better get these short people to bed."

"Say good-bye to everyone," Cindy added as she rounded up her not-quite-ready-to-leave children.

After the last of the guests left, Lee and Abigail, Lisa and Reno were left gazing at the dying fire. Reluctant to turn in themselves, they ended up chatting for another hour. Lisa held her questions for now and just savored the end of a wonderful family-filled day. At last Lee grabbed a hoe and snuffed out the last of the embers while the ladies went into the house.

27

Tuesday, September 4

"How many eggs?" Abigail asked Lisa.

"Two. You really don't have to make them for me; you've done so much already."

"It's not a problem. I like being Susy Homemaker."

Lee came in from making his early morning rounds, adjusted his cap, and planted a kiss on the top of Lisa's head before putting his arms around Abigail's waist and nuzzling her neck as she faced the stove. "Good morning, ladies! Did you sleep well?"

"Like a log," Lisa answered.

"So, what's next for you? Have you decided on graduate school or are you going to start making your millions?"

"Mom wants me to get my masters. Actually, I think the only reason she does is so that she knows I'll be living with her for at least two more years."

Lee kept silent for a moment and then asked with a slight edge as he tipped his head and raised one eyebrow, "I didn't ask what your mom wants you to do. What do *you* want to do? Have you prayed about it and gotten peace one way or the other?"

Lisa was unaccustomed to this dad who spoke so boldly and naturally about spiritual matters. *Abigail must be a good influence on him.* She blushed slightly and looked at her hands before replying, "I guess I hadn't approached decisions like that. But I will. Pray, that is." Lisa was uncomfortable. She went to church as a kid, but when she went to college she did not bother.

She had drifted from God, and in the middle of these vibrant Spirit-filled Christians, she was beginning to wonder if she was even saved.

"Here you go," Abigail announced as she slid Lisa's eggs onto her plate and broke her reverie.

"Thanks. I can't believe how dark these yolks are."

"Fresh eggs! Nothing like 'em." Lee beamed as he looked at the eggs on his own plate. Spontaneously grabbing each of the ladies' hands, Lee bowed his head and prayed, "Lord, thank You for another day that You have made. We will rejoice and be glad in it. Thanks for this great food; thanks for our friends and family; thanks for Lisa being here and please give her peace about whatever direction is best for her now. Amen!"

There was contented silence as homemade blackberry "jammie" was slathered on browned and buttered toast. Lee washed bites down with gulps of coffee while Abigail and Lisa sipped their juice.

"I guess you can help me be a farmer, Lisa, while Abigail goes to town. If there's anything special you want to do or someplace or someone you want to visit, just let me know. I don't exactly have a tight schedule these days."

"Thanks, Daddy. I think I'd just like to hang out here. It's so peaceful. I didn't realize how much I missed the country. Mom's got a nice condo, but it's just so noisy and crowded there all the time. Traffic! People! Asphalt everywhere!"

"Well, kiddo," Lee began softly, "I wonder if your discontent with the big city life isn't God's way of confirming that you need to move out to the country."

Lisa had a feeling in her chest that she had not quite felt before. It was like an adrenaline surge and yet different. It was a physical sensation and yet it was not. The astonished expression on her face was not missed by either Lee or Abigail.

"What are you sensing?" Abigail asked as if she were in a counseling session.

"I don't know. It's strange, but when you said that, Daddy, I felt ... I don't know how to describe it ... kind of like peace with a kick."

"In my experience, that's confirmation from the Holy Spirit," Abigail said.

Lisa teared up and quickly dabbed them away with a corner of her napkin. "I – I never felt anything like that before, but it seems right. I didn't think God would answer prayers like that." She began to gush her confession. "I mean, I've been so mad at God because of the divorce and all. I just didn't think He'd listen to me. He answered your prayer about me, but when I look at you and your friends, I'm not even sure that I'm a Christian." Lisa dropped her head and wept great sobs.

Lee immediately scooted next to her and enveloped her in a great bear hug. Stroking her hair as he did when she was a small child, he let her cry it out on his broad shoulder. When the crying shuddered to a stop, she looked up at her father said, "I'm sorry, Dad. I'm sorry that I bought everything Mom said about you."

"I guess you did the same thing to God that you did to me: pushed us away."

That registered with Lisa, too. "Oh, you're right. I never made that connection."

This was a sacred moment between father and daughter. Abigail was beaming as she quietly listened to her husband counsel his daughter.

"Well, kiddo, I forgave you a long time ago. I'm just tickled that you're back. God never stopped loving you any more than I did. We were just waiting for you to come home."

"I think I'm home," Lisa said as she looked at her father's misty eyes.

"You're home, baby."

"So, when did you get so smart?" Lisa perked up and broke the tension.

"Probably along about the time your brain got fully developed," he laughed as he lightly rapped his knuckle on her head. "Besides," he jerked his thumb in Abigail's direction, "I've been hanging around with this lady and she's full of all kinds of stuff I never even thought about."

"I'd like to take a walk and think, er, pray about this stuff." Lisa excused herself and headed outside and was pleased that Reno decided to tag along. She laughed as he stretched and yawned, shook off his sleep and trotted up to her expectantly.

Lee and Abigail high-fived and hugged after the screen door banged shut. "Thank You, Jesus," Lee whispered his prayer with misty eyes and a small lump in his throat.

"Praise God!" Abigail agreed. She lingered in his embrace for a minute and then pulled away after she glanced at the clock. "Well, I'd better clear up this kitchen and head to town."

"How long will you be gone?"

"Oh, I'd guess that we'll be done around one or one-thirty. I might chit-chat with a few people and get back around two or two-thirty. There's plenty of left-overs for lunch. And supper," she added with a grin.

Soon Abigail was heading to the northern end of the county. She turned right at the end of York Creek Road so she could catch route 1950 and by-pass Kingston. Oakvale was so small that it was said you would miss it if you blinked. Another sage cracked that the city limit signs were posted on either side of a central telephone pole.

Others were converging on Hawville Presbyterian Church and before long the parking lot was filled with clergy and lay people. All of them were dedicated to the transformation of this geographical area.

Urdang, the ruling territorial principality that was over this geographical area, dreaded these meetings. He felt like a toothless dragon, a fangless snake, a vulture divested of its talons. It infuriated him that he was losing his grip on his assignment. It terrified him. He was always watching his back. All he could do now was to stir up his minions to goad the unbelievers to sin, to tempt the unbelieving believers to fail in their faith, and hope to trip up believers so that their witness faltered. He delighted in besmirching the spotted and wrinkled Church.

"Welcome! Welcome!" Rev. Boardman raised his voice to get the crowd's attention. "Grab a seat if you haven't already found one and we'll get started." He paused for the minute that it took for the group of more than fifty to settle down at the tables. "We've got an assortment of sandwiches and two kinds of soup at the counter. I probably shouldn't indulge in dessert after yesterday, but these ladies have done a fine job. Let's thank them." He nodded toward the pink-faced ladies behind the counter and led the clapping. Once that faded, he asked a blessing on the food.

Chairs scraped on the antique mottled gray tile floor that was typical of church basements of the early 1900's. They all seemed to have that peculiar clean smell that accompanied the glossy waxed surfaces. Conversations were resumed as the group picked up their food and returned to their seats. Abigail sat at one of the large round tables that seated eight and was pleased to be able to catch up with news from Paula, her friend, and Wanda, her chicken lady. Richard York sat across from her talking with Pastor Crenshaw about his parents.

Soon Pastor Spalding stood up and cleared his throat. "Good afternoon, ladies and gentlemen. It's so good to see you and great to know that this county is being bathed in prayer. I know that some of you are curious about what happened at the last meeting, so I'll give you a Reader's Digest version." That engendered a ripple of chuckles.

"There is a young man who got suckered into the local cult when he was in high school. Thanks to God's intervention, he's out, but not without a cost. He's safe for the time being, but he's asked me to have you pray for him by name: Max." Seeing the nods, he continued, "The cult does not want to lose any of its members. We all know that our county government has been infiltrated by Satanists. They arrested him last month, but I'm tickled to say that our friend here intervened," he waved his hand toward Richard. "Richard York, has friends in higher places who rescued Max."

All heads turned toward Richard who nodded his acknowledgement. "Keep him in your prayers as well. His family has become a target as well as Abigail

Steele's, er, sorry, Abigail Norris. I understand that there was an attempt to abduct her not too long ago."

The sound of breaths being sucked in were heard all over the room with exclamations of shock. "So, keep these front-line folks in your prayers. Abigail, is there anything you want to add?"

Abigail stood and let her eyes take in the concerned faces before she spoke. "I am grateful that God spared me from what would have undoubtedly been an unsavory end. Don't mess with my husband!" she quipped with a quick smile. "I only want to reiterate that these people need Jesus. They're not the enemy. The enemy is the enemy. We do not wage war against flesh and blood but against principalities and powers. No weapon formed against us will prosper!"

"Amen to that!" Pastor Spalding beamed. "Let's get a report from the back-to-school event. Who's got it?"

Pastor Clara stood. She had excellent administrative qualities and had energetically headed the project while delegating various aspects of the endeavor to different committees. After a succinct report, she returned to her seat.

"What's next? How else can we continue to impact our communities? Why don't we take a few minutes in small groups to brainstorm? Look at your calendars and let's see what we come up with."

After twenty minutes, it was apparent that the people at one table were getting excited and animated about their idea. The consensus was that there would be no real opportunity until Halloween. They all desperately wanted to provide an alternative to the traditional Halloween activities without doing a lame

Christian substitution, so they were all in agreement when the lively group presented their idea.

"It'll take a lot of work, and we might need a carpenter or two, and some creative people, and a bunch of folks for live displays, but we've got about eight weeks to get it together. We'll need a fairly large church basement with access to different rooms where the different themes will be depicted."

"What will we call it?"

"How about 'Heaven or Hell?' or something like that? It'll be all about making an eternal choice. We'll need people who are comfortable with explaining the Gospel and salvation for anyone who wants to make a decision."

The group was getting excited about the prospect. Suggestions were thrown out and written down by Pastor Clara. Folks were volunteering themselves and thinking of others whom they could recruit. They agreed that their various church youth groups should also be involved. Pastors were evaluating how well their buildings might fit the bill.

"I'm ashamed to say it," Pastor Benjamin Morgan began, "but my church family isn't all that big. We're growing some now, but we barely use the basement. I think it'll be perfect for this and we're right on the main drag in Kingston."

"Okay," Pastor Spalding summarized, "we've got a great start on the who-what-where-when-why. Pastor Clara, are you willing and able to organize the various committees again?"

"Absolutely!"

They closed the meeting by one-thirty after discussing a few more minor issues. Abigail was besieged with curious people who wanted to know more about her near abduction. After extricating herself from the group, she was able to make her way out to her truck. There was just a hint of fall in the air despite the warm temperatures. Abigail breathed in the air and reflected upon how blessed she felt.

Richard decided that today would be a good day to get his oil changed and the tires rotated. He had a hunch. He had asked Cindy for Gary's work number and arranged to come in right after he dropped his father off at home and changed out of his dress clothes.

Rolling up to Gary's body shop and mechanic business, Richard walked into the office. "Hey, thanks for getting me in on such short notice."

"It's the least I could do. I appreciate you keeping my cousin around so I have someone to harass."

"I do have an ulterior motive for coming here," Richard confessed with a mysterious smile.

"Oh yeah?"

"Do you do business with the local junk yard?"

"I sure do. Sometimes my customers need some after-market parts or they don't have insurance so they need the most economical parts for repairs."

"What's the name of the proprietor?"

"Larry Robbins," Gary replied in a sour tone that indicated that he did not like the man. "He's kind of a weasel. Shifty eyes. Chain smokes. Foul mouth. But he's always given me fair prices on stuff. He's got acres of cars and trucks and junk. He also stores some campers, trailers, and boats on the side."

"Can I pick your brain?"

"Sure."

"Say I'm trying to find a particular car but it's been chopped."

"I'd say that you'd need an act of God to find it. Chop shops can dismantle cars in a couple hours and sell the parts. Sometimes they sell the whole car to someone overseas. No questions asked. Hard to trace. Insurance companies don't have the manpower so they usually just settle when a car gets stolen."

"Can I ask you a favor?"

"Sure."

"We're trying to track down the car that disappeared with that Romanowski fellow. It was a brand-new car with a custom engine and a custom paint job according to his wife. He was really proud of it. I've got pictures. I have a hunch that it was processed through Robbins' place." Richard took the hard copy photos out of the envelope that he had in his shirt pocket and showed them to Gary.

"Sweet!" Gary studied the photos and asked, "You think Robbins runs a chop shop? I know the sheriff uses his place for impound sometimes since he has fencing and the proverbial yard dog."

"Maybe. He's the only game in town, isn't he? What would Sheriff Bynum do with a car that he wanted to get rid of?" That question reminded him of another aspect of their investigations. *What ever happened to Carrie Sue's brother's car?* "I need to find another car, too. Do you remember that car that was abandoned on Lee's property?"

"Sure do." Gary had an incredible memory for cars. "Beat up old Chevy Nova with tinted windows. But it had a sweet six-banger under the hood." Gary snapped his fingers and cracked his biggest conspiratorial grin.

"You know, I just remembered that I needed to see if I could find a radiator cap for a Chevy Nova and a replacement front fender and door for a 2007 Camaro. Huh! What a crazy coincidence!"

"Do you have an extra cap?" Richard grinned at his new friend.

"Sure do. And the linen service just dropped off our shirts. Why don't you grab one out of the office? There should be a ton of grimy caps laying around."

Richard went to the office and exchanged his shirt for a McCord's Repair Garage shirt while Gary asked Rusty to make a priority of Richard's oil change and tire rotation. Richard chuckled at the crooked, faded sign over Gary's desk that said "The Busted Knuckle Garage – repair and despair under one roof" and featured several bandaged fingers.

Looking at Richard when he emerged from the office, Gary frowned.

"What's wrong?"

"You're too clean, man." Looking around, he picked a discarded oil filter off the top of the barrel and tossed it to Richard. "Here. Get some of that grime on your hands so you look like a grease monkey instead of a desk jockey."

Richard chuckled and complied. "Thanks. I should have thought of that." He sacrificed his nice denim jeans by wiping his grimy hands on them. *I hope Amy knows how to get grease out.*

"Nice touch," Gary laughed. "Let's go."

After settling into the truck, the two men talked about their prospects. "What do you say we pray about it?" Gary suggested.

"Uh, sure." It was obvious that Richard was unaccustomed to including God in his daily tasks. Out loud. With other men. "Can you start it?"

"Absolutely! Lord, we're asking for success on this little mission. We know that it's a long shot, but with You everything is possible. Lord, if either car is in that junkyard, would You show us where it is? As Richard prays in agreement, declare that it is finished so justice will prevail here on earth as it is in heaven, amen."

There was a momentary awkward silence as Richard swallowed nervously. "Yes, Lord, I'm asking that You would make it happen today like Gary prayed. We need solid evidence. Uh, er, amen."

"Ah, ha, ha, ha, ha," Gary chuckled easily with his infectious laugh. "You pray like I used to before my wife and I started hanging out with Abigail. You'll get used to it!"

Richard saw the humor and laughed at himself. "I hope you're right. I don't know if it's because of Dad's near miss and Mom's decline, but I think I've prayed more since I got back here than in all the rest of my life put together."

"Here we are," Gary announced as he down-shifted and pulled up to the trailer that served as an office for Robbins' Junkyard and Storage. "Wait by the truck and I'll see where he is. I'm not sure where Sadie is."

"Sadie?"

"His dog. I think it's short for Sadistic." Gary chuckled as he climbed the rickety wooden steps with the wobbly iron handrail that would not save anyone from a fall, and walked into the office calling out, "Hey Larry, you here?"

No answer. But he did ascertain that the big mongrel was enjoying the feeble output of the clattering air conditioning unit. Returning to his truck, reaching in through the open window, Gary tooted on the horn twice. "We'll just wait until he gets here," Gary said to no one. Removing his cap, he looked around, but Richard had vanished from sight.

Soon Gary heard the creaking of an old pick-up truck that could use a new muffler approaching on one of the narrow, dusty, one-lane rutted passageways that randomly crossed the property. It must have made sense to Larry and his sons. The man had every vehicle memorized. He knew where it was and what parts might be available to sell or trade.

The wiry man stepped out of his truck, wiped his brow and resettled his faded cap back onto what little stringy hair remained on his balding head. His hawk-like nose sat between two closely spaced beady eyes and over a thin mustache. "What can I do for ya today?" He seemed to like Gary and toned down his language unless others were around.

"I've got two things. The first one should be easy. I need a radiator cap for a '96 Nova. The other one I might have to find someplace else. I think it's a pretty long shot."

"I've got a couple radiators to choose from. What's the other one?"

"I've got a sick man I need to take care of," Gary said as he laid out his sad yarn. "He just bought a brand spanking new 2007 Camaro and would you believe that the first time he let his wife drive it, she smashed into the workbench inside his garage? I guess the front end was longer than she thought. Anyways, the guy doesn't want his insurance to go up so he asked me to see if I could try to find a new driver's side door and front fender for it. I don't know how she missed smashing the headlights. He said he'd pay top dollar 'cause it'd be cheaper in the long run."

Larry's greed button had just been punched. He removed his cap and scratched his bald spot as he considered his situation. *That's easy money for me. If Bynum finds out, I'll end up in the crusher. Of course, he never comes here; he just sends the tow truck.* "Well, now, I'll have to check my records. I'm not sure if anything like that came in. I was off a couple of days here and there. Somethin' mighta come in when I was gone and one of the boys coulda stashed it somewhere."

"I'd appreciate it. This guy's from out of town and he's in a bit of a hurry. He's a friend of the family and I told him I'd see what I could do." *As if he'd miss a hot car like that!* Gary knew that Larry Robbins was hiding something because that man knew this place like the back of his hand. He could name any make, model, and part and Larry would chug off in his old truck with the huge tool box on the back and return within a very short time.

Larry was not good at hiding his nervousness. He shook slightly as he lit up another cigarette. "Let me go get that radiator cap. I'll get you the best looking one. If it ain't right, just come back and exchange it for the other one."

"Great. I'll wait here."

Larry chugged off in the truck. It gave him more time to think about his next move. *It just doesn't feel right. But, dang, that's good money and under the table. I can trust McCord.* He quickly retrieved the better of two caps and stuck it in his shirt pocket. Eating the dust that had not yet settled, he bumped back to the office where McCord was talking with another man. *Where'd he come from?* Larry's internal alarms were going off.

Gary and Richard met him at the back his truck. "Perfect!" he said and transferred it into his own pocket. They agreed on a price and Gary paid him immediately.

"Hey, Larry, this is Rich, one of my new guys. I brought him along so he can find you when I'm busy."

Richard nodded and gave a short wave. The lowered bill of the cap hid his eyes. Larry nodded back and felt a little calmer. *Gary's straight up.*

"What about the Camaro parts? Any luck?"

"Well, as a matter of fact, I believe I have just what you're looking for." Larry nodded toward the area usually reserved for storage. "I called my son. He said he thought it was a storage customer waiting for a repair. He takes care of that end of the business. He said someone rear ended it. With the custom spoiler, mufflers, and paint job, it got totaled." Larry was lying through his teeth and he knew that Gary knew it but he wanted the money.

"Great! My friend will be so relieved. Do you mind if we take a look first?"

"Uh, sure. No problem. It's right over there." Larry waved in the general direction of the storage area. You can walk; I'll need my tools." With that, Larry hopped back into his truck and drove the short distance to the tarp-covered vehicle.

Once Larry removed the door and started working on the fender, Richard peered through the windshield and memorized the VIN. His excellent memory for

411

numbers and details served him well. This was the vehicle. He prayed that fingerprints would be useable. Nodding to Gary, Richard stepped around the car and furtively snapped a number of pictures with his cell phone. He watched Larry work.

Within minutes, Larry had the fender detached from the frame. He was quick. Chop shop quick.

"Thanks, man," Gary said with a disarming laugh as they carefully loaded the fender, "if this guy ever lets his wife drive it again, I might be back for more parts."

Gary's wallet was considerably lighter when he left. Richard's heart was considerably lighter. At last he had solid evidence of Barry Romanowski's last known whereabouts. They were still not quite sure where Billy Wagner's car was rusting in peace.

"Dad, could I ask you and Abigail for a huge favor?" Lisa asked as she looked intently at her father and then at Abigail across the dining room table.

"You can ask anything," he teased.

"I did a lot of soul-searching today and I decided that I'm really sick of school and I really am not a big city girl and I really don't want to rack up more student loan debt. I want to start my career."

"Well! That sounds decisive."

She hung her head a little as she resumed. "I guess I've been living Mom's dreams for me and I've been afraid to cross her so I've just gone along."

"Well, she can be formidable," Lee agreed. "I guess that can be both a blessing and a curse." He chuckled without a trace of bitterness. "So, what's the favor?"

"I called the university and cancelled everything. I'm not going back. I don't want to work for some big-time accounting firm. I want to go into business for myself. Somewhere around here."

"Really!" Lee exclaimed. He was thrilled. He had been sensing that this was the direction Lisa was heading.

"Can I crash here until I can get started and find my own place?"

"Absolutely!"

"Are you sure? I mean, you two are still newlyweds and all."

"Why do you think I built this great big house?"

"Oh."

28

Friday, September 7, Marriage to the Beast

The beast. The arrogant, blasphemous beast. This was his day. The dragon gave him his power and throne and great authority. This highly demonized mortal was not *the* beast spoken of in the end-time prophecies. This was *a* beast, a type. A human pawn had always been waiting in the wings for the very end of time. No one knew the day nor the hour. The prudent were prepared. Satan deemed himself prudent despite the declaration of Scripture that said that his wisdom had been corrupted.

Just as the antichrist is coming, and even now many antichrists have arisen, so the beast is coming and many beasts have arisen. Every region touted its candidates. The region that fell to Xerxes was no exception. Tonight, there would be an extravagant marriage ceremony. There would be blood sacrifices. There would be dismemberments of females from infants to age twenty-one. It would salve the fury of the most voracious appetites of these blood-thirsty agents of Satan. Only for a moment. If that.

Urdang was as close to delighted as a demon could be. Tonight, there would be action. He was certain that he and his underlings would be able to do severe damage in the territory. Already there were family squabbles, employees being fired, children needing stitches and casts from unusual falls, and several unfortunate traffic accidents. Several people who were teetering on the brink of death finally plunged over.

Teens skipped school and smoked weed. Miscreants conspired to rip off businesses. Jealousy and envy, bitterness and hatred, fear and anxiety were ratcheted up a notch or two and made for a miserable day for many of the citizens.

"You're deep in thought," Lee commented to Lisa over breakfast.

Blowing out a deep sigh, she said, "Mom's not happy. She's blaming you for brain-washing me."

"You're welcome," he said and gave her a bright semi-sarcastic smile.

"Da-ad! This is serious," Lisa complained and rolled her eyes at him. "I don't like it when Mom's mad at me. And I feel bad, too, like I'm abandoning her."

"Sorry. Lisa, every parent hates the day when their child grows up and leaves the nest. It's probably harder for moms than for dads, but it's what we're supposed to do. She'll get over it eventually. You haven't abandoned her. You can visit each other and talk on the phone."

"You're right. It just spoils all the fun."

"This is your mother and this is the way she is. Until God changes her, this is what you have to deal with. So, either you let her control your fun or you stand up like the sensible young adult that you are and move on. You may have to be a bit assertive and politely let her know that this is your independent decision and you're moving forward."

"You're right." Lisa finally let her face relax into a smile. "I'm going to fly back, pack up a car load of stuff, and then drive back here. As much as I want to get started, I think I'll take my time and hang with Mom for a week or two. I don't really need to rush."

"That sounds like a good plan. Hey, you're on your own this morning. I'm going to sit in on a session with Abigail and one of her clients."

Lisa was curious but she did not ask. "I'll use the time to arrange my flight and pack a little bag. I'll leave most of my stuff here if you don't mind."

Soon Abigail and Lee were heading down the road in separate vehicles. Lee would sit in on the session with the young Craig Jackson and then head to the feed store. Abigail hoped that Sherry Samuels would show up for her appointment. She could get an earlier start on her canning with Amy if she did not show. There were still plenty of beans and tomatoes coming in.

Grace was flustered. Her eleven-year-old son was slouched sullenly in the passenger seat with his arms folded. "I don't know why I have to talk to this stupid counselor."

"Just do it." Grace tried not to plead. "I think you need to talk to someone about your cousin. You've been so angry since he went to prison. She helped me and I think she can help you if you give her a chance. Her husband will be there, too."

The boy groaned. *Oh brother! All these grownups just ganging up on me.* "All right," he said as he rolled out of the car and shut the door with a little more force than was necessary. He was nearly as tall as his mother and looked very much like her. His voice had not yet changed, but the peach fuzz that was on his face was beginning to get coarser.

Lee and Abigail were already inside. After having Grace sign a consent form, she invited Craig into the office. "Do you want your mom to come in with you or can you handle it?"

"She can stay out here," he muttered.

"Come in and make yourself comfortable. This is my husband, Mr. Norris. I like to have a man in the room when I work with young men." Abigail tried to make him live up to a young man's standard rather than drop down to a young boy's standard.

"So, I take it that your mom brought you here and you're not real pleased."

"You could say that." His eyes shifted from Abigail to Lee and back to Abigail again before he found a spot on the floor. He wanted to bolt and run, but he was not sure about Lee. He looked nice, but he also looked like a man that would not tolerate trouble.

"Well, maybe if I talk fast and you listen fast we can get you out of here sooner."

He wanted to smile, but was determined to maintain a straight face.

"You're eleven?"

"Yeah. I'm in sixth grade."

"What's your favorite subject?"

He was not expecting that question so he hesitated before he responded. "Science."

"Yuk! That was one of my least favorite subjects. You have fun with that." Abigail tried to inject a little humor into the situation, but the boy was not buying it. *Lord, please grant me favor.*

"Let me ask you one more annoying question and then we'll get into stuff if you're up to it: What's your relationship like with God these days?"

417

Shifting his eyes nervously between Abigail and the floor, Craig finally said, "I go to church because I have to, but I don't get much out of it anymore."

"Did you get stuff out of it before?"

"Yeah, I guess it was a couple of years ago."

"What changed?"

Craig pressed his lips together. He really did not want to talk about anything and especially not about his cousin. He did not want to admit just how deeply the whole murder affected him. Craig was his hero. He was cool. He wanted to emulate him in every way. Now he was confused, drifting. He resigned himself to his fate and blurted out, "Everything."

"Everything? Like everything has changed because of your cousin Craig?"

"Something like that."

"Do your friends treat you differently?"

"They used to think I was cool. Now they make fun of me. They say that I'll be just like him and end up in prison. None of the girls will talk to me because they say I'll kill 'em."

"Ouch!" Abigail sympathized. "How does that make you feel?"

"Mad!" He sounded mad. He glared at Abigail.

Abigail sensed a presence in the boy. "On a scale of zero to ten with ten being the most intense, how mad does it make you feel when someone says something like that?"

"Twenty!" Craig spit out as his face reddened.

"That's a lot of anger." That confirmed to Abigail that there was some demon-fueled anger.

"It's how I feel. It makes me want to beat them up."

"But then you'd just prove their point."

"Yeah."

"So, you have all this anger stuffed inside and you don't know how to get rid of it."

He was amazed and relieved that someone could articulate his double-bind. She had his attention now. "Yeah," he said softly as he stared at that spot just beyond his shoes.

"Do you want to get rid of that anger and start feeling like yourself again?"

"I guess."

"Good. Let me talk to you about a couple of things and then we'll do a little praying and we'll see what Jesus shows you. Okay?"

"Yeah."

Abigail told Craig that Jesus was the same yesterday, today, and tomorrow and could show him things in old memories that he needed to see or hear or understand. She also told Craig that because of some things that happen in our lives, Satan takes advantage of it by having one of his demons oppress us. "Jesus wants to set you free. What has happened has already happened, but your pain and anger because of what happened can be healed. You want to try?"

"I guess."

"Great. I'm going to pray and ask God to bring you to a memory or thought that tells us where this kind of twenty-on-a-scale-of-zero-to-ten anger is coming from. You know that it really doesn't make sense that some stupid stuff your friends say should make you *that* mad, right?"

"Uh huh." Craig was following her reasoning and began to feel a little hopeful.

"Ok, I'll pray and then I'll shut up. You close your eyes so this room doesn't distract you and then just tell me the first thing that pops into your mind."

"Okay."

"Lord, Your word says that the spirit of the man is the lamp of the Lord and by it You examine the innermost chambers. Would You please show Craig where this kind of anger is coming from?" Abigail watched Craig for a minute and then noticed a change. "What's coming to you?"

He opened his eyes and looked at her with wonder as he said, "Well, I thought of a time when big Craig took me to the capital with him and his friend."

"How old were you?"

"Eight or nine. Craig just got his license and he wanted to go to the big city. Mom was really mad that he took me that far without telling her."

"What happened? Why did God bring you to that memory?"

"Um, well," Craig hesitated and squirmed. He was clearly uncomfortable with speaking about whatever had happened. "Big Craig and his friend told me that they'd kill me if I ever told."

"No one's going to know what you say. I can't even tell your mom what we discuss in here."

Craig looked Abigail in the eyes and made his decision. "Okay. It was summer time and we were just driving around in a bad part of town. It was hot and the windows were down. I think Craig got us lost and Jeff was mad. We were stopped at a light and there was a guy standing there. Jeff asked him for the quickest way back to the expressway." Craig hesitated, swallowed hard, and shifted his glance over to Lee before looking back at the floor.

"What happened?"

"The guy started cussing us out and flipped Jeff off. He told him that we were so stupid that we deserved to get bumped off."

"Not nice."

"When he walked away, Jeff pulled out a gun and shot him."

Abigail did not see that coming and tried to hide her shock. "Wow! Then what?"

"Big Craig peeled out of there and somehow we found our way back to the expressway."

"Did either one of them say anything?"

"Yeah. Jeff turned around and looked at me and said that we were both murderers because we were exceptories."

"Accessories?"

"Yeah. That's the word."

"Then what?"

"They just laughed about it. Then when I got out of the car, Jeff grabbed me and said, 'If you ever tell, I'll kill you, you little murderer.' Then he let me go."

"Wow! That's scary stuff," Abigail validated Craig's feelings. "So then, every time one of your classmates calls you a murderer, you're reminded of Jeff. That probably makes you scared and fear drives anger. Makes sense."

"Yeah." Craig connected some of the dots and it gave him more hope. He sat a little taller in his chair.

"Let's talk about some of these things I call verbal assaults." Abigail then explained about the power of believing lies and deceptions, making real or implied vows, and having curses and judgments pronounced over him. She explained about strongholds and the demons that hung out in them. He was tracking with her and eager to shed this man-sized burden.

"How about if I pray first and then you pray in agreement. I don't care if you just say, 'What she said, amen.'"

"Yeah." Craig sat up even straighter in his chair, folded his hands, and bowed his head.

"Lord, You were there that day, we ask that as Craig is focusing on that horrible memory, that You would manifest Your presence to him in the memory in whatever way You choose. Let Craig see You there with his spiritual eyes or hear You with his spiritual ears or just sense Your presence and the truth that You have for him that will set him free." Abigail paused and waited for Craig's response.

After a few moments, he slowly lifted his head and asked, "Is it true?"

"Is what true?"

"I saw Jesus, I mean, I think it was Jesus. He was sitting in the back seat with me and when Jeff shot the guy He put His hand over my eyes so I couldn't see it happen. And when Jeff turned around and said that stuff, Jesus put His hands over my ears and I couldn't hear him."

"Cool." Abigail was relieved that this little guy was able to find some peace. "What does that mean to you? What's the truth?"

"It means that Jesus was with me all the time and that He was protecting me from the bad stuff and that I'm not a murderer and Jeff can't kill me either."

"Let's look back at that memory. How does it feel now?"

"It's not so scary anymore. I think I should tell Mom and Dad."

"That's probably a good idea. Let me ask you one more question: Thinking about your friends calling you names and the girls saying that stuff, how mad does it make you feel on a scale of zero to ten right now?"

Craig cocked his head to the right and furrowed his brows. "I think only about a two."

"Good. I think that's a normal amount. You don't want to beat anyone up?"

"Nope!" Craig finally smiled a bashful smile that displayed his dimples.

"Jesus did a wonderful thing here. You did great. Let me close in prayer and get you out of here."

After Craig and his mother left, Lee walked over to Abigail, hugged her and said, "That was amazing. I don't know how you did that."

"Totally God! I wasn't sure that I'd get anywhere with him at first. Poor kid! That was a lot of junk."

Glancing at his wrist, Lee said, "How long before your next one?"

"Hopefully she'll be here by noon. If she doesn't show, I'll stop at home and change into play clothes before I head over to the old place. Amy and I are going to do some more canning. She's turning into a regular Susie homemaker."

As it turned out, Sherry Samuels did show up for her scheduled appointment. Abigail was relieved. The tall woman swept into the room, dropped her bag on the floor next to her chair, and looked expectantly at Abigail.

"I'm glad you could make it today," Abigail said. "How have things been? Both the inside and outside worlds? Were you taken to the ritual last Friday?"

"I don't think so, but maybe you need to talk to someone else about that."

"Is Sammy around?" Abigail hoped she could milk a little more information out of the young observer this time.

"I'm here!" the little guy cheerfully announced.

"Are you safe?"

"Yep."

"Did they make you go to the ritual last week?"

"Yeah," he said sadly. "Some guy came to our house and got us."

The thought sickened Abigail. "I'm so sorry. We need to get everyone healed up and back inside so they can't get accessed."

"They said it could never happen."

"Who's they?"

"Oh, Seimers and the outside guys."

"I happen to know that they're wrong, but it will take a lot of work. I'll work as hard as you guys do, ya know?"

"I know that but the big people in here don't believe you."

"Can you tell me more about the hospital? Where do you live?"

Sammy debated. He might get into trouble if he said the wrong thing, but he liked this lady and he believed her. "Well, I live on the third floor. Peeds."

"Is that short for pediatrics?" Abigail started to have a better idea about the hospital and started to wrack her brain for sinister counterparts to typical hospital departments.

"Yeah, that's it. I can't say that word very good."

"That's enough, lady," a gruff voice interrupted.

"Seimers?"

"Yeah. What are you doing grilling that kid?"

"I'm asking questions so I can understand and help more effectively. Besides," she shot, "he seems to be one of the few brave souls in there who's willing to talk with me."

"That's 'cause he doesn't know any better. He's just a kid."

"With good instincts." Abigail smiled pleasantly as if she were chatting with an old friend. "So, you're the administrator of this hospital?"

"What if I am?"

"That means that you know what goes on in all the departments. I'll bet your OB/GYN department is plenty busy."

He reacted as if he had been struck in the face. "How would you know about that?"

"I just figured that your buddies, the Satanists, would structure your system like a real hospital. I suppose the morgue is busy, too."

He was jolted by that remark as well. He was unnerved and angry. Actually, he was frightened and that fear fueled his anger. "You're going to get us all killed, lady! Why can't you leave us alone?"

"First of all, they can't kill you if the true Creator God who wrote all your days in His book doesn't permit it. Secondly, some of your people in there come here because they are tired of the Satanists' agenda and want out."

"I don't care what they want. It doesn't concern me."

"Yes, it does. Whether you like it or not, you all use the same body. If you go to a ritual, you drag all the little kids and grown-ups along."

"That's not my problem."

"Yes and no. Look! I don't want to waste your time arguing these points. Do you really want to rise up in the satanic kingdom and kill babies and rape and torture children and carry on your grandmother's legacy?"

"No! I hated her guts."

"I don't see any difference between you and her."

"There's a big difference," he retorted lamely.

Softening her voice when she noted the resignation, Abigail gently said, "I do believe that there is a difference in your hearts. Your grandmother was hard and she bought into all of it. You, on the other hand, seem to have a softer heart. Your biggest problem is that if you even appear to want to bail on Satanism, your demons will rat you out and you're not sure you could survive their discipline."

Sucking his lips in and clamping down on them as if to keep from saying something, Seimers stared at two different points on the floor – neither of which was focused on the external world. Finally, he heaved a resigned sigh and asked, "What do you want?"

"One step at a time, I'd like to discharge everyone from the hospital. There must be a bunch in the psych ward and whatever other floors and wards you have."

He did not flinch this time. "Yeah, you don't want to know what goes on in the psych ward and the secret department attached to it. Lobotomies."

Abigail could only imagine the horrors to which Sherry Samuels had been subjected over the course of her life from Satanists and witches and warlocks. Then there were all the medical situations that she alluded to because of her mother. Her mother sounded like one of those Munchausen's by Proxy Syndrome people. What a nightmare Sherry's childhood must have been.

Seimers and Abigail settled on a strategy once he decided that he was going to be all in. He was concerned by some of the doctors and nurses, aides and orderlies, maintenance guys and others who made up the staff of the internal hospital. He allowed her to pray for protection for himself and those who were willing to be saved, healed, and delivered. There were some spontaneous integrations. Many more remained in their beds recovering from various traumas.

It was a start. It was a very good start. Abigail was pleased as she finished the session by praying once again that Sherry would not get accessed and taken to the ritual tonight. After setting up their next appointment, Sherry switched into someone who could drive them home. Abigail closed down the office and also headed home.

All over the globe human sacrifices had been procured. Brides had been readied. The elaborate gowns thrilled the innocent little girls until they were walked through their marriage ceremonies and assaulted on their marriage beds by the representative beast of Satan. Their gowns became exceedingly spotted and wrinkled. The little girls split off new personalities as trauma after perverse trauma racked their young bodies. Some of them did not survive the night for some the beasts were indeed beastly. Death was a blessing in disguise. Their tormented spirits were whisked to the Throne Room to join the other martyrs. So many others had survived nights like this and had begged for death to swallow them up and release them from their agony.

———————————

The windows were open and fresh night-time breezes cooled the house. Carrie Sue and Amy talked long into the night with Princess curled in the doorway to the kitchen. They were both somewhat ill at ease, but were pleased that their former internal magnets did not draw them to the ritual. It was almost midnight when they decided to turn in.

"I'm heading for bed," Amy announced. "I hope David settles down. He's seems to be getting more active these days."

"Me too," Carrie Sue said reluctantly. She was feeling uneasy but attributed it to the fact that it was a big ritual night. Double checking the locks on the front door, she snapped lights off as she followed Amy back through the kitchen. Princess was rolled completely onto her side, stretched out on the cool floor, and barely acknowledged the two women as they stepped over her. Amy used the bathroom while Carrie Sue headed upstairs.

29

Saturday, September 8

By three o'clock in the morning, Xerxes and his comrades were spent. He was somewhat placated by the performance of his underlings so he was in as good a mood as he ever was. Curses had been sent out and he felt confident that they would strike their marks. Demonic messengers launched their diabolical attacks. Reinforcements had been called in. Those human and demonic reserves were not familiar with Urdang's territory and assumed that they would be as successful here as they were anywhere they were summoned.

It took nearly two hours to drive from the ritual site to the unincorporated rural area. Austin Anderson was a fireman in his other life in the capital city and had been sent out with Levi Blevins. Levi was familiar with these roads. He had driven them a number of times and he had been party to several attacks on the old farmhouse on top of the hill. He did not want to think about some of his former encounters with these women as he led Austin over hills and around curves until they arrived at Charlie Fletcher's place. He left his new SUV parked near the dust-streaked maroon pickup truck. It had not been driven since the day Charlie shot himself.

Austin skidded to a halt next to Levi's vehicle and immediately began scrounging around behind the seat in his truck where he picked up a glass soda bottle. Anyone looking into his cab would just see ordinary trash, but it was actually part of his arsenal. So were the rags. He was a smoker so the cigarette lighters were not out of place either. Funny how there was an increase in arson investigations in the big city since he joined the company!

"You think there's some gasoline stored around here somewhere?" Austin asked Levi as he looked at faint outlines of the barn and outbuildings. He could always siphon gas from Charlie's gas tank, but he would rather use an easier option. Basically a lazy man, he sought an easy life. He took short-cuts; he took the easy way out as much as possible. Fast food wrappers crumpled on the floorboards attested to that trait. Except when it came to arson.

"I'll go check his shed. He might have a lawnmower or something in there." Levi moved stealthily like a night creature and was nearly undetectable in his dark clothes. Austin was unable to track his movements in the pre-dawn darkness and was momentarily startled when the two-gallon faded red plastic gas container suddenly appeared on his tailgate next to where he had laid out the components for his Molotov cocktail.

"Perfect. One of these babies is enough to torch the place." Grabbing the grimy yellow spout with his grimy hand, he unscrewed it, removed the inner cap, put the spout back on, and poured gasoline into the bottle. Not bothering to replace the inner cap, Austin handed the container back to Levi and finished his task. Quietly putting his tailgate up, he said, "Let's roll." He did not pay attention to the quiet rattle of the plastic cap as it fell to the ground and bounced underneath his truck.

Parts of Levi were very eager and highly motivated to wreak havoc on those women, while other more cautious personalities were jumpy. The already high-strung young man was as taut as an over-wound guitar string and he was ready to snap. With very strong mixed feelings, he got into the passenger seat of Austin's unkempt truck. Levi's fastidiousness and meticulousness made them an odd pair. But an order was an order. He had failed before; he would not fail again. He set his jaw as he patted the dagger that was sitting in his pocket.

"Slow down. Make a sharp left just past that tree. When you get up next to the house, turn around so we can make a quick get-away." Levi remembered the odd sensation. The loss of power and concentration. Dread fell over him. There was something spooky about this property and he could not wait to leave. *Why did Herrak choose him? It should have been Max.* He was reminded of yet another failure. He could not keep his recruit either.

Austin followed Levi's instructions and soon his truck was crunching gravel and slowly creaking up the driveway without the benefit of lights. It was half way between the last quarter and a new moon so the silver lunar sliver was hardly a help in the predawn darkness. His youthful eyes quickly adapted and he went up to the house as planned.

They did not plan on Princess. She heard the first squeak of the truck's springs and scrambled to her feet, instantly alert. The low rumble in her throat was punctuated by several soft woofs which effectively woke both Carrie Sue and Amy who were extremely light sleepers.

Amy looked out the window at the head of her bed and saw the dark truck as it turned around. The bright red flash from the brake lights punctuated the soft glow of the yard light. Its movement triggered the motion-sensor lights once he got within range. She could see two men. Grabbing her pepper gel and cell phone from her night stand, she quickly moved to the bottom of the stairs and whispered loudly, "Carrie Sue! There's someone in the driveway! You call Abigail. I'll call Richard."

They had a plan. They worked the plan that they hoped they would never have had to use. Princess was now barking loudly and was furiously scratching at the front door.

"Should we let her out?" Carrie Sue asked.

"No. They might hurt her. She can protect us better if they get in."

Having been reminded by Lee to get to their safe zones, the ladies waited for rescue. And prayed.

Having triggered the lights, Austin and Levi had to put it in high gear now. "Give me the bottle!" Austin demanded with a string of expletives.

Levi's eyes widened as Austin flicked the lighter and started the end of the twisted rag on fire. He could already smell the faint odor of gasoline. Expecting it to explode in his hands, envisioning a blistering death, he snapped. Shoving the bottle into Austin's hand, Levi jumped out of the truck and started running down the driveway.

Austin was shocked that Levi had bailed on him. Anger rose like flames. Running to the front of the house he hastily hurled the bottle at the front windows of Abigail's former bedroom. There were two large side-by-side, old-fashioned farmhouse windows with an eight-inch gap between them. He hit the gap and the incendiary device shattered. Gasoline splattered all over the windows and screens before splashing and dripping onto the porch. *I can't believe I didn't break the window!*

What he could not know is that an angel of the Great Enemy had deflected his normally precise aim just enough to allow it to impact the least damaging place. He also sensed something odd about this place, but he could not put his finger on it. He did not have time to think. He had to move.

Austin cursed his bad luck, but could not keep from pausing long enough to enjoy the yellow and blue wave of flames as they hungrily consumed the gasoline fumes and then began to eat at the wooden structure. The screams of the women and the furious barking of the dog roused him. Jumping into the open door of his running truck, he slammed it into gear, hit the lights, and careened down the curvy driveway.

Levi was nearing the road and when he heard Austin coming, he stopped and waited on the side of the driveway expecting to be picked up. Austin had a different idea. He accelerated and swerved onto the grass. Levi underestimated Austin's fiendish rage and was unable to move more than one step after he realized his mistake. He could not avoid the front end of Austin's speeding pickup truck. His catapulting body glanced off the windshield and settled face up in the cool, freshly mown grass near the edge of the ditch.

Lee and Richard had gotten their respective phone calls at about the same time. Richard was far more practiced in going from sleep to combat-ready in a nanosecond. He took in the tailgate of the fleeing pickup truck at the same time that he saw the front of the house on fire and the silhouette of someone with a garden hose. He chose to fight the fire rather than to chase the truck. Driving hurriedly up the driveway and skidding to a halt, he took over the hose for Carrie Sue and told her to see if Amy needed help inside.

Amy was using the fire extinguisher that was kept in the corner of the kitchen and was able to put out the drapes and carpet. She ignored the cut on the bottom of her bare foot from the glass which had shattered with the intense heat. As the front porch was being hosed down, some of the water came through the screens. *Oh, this is going to be a mess to clean up!*

By the time Carrie Sue hustled around to the back door, Amy was satisfied that the fire was extinguished in the bedroom and was sitting in a chair in the kitchen with her foot propped up on the table. Blood-soaked paper towels were piling up.

"Amy! Are you, all right?"

"It's just bleeding a lot. I stepped in some of that glass. Can you check to make sure nothing flared up again? Watch out for glass!"

"Sure. Lee and Abigail just pulled up, I'll go get them." Carrie Sue remembered how Lee had cared for her sprains and bruises after her adventures last year. Unlocking and opening the front door, Carrie Sue called out, "Is it safe? Is it out?"

"Yes. Good job, ladies. Is Amy okay?"

"She cut her foot on some glass. She's in the kitchen and could use a little help."

Both Lee and Abigail dashed up the steps and crossed the unburned portion of the porch. Hurrying to the kitchen, Lee quickly assessed the cut and said that he thought that they could use butterfly bandages and avoid a trip to the hospital. Carrie Sue was already headed to the bathroom for the first aid kit.

"What's Princess barking at?" Amy asked. "She acts like she has a coon treed." The dog had slipped out at some point in the midst of all the confusion.

Richard had joined the group after making sure that the fire was completely quenched both inside and out. "I'll go check. Don't touch anything out there. I'll need to process the crime scene. Carrie Sue, do you want to join me? Princess might not appreciate seeing me without one of you."

"Uh, sure." Carrie Sue was not a big one for adventures and this seemed like yet another crazy escapade in an already big adventure. She was reassured by the presence of the very fit, very astute man who confidently walked down the front yard a few steps in front of her. Princess was still barking.

It was nearly dawn and the robins were trilling out their first songs. Cardinals chirped their one syllable notes while other unidentified birds added to the morning concert.

"Call her," Richard instructed quietly.

"Princess! Come here, girl!"

They heard her whine in protest. They got closer and in the dim light they could see her tensely approach an elongated dark object and then jump back barking ferociously with hackles raised. Charging and backing, the inexperienced young dog only knew that the unmoving entity was bad.

"Princess!" Carrie Sue commanded with more authority. This time the dog obeyed and trotted up to her. "Good girl." She reached down and held Princess by the collar while Richard investigated the find.

Squatting down next to the form, Richard placed two fingers on the left side of the man's cold and oddly twisted neck and could not detect a pulse. Pulling out his cell phone, he dialed his father's number.

David was aware that Richard left the house after receiving a phone call. He paced and looked out his windows. He saw flames. He heard a vehicle peeling out of a nearby driveway. He had been expecting a call. "What's cooking?"

"Got a body."

"I'll be right there. Call Diblassio."

"On it." Richard turned to Carrie Sue and said, "Do you think you might know this guy?"

"Maybe. I could take a look." Still holding the eager dog, Carrie Sue walked slightly bent over to the body. "He looks familiar, but I don't know his name. Maybe Amy does."

Richard gave orders – slightly gentler than if he were with his usual investigators – to Carrie Sue: "Take Princess up there with you and tie her up or keep her in the house. We can't let her mess up any evidence. See if Amy is patched up, and if she is, have Lee drive her down here so she can look. Tell him to take my truck. There's some stuff I need in the back."

Without answering the man, Carrie Sue shuffled as quickly as she could while still holding Princess by the collar. She was breathing hard by the time she burst into the front door. She immediately passed on Richard's message to the others and flopped down in her favorite chair to catch her breath.

"You good?" Lee asked Amy.

"Yeah, let me put my flip flops on. I don't think I can get this into my shoe right now." She looked at the bandages that Lee had applied to her foot and thought it was over-kill, but she did not argue. It beat a trip to the emergency room.

Carrie Sue filled Abigail in while she was looking at the shards of glass on the floor. Again. She thought about Charlie Fletcher's shooting spree and having to replace windows. Again. She thought about Charlie Fletcher shooting out her back door and having to replace that window. Princess barked to announce the arrival of another vehicle at the end of the driveway.

"That's probably Mr. York. Richard called him. Phew! It stinks in here!"

"Well, we'll see what happens after we get this burned stuff out of here. I hope that floor isn't charred under that carpet. It looks like we're going to get a new front porch, too."

The sun was peeking over the eastern ridge by the time Amy limped over to the body. She abruptly sucked in her breath and reflexively cupped her hands over her mouth. "Levi!" She did not have to look twice. She knew that evil man from the numerous abductions, beatings, rapes, and other violence that occurred both inside and outside of the rituals.

"Levi Blevins," she said with finality. "He's the jerk that beat me up, raped me, and probably torched my trailer."

Richard had reached into the man's back pocket and pulled out his wallet. Looking at the driver's license, he confirmed that it was indeed Levi Blevins.

"Well, I guess we don't have as many lawsuits to file now," Amy commented morosely under her breath. Looking at Richard with a serious face, she asked, "Can I kick him?"

"Ah, no. I can't let you do that. Sorry."

"Come on, Amy, let's get back up to the house and let these men do their job." Lee took her elbow and walked up to the house with her.

She was glad for the opportunity to walk through the cool, dew-drenched grass. Her mind was racing. *Is it over? Is it finally over? Can I stop watching over my shoulders now?* Logically she knew that she would no longer be stalked by Levi. *Who would they send next? They surely would want to exact some revenge.* The thoughts sent cold chills through her body.

In the morning sunlight, the charred porch looked like a huge black eye on the house. Lee and Abigail stayed with Carrie Sue and Amy. They took pictures. They hashed and rehashed the events of the early morning. They waited for Diblassio to show up.

Worried that Martha might wake up and need him, David had returned to his home, well satisfied that Richard had things under control. He checked on Martha and then went into the bedroom that had been turned into a command center. Making some notes, he added to the mounting piles of evidence.

Richard was relieved that Diblassio was on his way with a body bag and the van. He discretely covered Levi's remains with a dark tarp and placed leafy branches over it so the locals would not notice a body as they drove past. Joining the others in the charred farmhouse, he was pleasantly surprised to find that a steaming country breakfast was being made. The smell of coffee was detectable now that the stench of the fire was abating.

"I didn't realize how hungry I was!" Richard exclaimed. In spite of the nature of the business at hand, he relished the company of these extraordinary people. He missed family and fellowship.

"Have a seat," Abigail invited. "We're just about to sit down."

"Let me wash my hands and I'll be right there." Richard used the bathroom and then joined the rest of them in the dining room.

Holding hands, Lee prayed, "Lord, thank You for this wonderful day that You have made and in spite of the circumstances, we will rejoice and be glad in it. Thank You for sparing the house and Carrie Sue and Amy. Thank You for Richard and his team. Thank You for this food. Amen."

"Amen!"

"It could have been so bad."

"That porch can be fixed."

"I should have my old pry bar in the basement still. We can tear up that old carpet in no time," Abigail added.

"Are you going to call the insurance company?"

"No. I think we'll just repair this and keep it quiet. Besides, by the time we pay deductibles and have the premium jacked up for another incident, it'll probably be a wash."

They leisurely finished their breakfast as they waited for Steven Diblassio to show up. There were many thoughts that were not voiced audibly. Most of them were centered on safety issues.

"Do you think Levi rode with that other guy or do you think he stashed his SUV somewhere?" Abigail asked.

"There's an easy way to find out," Lee answered.

Richard looked at him quizzically. "How's that?"

"My guess is that if they met up around here, they'd leave it at Charlie's place just down the road."

"Good thinking. We can confirm or eliminate that possibility right now. What do you say we take a short drive? It'll give us something constructive to do while we're waiting. If we find it, we might be a while." Turning to the ladies, he said, "Tell Diblassio to call me if he gets here before we get back."

Richard and Lee hopped into his truck and headed back down the driveway past Levi's inert body. Carrie Sue and Abigail cleared the dining room and kitchen while Amy was relegated to the couch where she could elevate and ice her foot. And fuss.

Turning up the familiar gravel driveway that led to Charlie Fletcher's place, Richard and Lee were on high alert. Coming into the clearing, they saw what they had hoped to see: a dark green SUV with the license plates 1NG5050.

"Excellent!" Richard exclaimed. "Let's get this thing processed and get out of here."

Diblassio made good time once again despite hauling Lee's trailer behind his van. He pulled onto the grass alongside the driveway near the tarp and called Richard.

"I'm here. Where are you?"

"Just down the road about a mile. We've got the SUV that belongs to the dead guy. You want to come pick it up before we finish with the body?"

Diblassio expertly backed onto the road and followed Richard's directions to Fletcher's place. Bumping up the driveway made the empty trailer bounce and rattled the chains. They efficiently finished processing the scene, included the gas can and the yellow disk that had fallen under Austin's truck. Bagging evidence, they loaded the SUV onto the trailer, secured it with tie-downs that Lee kept in the silver box that was attached to the tongue of the trailer.

Within an hour, Diblassio and Richard bagged the body and loaded it into the van. Accepting an offer of a good country brunch, Steven drained the last of the coffee and collected fragments of the glass bottle that Richard had ready for him. He assured Lee that he would have his trailer back later in the week. He also collected the fingerprints that were obtained from the junkyard cars and copies of the motion sensor images. The truck and its plates were clear evidence. Stephen would be back soon to finalize some things with the Yorks.

The expressway had very little traffic and all of it was moving faster than the posted speed limits. Austin did not pay attention to the plain van that was hauling an empty trailer when they passed each other at seventy plus miles per hour in that early morning. Diblassio could not know how close he came to the arsonist.

The Satanist.

Austin's anger had died down and he had already put Levi out of his mind. His conscience was seared and he cared not whether Levi was injured or dead. Reporting directly to Amalek, the master who had been selected to carry on the legacy of Prinz, he exaggerated any semblance of success that they might have had and put the full blame for their failure to kill or capture the women on Levi Blevins.

Amalek, a state representative in his other life, had already contacted Zorroz. He had heard nothing of a fire. He would get Darod or Herrak to obtain Levi's report and get back to him. Amalek had big shoes to fill. Prinz had ruled effectively for over a century and his death was a reminder that no one was indomitable. That trouble spot at the far end of his region was still a mystery to him. Were his people incompetent? Or was there a superior power with which to contend? He would find out and rectify it. *Or die like Prinz.* Putting those thoughts away, he returned to his day job.

Richard returned to his father's house and efficiently debriefed him. Together they started to connect more dots. All fingers seemed to eventually point at Sheriff Bynum.

Earl and Jan had called because they noticed all the commotion. They rolled up the driveway to join the party just after lunch. Jan sat on the other end of the couch and commiserated with Amy.

"You're seven months along! You need to take it easy after all you've been through," the grandmotherly woman chided Amy.

"I know. But I feel responsible. I mean, if I wasn't living here, they wouldn't have torched the place."

"I heard that!" Abigail retorted from the bedroom. "They would have done that or even worse if I'd been living here by myself. They're after all of us."

Carrie Sue said nothing as she battled feelings of helplessness and fear.

Abigail sensed Carrie Sue's angst and announced, "All right! We're having a group session tonight. I'll put on my chaplain's hat and we're going to work through this trauma. It upsets me, too."

Lee and Earl were working on what was left of the porch. Crowbars and pry bars easily removed the charred remains. They had removed the warped siding that had melted in the fire. The window frames were burned and also needed to be replaced. The ceiling of the porch needed to be replaced and so did the floor boards. Fortunately, the joists were unscathed.

"How's it going out there?" Abigail asked when she noticed a lull in the activity.

"I think we have it all cleared out. We just need to take some measurements. The two by eight treated lumber is easy and I think I can match the ceiling pattern and the siding. We need to make a decision about this window."

"As old as this house is," Earl said, "you'd be better off taking the measurements and getting a whole new one-piece unit. We can fill in the gaps and that way you're not paying big bucks for a custom window."

"Works for me," Abigail said. "We can worry about replacing the carpet and painting in here later. Let's make the window a priority. Thanks to Amy's quick work, the woodwork on the floor is still good."

"You're welcome!" Amy yelled from the couch.

"What about Princess? She needs a new doghouse," Carrie Sue added.

"We'll get an extra sheet of plywood and make an even better one for her," Lee said.

"Want some company?" Earl asked.

"Absolutely." Lee had written down measurements, but he knew that Earl had more experience than he did in these matters. It was also a good opportunity to get to know each other better. After loading charred carpet and burnt wood into the back of his truck, Lee told Abigail, "We'll drop this at the landfill on the way."

By evening, all the new materials were sitting on the unscathed half of the front porch, the gaping opening where the window had been was sealed in plastic whereupon another impromptu party ensued followed by a short anxiety reducing session for Amy and Carrie Sue.

An escalating flurry of activity began on many other fronts since the Saturday morning fire. Lee, with Earl mostly supervising, got the new porch floor in. Once they had solid footing to walk on, the window unit was installed. Centering it and putting in the right sized shims was more time consuming, but they wanted a solid fit. By Wednesday morning, the front porch was fully repaired and the men went back to their normal routines.

Meanwhile, Abigail had gone to town and found an area rug to use in her former bedroom. They were delighted to find some beautiful oak flooring underneath the old carpet. With very little work, they would be able to restore its beauty. A fresh paint job and new curtains made the room look better than ever.

Richard and his father were tying up several loose ends now that Levi was out of the picture. He and Steven were in contact several times a day and were coming up with a strategy to execute all the warrants and make arrests. So many people were missing and presumed dead. It was not just Carrie Sue's brother Billy; it was Barry Romanowski, several runaways, and some of the prisoners who were hauled out of Bynum's jail at odd hours and never seen again. Violent crimes against Amy, Carrie Sue, Abigail, and their neighbors added up. They were all connected. Sheriff Bynum was definitely at the center of the nefarious spider web.

After receiving the call from Amalek, Sheriff Bynum had driven between Abigail's two properties on Sunday morning while everyone was in church. He shivered involuntarily as he glanced up the long lawn and saw that Levi and Austin had done a dismal job of destroying the property. Cruising past the York's home and on to Charlie Fletcher's place, looking for clues to the whereabouts of Levi Blevins, he was even more unsettled as a flock of crows settled in the branches of the trees just above him, eyeing him as if he would be their next feast.

"Get outta here!" he shouted. Stooping to grab a handful of stones, he flung them at the offensive birds.

They startled and flapped their wings before settling back down again. Their raucous caws seemed to mock him. Trying to ignore them, he walked into the barn in case Levi had decided to hide his vehicle there. He knew that they planned to rendezvous here. *Where was his SUV? Where was he?* Bynum was getting desperate. Not knowing, not being in control, was making him very irritable. He was angry. He was desperate. He was getting careless.

30

Wednesday, September 12

It was Wednesday. Sandwiched between yesterday's new moon ritual and tomorrow's ritual to celebrate the thirteenth, it was just the middle of an ordinary week for most people. Carrie Sue had gone to work as usual, but was extra vigilant and extra jumpy. She half expected to see her mother come into the store since the beleaguered woman had not been there for several weeks. She mentioned her concern to Amanda when her co-worker commented on her jitters.

Carrie Sue had finally told Amanda about some of her mother's issues. She did not mention Satanism but she did let Amanda know that her mother had multiple personalities which explained why Amanda noticed the different tone of voice and demeanor that changed with the switching. Susan Wagner did not drop in that day.

Both of the women were startled later that morning, however, when Sheriff Bynum opened the front door with more force than necessary, setting the bells jangling instead of tinkling. Scanning the large room, he saw Amanda by the cash register and headed her way through racks of used clothing.

"What can I do for you, Sheriff Bynum?" Everyone knew the sheriff. His smiling picture was in the local paper often enough.

"I need to speak to Carrie Sue Wagner. I understand that she works here." His impatient, angry voice shattered the normally serene atmosphere. The local

Christian radio station was playing a hymn softly in the background.

"Uh, sure, um, she's right there in the office. Let me go get her." Amanda turned and nervously walked the few steps from the front counter to the open door behind her where the office was located.

Carrie Sue had heard the exchange and was already on her feet and praying hard. "I heard." Under her breath she whispered, "Pray!"

"Hello, Sheriff." She said it in the same tone that she had used just before one of her internal protectors smashed his throat and broke his hyoid bone nearly a year ago. The Holy Spirit-fueled adrenaline rush gave her a boldness that surprised both of them.

He recoiled momentarily and automatically rubbed the scar on his neck. "Miss Wagner, I need to inform you that your mother's body has been found. You need to come with me to the hospital morgue to make a positive identification."

Panic gripped her. The last thing she wanted to do was to go to a morgue with this man! *Was this a set up?* "Oh my! She's dead? When?" Carrie Sue tried to stall. *Lord, I need some help here. What shall I do?* Instantly she had a thought. "Is it all right if I call a friend? I don't think I can handle this alone."

It was a reasonable request. It was a very typical request. As much as he wanted to refuse her, Bynum agreed. "Do you have anyone close by?" he demanded impatiently.

"Uh, let me think a minute. Yes. Can I call Pastor Spalding? He's real close."

"Fine. Make it quick. I have a lot to do today." He did not bother to disguise his animosity with a professional demeanor or an attempt to display any level of sympathy.

Carrie Sue went back into her office and retrieved her phone. *Oh, Lord, please let him be in today.* Ginny answered on the second ring and immediately put her call through. He was available and would be there within five minutes to pick her up. Carrie Sue relayed the information and waited outside for Pastor Spalding to come by.

It was worse than awful. Susan had been dead for about five days. She was decomposing. The gowned and masked morgue attendant tried to minimize the impact with coverings, but she had to look at her face and it was just not the kind of image that anyone would want to have as a last glimpse of a family member. The memory would remain etched in her mind for a long time.

Carrie Sue was grateful that there was a pane of glass between herself and the corpse. "Yes, yes, that's her. That's her; that's my mother." She was deeply shaken despite expecting that this day would come sooner rather than later.

"Thank you." Bynum nodded to the attendant who pulled the shade back down.

Pastor Spalding had been standing discretely behind her and had to steady her after the shade was pulled back down. She was shaky.

"Now what?" Carrie Sue had been familiar with the disposal of bodies from rituals, but had absolutely no experience in taking care of a body legally. Somehow her mother had managed to take care of her father's arrangements without her.

"Pick up her effects and get her buried," Sheriff Bynum snapped, turned, and stomped back down the hall to the elevators. In the back of his mind he noted that yet another one of his cult family was dead and gone. All of the deaths had something to do with Carrie Sue and Abigail Norris. Leaving the hospital, he immediately headed back to his office. He had to think. He was starting to feel more like the bug than the spider in the web.

"Come on, Carrie Sue," Pastor Spalding said gently, protectively, guiding her down the long hall with his arm lightly over her shoulder. He was astounded by Roger Bynum's rude and unprofessional behavior. *Well, he is a Satanist. His true colors are coming out.* "I'll help you. Let's go to my office and we can make some calls. Why don't you get a hold of Abigail and see if she'll meet us there?"

Driving back to the church, Carrie Sue realized that she had been both hoping for and dreading this day for a long time. Now that it was here, she was surprised at the mixed feelings. Regret. Dashed hopes. Confusion. Anger. Fear. Guilt. Relief. Mostly relief.

"Abigail?" Carrie Sue said in a shaky voice.

"What's wrong? Are you, all right?" Abigail knew immediately that something was very wrong.

"I'm at the church with Pastor Spalding. Mom died. Can you come? I need help making some decisions. I can't think straight right now."

"I'll be right there!" Abigail hung up and told Lee what Carrie Sue had said. "I'll be back as soon as I can." Grabbing her keys and wallet, Abigail hurried out the door and hopped into her truck.

Twenty minutes later, she entered Pastor Spalding's office. He was on the phone and Ginny was soothing the distraught woman. Carrie Sue broke down and began to blubber something that was indiscernible when she saw Abigail.

"What can I do to help?"

"Nothing really, I just need someone with me. I didn't think I would fall apart like this."

"No need to apologize. I'm not sure if I should say that I'm sorry for your loss or grateful for your loss."

Abigail both voiced and meant what she expressed sincerely. She happened to say out loud what Carrie Sue was already thinking and feeling which caused the woman to laugh and cry simultaneously. It was contagious and the slightly suppressed giggles broke the tension in the room. Once they settled down, Carrie Sue dabbed at her tears and smiled.

"Thanks. I needed that."

"Carrie Sue," Pastor Spalding said, "I just talked to Ed Wilson at the Damstra and Wilson Funeral Home. He said that he'd work with you. He's got time this afternoon at one o'clock. We have time to grab a bite to eat before we go."

"I'm not hungry."

"You have to eat. You've gone through a bit of a shock and you need to keep up your strength," he admonished her like a father, like a pastor, like a man who had too much experience in this area.

They settled on the little sandwich shop and ate. Talking between bites, they told Pastor Spalding about the latest assault over the weekend. They also apprised him of some of the things that Richard was free to share with them. He then assured them that he would pray more often and put this out on the prayer chain through the Ministerial Alliance.

Placing their trays on the shelf over the trash bin, they got into Pastor Spalding's sedan. Mr. Damstra was dressed in a suit but his shirt was open at the collar giving him a more informal look. He shook hands with each of them and gestured to the overstuffed chairs in the corner of his office.

"Can I get you something to drink? Water? Soda? Coffee?"

"No thanks."

"I'm good."

Very quickly Mr. Damstra understood that Susan Wagner would need to be buried or cremated as soon as possible. He also perceived that Carrie Sue was not at all close to her mother. He had her fill out papers and then asked, "Does she have a cemetery plot?"

"I don't know. She had Dad buried at the Tayler Mountain Cemetery. I just found out that she died this morning. I have her will back at the house. Maybe it says something."

"Does she have a life insurance policy?"

"Sorry, I don't know about that either." Carrie Sue was beginning to get anxious. How was she going to do all of this?

Abigail noticed her angst, touched her forearm, and said, "Carrie Sue, don't worry about that right now. I'll go with you to your mother's house and see what we can find out."

"Let me lay out some possible options for you," Mr. Damstra said gently. He proceeded to tell her the price difference between a burial and a cremation. He told her what coffins and burial plots cost on average. He let her know what a funeral service and an obituary would cost. He also assured her that if there was no insurance policy, he would be glad to take very minimal payments.

She promised to get back to him later that afternoon to let him know what she found out about her mother's final arrangements, that is, if she had any. They stood up, and once again, Mr. Damstra shook their hands. Carrie Sue was settling down as she marveled at the support of friends and even a friend of a friend. What a difference from the culture in which she was raised.

In the privacy of Pastor Spalding's car, Carrie Sue blurted, "As far as I'm concerned, I don't want a funeral or an obituary. Even if she does have a plot, it'd be cheaper to have her cremated. I'll sell her house. I'll sell her truck. I promise I'll pay him as soon as I can. I just want this done!"

"I think that's a good idea," Pastor Spalding said. He understood that this was not the typical death situation. "I'll do as much or as little as you'd like."

Rolling to a stop in his parking space at the church, they said their good-byes. Pastor Spalding returned to his office while Abigail and Carrie Sue got into her truck.

"Where to?"

"Oh, my! I need to get back to The Thrift Shoppe! I've left poor Amanda there all alone."

"Let's do that and then you need to be on funeral leave. We have a lot to do."

Carrie Sue rummaged through the bag of her mother's possessions that the morgue worker had given her and found the set of keys that she needed in the weathered leather purse. "Here's what we need," she held the keys up. "Let me see what else she has in here," she said mostly to herself from the back seat of Lee's truck.

Lee and Abigail heard her muttering a list of her finds: wallet, brush, cell phone, handkerchief, receipts, loose change, old mail, nail clippers, and some lipstick. She was busy examining the contents of the wallet as they pulled up to the neglected house.

"You okay?" Abigail asked as she turned around and noticed Carrie Sue staring at her mother's driver's license.

"Yeah, sure. As okay as I can be." Looking up with a resolute expression, she declared, "I'm not going to be Carrie Sue anymore. I'm just going to be Carrie. I don't want to have any part of her name associated with me."

"What part of your mother's name?" Lee asked. He was not sure if she meant Susan or Wagner.

"Susan. I guess I was named for her."

"We need to pray and renounce anything that may be attached to you because of the name thing. And before we go into that house, we need to pray."

"Good idea. I'm so glad I have you guys along! Can you pray?"

"We all will. I'll start." With that, Abigail led a short prayer for protection from anything that had to do with the name – first or last – as well as protection from any territorial or familiar or familial spirits that might be lingering on the property."

"Let's see what we've got," Lee said as he held his hand out for the keys. "Let me go in first." He was very protective and if there were any surprises, he wanted to be the one to find out.

Unlocking the door, pushing it aside, Lee pulled back just as a cloud of flies swarmed out of the door. "Phew!" he gasped.

"Ugh!"

"Gross!"

"Let's get some windows open and air this place out!" Lee exclaimed as he took a deep breath and plunged into the fetid house. It was clear that Susan Wagner had perished in the recliner in the living room. The putrid smell permeated the whole house, but was particularly strong in the living room.

Rushing from room to room opening windows, they took deep breaths through the screens before hurrying to the next window. Fortunately, a cool breeze was beginning to pick up and helped blow some of the rank stench of decomposition out of the house. Lee manhandled the recliner onto the front porch which helped immeasurably.

Abigail rummaged under the kitchen sink and found deodorizing products. After spraying the living room liberally, she finished the can on the recliner. "I think this house will be okay with some cleaning."

"Well, Mom never was much of a housekeeper." Carrie's flat-toned sarcasm brought rolled eyes and chuckles from her friends.

"Carrie Sue! Sorry. Carrie!" Abigail corrected her old habit and chided Carrie with a giggle.

"Now what?" Clearly Carrie remained somewhat unsettled because of the shocking turn of events.

"I guess we need to go back inside and see if we can find where she keeps her important papers."

"She has a filing cabinet in one of the bedrooms." Carrie took a deep breath and pinched her nostrils as if she were about to launch herself off of a diving board and hurried to the back of the bungalow with Lee and Abigail right behind her. The air was already much more tolerable.

Inspecting the key ring from Susan's purse, Carrie found the small key and unlocked the cabinet. "I wonder what all these other keys are for." Putting that thought aside, rifling through the top drawer, she found a check book and current bills. There were files for the various providers: electric, gas, telephone, cable, car insurance, and more.

"Here!" Carrie pulled out the file that was labeled with the name of a life insurance company. "Could it be this easy? She was so scatter-brained about everything. I can't believe how organized this is."

"She probably had one personality who did the bookkeeping. Besides, we've been praying for favor," Abigail reminded her.

"That would make sense." Carrie quickly thumbed through the file until she found a policy and a recent letter. "I guess I'll need to call these people and see if it's still in effect."

"Tomorrow is soon enough. Do you want to take a quick look through the rest of the drawers?"

"I probably should. Would you? I'm just not sure if I can handle any more shocks today."

Abigail found old tax returns in the next drawer. The third drawer had owner's manuals and vehicle titles. Some of them were probably from items that were long gone. The bottom drawer had an assortment of old documents, birth certificates, and envelopes stuffed with other papers. "It seems pretty benign. I can help you go through them whenever you're ready."

"Thanks." Carrie sighed as she surveyed the room. "What am I going to do with this place? I could never live here. There are too many bad memories." She shuddered involuntarily.

"Put that on your list of things to worry about later."

Lee had wandered outside and peeked through the window of the two-car detached garage. There was an old Nova with tinted windows wedged in one side with boxes and barrels, lawn care equipment and tools jammed into the other bay. It looked as if it had not been opened for quite some time. The windowless shed was locked. Looking at the overgrown lawn, he wondered how long ago it had been mowed. The only thing that seemed to be disturbed was the rose bed. It was weeded and nicely pruned.

31

Thursday, September 13

Carrie's eyes popped open earlier than usual. It took all of two seconds for the events of yesterday to settle down on her like a sodden blanket. *Mom's dead. Dad's dead. Billy's dead. Danny's dead. I'm the last one standing.* She was not entirely sure how she felt about that. The deaths of her family members brought relief, not grief – especially her father's. He was her primary perpetrator and had abused her severely both at rituals and at home. He had trained his sons to do the same.

Rolling onto her stomach and looking out of the window at the head of her bed, she could see the Milner's house across the valley through the thin stand of trees. Thinking about all that had to be done, Carrie finally pushed herself out of the bed, hastily made it, dressed, and tip-toed down the stairs so she would not awaken Amy. They had stayed up late last night talking. Amy liked the idea of dropping Sue from Carrie's name. They usually called each other "Care" and "A" anyway.

Princess greeted her with a full-body wag and with a glistening tongue hanging out of the side of her mouth. She was looking for some ear scratching and breakfast.

"Come on, girl, let's go let the chickens out."

Always eager to go anywhere and do anything, the frisky dog dashed out the back door ahead of Carrie. She immediately went to the fence line and did her business and then romped in energetic circles around Carrie.

"Stay!" Carrie commanded when she got close to the chicken coop.

Princess obediently settled down and waited for the squawking, flapping, cackling hens to be released and fed their morning ration of cracked corn. Carrie double-checked the water supply and feed as she gathered some early eggs. They were still warm.

"Thank you, ladies."

By the time they got back up to the house, Amy was awake and moving slowly through the kitchen. "Good morning. You okay? Sleep well?"

"Yeah. I guess. I'm mostly relieved. I wish I could just walk away from having to take care of all these final arrangements or whatever they call it. I guess I'd better call that insurance company and see if it's paid up and how to file a claim if it is."

"Well," Amy quipped, "if I can be of any help at all, you're in worse shape than you thought."

"Funny. At least that funeral home guy said he'd take care of a bunch of details for me."

They ate a leisurely breakfast. The life insurance company would not open until nine o'clock. When it did, Carrie was delighted to find out that the three thousand dollar life insurance policy was valid. It was not much, but it would help. The woman on the other end of the line was accustomed to working with grieving family members and compassionately walked Carrie through the steps that she would need to take. Carrie would receive official paper work shortly, but in the meantime, they would fax the information to Mr. Damstra at the funeral home.

Carrie made several more calls. The one to the Taylor Mountain Cemetery where her father was buried confirmed that only one burial plot had been purchased. Her mother had none. That simplified her decision. Calling Mr. Damstra, she informed him that a fax would be coming in to confirm the life insurance policy. She told him that she wanted absolutely no frills, no service, just a cremation – and she did *not* want the ashes.

"What are you going to do about the house?" Amy asked when she got off the phone.

"I'm not sure. According to the will, I'm the sole beneficiary of everything. I do know that I don't want it. Too many bad memories! Too many buried bodies. Literally."

"Hey! You said you were curious about who was buried in the rose bed."

"Ooh, that's right. I guess if I own the property, I can have Richard dig around a little."

They were quiet for several minutes as they were lost in thoughts about discovering tangible evidence. Carrie finally broke the silence. "I don't really care about any proof that they were Satanists, but I've always felt bad for the neighbor who never knew what happened to her husband. I mean, all these years and she still doesn't know."

"Does she still live down the street?"

"Just a few doors down. I think she always suspected something. I mean, she had to know that her husband was going to talk to the dad, but she's just like all the other neighbors who were intimidated by him. They all hated us. I could never live there."

"How soon can you sell it? Don't you have to go through probate or something?"

"Pastor Spalding said that he's going to ask Al Chambers to talk with me. He's an attorney who goes to our church. Lee and Abigail are going to help me start cleaning it up today."

"It sure sounds like God's put a lot of people in your path to walk you through this stuff."

"Yeah. He sure has. I'm blessed."

Sheriff Bynum was not feeling particularly blessed this morning. In fact, he was feeling down-right cursed. Doomed. He had a strong inclination to double-check on a number of things. Charlie Fletcher's body had been discovered and his own fingerprints could easily be found on the body bag. There was nothing he could do about that except infer that he was the one who gave the bag to Andy Lockman. Let Lockman take the hit.

Then there were the cars. He had to make sure that Larry Robbins actually did chop every vehicle that went his way over the years. There was no way to prove it, but Bynum suspected that the shifty-eyed weasel would try to keep some of the prime parts for himself. It was imperative that not one hubcap was left in that junkyard. Not one title or registration, license plate or bill of sale had better be there! Especially not for that hot Camaro.

Before he could do any of that, he had to answer the summons that Daggett had issued. Normally he would just head over to the courthouse where he and the judge would confer. It never roused any suspicion. What would be so unusual about the county sheriff and the county judge getting together? Not today. Today he was told that they would be meeting in the windowless lodge.

All of his senses were on high alert. He did not have a very good feeling about this ill-omened meeting. Although they had met here on ritual days in the past, he had never had a sense of foreboding like this before. Calling on his higher powers, Zorroz parked his car next to two others and warily entered the building.

"Be seated," the gruff voice of Amalek ordered.

Adrenaline flowed. His pupils dilated, his heart beat faster, and his stomach knotted as he bowed toward the master before taking his seat. He suppressed the urge to rub the scar on his neck.

"We have word from our sources that the DOJ is about to launch a thorough conspiracy investigation. Your carelessness has exposed more than yourself."

Zorroz' face grew pale, his thoughts alarmed him. He felt the slackness in his hips and tried desperately to keep his knees from knocking.

Amalek pronounced, "You have been weighed and found deficient."

The words were spoken in an even tone, but they slammed into Zorroz like blows of a sledge hammer. His intuition was correct. He was going to go down. It was just a matter of time. Clearing his throat, Zorroz hoarsely pleaded, "I can take care of it. They don't know anything."

"On the contrary," Amalek uttered loudly, "your fingerprints are literally and figuratively all over everything and many of them are pointing at us as well. Just remember that we have eyes everywhere."

Zorroz was keenly aware that he was being watched by human and celestial beings. He was sensing that his own demons, the ones with whom he made binding contracts, were beginning to turn on him. They had more loyalty to themselves than to him. They were supreme liars and deceivers. Zorroz sensed that the walls of demonic security that he had built around himself for protection were now his prison walls. *There has to be a way out. There just has to!*

Having come as close to groveling as he ever had in his proud life, Zorroz promised and swore and bargained. He would come through. The only thing he could think of would be to bring in the most sought-after prize in this region: Abigail Norris. If that did not work out, then that Wagner woman would suffice.

Cruising down the highway to tie up one loose end, Sheriff Bynum's volcanic demon-fueled rage was escalating to the point of eruption. He heard the voices in his head. "Kill him!" "Teach him a lesson he'll never forget!" Like Charlie Fletcher before him, he was feeling desperate. Adding more demons to the mix was supposed to have given him more power, more resources, but right now he was not feeling it.

Those very demons knew the truth of the Bible. The god of this world blinds the eyes of the unbelieving. The god of this world steals and kills and destroys. The god of this world manipulated everyone, including the most devoted Satanist. Zorroz was no exception.

Skidding to a halt in front of Robbins' Junkyard and Storage office, Bynum slapped his hat on his head and stood in the cloud of dust that he had just raised. Stalking up to the office, clomping up the shaky wooden steps, he jerked the door open. "Robbins! Where are you?"

"Right here! Whaddya want?" the shifty-eyed man answered from his position behind the desk.

A low growl came from the corner of the unkempt room. Having been rudely awakened, the Rottweiler mix scrambled to his feet with his hackles up and his teeth bared.

"Shut up, you miserable cur!" Bynum added a number of curses that only served to further arouse the dog's ill temper.

Charging at Sheriff Bynum, the dog was in mid-air when the shot rang out. His momentum carried him into the large man, causing him to stumble over the trash can and land on the floor in an undignified heap with a loud thump.

"You shot my dog!" Robbins scrambled over to the whimpering dog. "Whatcha have ta go an' do dat for?"

The sound of the shot was heard by two of Larry's sons and they came running. Bursting through the door, they looked questioningly from Sheriff Bynum to their father to the growing puddle of blood that was coming from Sadie.

"He shot Sadie!" Larry let another bitter mouthful of very colorful cuss words fly.

"He attacked me!" Bynum exclaimed as he holstered his weapon.

Jimmy, the youngest of his sons, had been raised with Sadie. They had a special bond. Everett was the oldest. He had a fiery temper and had spent many nights in Sheriff Bynum's jail over the years for everything from disorderly conduct to attempted murder. He was a brawler and he was not quite right. Somehow the charges always got dropped.

Jimmy dropped to his knees and cradled the dying dog's head in his hands. Everett stormed out of the office. Jumping into his father's pickup truck, heading to the back of the yard where the engine biter was parked near the crusher, he skidded to a halt. Leaping out of the truck and into the machine, he fired up the huge tractor that looked like a cross between a dinosaur and a bulldozer on wheels.

The five-foot-tall wheels churned back toward the office. Lowering the flat forks, opening the gaping jaws, Everett neatly slid the forks under the frame of the sheriff's car. Securing his load by crunching the huge incisor-like hooks into the roof, he effortlessly lifted the load high above his eye level, turned, and headed to the back of the lot cursing all the way.

Aware of the racket outside, Sheriff Bynum looked out of the window just in time to see his car lifted off the ground. "What the...?" Jerking the door open, he helplessly stood there watching in disbelief as the rust and yellow lion of a machine pivoted and retreated with its prey to its lair.

Pausing to fire up the old hydraulic crusher, Everett returned to the cab of his engine biter and neatly stacked the car on top of the others that were waiting to be crushed. Sheriff Bynum sprinted down the lane and arrived just in time to watch the crusher reduce his car to a fraction of its original size. The violent sounds of crunching metal, shattering glass, and blowing tires filled the air.

Everett turned off the crusher and hopped into the pickup truck. Ignoring the presence of the sheriff, he chugged back to the office as if he were just doing his normal job.

Sheriff Bynum was left in the settling dust cloud trying to wrap his mind around what just happened. The wheels were coming off more than just his vehicle. Stalking back up to the office, thinking furiously through his options, he could only see one outcome. This day would crescendo into the worst that anyone with triskaidecaphobia – fear of the number thirteen – could imagine.

By the time he got back to the office, Everett had disappeared. Jimmy had carried the dead dog out to the truck. He would bury Sadie. Larry was back at his desk nervously smoothing his stringy hair and replacing his greasy cap as he tried to sooth himself with the repetitive action.

"You're in deep trouble, Robbins! I came here to make sure you got rid of all those vehicles I brought in here, especially that Camaro."

Larry could not control his reaction and Sheriff Bynum had years of experience reading body language. Larry's language said that he was hiding something. "I chopped some of it. Honest, I did!" Larry protested. "I put some new parts on it and had it repainted. Who's gonna know?"

"You were supposed to make it completely disappear! That was the deal! Where is it now?"

Larry hung his head and groused, "I'll check with Everett. He was taking care of it."

"Check with him now!" Bynum roared.

Larry catapulted out of his rickety swivel chair, slid past the glaring man, and headed out the flimsy door. Skipping the bottom step, he hurried over to the shed that served as an office for the storage area. Bynum was right behind him. Everett was nowhere to be

465

found. The space in which the Camaro had been parked was empty except for the tarp that used to cover it.

Bynum was hot. He knew that Everett was unpredictable and yet savvy enough that he would know that he needed to get out of town. If his recklessness got him into an accident or some other trouble, that car would point right back to Bynum. Bynum could not utter enough curses. Returning to the office, he called his office and ordered the bewildered deputy to come get him at the junkyard.

"You get that miscreant son of yours back here with that car and take care of it right!" he ordered the rattled Larry Robbins who was staring at the worn blood-stained carpet.

Sheriff Bynum had another car to check on.

Carrie was clearly overwhelmed by the enormous task of straightening her mother's house. She did find out that she could take immediate possession because she was named the sole heir in a valid will. At least she did not have a legal hassle on top of everything else. Mom was a hoarder, or at least, parts of her were. Every room was cluttered. Walls were cluttered with pictures and various hangings. Garbage was spilling over all of the jam-packed trash cans. Papers were piled on floors, tables, and chairs. Burns stained the furniture around the ashtrays. It still smelled faintly of death.

As if that were not enough, Carrie was uneasy thinking that she might turn up something sinister. It was a comfort to have Lee and Abigail with her today. They brought a large box of trash bags. Carrie's job was to bring all the papers and mail to the dining room table. She would sort through it later and separate the obvious trash from any important papers.

Abigail busied herself with cleaning up the kitchen. It was a challenge, but within a couple of hours, the counter tops and kitchen table were clear. Dishes were put away in hastily cleaned cabinets. The refrigerator was relieved of indistinguishable foods. She threw the plastic or Styrofoam containers away along with their fuzzy contents.

Lee went out to the shed. Having found the key to the padlock on Susan Wagner's overloaded key ring, he found enough gas in a gas can to fill the mower. He set the wheels as high as they would go and mowed the lawns on the large lot that was surrounded by tall privacy fences. After that was done, he went into the garage and began moving boards and old lawn furniture to see about the car. It looked familiar.

Sheriff Bynum could hardly believe his eyes when he saw the truck in the driveway and the front door wide open. "Well, what do you know? Maybe my luck is changing after all. I'll bet both of them are in there."

The deputy next to him was uneasy. He had been indoctrinated into the cult shortly after he joined the force. He was a godless man, but some things went too far. He was as afraid to cross Bynum as all the others were, so he quietly awaited his orders.

Cars had been going up and down the residential street at irregular intervals all morning, but Lee remained vigilant as he worked. He was inside the garage when he heard a vehicle turn into the driveway. He sensed that something was wrong. Sliding out the side door, he angled toward the back of the house, ducked past the bedroom windows, and took a peek inside the living room window. Sheriff Bynum was towering over Carrie and another man had Abigail by her upper arm. Guns were drawn.

Quickly stepping back, Lee speed dialed Richard York. The Wagner place was in a neighborhood just off the back road that led to Kingston near the three-way intersection. He estimated that it would take Richard a minimum of ten minutes to get there. *If he knew exactly where he was going.*

Fortunately, David jumped into action and went with him, calling Amy as they peeled out of the driveway. She would come down to stay with Martha for the duration. Driving as fast as he could safely maneuver around the blind curves, Richard followed his father's directions.

I could get one of them, but not both. I might hit Carrie or Abigail or they might just shoot them. Oh, Lord, get Richard here quick! Give me a strategy. Lee's brain was in high gear as he ducked under the windows and stayed in the shelter of an overgrown hedge that lined one side of the driveway. Squeezing through a break in the shrubbery, pulling out his knife, he cut the valve stems on all the tires of the sheriff's SUV. They'd be riding on their rims if they got that far. *Come on, Richard!*

"Okay, ladies, nice and quiet. If you try anything you're going to end up like the last occupant of this house. We're going to walk out to the SUV and you're going to get into the back seat without making a fuss," Bynum ordered. The malevolent glint in his eyes was exacerbated by the demons that were fueling his rage. "We're going for a little ride."

Manhandling the terrified women through the front door, across the porch, and down the driveway to the SUV, they threw them into the back seat.

"Buckle up!"

Bynum was not interested in their safety, he just wanted to be sure that they would not try anything. Moving to the back of the SUV, he opened the hatch and rummaged through his supplies. Finding the needles and sedatives, he arrogantly savored the moment as he injected a dose into Carrie's arm.

Abigail watched Carrie slump in her seat and was determined not to go down without a fight. He had to contend with her punches. Laughing dementedly, triumphantly, he smashed his huge fist into her face and then administered a dose to her as well.

"Uh, boss?" the deputy interrupted. "All the tires are flat."

"Huh?" Bynum looked at the tires and cursed. He was in sight of a redeeming victory, and now this! Nothing was going right! Nothing! The sinking feeling in his gut was indescribable. Looking around in a panic, he said, "Let's take their truck."

"No keys, boss."

"Go find them! They have to be in their pocket or a purse or something."

He searched Abigail while the deputy searched Carrie. No keys.

"Look in the house. They must be in there."

The deputy obediently went back into the house and searched quickly through the living room and the kitchen. Nothing was apparent. He searched again. He did not want to risk coming out of the house without the keys.

"Looking for these?" Lee said as he suddenly appeared behind Sheriff Bynum dangling the keys to his truck.

The shocked man had a fraction of a second to react. It was not long enough. Lee's powerful punch to his throat put the man on the ground. Once again, the hyoid bone fractured. Once again, slivers of bone punctured critical blood vessels. Once again, the large man grasped his neck and tried to breathe and talk while his vocal cords were being flooded with blood. He could only gurgle and rasp as he rolled onto his side and dribbled crimson onto the driveway.

Lee took the man's service revolver from its holster and fastened handcuffs on Bynum just as Richard pulled up and squealed to a stop. Exiting the vehicle, he stayed behind the door. Lee kept his head low, hurried to his side, and said, "Bynum's out of commission. The deputy is inside. Got a gun. Abigail and Carrie are in the back seat of the SUV. We need a couple ambulances."

"Call them. Stay here with Dad, I'll see how the deputy wants to handle this."

David was standing behind his door with his weapon drawn. "I'll cover you, son."

Lee assumed a position behind Richard's door despite desperately wanting to check on Abigail and Carrie. He saw the knock-out punch that Bynum had administered to Abigail and he wanted to sin. Very badly. His training and discipline kept him from doing anything rash. He dialed 911.

"Deputy! It's over. Throw your weapons into the yard and come out. Now!"

"I'm coming out. Don't shoot!" The deputy wanted no part of this assignment. He just happened to be the only one on duty when Sheriff Bynum stormed into the office in the foulest mood anyone had ever seen. Tossing his main weapon and a backup onto the ground, walking tentatively out the front door with his hands raised, he submitted to being cuffed by Richard – with his own cuffs.

"All clear!" Richard yelled.

Lee bolted to the SUV and gently took Abigail's face in his hands. Lifting her eyelids one at a time, he looked at her pupils. *Thank you, Lord, equal and reactive. No brain damage.* She was still knocked out by the blow as well as whatever Bynum had injected into her and there was a cut in her eyebrow that would benefit from a couple of stitches.

Carrie was groggy but starting to come around. Richard checked the back of the SUV for the vial. Sheriff Bynum had stopped writhing. David slowly walked over, slowly stooped, and checked his carotid. Standing erect, he shook his head and walked away.

32

Sunday, September 16

Lee opened his eyes, rolled onto his side, and looked at his sleeping wife. The cut was neatly stitched, but the shiner that she sported would take some time to fade. Her face was still swollen and looked as if she had put too much dark eye shadow on one eye.

Eyes fluttering open, Abigail smiled at Lee. "This is the day," she began.

"That the Lord has made," Lee continued.

"We will rejoice and be glad in it," they finished in unison.

"How's your headache?"

"Right now, it's okay. We'll see what happens when I get up."

"Stay down then. Are you hungry?"

"Still a little queasy."

"That's a nasty concussion he gave you. What can I get you?"

"Can you go back to the herb garden and get a couple lemon balm leaves for tea? It should settle my stomach."

"You got it. Stay there. You might just have to spend another day in bed."

Both Abigail and Carrie felt like they had hangovers because of the cocktail of drugs that was injected into them. Each dose would have sedated several large men. Carrie was able to go home the first night, but Abigail had to stay longer for observation. Lee never left her side.

The tea helped and soon Abigail was sitting in her favorite chair watching the hummingbirds hover and swoop and squabble over the feeders. Fresh air was blowing through open windows. The smell of autumn was in the air.

"Richard called and wanted to know when he could come and talk to you. He's got some reports to get in."

"Today's good. Wait a minute. What day is it?"

"Sunday. I'll call him right now."

"Oh, my! What about my appointments on Friday?"

Lee brought her up to date on the things she had slept through: "I found their numbers in your datebook and cancelled them. I told them you'd reschedule when you felt better. It's all over the news. I'm kind of glad we don't have a television. Cindy and Gary want to stop by after church. She's bringing a meal so don't worry about that. Oh, and Lisa should be arriving any time now. And the Spaldings want to come and check up on you, too."

"It sounds like we're having another party."

"Yeah," he said ruefully, "a ding-dong-the-witch-is-dead kind of party."

"What?"

"Oh, sorry, I forgot you didn't know. Sheriff Bynum a.k.a. Zorroz didn't make it. He was gone before the ambulance got there."

"How did he...?" Abigail looked sharply at Lee. "Did you...?"

"He was going to kill you, sweet. I had to stop him. It was just one punch."

Abigail sat in stunned silence as she absorbed the news. *Zorroz was dead. Now what? Will they send in more troops? Or were their prayers finally answered?* "Are you okay?"

"I'll be fine, but I just might need to make an appointment with a counselor. I never killed anyone before. Know any good ones?"

Abigail pestered Lee until he filled her in on every nitty-gritty detail that happened after she was knocked out. By the time he was finished satisfying her curiosity, Richard York and Steven Diblassio were at the door. They had enough information to put the entire sheriff's detachment away on conspiracy charges. Declining the invitation for lunch, they headed back to the York's residence.

Light was shining in this territory and cock roaches were scuttling for darker sites. Demons were gnashing their teeth. Urdang caught a back full of talons because his territory was no longer firmly in the grasp of the Satanists, and therefore, no longer in the grasp of Satan. Zorroz' personal demons were punished for their failures as well. Dog eat dog.

The local Satanist masters had met at the windowless lodge after their night of revelry in the wee hours of the fourteenth. They were backpedaling. They were disappointed that they did not have the personal pleasure of punishing the man who had jeopardized their positions by his arrogance and ineptness. Their demons had brought messages back from earlier in the day when Zorroz' spirit was unceremoniously escorted to his final destiny where he would be judged because he did not receive the truth, but took pleasure in wickedness.

They were blinded by the god of this world and could not grasp the fact that they were seeing in a mirror dimly. Someday they would fully know truth. But then it would be too late. Their own arrogance kept them believing Satan's lies. Those deceptions kept them working their way up in Satan's kingdom so that they could taste the fruit of their success when the final assault on the Great Power was completed.

"We'd better invite Earl and Jan and Carrie and Amy while we're at it," Abigail said.

"Good idea. You sit there and I'll take care of it."

"I'll let you. I think I'm going to milk this one for all it's worth. I mean, it's not every day that one is nearly murdered." *There I said it. I was nearly murdered.* Abigail shuddered involuntarily.

By one o'clock the Norris' driveway was lined with all kinds of vehicles. Cindy took charge of the kitchen and organized the food. For an impromptu gathering, the meal came together as if it had been custom ordered. Cindy's two large pans of lasagna were complimented by salads, vegetables, and desserts.

During the informal dinner, conversations were light. Neighbors and friends got caught up on news. It was as if they were waiting for a signal that would let them know that it was all right to talk about the reason for the gathering in the first place.

"What do you think is going to happen to the cult now?" Pastor Spalding broached the subject.

"It's hard to say," Abigail spoke slowly as she organized the jumble of thoughts that clouded her mind. She had been thinking and praying about it for a long time. "I just know that the cult doesn't ever want to lose any territory, whether it's a person or a place."

Carrie nodded in agreement.

"Look at how many of them have died lately," Amy reminded them. "There's Carrie's whole family. Now Sheriff Bynum is dead and the other deputies are in jail or wherever Richard put them. Max has defected. Charlie Fletcher is dead. Levi's dead and gone."

"I wonder if any of the local ones are still around," Carrie mused.

"I heard that the Parkers have closed their appliance store. They were retiring and moving to Florida."

"They're Satanists?" Jan asked incredulously. "We bought all our appliances from them. They seemed so nice."

"And I'm working with another local lady. She's still iffy, so pray that she'll get healed soon," Abigail added.

"How many are there?"

"I don't know, but Max has that program going at his dad's business. He's been trying to keep kids from getting recruited like he was."

"We have two things going on at the same time," Abigail continued her original train of thought. "There's the whole legal and criminal thing that will probably nail most of them, and then there's the whole spiritual angle."

"It just reminds me of all the wars that Israel fought," Cindy added. "It's like they had to reclaim the land that God had promised to Abraham. If they followed all of God's laws and statutes and ordinances, they'd be successful. God gave them strategies for each battle."

"That's right!" Pastor Spalding's irrepressible enthusiasm erupted. "I've been reading through the book of Deuteronomy lately and I came across a couple of interesting verses. I don't know why, but I sense that there's something about them that pertains to this whole situation." He had no idea how right he was.

"Deuteronomy? Interesting?" Gary quipped.

"You ought to read it sometime; it's got some amazing stuff in it," Pastor razzed back as he reached for his Bible and thumbed over to Deuteronomy 25. "Here it is. It's only three verses at the end of the chapter. Let me read it real quick." He cleared his throat and read, *"Remember what Amalek did to you along the way when you came out from Egypt, how he met you along the way and attacked among you all the stragglers at your rear when you were faint and weary; and he did not fear God. Therefore, it shall come about when the LORD your God has given you rest from all your surrounding enemies, in the land which the LORD your God gives you as an inheritance to possess, you shall blot out the memory of Amalek from under heaven; you must not forget."*

That opened up an animated discussion amongst the close-knit group.

"Wow! That sure sounds like the way the Satanists operate!"

"Yeah. They go after the weak and weary."

"That's me."

"And the stragglers."

"We can't get complacent and forget that there's a prowler out there."

"That's why it's so important for all Christians to stay together. Unity in a bond of peace."

"Well, I think we've made a lot of progress over the last year with the Ministerial Alliance."

"The tide is definitely turning," Pastor Spalding agreed. "I'm hearing from the other pastors and ministers that attendance is up for all of them. And it's not just from sheep swapping either."

The afternoon passed quickly and soon the various families began to head for home. Cindy and the other ladies cleaned up the kitchen much to Abigail's consternation.

"Oh, no!" Lee reminded her when she tried to get up, "You promised to milk it!"

33

Sunday, September 23, Equinox

What a difference a week makes. Abigail's shiner was almost completely gone and the symptoms of the concussion had abated. She was finally able to get back to work on Friday as well as get back into her routine around the house. Reluctant to get up yet, she listened contentedly to the soft twittering of the songbirds that lived in the woods all around their property. One of the cows was unhappy about something and her distant mournful bellow broke the quiet. Lee stirred. Stretching and yawning, he wrapped Abigail in his embrace without opening his eyes.

Lisa was already in the kitchen and by the smell of it, she had the coffee brewing. She had caught snippets of conversations in the past, but with this latest episode, she sat down with her father and Abigail and asked many pointed questions. She was like so many people, even church-goers, who struggled through life without ever sensing the greater battle that was waged in the invisible realm. She was catching on and catching up.

"Hey, sweet," Lee greeted his daughter with a kiss on top of her head. "Thanks for making the coffee." Pouring a mug, he sat at the table while he tried to wake up.

"Sleep well?"

"Yes. It just seems like the whole atmosphere has changed around this community."

Lee agreed.

"I didn't really think much about it, but now that you mention it, it does seem more peaceful. It's like you can't tell that something's missing until after it's gone."

"What's missing?" Lee asked.

"I don't know; it just felt heavy. I'm not sure if that's the right word or not, but it feels lighter now."

"Oppressive?" Abigail wandered into the kitchen and caught the end of the conversation.

"That's the word I was looking for." Lisa looked up at the intriguing woman who was quickly becoming her second mother.

"What's everyone want for breakfast?"

"Eggs!"

It was exactly what Carrie and Amy were having. Carrie took less time to mend than Abigail and had gone back to work on Monday. They had a very ordinary week that week. They, too, felt the absence of the ever-present oppression that lurked around them as they traveled through the community. As ritual abuse survivors, they had been gifted with keen discernment. It was one of the many ways that God equipped and recompensed these amazing survivors.

Meeting at the church in "their" pew, the friends worshiped together. Carrie and Amy were becoming less shy around the friendly and sometimes overly friendly church members. Amy had brought along her latest ultrasound images and they celebrated David being thirty weeks along.

"Two more months," Cindy said. She gave Amy a quick hug as they walked up the aisle after the service. "How big is he now?"

"Oh, the tech said that he was about three pounds and about fifteen inches long." Amy held her forearms next to each other with her palms up and looked down as if she were gauging whether or not David would fit in her arms.

"I can't wait to hold him. I think he looks like you."

"I've been praying that he doesn't look a thing like his biological father."

Later that afternoon, Lee, Abigail, and Lisa wound up the driveway to the old farm. Lee gave the double toot that had become the signal that friendly folks were coming up to the house. Carry and Amy had invited them over for a cook out. The weather was clear. The full moon was only a couple of days away so it would be a beautiful evening.

Relaxing on the deck after stuffing themselves with barbequed chicken and double-baked potatoes and grilled vegetables, they enjoyed watching the sun set. There were just enough cottony clouds in the sky to catch the last rays on this Equinox to add shades of orange and peach which eventually toned down to purple and gray.

Somewhere in the distance the sound of four-wheelers was heard in the river bottoms. Princess stretched and whined her high-pitched yawn as she got up from her place under the deck. Sitting between Amy and Carrie, the thump of her tail could be heard on the decking as the two ladies stroked her glossy fur.

"It's just night riders, girl," Amy said.

A year ago, it was Abigail and Dude on this very deck listening to the night riders. How very different it was. She reflected on the changes that had come over the last year and was interrupted by Lee.

"Penny for your thoughts?"

"I was just thinking about all the changes since the Equinox last year."

"Let's see now," he said as he started counting items on his fingers, "you're married. You're living there and not here. You have a fabulous step-daughter. You have a different dog. You have chickens down there instead of Buster. You've survived a bunch of attacks. Need I go on?"

"No. How many changes have *you* had in the last year?"

"I traded a ranch for a little farm. I'm connected to my immediate and extended family. I know a whole lot more about spiritual warfare. And not the least of which, I'm married."

"Lisa?"

"I traded city life for country life. I quit college and I'm starting my own accounting business. I moved away from one parent and to another one. And most importantly, I changed from a church-goer to a real Christian."

"Well, I'm living here and not in my old trailer," Amy joined in. "I'm pregnant and not worried that he'll be sacrificed. I'm not delivering pizzas anymore. I have a thriving egg business and house-cleaning business and elder-care business sometimes. I know how to cook and can. I can take care of a garden and an orchard and a vineyard."

"Don't forget the chickens," Carrie reminded her. "I've had a bunch of changes, too. I live here instead of an apartment in town. I don't have a biological family anymore, but I have a huge spiritual family now. I was on disability and now I have a real job. I'm a manager. I could hardly take care of myself let alone a business."

"Or chickens or a dog," Amy added with a grin.

"And, best of all, I'm whole. No more dissociation."

"Me too!" Amy exclaimed. "How could I leave out the most amazing thing?"

"Hey, and don't forget that you know how to pepper spray people," Lee laughed.

"We have gotten better at self-defense, haven't we? No more victim mentality."

Soon they grew quiet as they each pensively reflected on the conversation. The distant hoot of an owl was answered by a closer one. Crickets and frogs kept up their separate cadences. The gentle breeze brought tangy scents of autumn.

Tonight, the night riders were just night riders. No one was going to Charlie Fletcher's abandoned farm. People were simply taking advantage of the fair weather, the bright moonlight, and the dry trails. There would be no ritual abuse to mark the end of summer and the beginning of autumn.

Not here, at least.

Epilogue

"David Elia!" Amy called out the back door. "David, you need to hurry up. The bus will be here in ten minutes."

"I'm coming, Momma," the sandy-haired, freckle-spattered kindergartner called back. His morning chore was to let the chickens out, but only if he managed to get ready for school first.

"Change into your school shoes."

"Yes, ma'am." David kicked off his boots and slid his growing feet into shoes that flashed blue and red lights with each step. Fastening the Velcro straps, he announced that he was ready for school. Grabbing his backpack, he and his mother walked down to the road to wait for the bus with Princess romping beside them.

The bright little fellow loved his teacher, Miss Binkley, and showed great promise as a student. Amy remembered her own dismal school records. What a contrast to the way she was raised. She stopped worrying that he might have inherited traits from Prinz. David was a mighty man of God in the making. He had responded to the Gospel during the vacation Bible school week at church this past summer.

She stopped worrying about whether or not David had a strong male role model. He was as attached to Lee as Bryan McCord was at that age. He and Princess crossed the road under Amy's watchful eye nearly every day. He had chores to do with Lee, after all, and Princess wanted to romp with Reno. The inseparable pair also scooted over to visit Richard York whenever the official vehicle was parked in his driveway.

Lee continued to develop his eighty-acre farm. His original herd of heifers had been very productive. They were now in the fourth generation of Black Angus cattle. He and Abigail tried their hand with pigs. Once. The bacon was a nice addition to their constant supply of eggs. He and Abigail had a busy life, but it was not hectic.

Tonight was one of those special nights. It was one of the last of the balmy late summer days and the usual crowd of neighbors, friends, and family would gather. David and Richard would be there, but sadly Martha had continued to deteriorate and eventually stopped eating. David insisted on home health care rather than a hospice in a distant city. She stepped peacefully into her Father's house nearly three years ago. David York was fully recovered from his gunshot wound and was as energetic as ever.

"Are the McCords coming?" Abigail asked.

"Gary said that they'd be a little late, but they wouldn't miss it for anything," Lee answered and chuckled. "Actually, Bryan wouldn't let them miss it." Bryan was nearly nine years old and he never tired of visits to Cousin Lee's farm.

The grill was sending up its smoke signals and drawing the friends and family. It was not long before tires crunched over the gravel alerting Reno. He bounded toward the road and escorted each guest up to the house much like Dude had done years ago when Abigail lived across the road. Dishes were arranged on the island in the kitchen for an easy buffet-style dinner.

Laughter punctuated the chatter. Abigail sighed contentedly and when the steaming burgers and hot dogs were ready, she announced, "Okay, everyone! Gather 'round."

"Where'd Bryan and David go?" Cindy asked.

"I saw them heading to the barn," Amy answered. "They're probably in the hay mow."

Lee had finished his barn and the sturdy hay mow was nearly filled with a winter's supply of hay bales for the horses. He stored the round bales in the covered lean-to for the cows.

"I'll get them," Lee volunteered. "I know where the fort is." He jogged off to the barn and soon had the dusty boys in hand.

After Lee opened with prayer, the conversations began to flow again as the sun started to go down and the mild evening breezes came up. They gathered around the fire pit in chairs or sat at the twelve-foot-long picnic table that Lee and Earl built a couple years ago for just such occasions as this.

"Jan," Cindy addressed the new widow. "How are you doing these days?"

"Oh, I'm mostly fine. I miss Earl, but he's with the Lord, so I don't wish him back. Michelle and her husband fixed me up with a real nice bedroom that I can retreat to when the kiddies get too rambunctious."

"I miss Earl, too," Abigail said. "He taught me to shoot and split wood."

"I'm so glad he was a sharp-shooter," Lee agreed. "He saved Abigail's life!"

"Me too!"

"We put away a lot of criminals; that's for sure," Richard added.

"Well, with you as the sheriff, and your dad as a deputy, the crime rate in this county should stay nice and low."

"Well, Richard," Jan addressed the young man, "How do you like the house?"

"You and Earl kept such good care of it. I love it." After all the trials and investigations, Richard decided that the hectic life that afforded him too little time to enjoy his little farm in Eldersburg was getting to be too much. He yearned for a simpler life. He yearned for his roots. After Earl died, Richard sold his house and purchased the Milner's home.

"Works for me," Amy piped up. "I've doubled my house-cleaning services." Actually, she more than doubled her cleaning services. She added several new clients and was able to bring in an irregular, but steady income that provided enough to support herself and her son.

"Well, I don't know what I would have done without you guys with Mom's old house. What a mess that was!" Carrie added.

After all the investigations were finished – including the official notification to the neighbor regarding the remains of her husband that were exhumed from the rose bed – Amy and Carrie, Lee and Abigail cleaned and scrubbed, painted and repaired the house. Their prayers and anointing oil cleansed the foul spiritual filth. It sold quickly and after everything was settled, she had nearly fifty thousand dollars. Lisa had opened her accounting business and was able to help Carrie through the daunting financial maze.

Carrie kept her position at The Thrift Shoppe and was able to hire Sherry Samuels. Abigail was still working with Sherry, but she was nearly whole. The transformation in the woman was remarkable. Her wall-eyed condition was healed after the programming was broken and the demons were renounced. She continued to live in her grandmother's house and attended the Hillsdale Baptist Church where Don Wilmore was still the pastor.

The group talked about the next Ministerial Alliance meeting. It was growing and now included nearly every church in the county as well as some from the surrounding counties. Pastor Spalding's church had grown so much that they had to go to two services. Jason Miller, a recent graduate from Bible College, returned to the area with Kristin, his young bride. He was hired as the new youth minister.

"Isn't it amazing, actually, ironic, how Jason and Max are working together again? This time *for* God." Abigail remarked.

Max's apprenticeship program was very successful. He was able to connect with those young men who were on the edge of rebellion like few others could since he was once one of them. He would invite them to church and introduce them to Jason. Jason had graduated with a minor in counseling and was being mentored by Abigail. He also recruited these young men to help with his local ministry projects and would slip in some counsel in the process.

Orion was peeking over the ridge. The night skies were clear. Urdang and his minions kept their distance. It was too painful to gaze at the light that emanated from the region. It pained their eyes and it pained them because they lost. Their former territory had been transformed. The Great Enemy had won this battle.

"You sleeping?" Gary asked Amy. "You're awfully quiet tonight."

"Just thinking."

"That's scary," he teased.

"You know? I think everyone here has been shot at or assaulted. I'm sure glad that's over!"

"No weapon formed against us will prosper!" Abigail exclaimed.

A chorus of friends and family shouted their agreement in unison, "No weapon!"

Author's note

These books are part of a spiritual footprint that I hope to leave behind. It has been a four-year journey writing these four novels which are loosely based on my own experiences of the last twenty-five years. Some of the most incredulous things that have been included in these novels are based on actual events that occurred in my life. I have always joked that I would have to write about Ritual Abuse in novel form because no one would believe it if it were written as a memoir.

Ministry came with a price. It was frightening to get a gravel-voiced threat over the phone that said, "We know where your daughter goes to school." It was intimidating to hear, "If we can't kill you, we'll ruin your reputation." It has been arduous, but in the midst of the threats and attacks, I clung to the precious Word: No weapon formed against me will prosper. I will continue to minister as long as the Lord allows. There are far too many survivors and far too few experienced counselors. Pray that the Lord would raise up more.

The battle is real. The war has been won. In the meanwhile, pray for these incredible, amazing survivors. What a privilege it has been to be able to minister to them!

Counseling related E-Books by this author

I am a Cutter, Please Help Me
Yo Soy un Cortador Ayudana Por Favor (Spanish version of I am a Cutter)
Emotional Abuse and Verbal Assaults through Lies, Vows, Curses, and Judgments
Battling Anorexia, Bulimia, Binge Eating, Health Food Obsession
Panic and Anxiety Attacks
Heaven or Hell – Have I Lost My Salvation?
Mad at God, Self, and Others
Dissociative Identity Disorder
What's in Your Family Tree? Battling Generational Curses and Familial Spirits
Spiritual Gifts – Discovering Your Spiritual Gifts
Seeing, Hearing, Sensing God through His Brokenhearted Children

Watch for paperback versions of the above books.

Novels by this author

Available as E-Book or paperback

Ritual Abuse - Autumn
Ritual Abuse - Winter
Ritual Abuse - Spring
Ritual Abuse – Summer

Send questions or comments to:
ironsquillreader@gmail.com

www.ingramcontent.com/pod-product-compliance
Lightning Source LLC
Chambersburg PA
CBHW050841030726
47503CB00007BA/2267